WINGS OF PREY

WINDSTORM
PRESS

Praise for Wings of Prey

Wings of Prey *is the sixth book in McLean's The Gift Legacy, an urban fantasy series for adults, and as such it brilliantly achieves what seems to elude many authors of multi-book series: it deftly manages to further deepen and intensify Emelynn Taylor's story of her gift and the dangerous world she must face as a result. The tension within Emelynn, a character I have not forgotten since reading the first book in this series, is taut and intimately drawn by McLean. A profoundly intelligent story of a captivating young woman whose victories and struggles with a unique gift will grab your every emotion.*

—Jennifer Manuel, award-winning author of
The Heaviness of Things That Float

Wings of Prey *simmers with tension from its first pages and builds to an epic battle that sets your heart racing. McLean's expertly drawn world of Fliers with Emelynn at its heart, is filled with intriguing characters and near-familiar settings that draw you into this compelling read.*

—Katherine Prairie, author of the Alex Graham thriller series

Unique and compelling—a must read for fans of supernatural thrillers!

—Lisa Voisin, author of The Watcher Saga

Praise for The Gift Legacy

❝ JP McLean possesses her own unique gift: the ability to bewitch her readers with her boundless imagination.
—Elinor Florence, Globe and Mail bestselling author of
Bird's Eye View

❝ Extraordinary heroine—awesome world-building.
—Roxy Boroughs, award-winning author of
The Psychic Heat series

❝ The story pulled me in from the first page and kept me hooked until the very end.
—Ev Bishop, award-winning author of the River's Sigh B & B series

❝ JP McLean at her six-star best.
—Pat McDonald, British crime author

❝ Exposed secrets, hidden enemies, and a new, gut-wrenching reality for Emelynn create a gripping read you won't want to put down.
—Debra Purdy Kong, award-winning author of
The Casey Holland Mystery series

❝ This story has all the elements of an engrossing thriller—dynamic characters, secrets, suspense, sex, violence, and a believable and likeable protagonist.
—Diana Stevan, author of *A Cry from the Deep*

❝ The story is a very nicely woven combination of several genres, has a wonderful flow; it was easy to get hooked.
—Karen Oberlaender, author of *In a Small Compass*

❝ A thoroughly enjoyable read.
—Island Gals Magazine

Titles by JP McLean

The Gift Legacy
Secret Sky

Hidden Enemy

Burning Lies

Lethal Waters

Deadly Deception

Wings of Prey

The Gift Legacy Companion
Lover Betrayed (Secret Sky Redux)

WINGS OF PREY

THE GIFT LEGACY
BOOK 6

Jo-Anne P. McLean

JP MCLEAN

Wings of Prey
The Gift Legacy ~ Book 6
First Canadian Edition

Copyright © 2019 by JP McLean
All rights reserved.

ISBN
978-1-988125-23-7 (Paperback)
978-1-988125-24-4 (MOBI)
978-1-988125-25-1 (EPUB)
978-1-988125-26-8 (PDF)

Edited by Nina Munteanu
Copy edit by Rachel Small
Book cover designed by JD&J with stock imagery
provided by Konstantin Kamenetskiy © 123RF.com
Author photograph by Crystal Clear Photography

This is a work of fiction. All of the names, characters, places, organizations, events and incidents, other than those clearly in the public domain, are either products of the author's imagination or are used fictitiously. Any resemblance to actual persons, living or dead, is entirely coincidental and not intended by the author.

No part of this publication may be reproduced, recorded, stored in a retrieval or information browsing system, or transmitted, in any form, or by any means, without prior written permission from the publisher or, in the case of photocopying or other reprographic copying, a licence from Access Copyright, www.accesscopyright.ca, 1-800-893-5777, info@accesscopyright.ca.

Excerpt from *Lover Betrayed* copyright © 2019 by JP McLean

Cataloguing in Publication information available
from Library and Archives Canada

WINDSTORM PRESS
BRITISH COLUMBIA, CANADA
WWW.WINDSTORMPRESS.COM

For John.

Nothing is more sad than the death of an illusion.
—Arthur Koestler

Chapter One

Three weeks had passed since my mother learned that another world existed within her own. A world where the laws of gravity weren't so much laws as suggestions. A world where a select few who shared the right gene could dissipate into molecules too tiny for the human eye to see and then re-form, unaffected. A world of Fliers and Ghosts.

Years of hiding the truth from her were behind us, and yet I felt her doubt, her skepticism. It seemed as if she was waiting for me to say *just kidding* and then life would return to normal. Normal: the most overrated place in the world.

"Where's your mom?" James said, leaning against the kitchen door jamb. He raked his hand through still damp hair that touched his shoulders. Last night it had been my hands running through his hair. He was dressed in dark colours. They made him look leaner, lankier. Sexier. He stared at the belt of my robe.

I pulled my mind out of the bedroom and picked up the note she'd left. "At the university again. 'Back tonight,' it says. You know what she's doing, right?"

He pushed off from the jamb and sauntered over. "Looking for proof?"

"It's the scientist in her. She can't help herself."

James pulled two mugs from the cupboard and reached for the coffee pot. "There's always the hope the university will pull her library privileges."

"With her credentials? Fat chance." We took our coffees to the living room and settled on the sofa. Outside, the Pacific shimmered under a weak May sun.

"I did the same, you know," I said. "Before I knew. Back in Toronto."

"Did you find anything?"

"Not unless you include witchcraft and mystical rapture. Then there's always demonic possession and shamans. And let's not forget cults and alien space invaders."

James gave me the laugh I was looking for. "Abnormal behaviours are your mom's forte, are they not? Maybe she'll be the one to figure out the science behind the *gift*."

"More likely a drug to cure it." My mom, Laura Aberfoyle, was a respected behavioural research Ph.D. She'd resigned from her post at the University of Toronto a few weeks ago.

"Cure it?"

"It wouldn't be the first time she pioneered an anti-psychotic med. Mom's furious that Jolene did this, gifted me, put me in this position. She thinks the gift is dangerous." I traced a dribble of coffee up the side of my mug and licked my finger. "She doesn't know the half of it."

"When are you going to tell her?"

"I don't know. I'd hoped the gift would win her over. She should be curious, but she's resisted every offer to experience it for herself—from Stuart, from me. Without that cushion, it's going to be a blow when she learns about the Tribunal Novem and our enemies."

"I wish I could stay and help, but it's going to take from now until the caucus to set up the security."

Next week's caucus was a big deal. The entire Tribunal Novem, their families and allies would be in attendance. Security measures would be unprecedented.

"I have to tell you, I'm surprised Mason asked for your help."

"I sense Stuart had a hand in that."

"He tells me you two work well together."

"The guy's got balls. Pretty nimble for an old cowboy. I owe him."

That old cowboy was becoming more like the grandfather I never had with each passing day. He'd pressed James's right for revenge with Sebastian and then helped James track down and assassinate the two amoral vultures responsible for stealing our genetic material. He'd then helped dispatch James's handler, Tim Beale, the man at International Covert Operations who'd set James up.

I smiled. "Stuart's probably taking advantage of your new unemployed status."

"Unemployed. I like the sound of that. But I'm not idle. Took a private contract before I showed up on your doorstep."

James toyed with one of the lockets on my bracelet. Inside the locket was the RF transmitter International Covert Operations had implanted in my arm. James had one just like it—not the bracelet, the transmitter. ICO wasn't aware we'd found them, and we were counting on them not knowing we'd had them surgically removed. Now we were in control of how much they knew of our whereabouts.

James twisted the bracelet and checked the second locket—his locket. I'd agreed to keep his tracker with me while he was working with Mason on security for the caucus. We couldn't risk ICO knowing where the meeting was taking place.

"I'm glad you came."

"Me too." He took my hand in his. "I was worried your mom would toss me out when I showed up."

"Are you kidding? She thinks you can do no wrong. I was the one who kept her in the dark and insisted everyone else do the same. You, she loves."

A playful smirk crossed his lips. "I *am* damn near perfect." I rolled my eyes. He raised the back of my hand to his lips. "Thank you for saying yes."

My smile faded. "We're taking it slow, remember?"

"Like I'd forget that conversation."

An awkward silence fell. He rubbed his thumb over my knuckles. "We aren't the first couple to have to work out a few snags, Em."

"Snags?"

"Tiny," he said, squinting at the small gap between his thumb and forefinger. "My father's law firm will work out the legal issues with me being American and you Canadian. And as far as the Reynoldses go, I've already made my peace with Stuart, and Mason will come around when we tell him."

"And that little snag to do with children?"

He cocked his head to one side and frowned. "You want kids, right?"

"Eventually."

"Then it's just a matter of timing, that's all."

That's all. He said it as if it were an easy fix, a little tweak. I wasn't so sure. The thought of having kids sent me into cold-sweat territory.

"Speaking of kids, isn't Short, Dark and Bubbly about to pop?"

"Next month if she can hold on, but I don't think it's contagious," I said.

James laughed, knowing I'd caught his not-so-subtle play. Short, Dark and Bubbly was James's nickname for Molly Connolly, though she was Molly Meyers now. She and I had been best buddies when we were kids. She was still my closest and dearest friend in the non-Gifted world.

"I've got to get moving," James said.

"You'll keep in touch?"

His gaze dropped to my hand. "As much as I can. Yes."

James was a man of few words, but his habit of cutting off communication when he worked a case had moved beyond annoying. I had the same job, so I understood the risks, but not knowing if he was alive or dead, not being able to reach him or warn him, had cost us both—dearly. Now someone at ICO had a piece of us they shouldn't have, and the Tribunal had issued a death warrant for the operatives within ICO who knew of our existence.

After breakfast, James put his Dopp kit in a black leather satchel that sat on the floor inside my bedroom door. I tried not to take offence that he kept it perpetually packed, ready to grab and go at a moment's notice.

"If the Tribunal doesn't deal with ICO before you head to the caucus, leave the trackers here."

I nodded patiently at his reminder, the third one he'd given me since stringing his tracker on my bracelet. He kissed me one last time and then left for the airport to board a plane headed to San Francisco, where he'd meet with Mason. The exact location of the caucus wouldn't be disclosed until twenty-four hours beforehand. After the massacre at Cairabrae, no one on the Tribunal was taking any chances.

The home gym I'd set up in the third bedroom of the condo would feel too confined today. I needed space to burn off energy. I dressed in workout gear and ran a ten-kilometre circuit around the university.

At six o'clock that evening my mother still hadn't returned. I ate a dinner of ham and scalloped potatoes alone and then dished her a plate. This felt like our old life in Toronto, when I was going to university and she worked at the lab. Once again we occupied the same home but rarely saw each other. I texted her but it went unanswered. If she was in the library, she probably had her phone turned off.

When Mom finally came home, it was eight thirty. I set my book aside and listened to her slow footsteps approaching from down the hall. She plodded into the living room and dumped her shoulder bag as if it weighed fifty pounds.

"Tough day at the office?" I asked.

She shrugged out of her trench coat. "Has James left?"

"This morning."

Mom headed to the kitchen. I heard the creak of the oven door and the wrinkle of tinfoil. Moments later, she carried the plate I'd kept warm to the dining room table and took a seat. "This is good," she said, swallowing a mouthful. "Thanks."

"How was the library?"

"Good. I hired a grad student today. He starts tomorrow."

"Why?"

She raised a sardonic eyebrow. "Have you seen UBC's library?"

"Which one?"

"Exactly. I'm spending more time running around buildings and stacks than I am researching."

Alarm pricked the back of my neck. "You haven't told him anything ... about the gift ... have you?"

"No! You think he'd agree to work with a woman of questionable sanity?"

"Tell me what you're looking for, Mom. Let me help."

"Thanks, sweetheart, but the young man I hired is a master of library sciences student. He'll be far more efficient than either of us, and I'm only here until the end of the week."

Her avoidance of my question reinforced my belief that she was looking for evidence of the gift. I wanted to tell her she wouldn't find it, but she'd learn that for herself soon enough. "You're coming back, right?" I'd invited Mom to move in with me, at least until she found her feet on the coast.

Mom screwed up her face as if I'd asked a ridiculous question. "Of course. I'm going to hand off my research and pack up the condo. Shouldn't be more than ten days."

"You planning on working late again tomorrow?"

"For a few more days, yes."

"How about I meet you tomorrow? Say eight o'clock? We'll go for dinner."

"Tired of cooking?"

"Tired of not seeing you. It feels a little too much like our time in Toronto."

"Well then, let's try to fix that. Dinner tomorrow it is."

The next night, I took the usual precautions to ensure I wasn't followed. ICO knew where I lived, but I'd gone to extreme measures to hide who my mother was. I didn't trust them not to use her to get to me. Koerner Library was a twenty-minute walk away. I pulled my collar close, stayed alert and made it there without incident.

"Impressive," I said, when I found Mom. She'd managed to commandeer a carousel in a study room on the first floor, two floors below the main entrance.

Mom jerked her head up from behind a stack of books and journals. "Is it eight o'clock already?"

I tilted my head to read the books' spines. Mom twisted the pile away from my quizzical gaze. "You're researching ocean tides?"

"You should have called. I'd have met you upstairs." She scraped her chair back and grabbed her coat and bag. "Let's go," she said, nudging me ahead of her.

How did ocean tides tie into the gift? Perhaps I'd been wrong about her research subject. I dismissed the matter and we started out for the Point Grill, a ten-minute walk away. James and I had eaten at the Point a few times. We liked the casual atmosphere, and most nights the restaurant was busy enough to render us anonymous and mask our conversations.

After we were seated, Mom pulled out her tablet and showed me the real estate listing for the Toronto condo. "It went up this afternoon," she said. "The agent's showing it this weekend. She figures we'll have offers by Sunday."

Through dinner, we talked about her upcoming trip and impending move. The gift was the impetus behind all of it and yet that very subject never crossed our conversational threshold. It wasn't because of the public venue; the gift had somehow become a taboo topic. *Verboten.* As if talking about it made it more real.

We left the Point and stepped into a cool, starlit night. Mom tucked her hand in the crook of my arm as we strolled along the street, our footsteps the only sounds.

"I'll head off at the next corner," I said. She nodded, having gotten used to my routine. "Meet you back at—"

High-pitched yips startled us. A woman screamed. I dropped my mother's arm and raced toward the ferocious snarling around the corner.

At the forested edge of a small greenspace, a coyote had cornered a small fluffball of a dog. The dog held its ground, but it had been hurt and the coyote smelled blood. The only things keeping the coyote at bay were the screams and cartwheeling arms of the young woman standing too close. She stood to my right gripping an empty leash. The coyote was on my left and the injured dog straight ahead.

Without a second thought, I drew on the gift and, with a toss of my head, drilled a potent *spark* into the coyote. It yelped and turned on me, baring its teeth.

"Go on! Git!" I said, and stomped my feet. But the coyote had a meal within reach and wasn't keen to let it go. It lowered its head and snarled. I hurled another spark. It yelped again, and this time it charged me.

My next spark wasn't a warning. Its hind end collapsed, stopping it in its tracks. I took a step forward and the animal quickly righted itself and limped off into the bushes, abandoning its dinner. I bent over with relief.

The young woman raced for her dog and scooped it up. "Thank you," she said. Tears streamed down her face. Blood stained the white fur of the dog that quivered in her arms.

"He's probably in shock. Keep him warm," I said.

Mom appeared at my side. "I called campus security," she said, and to me she whispered, "We gotta go." She tugged my coat and I stumbled to follow. I stole a glance behind me. The woman ran to the street, where a vehicle with flashing lights approached. I turned and hurried after my mother into the shadows.

She marched west, opposite the direction of the condo. Neither of us said a word until we were across Northwest Marine Drive.

"What the hell was that?" she said, still marching forward.

Even with a brisk stride, I could barely keep up with her. "Have you not seen the warning signs around campus? About coyotes?"

"That's not what I'm talking about and you know it!" Anger fuelled her pace.

"Mom, stop," I said, and halted in my tracks. The *no good deed* axiom ran through my mind. My actions had forced a conversation I'd been dreading, but there would be no stopping it now.

The moment Mom realized I wasn't following, she turned. "I thought you were done keeping secrets."

I closed the distance between us and blew out a breath. "It's another facet of the gift. It's called a spark."

She frowned. "Another facet? How many more *facets* haven't you told me about?"

"I can't change any of this, Mom. Only Fliers born with the gift can give it away. I don't have that option. There's no getting rid of it. It's part of me."

"None of that has any bearing on you lying to me. Again. Or should I say *still*?"

"It has everything to do with it. I know you hate Jolene and what she did to me, but it's not curable. I can't be fixed. This is me now, warts and all, and it would be a lot easier for me to tell you about the warts if you'd accept some of the good things about this damned gift."

Mom stepped close. "There are no good things about that gift. Everything it allows you to do will get you killed."

"That sweet dog would be dead if I hadn't been able to scare off that coyote. That's something good."

She flung her arms into the air. "And what if you hadn't been able to scare it off? It could have been rabid. What if it had attacked you or that young girl?"

I lowered my voice. "Then I would have killed it."

My mother's face went slack. I'd gone too far.

"How?"

I straightened, confused. "What? You want a demonstration?" She jutted her chin. Not once had she asked for a demonstration of the gift, and she was choosing this?

She jutted her chin. "Show me. I want to see."

I knew that look. It meant there would be no escaping her stubborn determination. Exasperated, I blew out a breath. "All right. There," I said, nodding toward a sign with a white *H* on a blue background; a directional sign for the hospital. I called on the crystal that powered my gift and gathered the strength I needed for a powerful *jolt*. Mom's gaze turned slowly toward the intersection where the signpost stood. When the jolt was molten hot, I hurled it at the sign with a flick of my head. The post snapped and the sign blew loose and landed with a crash in the bushes.

Mom gasped and stared at the jagged stump of the post for a long minute. "I suppose that explains why your father was so fascinated with that second lens in Fliers' eyes."

"He never intended to share that information." It was Mom who'd unwittingly passed on his research to one of her colleagues.

"I know that now." She turned to face me. "We need to talk. I'll meet you at home." She stuffed her hands in her pockets and walked away.

I watched her until she crossed the street. Indeed, we needed to talk. Tonight she'd learn the rest of the terrible truth. For her, there would never be the awe and wonder of the gift to offset the Tribunal and what it did to protect us from those who would do us harm.

Unseen, I stepped off the path and into the forest, squeezed the crystal that lived alongside my soul, and ghosted.

Chapter Two

Waiting for my mother to arrive felt like backstage on opening night. I paced in front of the windows, palms sweating, and rehearsed what I needed to tell her. A pot of camomile tea steeped on the coffee table, though I suspected nothing less than Valium would reduce my anxiety.

A key turned in the lock. I forced myself to take a seat on the sofa and took a deep breath. Mom's footsteps came down the hall. Her bedroom door opened then closed, and a few moments later, she joined me. I tipped the teapot and poured two cups of tea without asking. Mom ignored my offering and walked to the bank of windows.

She stared out, rubbing her arms as if chilled. "I need to know everything you've been holding back," she said. "It's important."

"Important?"

She didn't turn around. "Yes."

"That's all you're going to tell me?"

She didn't answer. I couldn't guess at what she meant, but it didn't matter. Even if she never accepted what I was, she was a part of our world now; there were rules she had to heed, consequences she had to understand, and I'd put off telling her for long enough.

I swallowed a mouthful of tea and carefully set the cup back on the coffee table. Mom remained standing, her gaze focused on something outside. I started at the beginning and retold the history that Avery and, later, Stuart had imparted to me.

"When Fliers come of age, they become part of a local group of Fliers we call a covey. Dr. Coulter is the head of our covey here in

Vancouver. Coveys train together, protect one another and most importantly, maintain the secrecy of the gift. It's been that way for more than two hundred years."

Mom's shoulders remained stubbornly set. She kept her back to me.

I continued. "Before coveys, Fliers were unrestrained. Those who weren't guided by morals and the law grew rich using their gift. But it wasn't just wealth they were after. The biggest prize was the gift itself, and the most valued gift of all was that of a Ghost. Like me."

My mother shifted but didn't turn around.

"More times than not, gifting ends up killing the donor. That's one of the reasons for keeping the gift a secret. No one in Stuart's family has heard from Jolene since she gifted me. But secrets have a way of getting out, and back then, with no one to stop them, unscrupulous Fliers absorbed the gifts they stole, grew stronger, and passed those enhanced genes on to the next generations.

"Eventually, nine of the most powerful families of Fliers grew a conscience and put a stop to the practice. They formed the Tribunal Novem to police the ranks because no one else could. They put laws in place to control gifting and to protect the secrecy of the gift.

"But what no one knows is that each of the nine founding families carries the ghosting gene. In fact, most Fliers don't believe Ghosts actually exist. Long ago, the Tribunal wiped out all records of their existence, and what they couldn't erase they turned into folklore and fairy tales.

"But Carson Manse found out."

Mom's head pricked up at the mention of Carson. She turned around.

"He didn't like the way the Tribunal operated. He recruited like-minded Fliers and formed a group who called themselves the Redeemers. Their goal was to eliminate the Tribunal and replace them. That's the reason Carson targeted me. He'd known Jolene. He learned I had her gift and thought he could steal it, become a Ghost and then be able to fight the Tribunal. But he didn't know a gifted Flier can't relinquish the gift. I couldn't have gifted him even if I'd wanted to. Before the Redeemers were wiped out, they attacked the Tribunal at Cairabrae. I was there."

Mom raised her hand to cover her mouth.

"Cairabrae was the safe house Detective Jordan sent me to after Carson burned down the cottage. The Redeemers killed Stuart's wife, their cook, the wife of another Tribunal member, and others. They shot

James and my bodyguard and they would have killed everyone else, but we managed to stop them.

"I'll spare you the gory details of how—I don't care to relive them—but there is something you should know." I paused and steeled myself. "I was the one who killed Carson Manse."

I searched her face, waiting for the words to sink in.

"Good," she said with a conviction that startled me.

"Good?"

"After what he did to you? Yes. Good."

It wasn't the reaction I'd expected from her—far from it. "How is that okay with you?"

Mom came around the end of the sofa and sat beside me. Her gaze fell on the wedding ring she'd never abandoned. She twisted it slowly and looked up at me. "One day, when you have a child of your own, you'll understand."

The relief I wanted to feel remained out of reach. "I've come to terms with what I did, but I can't believe you aren't horrified by it."

"Horrified? No. I'm heartsick for you. You did what you had to."

I took her hand and squeezed it. "Thank you." Carson had paid with his life for the scars on my back and his attack at Cairabrae. Some days it didn't seem a high enough price.

After another mouthful of tea, I cradled the cup and continued. "Our secret got out that night at Cairabrae. Sam Jordan bore witness to it. So did a handful of police at the scene. Paramedics were called in to treat the injured, but the police couldn't detain the Fliers. They flew off in the chaos and disappeared. Mason and Stuart didn't have that option given the location.

"Later that night, before the bodies were removed, a helicopter arrived with a representative of a government-sanctioned organization none of us had ever heard of called International Covert Operations. ICO is as secretive, powerful and well funded as the Tribunal. They manage the inconvenient details governments can't using operatives they've embedded at all levels of law enforcement, government and the military on both sides of the border. The ICO rep was willing to overlook the bodies, to cover up what had happened and to keep our secret, but only if we joined forces with them.

"The Tribunal made the deal. ICO created a small dedicated division. James and I were *volunteered* to join them, and they recruited Detective Jordan because he'd already been exposed."

I stared into my cup. "I don't work with Avery Coulter. I work for ICO. Sam Jordan is my handler. Avery provided the job cover because you weren't cleared to know about ICO."

Mom inhaled a deep breath. "You never worked with Dr. Coulter?" she asked. I shook my head. "He had me fooled." She looked away.

"It was never a matter of fooling you. It was cover. But ICO won't be a factor much longer. Someone in their organization got greedy and ambitious. It's behind us now, but a few weeks ago they captured James and used him as bait to lure me into a trap. They betrayed us, and what they did to us threatens our existence—"

Mom's head shot around. "What did they do to you!"

I reached for her hand. "They didn't hurt me, Mom, but I don't know, exactly. They drugged us, took blood samples ... The worst of it is ... they extracted an egg, maybe two, and took James's sperm."

"Oh my god." Mom's shoulders slumped, as if my words had hollowed her out.

"That part hurts. When I think about what—" I stopped short, as I always did when the possibilities ran through my mind. "I just can't dwell on it. We have some leads, and good people are looking for what was stolen from us, but they haven't found it yet."

"You could have a child, Emelynn."

"Avery thinks the odds are quite low, but yes, it's a sobering possibility."

Mom straightened. "This is Jolene's fault. She should never have done this to you."

"Mom, please. Jolene paid a terrible price for what she did. I'm lucky her family doesn't hold it against me."

"*Lucky*? That's not the word I'd use."

I swallowed and Mom took a breath. "Because ICO crossed us, any day now, everyone in that organization who knew about Fliers will be gone. All their documentation will be destroyed and any data they have on us will be wiped clean."

She drew her eyebrows together. "Are you saying those people will be killed? By the Tribunal?"

"Yes. Like the Redeemers before them."

Mom jerked her head back. "What they did was horrible, no question, but what you're suggesting is murder."

"It is. So was killing Carson Manse."

"That was self-defence."

"I appreciate the benefit of the doubt, Mom, but no. It wasn't. And if he'd lived and been found guilty of a crime, there isn't a prison on the planet that could have held him. Or us. This is my world, Mom. This will be the world of my children because they will inherit the gene. The ghosting gene. Very few people outside of the Tribunal know about Ghosts. Sam Jordan knows, James's family knows. Avery Coulter knows. And now you know."

Mom pushed at the cuticle of her thumb. "And my knowing makes me a threat."

"Not as big a threat as ICO, but yes. You'll be expected to keep our secrets. It's not only for the Tribunal's sake; you'll be a target for anyone who thinks they can get to me through you. That's why James encrypted our phones, why we have to keep his communication protocols in place. It's why this condo, my cars, even the parking spaces downstairs are all owned by a maze of companies. None of it can be traced back to me, or you."

Mom grew quiet. The silence between us felt heavy.

"The Tribunal operates with impunity." She wasn't asking a question. It was a statement. She understood.

"You saw the damage I caused to that road sign. Any one of the Tribunal can deliver far more powerful jolts than that. The Tribunal were, and still are, the strongest of our kind. The Reynolds family—Jolene, Mason and Stuart—are descended from one of those nine founding families."

"Can you protect yourself from them?"

"Most of us can produce what's called a *block*. It will stop the jolts and sparks from weaker Fliers. But there's no protection from those who are stronger."

"What's the effect of one of these jolts?"

"Depends on its strength. They're all painful. Weaker ones knock you out. Stronger ones cause brain hemorrhages that can kill."

Mom looked away and stared blankly at the teapot. After a moment she stood and walked into the kitchen. A cupboard door banged, and then another. I heard the unmistakable glug of liquid being poured from a bottle. When she returned, she held two tumblers of amber liquid and handed me one. I sniffed it. Scotch.

She sat down beside me and swallowed a sip. "Is there more?"

"Nothing critical. You now know the worst of it."

Mom's gaze remained fixed on her glass as she gently swirled the liquor.

"What is it?" I asked.

"Remember the letter you found? The one from Jolene to your father?"

"Of course." I'd never forget it. That letter was how I learned that Jolene and my father had a relationship long before he met my mother. Jolene had written about the son she and my father had had, who'd died. It answered the question of why Jolene had chosen to gift me.

Mom took another sip from her glass. "I'm going to tell you something I've never told another soul." I stilled at the sombre tone of Mom's voice. "I remember Jolene's visit all those years ago—the one she wrote about in that letter. After I told your father she'd been to the cottage, he couldn't sleep for days. I'd never seen him so rattled. He warned me about her family's power and influence. I never understood his terror until now."

"Terror? What are you talking about?"

She raised her hand to silence me. "He made me promise if he should die unexpectedly, or of unnatural causes, I was to take you and run, that the police wouldn't be able to help us."

Chills turned my skin to gooseflesh.

She continued. "I thought he was being irrational—blamed it on sleep deprivation. Jolene's visit would have opened old wounds." My mother swallowed. "And then he died in that plane crash."

My mind spun back to that terrible time: an empty casket; a framed photo of my dad with a wide smile that seemed out of place for the occasion; my mother dressed in black; and tears. So many tears.

"I didn't remember his instructions at first. It had been twelve years since Jolene's visit. It wasn't until I read a newspaper account of the accident and saw the words in print that I recalled his warning of an unexpected death. That's why we abandoned the cottage, why I left Laura Taylor behind and became Laura Aberfoyle again. The only person who knew where we'd gone was Nanny Fran, who I swore to secrecy. You were furious with me, but I had no choice. You were the only thing I had left of him, and I had to keep you safe."

"Are you suggesting Dad's death wasn't an accident?"

"The investigation was inconclusive. They never found his plane."

"That doesn't mean—"

"Jolene didn't come to the cottage to introduce herself, Emelynn.

She came to reconnect with your father. Imagine how disappointed she must have been to find he'd married me, that we were expecting a child."

"Disappointed, yes, she said as much in her letter. If it hadn't been destroyed in the fire you could read it for yourself and you'd know. She held no resentment. She was sad, but she wished you both well. She understood that Dad had moved on."

"And yet she returned when you were twelve. Did her brother know? Her father? How many times before that had she returned to check on us? To see if your dad was still married. She was a Ghost. We would never have known if she'd been there."

"Even if she had, it wouldn't have mattered. Dad loved you. He loved me. He was happy. Even if Jolene had it in her to mess with that, and I don't believe she did, she wouldn't have been able to tear our family apart."

"But she did. She planted the gift in you and then disappeared. Two months later your father's plane vanishes. Makes me wonder if someone in Jolene's family knew she'd been visiting your father and blamed him for her disappearance. The timing of her gift to you and your father's death is too close to not be connected."

"You think Dad was murdered? That Mason or Stuart had something to do with it?"

Mom stared at me, her eyes set in hard lines. "Yes."

I scrambled up and made my way outside into the cool night air. She followed. I had no illusions about Mason. He was Tribunal. He'd wiped blood off his hands many times, but he had no reason to harm my father. And neither did Stuart.

I wrapped my arms around myself. "Mason loved Dad like a brother. Stuart respected him. They couldn't have done it."

"Your father's plane went down without warning on a clear day. No crosswinds, no dangerous weather of any kind, no other air traffic. The pilot had no prior accidents on his record, not even a near miss. They searched for days and never found a scrap of wreckage."

I turned to face her. "This is what you've been researching? There were five people on that plane. Any one of them might have had enemies who were responsible for the crash."

Mom fisted her hands. "How many of them had warned their wives of an untimely death?"

"Mason would never hurt me like that."

"The Reynoldses wouldn't have even known you."

I stormed away from her, back inside, and ended up standing in front of the windows facing the ocean. All these years later, my dad's death still hurt; the hole it had left in my heart had never healed. The thought that Mason or Stuart could have had a hand in his death made me want to vomit. The urge to escape, to take wing and fly away from the pain, overwhelmed me.

My mother approached and stood beside me.

I spoke to her reflection. "Why do I feel like you're on one side and I'm on the other?"

My mother quirked an eyebrow. "I don't feel that way. Why do you?"

I looked away. I couldn't hold her gaze because I knew why: I'd come to love Mason and Stuart as if they were my family, and that love now warred inside me, pitted against the love for my father.

I crossed over to the sofa and folded into it. Jarring thoughts ripped through my head. What had prompted my father's warning? Did he know about the Tribunal? I couldn't fathom Mason or Stuart being responsible for Dad's death, but they'd deceived me before.

"Did Dad ever tell you why he feared for his life?"

"No. Other than the warning about Jolene's family, he wouldn't discuss it. But it makes sense now. After what you just told me."

"I don't believe Mason or Stuart would do anything to hurt Dad. And I won't believe it. Not without proof."

Mom sat beside me and reached for her glass. "I think we're finally in agreement."

I cocked my head. "How do you figure?"

"You need proof, so do I."

"I take it you have a plan to get this proof?"

"The investigation of your father's accident was—is—inconclusive. Because no wreckage was ever found, the cause of the accident remains unknown. I think we might be able to pressure the authorities to reopen the file."

"How?"

"I've reviewed the original search results, the methodology, the equipment they used. Technology has advanced since then."

"You think a new search might find the wreck? After all this time?"

"There's a company called the Mansfield Group. They've developed radar technology that can find shipwrecks in cases where the old technology failed. The Transportation Safety Board hasn't used Mansfield's technology before, but we could make a case."

"You think if the Mansfield Group finds it, the Transportation Safety Board investigators will be able to tell if it was an accident or sabotage?"

"It's what the TSB does. I think it's worth a shot."

"A long shot."

Mom straightened. "If we find the wreck and the investigators conclude it was an accident, I will make peace with this gift of yours, warts and all."

"And if it turns out to be sabotage?"

"Then I will point the authorities in the right direction," she said, and crossed her arms with a look of self-satisfaction on her face.

I buried my face in my hands. Mom didn't quite grasp the problem. I pushed my hair back and blew out a breath. "That's where your line of reasoning falls apart. If a Ghost is found responsible, they'll make sure the proof disappears." Mom started to interrupt, but I cut her off with a shake of my head. "Even if by some miracle the proof remains intact and a Ghost is found guilty, where do you imagine they could be imprisoned? Locked up?"

Mom's face reddened. "There have to be consequences! They killed your father, I know it. They have to pay for that."

"They won't in the regular judicial system. Never."

Mom leapt up and stormed to the windows.

"But ... there is a way," I said.

Mom turned and tipped her head, waiting.

"Just so we're clear, I don't believe Mason or Stuart had a hand in Dad's accident." I raised my hand to cut off Mom's protests. "But, if it's proven that a Flier or a Ghost did have a hand in Dad's death, the only body that can hold them responsible is the Tribunal."

"The same Tribunal that sanctions murder? What if it was this Tribunal that sanctioned your father's murder?"

A headache threatened. I rubbed my temples. "I suppose it's possible, and that's more reason why this can't be a public investigation. The TSB can't be involved. Nor the police. We have to do this privately and quietly."

"To what end? If the Tribunal are guilty they won't be punished. Why not make as much noise around an investigation as possible. Publicize it. Sing the praises of the Mansfield Group and turn the search into a high-profile news event. Make it so public that the Tribunal won't be able to defuse it."

"If the Tribunal sanctioned the accident, a new investigation would threaten their exposure. They wouldn't tolerate that. They'd find a way to shut it down, or destroy Mansfield's technology. They might even plant proof of the results they want. There is no winning if the Tribunal are responsible. No, if this turns out to be sabotage, our only hope for justice will be if someone acted without the Tribunal's blessing. And we'll need to prove it without threatening to expose them."

"And if it turns out to be the Reynoldses, do you really believe the Tribunal will hold one of their own responsible?"

"They've done it before."

"Promise me then. If your father's accident is proven to be sabotage, you'll take the results to the Tribunal? Make the Tribunal hold those guilty responsible?"

"Do you know what that means, Mom? Whoever may have done this will die. The Tribunal will kill them."

"Like they killed your father?"

I stood and walked to the windows. I'd never seen this side of my mother before. Her grief for my father I knew well, but this vengefulness? She stared at my reflection.

"There will be no going back, no appeals. Are you absolutely certain you can live with that?"

"I'll sleep just fine," she said. "Promise me."

Though I wasn't at all sure I'd sleep just fine, I made that promise. "I will."

"Even if the investigation implicates Mason or Stuart?"

My hesitation was born of unfathomable dread. "If they killed Dad, they'll pay."

Chapter Three

In my room, I opened the drawer where I kept the crystal Mason had given me. Because his sister had gifted me, he considered me his niece. He'd asked me to think of him as my uncle, and I did. Likewise, his father, Stuart, treated me like a granddaughter. The crystal had belonged to Mason's mother, Jeannette. It rested in a white-gold case of fine filigree. The necklace's chain was attached to either end of the case. A latch on one side of the case opened to reveal the clear, six-sided crystal. It was an heirloom. Most Ghosts' crystals were, passed down from grandparents to grandchildren.

In the hand of a Ghost, with a bit of pressure, the crystal would melt. When it did, the Flier would achieve that state where his or her physical form dissolved into molecules. Every Ghost needed a crystal to achieve that state—every Ghost except me. My crystal lived in my soul. It wasn't a physical thing I could touch, and this kept it safe. No one knew the secret of my crystal and I planned on keeping it that way.

To me, Jeannette's crystal was simply a beautiful piece of jewellery. I pulled it out of its case and warmed it in my palm. I refused to believe that the man who had given this to me, or that his father, Jeannette's husband, would harm my dad. They had loved him. I felt it with all my heart.

When I finally crawled into bed, sleep played hard to get. Mom had stirred up a whirlwind of emotions that fought for space in the sleepless hours. I felt like a traitor to Mason and to Stuart. But if Mom was right, and Dad's crash wasn't an accident, then someone had to have set it up.

Loyalties warred in my conscience, tearing me in two. Sleep only came after I stopped thinking about who would have wanted my dad dead and focused instead on the possibility that one of the other people aboard the plane was the target.

In the morning when I stumbled into the kitchen, the coffee was already made. I poured a cup and found Mom with a large nautical chart spread out on the dining room table. The shadows under her eyes made me think we looked like matching poster girls for uncomfortable mattresses.

"What's that?" I asked.

"The Queen Charlotte Islands. Haida Gwaii. This is the area where investigators figured your father's plane went down." She pointed to a north-south rectangle the size of the islands themselves.

"That's huge."

"Two hundred and fifty kilometres."

I took a sip of the coffee. Barely seven in the morning, we hadn't even started the search, and already the task looked hopeless. "No wonder they couldn't find it."

"The pilot radioed twice before the plane dropped off the radar." She pointed to an X drawn an inch inside the top of the rectangle. "They concentrated the search in this area when they still had reason to believe they'd find survivors." She drew her finger around an area one third the size of the whole rectangle. "After two days, the search expanded based on calculations of the plane's departure time, the route they expected the pilot to follow, typical speeds and the timing of the two calls."

The smaller area was only fifty kilometres long and ten across but still a formidable search grid.

"I'm going to ask Sam to help us," I said. "He can put his detective skills to work. Plus, he knows all the players and the risks."

"I thought I'd approach the Mansfield Group. See if they're interested."

"No. It's too risky. Your name can't be connected to any part of this. If Sam agrees to help, let him handle the Mansfield Group."

"Risky? How?"

"If word of a new search leaks out, I don't want anyone thinking they can shut it down by threatening you. You can't defend yourself. They can come after Sam or me."

"I'm not comfortable with that."

"Mom, be reasonable." I pointed to the chart. "You've already done the legwork, reviewed the investigation and found the Mansfield Group. You've done everything. Besides, you're leaving for Toronto in two days."

"Don't shut me out."

"I'll tell you everything I learn."

After a bite to eat, I drove Dad's old red MGB to my rendezvous with Sam. Our usual protocol was to meet at Denny's, but both ICO and the police department where Sam was embedded were familiar with that routine. Instead, we met at Grounds for Coffee on Alma, in Point Grey. We'd used the coffee shop before without raising suspicion, and as a bonus, Grounds for Coffee made a tasty cinnamon roll.

I balanced a tray with our coffees and two of the signature sticky buns and claimed a small table at the back. Sam arrived and pulled off his aviators just inside the door. At six foot two with shoulders as wide as the door, people looked. They'd see a cop, maybe a military man. It was the brush cut. Without that, they might guess football player or pro wrestler. Sam didn't move toward me until he'd surveyed each and every customer in the busy coffee shop.

He took a seat with his back to the wall, and only then did he look at me. "How many people are joining us?" he said, staring at the cinnamon-laced pastries.

"Wow, Sam. Leading with humour? Things must be going really well with you and Naomi." Sam reached for his cup. He had the hots for an accountant named Naomi Russel. He wouldn't admit it, but I'd seen it when he hired her to do a forensic audit a few weeks ago. "She still working on the Chinese embassy case?"

"As far as ICO knows, we're all still working the embassy case. But no. Naomi finished up. I don't want her anywhere close to us when ICO gets dusted. I don't suppose you've heard anything?" Sam pried the lid off his coffee.

"No. The Tribunal's keeping us in the dark. Sebastian's worried we might do something to tip their hand. I swear he thinks we're morons." Sebastian Kirk was the man who'd *volunteered* me to work with ICO. Not only did I report to him, he was also the current head of the Tribunal Novem.

"And James?"

"He hasn't heard anything either, but he's hoping the Tribunal makes their move before ICO read in a new handler for him. One less person exposed."

"I never imagined this would be the note my career ended on."

"Your career doesn't have to end with ICO's demise."

"You think I can go back to being a cop knowing what I know, condoning what's about to happen?" He picked up his knife and fork and stabbed into his sticky bun as if it had offended him.

"ICO set you up. General Cain may not have done it himself, but he didn't stop them either. He didn't even tell you we'd been compromised until months after the fact." Cain was the man Sam reported to. He should have protected Sam. "You're a disposable asset to Cain. You made the right choice."

"Doesn't make it any easier to live with."

"No. You're right. It's not easy. But I'm glad you chose us."

He nodded as he speared a piece of bun and stuffed it in his mouth. After he'd swallowed, he said, "You called this meeting. What's up?"

Between sips of coffee and bites of sticky bun, I told him about the latest developments with my mom, starting with the coyote encounter and ending with her revelation about my father's warning.

"Mason and Stuart are like family to me. I don't want to think they had anything to do with my father's death, but you know what they are, what they're capable of. My father was afraid for his life, and he named them. I need to learn the truth about what caused Dad's plane to go down."

"Your father's death was ruled an accident. No agency is going to reopen the investigation without compelling new evidence."

"Which we don't have, but we don't want it reopened, at least not officially. We want to hire someone to conduct a private search for the wreckage."

He lifted his eyebrows. "There's nothing stopping you, but it'll be expensive."

I nodded. "I figured as much. Mom's found a company with the technology to look for the wreck, but her name can't be attached to this in any way. And that brings me to the crux of this meeting. How do you feel about taking on a new job?"

Sam licked glaze from his finger. "Considering my pending unemployment? I'm interested."

"I was hoping you'd say that." I dug into my purse and handed Sam a piece of paper. "The Mansfield Group is the name of the company Mom found. That's their website."

Sam read the name and tucked the paper away.

"There's more. My father was one of five people on that plane. If the accident turns out to be sabotage, any one of those five may have had enemies capable of murder. I want to investigate everyone."

"I agree. You said your mom has the original report?"

"She has everything: the detailed investigation, newspaper clippings, the notes from the search team, charts, you name it."

"I'll need to talk with her."

"Great! Why don't you come for dinner tonight? Mom and I can be Jordan Investigations' first clients."

"Jordan Investigations?" With Sam's chuckle, some of the weight lifted from my conscience. "You going to be my partner in this new company?"

I frowned, contemplating the idea. "If I do we'd have to rename it. Jordan Taylor Investigations."

"At least you put Jordan first."

"Don't let it go to your head. It's strictly an alphabetical arrangement."

Sam and I shared a laugh. Even though the company was a lark, it felt good to have him on board. I trusted Sam. He had no twisted Flier agenda, no ego. Even back when he'd been investigating me, he'd been fair. Tough but honest. Just the kind of man you'd want to have your back.

He thanked me for the coffee and was halfway to the door when my phone rang.

It was Mom. "You've got company, sweetheart."

"Who is it?"

"Sebastian Kirk. He says he'll wait if you're coming home soon."

Crap! "I'll be there in twenty minutes. And Mom, don't let him see your charts."

I rushed from the coffee shop and made it home without a speeding ticket despite my efforts.

Mom's voice carried down the hall as I closed the door. "There she is."

Sebastian stood as I came into the living room. "Sebastian. This is a surprise." He wore his hair short and brushed forward. It reminded me of images I'd seen of Julius Caesar. Perhaps that's the comparison he'd intended.

He leaned in to kiss me on the cheek. "A pleasant one, I hope."

Never, I thought, but I managed an agreeable smile. Sebastian excelled at the gentlemanly manners game when it suited him. "I see you've met my mother."

"Yes. Laura was kind enough to make me a coffee."

"Thanks, Mom."

"We've been chatting about Toronto." He looked at my mother with a smarmy smile and a twinkle in his small, dark eyes. "Looks like I have to visit the Royal Ontario Museum next time I'm there."

"Oh?" The ROM? Mom must have been dipping into the reserve fund to come up with conversational fodder. "Did you tell him about your move?"

"I haven't had a chance." Mom stood and smoothed her slacks. "You'll have to fill him in. If you'll excuse me, I must be going."

"It's been a pleasure to meet you, Laura," Sebastian said, and offered his hand. When she clasped it, he covered it with his other hand and smiled as though he wanted a donation. "Until next time."

Mom schooled her face in a pleasant smile—the one I called her smile mask. Sebastian hadn't fooled her. She turned to me. "I'll be at the library if you need me."

"Take the MGB if you want, Mom. I won't need it."

Sebastian waited until the door closed behind my mother before he spoke. "She's a lovely woman."

"She is. I thought you were in Ottawa." *Taking care of eliminating ICO* went unsaid.

"Yes. I was. May I?" he asked, as if he needed permission to sit.

"Of course." I took a seat opposite with my back to the windows. "Is it over, then? With ICO?"

"In a minute," Sebastian said, ignoring my prompt. "First, tell me about your mother's visit."

Casual questions from Sebastian were never wholly casual. "There's nothing to tell. We've had a wonderful visit. Thank you, by the way, for arriving through the lobby."

"Simply doing what you asked," he said. "I have no desire to destroy your mother's illusions."

Illusions? I took a breath. Did Sebastian have to work at being caustic, I wondered, or did it come naturally? "I'm finished lying to my mother. She knows about us."

"And you didn't tell me she knew? I'm sure she's wondering why I didn't address it."

"I'm sure she's not."

WINGS OF PREY 25

He arched an eyebrow. "I've been here ten minutes and already you're being impertinent."

It was dangerous to forget what Sebastian was capable of. "You're right. I apologize. Mom only learned of the Tribunal a few days ago. She has no idea that you're on it, let alone the head of it, so there's nothing for you to address."

"I assume you advised her on the need for caution, complete secrecy."

No. I gave her a bullhorn. "I have. She's handling it remarkably well, considering. She also knows that Dr. Stein was responsible for the break-in at her condo. That's why she's moving. She's returning to Toronto in a few days to wrap up her work and sell the condo and then she's moving in with me."

"Dr. Stein's the man she gave your father's research to?"

"Yes. He's a colleague. Mom doesn't feel safe around him anymore. With good reason."

"Indeed."

Sebastian's focus on my mother left me uncomfortable. "At the risk of sounding impertinent again, why are you here?"

Sebastian tugged at the cuff of his jacket. "There was a hiccup in the execution of the plan to eradicate ICO."

He said it as if in passing but alarm registered. I straightened and waited for him to enlighten me.

"Cain has escaped our net. Disappeared."

"What!"

Sebastian whipped his head up and narrowed his eyes in warning.

I softened my tone. "What happened to the bug I planted on him?"

"He found it. Used it to misdirect us. He wasn't where he should have been when the time came."

That trick shouldn't have surprised Sebastian. It was the same ruse James and I were playing with ICO's trackers, and Sebastian knew all about that. "When did he go missing?"

"Yesterday. The rest of the plan was executed beautifully. The data they held concerning us has been destroyed."

Only Sebastian would gloat in the face of a major screw-up. "Where is Cain now?"

"I don't know."

I closed my eyes and inhaled a deep breath.

Sebastian continued. "From what I've observed, Cain's not the type to run. He'll try to negotiate."

"Which means he'll contact Sam." Sam was the conduit between General Cain and me.

"I suspect he'll target you. You have the link to us, not Detective Jordan."

"Terrific. He knows where I live. Now my mother's in danger and so is Sam."

"Jordan signed up for this. As for your mother, perhaps she could be convinced to leave for Toronto sooner than she planned."

"Cain could be out there right now, picking her off."

"After all I taught you? He couldn't possibly know she has a connection to you. Unless you've been careless."

"I haven't." Sebastian's mentorship wasn't one I'd sought. Mason had foisted Sebastian on me to get the man out of his hair in the run-up to his assuming the Tribunal's leadership, a handover that occurred every five years. As arrogant as Sebastian could be, he'd taught me techniques thieves and spies would pay good money to learn.

"Then she's just another tenant in the building. You have nothing to worry about."

"Until Cain shows up at my door."

"Yes. Which is why your mother should leave as soon as possible."

And I'd told Mom she knew the worst of it. Damn. Telling her she had to leave, and why, would smack of my not telling her the whole truth. She'd worry about me, but not before she ranted and railed against the gift ... again.

"I'll talk to her."

"Good. And another thing. I'll need to install tracing software on your phone in the event Cain elects to negotiate by phone."

"You'll have to organize that with James. He's made my phone impenetrable. I can't even download an app without his help."

He offered me a politician's smile. "In that case, perhaps you can have James call me."

Far be it for Sebastian to make the call. "I'll do that. In fact, I'd prefer Cain to contact me by phone."

"Don't count on it. You're wearing his RF transmitter aren't you?"

Damn it! I pulled back my sleeve and dangled the lockets on the bracelet. "If you'd told me about Cain's escape yesterday, I wouldn't also be wearing James's tracker."

Sebastian blinked. Once, twice. "Then Cain will be expecting both of you. What are you going to do about that?"

What a piece of work. "I'll deal with it," I said, shaking my head. "How?"

Urgh! He'd donned his mentor cap. "Another lesson?" Sebastian hollowed his cheeks, clearly impatient for me to play pupil. I went with the flow. Not doing so would only prolong his visit. "We can't destroy it yet. As long as Cain thinks he has something on us, we can use it. I'll plant James's tracker in a hotel. Cain can think what he will."

"Lovers' quarrel?" Sebastian said with a nod, and stood. That I was annoyed with him didn't even hit his radar. My annoyance was beneath him, like a lower life form on the underside of his shoe.

Sebastian said goodbye and left. This time, it wasn't through the lobby. He lingered a moment in ghosted form and then he was gone. When I could no longer sense him, I reached for my phone and dialled James.

"Sebastian just left," I said. "Have you heard the news?"

"About ICO? Yeah. Mason had a report this morning and filled me in. A few glitches, but otherwise a smooth rollout."

"A few glitches? A smooth rollout? Is that what he said? Who reported to Mason?"

"Don't know. What have you heard?"

"Cain's on the loose and Sebastian doesn't know where he's gone."

James cursed under his breath. "What's Sebastian's plan?"

"He's playing a waiting game—waiting for Cain to contact me to try to negotiate."

"You? What about Jordan?"

"I'm closer to the power brokers than Sam. Besides, Cain knows exactly where to find me. I'm the one with the tracker."

"Shit!"

"Yeah. Sebastian didn't know I had yours on me."

"Get rid of it."

"Not yet. We may need it yet to redirect Cain. For now, I thought I'd plant it in a hotel somewhere ... unless you've got a better idea?"

"I do. After I tell Mason what's really going on, I'll catch a red-eye and see you later tonight."

"No. As much as I appreciate the whole knight-in-shining-armour idea, the caucus is only days away. Mason needs you there. I can handle Cain."

"Cain will be desperate, dangerous. His entire network just evaporated."

"I know. But I've got Sebastian on speed dial. Speaking of which, Sebastian would like you to call him. He wants to install tracing software on my phone to help him find Cain if and when he calls."

"That'll give him access to your calls. All of them."

"Shit."

"I'll send you another phone, but until you get it, know that he'll be able to listen in and collect phone numbers."

"If that's the case, don't install the trace until I get the new phone."

"I'll overnight it today. Text me when you get it. And Em, I hope you were kidding about speed-dialling Sebastian. You can't count on him to help you. You have to be prepared to handle Cain on your own."

"I am and I'll be careful. Besides which, I can do this nifty disappearing trick."

"That nifty trick didn't help you out the last time."

His words caught me by surprise. I sucked in a breath. "I didn't need that, James."

"You can't take Cain lightly. He's a professional soldier. Stay alert. Please. You'll keep in touch?"

The screech of the turning tables was deafening, but his concern felt genuine. "Of course."

When we disconnected, I immediately dialled Sam. Ping-ponging from one crisis to another gave me indigestion.

"Sebastian just left," I said, when he answered.

"What did he want?"

"They pulled the trigger on ICO yesterday."

I heard him blow out a breath. "Well, I guess that's that."

"Not quite. Cain escaped."

"What?" Sam said, raising his voice. "How'd that happen?"

"Seems he found the bug we planted," I said. "Used it to make it look like he was somewhere he wasn't when they went looking for him."

"They underestimated him."

"Sebastian thinks Cain's going to approach me. Try to negotiate a way out. I've got to get my mom out of here."

"Where is she now?"

"At the university, but I know her. She won't want to leave me. She's more likely to go if you're here."

"I can be there in half an hour."

"I'll book her a flight."

Booking the flight was easy. Reaching my mother was another

matter entirely. By the time Sam arrived at the condo, I had my mother's things packed and by the door. The charts she'd shown me of Haida Gwaii were rolled up and neatly stowed in a weatherproof carry case.

"Mom's not answering," I said, when Sam questioned the luggage in the hall. "We'll have to find her at the university and hope she listens to reason. She's in the Koerner Library on the Main Mall." We agreed to meet inside the front entrance.

Sam grabbed my mother's things and I closed the door behind him. I made a final check to make sure I hadn't forgotten anything and then ghosted up to the rooftop. The daylight left me no option but to remain in ghosted form. My stamina was improving, but I could still only hold that form for thirty minutes or so before exhaustion forced me to re-form. I got my bearings and flew a straight line to the library. When the glass-and-steel building was in sight, I dove down, passed through the main doors and re-formed in a vacant meeting room.

I smoothed my hair, opened the door and nearly knocked over a skeleton of a man looking down at me through eyeglasses perched on the end of his nose. Keys dangled from his outstretched hand. "This room is booked. You'll have to clear out."

"All done," I said, and whisked out of there before he wondered how I'd gotten in. Sam stood in the lobby looking like a guest lecturer in the criminology department.

"Hi," I said. "This way." Sam followed me to the stairs and down to the first floor. We wordlessly made our way to the study room where my mother had managed to appropriate a cubicle. She was hidden behind a stack of books, each one flagged with colour-coded index cards.

"Mom?"

She lifted her head, but her smile dropped at the sight of Sam by my side. "What is it?"

"We need to talk."

Mom stood and reached for her purse. "Not here. Follow me." She led us into the stacks and to the end of a lonely row of books that reached to the low ceiling on both sides. Sam played sentry at the head of the aisle and tipped out books as if he were looking for something.

Mom squared her shoulders as I explained what had happened. Her gaze kept flickering to Sam.

"Cain knows where I live, Mom. You're not safe there until he's dealt with."

"Killed, don't you mean? Using euphemisms doesn't change that."

"Would you rather not know?"

Mom shook her head. "How could Jolene, a mother, have done this to you? A child."

"I've packed your things. They're in Sam's car. Your flight leaves at four o'clock this afternoon."

"Did you fill in the detective on our plans to find your father's plane?"

"Yes. He's interested. But it'll have to wait now."

"No. I'm not waiting another moment. You say you packed my things. Did you bring the charts?"

"They're in Sam's car."

"Get them. I'll book a meeting room."

"Mom, we don't have time for this."

She checked her watch. "We have thirty minutes. You'd better hurry." She turned on her heel and beetled away.

Sam stared after her and shot me a quizzical glare.

"She's not going anywhere until she gets you up to speed on my father's plane crash. You know that canister in her luggage?" Sam nodded. "Bring it in. And her luggage. Meet us back at her cubicle."

By the time Sam returned with the charts, Mom had a key for one of the meeting rooms and a portfolio stuffed with papers. She didn't say a word as she marched us into the windowless room and closed the door. She took the canister from Sam and explained the reasoning behind the search area as she unfurled the charts. Sam held a palm against the top edge to keep it from rolling up. Two stars marked the plane's position when each radio call was made. Mom shuffled through her papers and showed Sam the investigator's calculations.

"Take the charts and my notes," Mom said, repacking the portfolio. "The research paper on the Mansfield Group's technology is in here, too. I'll email you everything else."

"Send it from the phone James programmed for you," Sam said. "It's encrypted."

Mom nodded to Sam and turned to me. "I don't like this one bit."

"I know. I'm sorry."

She leaned in and we embraced. "I love you, Mom."

"I love you, too. I must go," she said, and pushed away. "I need to find my student and give him some direction before I leave. Take every precaution, please."

I nodded. She spun around and rushed out.

"Looks like I have some homework," Sam said. He rolled up the charts and stuffed them back in their carrying case. "Your mother is one determined woman."

"Maybe a little too determined." Sam cocked an eyebrow. "I'm not convinced she understands who she's dealing with."

"The Tribunal?"

"I'm worried she'll cross them if this doesn't turn out the way she wants it to."

"Laura doesn't strike me as careless. And I don't think she'd do anything that might jeopardize you."

I hung my worry on that reassuring thought and we went our separate ways.

Chapter Four

Back inside the condo, I felt my mother's absence like a chill. I pulled on a sweater and filled the kettle.

When the tea was ready, I poured a cup, settled in a club chair in the living room and swivelled to face the floor-to-ceiling windows. Darkness fell with no word from Cain. I called Sam. He hadn't heard from Cain either.

"You being careful?" I asked.

"Don't waste your worry on me. I'm bunking in the station. Cain can't pull anything here. Not without his team, and they're gone. You should come in, help me beat through your mother's paperwork."

"Maybe I will. Later though. I have to drop James's tracker somewhere convincing, and after that, there's someone I have to talk to."

"The doctor?" Sam knew Avery was one of us, but he respected that I wasn't at liberty to confirm that information.

"Yeah. I don't want to do it over the phone. I'm going to fly over there."

I hung up relieved to know Sam was safely ensconced at the police station with a project to keep boredom at bay.

Next, I dialled Avery and invited myself over. I changed into the dark clothes that would mask my flight, set the condo's security alarm and ghosted to the rooftop for the second time that day. The evening was cool but dry. Perfect for flight. Avery lived in St. George, an old-money neighbourhood thirty minutes south of me. I checked my ponytail, fastened my Ryders and lifted off, desperate for the release that flight always provided.

Once over the Pacific, I let loose the speed that marked my gift as Jolene's. The wind cleansed my mind, cleansed my body. There wasn't a drug in the world that came close to the euphoria that flight instilled in every fibre of my being.

South of the Vancouver airport, I flew inland and used my wrist-mounted GPS to zero in on the Marriott Hotel. After landing on the roof, I tucked James's tracker under a loose piece of flashing and resumed my flight to St. George.

By the time I'd arrived at Avery's, the day's stress was flushed out and I felt invigorated. I dropped into the tree cover in Avery's backyard and brushed myself off as I approached his back door. The lights were on but through the French doors, I could see that he wasn't in the kitchen. I removed my Ryders and tapped on the door.

He appeared from his study on the left. "Emelynn," he said, holding the door. "Come in."

I kissed his cheek as I passed. Avery was a physician to most in the covey, but to me, he was much more than that. "Hope I'm not ruining your evening."

"Never," he said, and pulled the door closed. "Victoria will be home shortly. Will you stay for dinner?"

"If I'm not imposing, I'd love to."

"Not at all. It's lasagna. We'll be eating it for a week. What brings you by?"

I hated that more times than not, what brought me by was unwelcome news. Avery had found me when I lay broken in a hospital bed before I knew what I was. He'd taken me under his protection and taught me most of what I knew about Jolene's gift. He was the closest thing I had to a father and I loved him dearly. The update could wait a few minutes. "How are the wedding plans going?"

He examined the reading glasses he held in his hand. "That bad, huh?"

"That obvious?"

He offered a sympathetic smile. "You need to work on your deflection technique. But since you asked, our idea of a small affair did not sit well with Victoria's family. They asked us to consider Christ Church Cathedral. Victoria's an only child. Hard to say no. We'll have to push the date to next spring, and you can't imagine how many details need sorting out, but Victoria's got a good handle on it."

Avery opened the oven door to check on dinner. The room filled with the rich scent of tomato and basil. The cheese wasn't yet bubbling.

He poured us each a glass of wine and we took them to his study. Behind the desk, the curtains to the back garden were drawn. We settled in the wingback chairs in front of the fireplace.

"Might as well get it over with," he said, urging me on.

Avery and I didn't keep secrets. Not about anything important. I couldn't always tell him about Tribunal affairs, which he understood, but I probably told him more than I should.

I unloaded the latest news: about my mother, the investigation, Sam's involvement and, finally, the business with ICO and Cain. He probed about Cain, and I knew he'd share with the covey what he needed to ensure their safety, but nothing more. Not without my permission. He'd earned my trust completely.

"And James?" he asked.

"He's in California helping Mason with security ahead of the caucus."

"He and Mason are getting along?"

"For now. Stuart's been encouraging Mason to make an effort."

Avery frowned. Doubt flitted across his features.

"There's a reason for that." I drew my fingertip around the edge of my glass. "James asked me to marry him." Avery's face lit up, but I stomped on his exuberance. "We're keeping it quiet."

"You said yes?"

I nodded and watched his gaze slide to my left hand. "No ring." James had given me earrings instead. Exactly James's style. He valued his privacy and shunned public displays of affection. He'd said the sparkling grey-green stones reminded him of the colour of my eyes.

"Why the big secret?"

"That's on me. Having kids has become a priority for James now that his family is free of the Tribunal's control. I need some time to get my head around that."

"You'll be a terrific mom."

My appreciation leaked out in a thin smile. "Thanks, but it's not just about kids. My connection to the Reynoldses rubs James raw. The fact that I accepted Jolene's inheritance drives him crazy. He hates that I'm a Ghost, and that's despite the fact that our children, the kids he wants so badly, will be Ghosts."

"Whoa, Em. If these were issues for James, he wouldn't have asked you to marry him."

"He's convinced we can work them out."

"And how do you feel?"

"I know he loves me, but he's not being honest with himself."

"You think he's going to change his mind?"

"I don't know. Maybe he should."

"And yet—you said yes."

"I thought I'd lost him when ICO had us cornered at Vector Labs. It scared me. Made me rethink some things."

"Answer me this: can you imagine your life without him?"

"No. At least, I don't want to."

"That right there is your answer. The rest of it's just noise."

Victoria's arrival ended our conversation. At the sound of her footsteps down the hall, Avery called out, "We're in the den."

She arrived through the kitchen entrance and dropped an armful of shopping bags on the desk. "Hi, Emelynn." She bent her willowy frame to kiss Avery, and her long blonde hair fell forward. She straightened and with a flip of her head, flung the hair back over her shoulder.

"How'd it go with your mom?" Avery asked.

"She finally settled on a dress." Victoria turned to me. "She's taken longer to choose her outfit than it took me to find my entire trousseau. I had to threaten to elope if she dragged me to one more shop." She handed Avery a folded newspaper.

"Sounds like she's enjoying it," I said, thinking of my own mother. Would she enjoy the mother-of-the-bride spotlight?

"A little too much, but as she reminds me, she's only doing this once."

"And she'll have to live with the photos for decades," I added.

"True. She wants my seal of approval on her choice, and I grumble about it, but I love that she's so keen on Avery. We really are fortunate." She beamed a smile at Avery that would have melted Boreas, the Greek god of the frozen north.

"Have you seen that?" Victoria asked, referring to the newspaper she'd handed Avery.

Avery unfolded it and scanned the headlines. Something caught his attention and he straightened. His gaze fixed on the front-page teaser. He opened the newspaper and found the full article. "Interesting," he said with a poker face, and handed the newspaper to me.

The headline read, "American Tax Dollars at Work: Clandestine Government Organization Funds Paranormal Research." Victoria's voice faded into the background as I read the article. An unnamed source within the CIA was whistle-blowing from the grave. The article speculated the whistle-blower must have had high-level clearance to provide the details, which were released to the press when he died.

I looked up from the newspaper and met Avery's stare. Victoria hadn't noticed our diverted attention and collected her bags from the desk. "I'll be back in a few minutes," she said, and excused herself.

Avery waited until her footsteps faded away. "You thinking that's the CIA director who infiltrated ICO?"

"A posthumous poisoned pill?"

"It might not have anything to do with us."

"But the timing's right," I said. "Too coincidental not to be. I have to call Sebastian and make sure he knows about it."

"I'll give you some privacy." Avery stood. "Need to check on dinner anyway."

When the door closed behind him, I dialled Sebastian.

"Hello, Emelynn," he answered. "What is it?"

A rude retort popped into my head. I counted to three. "There may be another hiccup. Have you seen the story in the paper?"

"The paper is full of stories. Which one?"

I fought the urge to define *impertinence*. I read him the headline. "The reporter says someone in the CIA had the documents, which were released posthumously."

There was silence on the other end of the phone. "Sebastian?"

"One moment!" I heard his footsteps and then a door closing. More silence. I waited. "Did Mason ask you to bring this to my attention?"

"No. I haven't talked to Mason yet."

"You sure?"

"Why are you asking, Sebastian?"

"This scenario plays right into his foolish notion of going public, does it not?"

Though I hadn't thought of it, Sebastian had a point, but I quickly dismissed it. "Having our hand forced is exactly the type of situation Mason is trying to avoid. This sounds like the work of the CIA director who infiltrated ICO and set us up."

Silence again. "Perhaps," Sebastian said. "Stay close by. I may need you."

"I'm not—" I'd been about to say *at home*, but the dick had hung up on me.

I tucked my phone away, upended my wine glass and joined Avery in the kitchen.

He stood in front of a chopping board preparing a salad. "How'd it go?"

"Sebastian is such an ass."

"You've mentioned that once or twice before," he said with a chuckle.

"He wants me at his beck and call tonight. Sorry, Avery, but I'd better go. I'll head to the police station and wait with Sam. May I take this?" I said, referring to Victoria's newspaper.

"Go ahead. You sure Sebastian can't wait until after dinner?"

"Sebastian and wait don't really go together. Will you say goodbye to Victoria for me?"

"Of course."

Avery saw me out the back door and wouldn't let me leave empty-handed. I waved before ascending through the trees. Skirting the suburban lights, I made my way into the city then used rooftops to hide my presence until I was able to drop down to street level and re-form a few blocks from the station where Sam worked, off Cambie Street.

I presented myself to the officer at reception. Sam showed up moments later and signed me in. He handed me a visitor badge on a lanyard, which I slipped around my neck. Then his gaze fell to the package in my hands. He tipped his head in question.

"Dinner," I said. "Avery's lasagna." Neither of us spoke in the elevator, or in the kitchen, where we stopped to collect dishes on the way to his office.

After he closed his door behind us, he spoke. "What happened?"

I pulled the newspaper out of my jacket and handed it to him. While he read, I manhandled a slice of lasagna out of Avery's dish and inadvertently decorated Sam's desk with cheese strings.

"Shit. This the CIA director who sold us out?"

"Don't know. The article doesn't ID him."

"Doesn't matter. The CIA's not going to claim him now." Sam tossed the paper on his desk. "Funding for the CIA's black ops is as secure as ICO's. Even with the whistle-blower's detailed accounting, those funds will be untraceable. Whoever the dead guy is, he'll be a joke come tomorrow's paper."

"Sebastian seems worried about it."

"Waste of energy. There won't be any tracks to cover by now." He rounded his desk and dropped into the big swivel chair. "This for me?" he said, pointing to the plate I'd dished.

"Yeah. You sure about that?"

"Uh-huh," he mumbled, his mouth already full.

"Just the same, I'm going to call Mason. Lord knows I can't trust Sebastian to do it. He seems to think this plan of his to deal with ICO has rolled out *beautifully*."

I took a seat in one of the two guest chairs in front of Sam's desk, and while Sam ate, I found the article online and emailed it to Mason. Then I phoned him. "Sam thinks it'll blow over. Says there won't be any way to tie the funding back to the CIA or ICO."

"The detective's right. I'll pass that along when I hear from Sebastian. Thanks for the heads-up on his suspicion. I'll quash it. James told me about Cain. Any word from him yet?"

"None. James is putting a trace on my phone so Sebastian can locate Cain if he calls. I'll have to divert the calls I don't want Sebastian to overhear to the new phone James is sending. I'll call you with the number."

"And Laura?"

"Sam helped me get her out of here. She's left for Toronto. How's the prep for the caucus coming along?"

"We'll be ready. And if Cain hasn't made his move before the caucus, you come anyway. I want you here."

"I know. I'll be there."

After I disconnected, Sam asked, "You'll be where?"

"At the caucus. Not that I can influence anything—the leadership is preordained to change hands every five years—but it's important to Mason. Moral support, I think."

I took a bite of the lasagna. If Avery ever had to hang up his lab coat, a chef's jacket would fit him nicely.

"How long can you stay holed up here?" I asked, gazing around Sam's office.

He shrugged. "The sofa's comfortable, and there're showers in the locker room." He pointed to a duffle bag on the floor at the end of the sofa. "I've got clothes. I'm good."

Between mouthfuls, Sam caught me up on the research he'd done on the other passengers on Dad's plane. He'd already dismissed one of them, a family doctor with a practice in Richmond. He pulled a notepad out of a desk drawer. "After the crash, his practice folded. The doc's seventy-three-year-old widow died two years ago. When her husband died, she received a payout from an old life-insurance policy. No evidence of changed spending habits or new wealth before she died. She didn't remarry. They had two kids, both married, both on good terms with the parents. Nothing surprising in either kid's finances."

"And the others?"

Sam raised an eyebrow and made a point of looking at his watch. "I've been on the job eight hours and already cleared a name. You aren't going to be one of those pushy clients, are you?"

I wrapped my lips around my teeth to hide a smile. "Not me. Great job, Detective."

"That's better." Sam wiped his mouth and balled up the napkin. "Your mom's dossiers on the passengers cut my work in half, and I still have ICO's resources at my disposal. Might as well use them while I still can. I've ordered new financials on everyone. Should have the rest of them in a day or two."

I left Sam after midnight and returned home. Sebastian never called. Maybe he'd put the call in to Mason and decided the leaked documents wouldn't amount to anything. An update telling me I could stand down would have been nice, considerate even, but that wasn't Sebastian's way.

Chapter Five

Sam called from the station at noon the next day. "I've eliminated another passenger. A thirty-five-year-old realtor from North Van. Partner in a larger firm. Specialized in high-end residential. No controversial sales in his last year. Had a sizable life-insurance policy, but purchased it before the birth of his first child. Wife was the beneficiary. She remarried five years ago. Met the new guy two years before that. Nothing sketchy in there."

"So two left?"

"The pilot and one passenger, other than your father. No word from Cain?"

"None. I'd thought one of us would have heard from him by now."

"Assuming he wants a deal. Could be he's comfortable hiding out."

"Yeah, but for how long? It's not like the Tribunal is going to give up looking for him."

"It's out of our hands. Did your mom get to Toronto?"

"Yeah. I talked to her this morning before my run. Told her you'd already eliminated a passenger. Of course, she thinks looking at the other passengers is a waste of your time. She's more interested in your contact with the Mansfield Group."

"That's actually why I'm calling. I spoke with a man named Peter Caulfield. After I convinced him I wasn't a whacko, he agreed to look at your mother's charts. I'm expecting to hear back from him this afternoon, but Em, he already told me they wouldn't touch it for less than a hundred and fifty grand—up front—and he said the cost could climb to over five hundred thousand."

"When can they start?"

"Did you hear me, Emelynn? Five hundred grand."

"I'll cover it." A slice off the top of Jolene's inheritance would either clear her family's name or condemn them.

Silence.

"Sam?"

"Yeah. Okay. I'll let you know what they come back with."

The next morning, I wired a hundred and fifty thousand dollars to the Mansfield Group. After they received confirmation of the funds, they marshalled their people. Peter Caulfield's team and their specialized equipment would arrive within days, and Sam had their assurances that the search would be underway by next week. Mom was ecstatic.

When Mason called in the afternoon, guilt once again crawled under my skin and set up house. Would he understand my disloyalty when he learned about the Mansfield Group? Because, one way or another, he would learn. Either when he and Stuart were exonerated, or when ... no. I refused to think about the *or*.

"I've sent the jet to Vancouver to collect you and Sebastian. James will meet you at this end. Thought you and James might like a night alone before the caucus."

The guilt that was making itself at home kicked me in the ribs. It almost sounded as if Mason was softening to the idea of James in my life. "Thank you. You sure you can manage without him?"

"Yeah. He's worked his ass off. We're all set."

"All right. I'll pack. It's a formal affair, right?" The Tribunal's assembling to witness the leadership change hands was the social event of the half-decade. I knew that Tribunal members, their families and influential guests would be there.

"No. Wear the usual."

"It's not black tie, like the annual gatherings?"

"Not for us. Leather is as formal as we get."

Leather? "All right." My boots were leather, as were my gloves, but that was as much black leather as I owned.

Mason told me to meet Sebastian at the Vancouver International Airport at five o'clock.

I packed a small bag and collected the courier package with my new phone on the way out the door. During the taxi ride to the airport, I texted my contacts to give them my new phone number.

Sebastian didn't arrive alone.

"You remember my wife, of course," Sebastian said, touching Kimberley's elbow. She bobbed her head as if she were royalty. She certainly looked the part in a pale-green dress with matching coat.

"Nice to see you again," I said, hoping my face didn't betray the lie. A few weeks ago, I'd eavesdropped on a conversation in their Point Grey home. Kimberley had referred to me in unflattering terms. That was the price for eavesdropping, I supposed. Regardless, it wasn't *nice* to see her. I wondered for a moment if I wore the same smile mask as my mother.

"And my daughter, Tiffany," Sebastian said.

I nodded. "Tiffany." She was going for something more casual than her mother: flouncy layers over tight jeans. Shabby chic, perhaps. It was a refreshing improvement on the hooker-look I'd last seen her in, on the night of the massacre at Cairabrae.

The co-pilot introduced himself then escorted us onto the tarmac. The executive jet awaiting us was one of a dozen scattered on the apron near the terminal. Kimberley and Tiffany boarded first and headed to the rear of the plane and the sofa that lined one wall. Sebastian followed them and took one of the two chairs facing the sofa. With no desire to make small talk for the flight's duration, I settled into one of the lounge chairs up front. Thankfully, Sebastian didn't insist I join them.

After the jet was in the air and levelled off, I found my earbuds, plugged them into the jet's sound system and closed my eyes. I got lost in the music until a few songs later, when I sensed someone nearby and opened my eyes. Sebastian stood in front of me with a glass of wine in each hand. I straightened in my chair and stole a glance at his wife and daughter. They weren't paying us any attention.

He extended one of the glasses to me. "May I?" he asked, tipping his head toward the chair facing mine.

"Sure," I said, accepting the wine. Note to self: check weather app for the temperature in hell.

The leather creaked as he sat. "Did Mason fill you in on what to expect at the caucus?"

"He mentioned a formal meeting followed by a reception."

Sebastian swirled the wine in his glass. "It won't be the affair it used to be. The numbers are down. Families are still in hiding because of what happened at Cairabrae."

"They'll be relieved to learn the Redeemers are no longer a threat."

He nodded. I'd never known him to be contemplative, but he was now and it worried me.

"Will you miss it? Leading the Tribunal?"

He stared across the aisle, his gaze on the small window. "Your uncle will make a fine replacement."

"He will. And you'll have more free time. Any plans?" Like moving back to the States?

He swivelled his head back in my direction and smiled. "As soon as Cain is dealt with, I'll resume mentoring you. I've been remiss these last few weeks."

I nearly choked on my wine. That explained Sebastian's cordial act. After he handed over the Tribunal's reins, he'd no longer have authority over me. I'd never wanted Sebastian's mentorship, and I had no intention of continuing it beyond the caucus. I considered my next words carefully. "You've been very generous, Sebastian. I know how fortunate I am to have had your mentorship, but it's run its course."

He tilted his head and frowned, as if he were genuinely confused. "After just three months? Surely you don't think your skills are where they should be."

"You and I are like oil and water. Opposing magnets."

"I agree. You can be difficult. However, you'll soon be responsible for your mother's safety. There is still much I can teach you."

His motivation had nothing to do with my mother's safety. He wanted to keep me close. He was about to lose access to the Tribunal's inside track and its power source. But I wouldn't; Mason was family. "I appreciate your offer, but no."

His expression gave nothing away. One of these days I'd have to define *mentorship* for him, and emphasize how trust and respect fit into it. He studied me as he took another sip of his wine. I decided to change the subject before he thought up another way to sell the mentorship idea. "There's something I've been meaning to talk to you about."

"Oh?"

"Redeemers. The current threat may be gone, but the reason they formed in the first place remains."

"Greed is the reason they formed. They wanted to usurp our power and our wealth. That they no longer exist will serve as an effective deterrent to anyone who gets the notion to repeat their mistakes."

"I disagree," I said. "The Tribunal operates in secret, making decisions that impact us all. Most Fliers never learn the reason behind those decisions, and that vacuum breeds distrust and fear. The way to prevent another rebellion is to include all Fliers in the process."

"What are you suggesting? We give everyone a vote?" He flared his nostrils and scowled, as if he'd caught a whiff of sewage.

"Yes, Fliers or their coveys. Shed some light on the Tribunal. Humanize it."

He rested his glass on the armrest and twisted it a quarter turn right then left. "Your naïveté surprises me, Emelynn, but it reminds me that you weren't born to this. Keep in mind that there is a natural order with us. We are the hunters, not the prey. Ghosts are more powerful than Fliers, Fliers are more powerful than everyone else, but *everyone else* outnumber us many hundreds of thousands of times over. Even hunters are vulnerable when outnumbered. We exist and remain free only because the masses don't know about us. They did, centuries ago, before the Tribunal Novem. Back then our kind were tracked down. We were killed like nature's predators—lions, tigers, grizzlies. Now we're safe. Secrecy is and must remain the Tribunal's core principle. You will come to understand this in time."

If Sebastian's attitude was any indication then Mason had been right when he warned me the Tribunal would be opposed to democracy. "Perhaps in time it won't be necessary."

"Yes, perhaps," Sebastian said. He raised his glass to his lips and swallowed. "Your mother told me you were considering rebuilding the home you lost."

I hesitated, surprised she'd shared that with him, though I didn't suppose it mattered. "Yes. I took her to the property a few weeks ago. She and my father lived there before he was killed."

He looked away. "Laura mentioned it was built in the Arts and Crafts style. Is that what you had in mind?"

"I've nothing in mind yet but lots of ideas."

"You don't have an architect?" I shook my head. "I'll make an introduction. The people who remodelled our home in Point Grey were very good."

"That's kind of you, but I'm a long way yet from needing an architect."

"Ah, but early in the process, an architect can open up possibilities you can't imagine." Sebastian stood, his wine glass now empty. "That's exactly what a mentor does, Emelynn. Opens up possibilities. You and I are not oil and water. Granted, we may need to have a little more patience with one another, but I'm not prepared to let you discard my offer." With that parting comment, he returned to his family.

Had he taken some No Only Means Not Right Now sales course? If he had, he'd aced it. Admittedly, he'd made a good point about hiring an architect, but I was finished with his superiority complex and letting him belittle me under the guise of a mentorship I didn't want.

The smell of jet fuel permeated the cool night air as we disembarked. Two vehicles waited on the tarmac. One was a stretch limo with a uniformed driver and the other a minivan circa 1990.

Kimberley and Tiffany were first off the plane. They walked directly to the limo's open back door and climbed in.

Sebastian got out last and walked with me to greet James. "How is the lovely Grace Shipley?" he asked.

James stopped short, as did I. Grace was an American detective with a reputation for undercover work. Last September, she'd impersonated me in the hunt for Carson Manse. She was also strikingly beautiful. And James hadn't mentioned her recently.

"You keeping tabs on me, Sebastian?" James said.

"Not at all. One of my companies owns the warehouse in San Diego that Miss Shipley needed permission to use. I simply recognized her name. Sent someone over to check it out."

A baggage handler wheeled a cart of luggage past us and stopped at the limo. He and the driver began shoving matching bags into the trunk.

"Well then, thank you for your cooperation," James said, and offered his hand.

A benevolent smile crept onto Sebastian's face. He shook James's hand and nodded. "I'll see you both tomorrow." He then stepped away and slid into the back of the limo.

After the limo started rolling, James took my hand and pulled me close for a kiss. "How was the flight?"

"Fine. You didn't tell me you were working with Grace again."

"Didn't I? I thought when I was in Vancouver I mentioned I'd taken a private contract."

"I suppose you did." But he hadn't told me about Grace. Then again, they were colleagues. And professionals. Who had unmistakable chemistry and a prior relationship I'd never asked about. Crap. I stomped on Jealousy's green-toed intrusion and bucked up. I was not going to be *that* girlfriend, or rather, fiancée.

"Where are we going anyway?"

James slipped a tip to the baggage handler and took my bag. "North of Napa. A ninety-minute drive."

We started toward his ride. "A family van? Is this your idea of a hint?" I asked, giving the minivan the once-over. Faded blue paint, wheels with no hubcaps and a rusted dent on the rear quarter panel didn't inspire me to ditch the contraceptives.

He grinned. "Flashy transportation invites attention. Not my style." James tossed my bag in the back then opened the passenger door for me. The hinge groaned.

"If this thing has a car seat in the back, I'm calling a cab," I said. James's laughter kicked my lingering jealousy to the curb.

He negotiated a maze of ramps and overpasses that dumped us northbound. I cracked the window to let in fresh air. "You've made an impression on Mason."

"Yeah? Good or bad?"

"Good, of course. Why would you doubt that?"

"Mason doesn't say much. Never asks for advice and I don't give it."

"Is he treating you all right?"

"Sure. Like an employee he wants to fire but can't."

"That's not how he describes it. He told me you've been working your butt off."

"I have, but not for him. I want this caucus over with so you and I can get away from here. If Mason succeeds in getting the Tribunal on board with his agenda, he'll be too busy to interfere in our lives."

"Interfere? You volunteered for this, remember?"

"Only because your name is on the caucus agenda, along with the seat they offered you." The Tribunal seat was a thank-you for the role I'd played defending them at Cairabrae. "When you formally turn it down, we'll be free of them."

I wanted to argue with him, to remind him that Stuart and Mason would always be a part of my life, but I couldn't. Not with the Mansfield Group on their way to Vancouver and about to start searching for Dad's plane's wreckage. I stared out the side window, watching the houses rush by.

"You going to tell me what's bothering you?" James said. I realized I'd been quiet for a while.

"There's something I need to tell you, but you have to promise me you'll keep it to yourself."

"All right. What is it?"

I told him about my father's warning to my mother, about my

mother's research into my father's crash and finally about involving Sam and hiring the Mansfield Group to find Dad's plane.

When I finished, he looked over and searched my face. "What will you do if they determine it was sabotage?"

I looked away. Ahead, the art deco span of the iconic Golden Gate Bridge approached. "I promised Mom I'd report the findings to the Tribunal."

James let that sit in the air between us. As we exited the north end of the bridge deck, he spoke. "Even if they find it's sabotage, the Reynoldses may not be responsible. You know how the Tribunal are. Bunch of manipulative, back-stabbing, glory seekers. Any one of them could have done it."

"But who besides the Reynoldses would have had a motive?"

"Jordan's research may turn up someone else." James reached across and squeezed my shoulder. "Put it out of your mind for now. Let's just get through tomorrow."

I nodded, inhaled a deep breath and tried to clear the negative thoughts on the exhale. It didn't work. "Any word on Cain?" I asked, changing the subject.

"Nothing. Did Sebastian say anything about him on the flight?"

"Not a word. I think we were wrong about Cain. He doesn't want to negotiate."

"Maybe, but living in hiding isn't much of a life."

We passed through long stretches of residential neighbourhoods. Eventually, vineyards took over the hillsides. Row upon row of perfectly spaced vines stretched far into the distance. Even in the dark of night I could see the patterns repeat to the horizon. Where did the water come from that fed them all? I wondered. In some fields, large fans towered over the vines, ready to blow away damaging frosts.

James exited onto Highway 29, and we continued north to Napa. Endless miles of grapevines grew on both sides of the road, broken by the occasional Spanish- or Mediterranean-style villa. Some were wineries with signs advertising wine tastings, others looked like private residences. Sometimes, it was a modest farmhouse or a large barn that broke the pattern. Traffic was sparse along the newly paved two-lane highway.

At the ninety-minute mark, we passed Napa and kept going. I absently noted the signs, until one jumped out at me. "Reynolds Family Winery? Did I read that right?"

"Yup."

"Mason and Stuart own a winery? Is that where we're going?"

"No. No one knows where we're going tonight. As for the family winery, you'll have to ask them."

I didn't know why I was surprised. We weren't far from Cairabrae, in Bodega Bay, and I'd known they owned properties elsewhere.

We'd been on the road almost two hours when James finally signalled a turn and pulled into a wide concrete driveway. Two hundred yards ahead stood a modern two-storey home. The size put it into the estate category.

"Wow. Who owns this?"

"Clients who owed me a favour. They're away right now."

Instead of driving to the front door, James drove past the house on a lane to the right. The lane circled around a well-maintained outbuilding, behind which were stored large stainless steel tanks and racks of weathered oak barrels. We carried on over a ridge. A small home came into view, likely the original dwelling on the property. It put me in mind of a 1950s ranch house from a time when a thousand square feet was considered large. James rolled to a stop in front of it and cut the engine.

"Home sweet home," he said.

"Not flashy," I said, repeating his earlier words.

"Exactly." He opened his door and walked around to my side. I'd already gotten out and was stretching my legs after the long drive. James opened the back door and started loading up: a cooler strap over one shoulder, my bag over the other, several shopping bags in his hands.

"I'm not an invalid. Give me some of that," I said, tugging my bag off his shoulder. I grabbed his black leather satchel, closed the van's doors and followed him to the darkened porch. He juggled his load to fish a key out of his pants pocket and fitted it into the lock.

"Bedroom's through there," he said, nodding to the right. I walked in that direction and found a comfortable bedroom—small but tidy and clean. The old iron bed was centred on the wall to the left. On the far side was an ensuite bathroom, and facing the end of the bed was a dresser with a large mirror. I dropped our bags on the floor and went to find James.

He was crouched behind the open refrigerator door unloading the cooler. The shopping bags were propped on the counter. I strolled over and peeked inside. "How long are we staying?" I said with a laugh. Three bottles of wine, a baguette and a jar of olives suggested a three-day stay, but I knew we had to leave for the caucus the next day.

James rose and closed the refrigerator door. I turned my back to the counter and he stalked toward me, stopping when he had me pinned with his hips. Even with the added height of my boot heels, he stood taller than I was. I slid my hands around the soft leather of his car coat and tipped my head up. A day's beard stubble darkened his angular features. I had an urge to loosen the elastic band that held his hair but resisted. There'd be time for that later.

Pale-blue eyes took in every nuance of my face. I closed my eyes to his scrutiny and inhaled the scent of him.

"I've missed you," he said, then bent his head down and kissed me. It wasn't a casual kiss, and definitely not a kiss for public consumption. It was the kind of kiss that hardened a man and made a woman want every inch of him.

He stopped and pulled back with a smirk that told me he'd intended all that and more.

"Tease," I said.

"How about a glass of wine?" He reached behind me and pulled a bottle of red from the bag. It was a Chateau Margene reserve cabernet.

"I suppose we should. When in Rome and all that," I said, feigning umbrage.

He pressed in and dropped a chaste kiss on my lips before going in search of a corkscrew. While he rattled around in the kitchen's drawers, I found two glasses.

He poured and then proposed a toast. "To seeing the tail end of this caucus."

I touched my glass to his and tasted the wine. It was full-bodied and rich, just how I liked my reds. "What do you know about the caucus?"

"I've seen the agenda. I know what Mason has planned. I'd say it's going to be an education for most of them."

"You think Mason will change any minds tomorrow?"

He shrugged. "In my experience, they aren't what I'd call flexible or open-minded. No offence, Emelynn, but they're all Ghosts. Ghosts tend to think they're untouchable."

"If only that were true," I said.

Wine in hand, James toured me around the house. The owners used it as a guest house. The vineyard was leased out. At my insistence, we went outside and I got a close-up look at the vines, which crowded the house. The grapes were still flower clusters that only hinted at the fruit to come. Soon enough, the cool evening air pushed us back inside.

While I refilled our glasses, James pulled a bag from the refrigerator and unpacked it on the counter beside the stove. He found a cast-iron skillet and set it over a flame on a burner.

"What's for dinner?"

"Chicken puttanesca."

"Yum. Can I help?"

He assigned me table-setting duty and baguette slicing—cook-speak for *don't interfere*. When my chores were done, he placed browned chicken breasts back into the skillet that now bubbled with sauce dotted with fresh cherry tomatoes and black olives. The kitchen smelled like a fine Mediterranean restaurant. He replaced the lid and set a pot of water on to boil.

While we enjoyed his savoury meal, and a second bottle of Chateau Margene, we tossed around destinations for our dream trip after the caucus.

"We'll be gone for a year if we visit all of them," I said, but my smile failed, dragged down by the weight of the axe swinging over my head.

James pushed his plate away and leaned back, stretching his long legs under the table. "Did the Mansfield Group give you a timeline?" I loved that he knew what was bothering me.

"They start searching next week, but they've not promised results."

"Understandable. It's been years. The wreckage may have drifted."

"I'm sorry. I know you wanted to leave after the caucus, but I can't." What I didn't say was that I had no idea when I might be able to leave because I didn't know what my future looked like if Mansfield's search turned up sabotage. "Can you wait a few weeks?"

"For you?" His smile said yes. "Cain's disappearance will likely delay us anyway. I'd rather he's dealt with before we start travelling on passports he can easily trace."

"Good point." My anxiety eased somewhat. I yawned and checked the time. It was almost two in the morning. I stood and cleared the table. "I'll wash up tomorrow. How about we go to bed?"

A slow smile spread across James's face.

I used the ensuite, and when I opened the bathroom door, James lay naked on the bed, propped against a stack of pillows with his hands behind his head. I bit my lower lip and walked to the end of the bed admiring the sight.

He was lean and muscled with an honest-to-god six-pack and a fine dusting of chest hair that ran into a funnel at his belly button and poured out in a tempting line, like an arrow pointing to a fine-looking erection. "Been thinking about me again?"

"Always," he said, shifting his hips under my glare. "Now, how about you get naked. Slowly."

Stripping for a man didn't come naturally. It had taken me ages to get comfortable being naked, let alone putting on a show to get there. But James loved it, and whether it was the show itself or the fact he liked ordering me to do it, it didn't matter. The results were worth every impish instruction.

He had me take off my pants first, and then my socks, which completely undid any sexy I might have had going on. After that, I unfastened my blouse, one button at a time. I was ready to shirk out of it when he stopped me.

"No, don't open it. Turn around." I did as he asked and waited, watching his reflection in the big mirror above the dresser. "Fold the cups of your bra under your breasts." I complied. "Face me." His right leg was bent and he held his erection in his hand. I wanted to jump his bones right then, but I knew better.

"Now you can take the shirt off." I slid it off my shoulders first then let it fall to the floor. Watching the lust on James's face was all the encouragement I needed. I stood before him in a thong with my breasts thrust out. "Rub your nipples."

My breath hitched with his words. My nipples were already hard, and the warmth of my hand brushing the hard nubs sent shivers up my spine. His hand slid up his shaft and back down. "Turn around and remove your thong."

I did as he asked, knowing he was watching my ass. The bedsprings squeaked and a moment later, James was at my back, his hands all over my ass, my breasts. I rested my head against his shoulder and enjoyed the caress. "Open your legs," he said. I shifted my feet and he immediately slid a hand between my legs and circled my clitoris. I nearly collapsed in ecstasy.

He turned me toward the iron footboard. With his chest to my back and his lips at my ear, he said, "You'd better hold on." He stepped away and immediately, cool air skimmed my back. The tip of his erection slid between my legs. He dragged it up my backside and went back for seconds. I reached my hands to the iron railing and pushed back against him. He probed again, slipping through my wetness, and then he pushed inside me with a sharp thrust that took my breath away.

He tried to go slow, but he'd gone too far with the foreplay. "I'm not going to make it," he said, as he pounded into me. He pressed his fingers to my clitoris and worked that magical knot of nerves like a reiki master. He brought me to a climax moments before he cursed and groaned to his own conclusion.

Chapter Six

Sex and the late hour proved effective sleep aids. I thought of Grace only once before I drifted off. We didn't stir until the sun was well on its arc through the morning sky.

We made sleepy morning love, slow and indulgent, like licking drips from an ice cream cone on a hot afternoon. When James left our bed for the shower, I donned his shirt, revelling in the scent of him, and ambled to the kitchen to make coffee. It was already past noon.

Sun shone in through the windows above the sink. In the distance, birds fluttered amongst the vines, their faint chirps the only sounds other than the coffee gurgling through the old drip coffee maker. I cleaned up the dinner dishes and started breakfast.

As I flipped bacon in the freshly washed cast-iron skillet, James sauntered up behind and wrapped me in an embrace. "My shirt doesn't quite cover your butt."

I turned in his arms. "I know." I stood up on my toes and kissed him. "Will you finish making breakfast? I'm going to shower."

"Sure," he said, smacking my behind as I left his embrace.

I loved lazy mornings like this with James. It felt right. Comfortable.

After showering, I dressed in a long-sleeved T-shirt and capris then packed my small bag and set it on the floor beside James's satchel.

James was on his phone in the kitchen. He hung up when I arrived. "Last-minute checks. Mason wants to see you before the caucus."

"All right." I took a seat at the table. "Have you been to one of these caucuses before?"

"No," James said, dishing up our eggs and bacon. "The Tribunal isn't keen on having the help mingle with the upper crust."

As much as it bothered me that he thought of himself as *the help*, it was probably better than the truth. His family had been coerced into participating in Tribunal interrogations. And all because long ago one of James's ancestors had inadvertently revealed that the males in his family could read memories, a skill that made interrogations less messy. Sometimes.

"That's in the past. You're not the help anymore."

James shook his head. "Not for the last eight months, but we were for more than a hundred years."

"I still find it hard to believe the Tribunal thought using your family like that was okay. The changes Mason is proposing will make it impossible for them to ever do it again."

James set a plate in front of me. "You think going public is a good idea?"

"I'm not sure about that. It's moving toward some form of democratic representation that I was thinking about."

"There's not a chance in hell of that happening," James said, and took his seat.

"I'm trying to be optimistic. You should give it a try."

After eating, we cleaned up and left the place the way we'd found it. We got back in the minivan and I reached for my seat belt. "Where's the caucus meeting?"

"At a winery, but I want to take you someplace else first." James started the engine.

"Where?"

"To meet my family. They're staying in St. Helena. It's not far."

I swung my head in his direction. "You waited until now to spring this on me?"

"Not exactly." He turned off the engine and met my gaze. "They weren't sure they'd come at all. It's the first time they've been invited. A show of good faith, I think. Dad didn't want any part of it, but Mom did. She wanted the chance to put faces to names and look each one in the eye. They arrived this morning."

"Brave woman, but still. You could have warned me."

"And have you worry for nothing? I honestly didn't think they'd come. They phoned as I got out of the shower this morning."

I took a deep breath and settled back in my seat.

"You would have met them tonight anyway, but I'd rather you meet them someplace private."

"You mean somewhere you can intervene if blood's drawn."

"That's a little melodramatic don't you think?"

"Your father isn't my biggest fan." The first time I met James's father, he learned I was a Ghost. He equated Ghosts with Tribunal, so yeah, that hadn't gone well. The second time I met him, he jolted me. If he'd been stronger, it would have killed me.

"He'll come around. So will Mom."

I gazed down at my shabby capris. "I'm not even dressed nice."

"That's what you're worried about?"

"Don't be an ass."

"Would you rather meet them tonight when the others are there, standing around watching?"

"No."

"All right, then." He reached for the ignition and restarted the engine.

He drove north until Highway 29 turned into Main Street, where the homes were turn-of-the-century and well maintained. Three-globe antique street lights rose over manicured lawns. A short fifteen minutes later, he turned into a driveway surrounded by river-rock walls.

The sign read Las Alcobas. "The Alcoves," James said. A Georgian-style mansion was visible from the street behind a row of palm trees. We drove past the mansion and pulled into a spot close to one of two modern annex buildings at the rear. Las Alcobas was flashy. James didn't get his taste from his father.

He pulled out his phone and sent a text before looking over at me. "Ready?" he asked, with his hand on the door latch.

"You've never talked much about your mother. What's she like?"

"She's a proper Southern woman, soft on the outside, hard as iron inside."

"That's not reassuring."

"*Hard*'s the wrong word. *Strong* is better. Like you. Now stop worrying and get out of the van."

His compliment stole my words. I floated on top of it, hiding a grin, then took a deep breath and opened my door. James met me at the back of the van and took my hand. Ahead, I spotted his father, Redmond. He'd come out a side door to greet us. Redmond Moss stood shorter than his son by a few inches. He wore a cashmere sweater under a suit jacket despite a day already into T-shirt temperatures; a lawyer, through and through.

"Son," he said, shaking James's hand.

"Dad. You remember Emelynn?"

"Of course. Emelynn." He offered his hand. "Good to see you again." He had the physique of an athlete, and it readily defied the grey in his hair that hinted at his age—mid-fifties was my guess.

I established my block. It was my only defence to prevent Redmond from using the physical contact to read my memories. I shook his hand and mumbled something polite. He held the door for me. We climbed to the top floor and a corner suite. Redmond led the way inside. James's mother sat on the sofa with her ankles crossed and her hands in her lap. She looked up, and a perfect smile animated her fine porcelain features. She stood and smoothed her dress, waiting for us to approach. I wondered what had made James describe her as soft. She looked five pounds short of skeletal.

"Mother," James said, bending to kiss her on the cheek. "This is Emelynn Taylor. Emelynn, my mother."

"Mrs. Moss," I said, and offered the petite woman my hand.

Her grip was light and brief, her eyes sharp and penetrating. A queen holding court with a demure tip of her head. "Diana, please. No need for such formality. Have a seat."

I sat where she suggested, opposite her. Redmond sat beside me, leaving me feeling penned in.

"Darling, would you mind serving coffee?" she said to James in a sweet, sing-song voice that I imagined he rarely said no to. Diana wore her hair in a smooth bun that sat at the nape of her neck. Not a single strand strayed from its place. I got the feeling it wouldn't dare.

"James tells me you live in Vancouver?" She spoke with the same measured cadence and Southern drawl as her husband.

There was an art to small talk I hadn't appreciated before. Chatting with Diana felt like a waltz with predetermined steps and a predictable rhythm. The conversation moved back and forth, and the circle of her questions grew tighter with each round. I began to appreciate James's description of her. *Soft* didn't refer to her physique but to her silken manners.

As James served the coffee, Diana started pecking on the frayed outskirts of my life. Where did I grow up? Which schools did I attend? How did I end up in Vancouver? Then she moved in closer. Who were my parents? What were their backgrounds? What did I do for work? And finally, she asked the question I suspected she'd wanted to from the moment I walked in the door. How did I meet her son?

I glanced at James, who had taken the seat next to his mother. Was it a trick question? Surely James hadn't told her the truth—that I'd been the unwitting mistress to his brother-in-law, Jackson. "James hasn't told you?" I asked, praying James hadn't painted that unflattering picture of me in the arms of his sister's husband.

James intervened. "She's from the Vancouver covey, Mother. Emelynn is the one who was injured during Sandra's rescue."

Injured? I'd been shot.

"Forgive me," Diana said, pressing her hand to her heart. "We are ever so grateful." She tipped her head and presented me with a thankful smile. My inner skeptic kicked me in the shin. Diana seemed far too polished to have missed such a big detail. "I'm sure I would have remembered if it weren't for the occasion."

I raised my eyebrows in question. "Occasion?"

"Why yes. This is the first time James has brought someone to meet us."

Heat rushed to my face.

"You would have met tonight, regardless," James said, trying to take some of the weight out of his mother's revelation. But what he'd done was unintentionally drop a gold nugget in her palm, and she went mining for more.

"Oh? You must have some influential connections, Emelynn." From the corner of my eye, I saw James raise his hand to his forehead.

I didn't for a minute believe Diana was unaware of my relationship to the Reynoldses—I was the one who'd told her husband, after all. I also knew from James that Diana had a keen interest in the Tribunal, who had impacted her life so severely. She probably knew more about them than I did, and she most certainly knew the Reynoldses were one of the founding families.

Even so, I could have brushed her off. But I also had a keen interest; this woman would be my mother-in-law someday. If she had a problem with the fact I was a gifted Flier and not born, or that Jolene's gift had made me a part of the Reynolds family, it wouldn't be because I hadn't been up front with her right from the start.

I told her everything. Surprise didn't flit across her features once. She was either very good at checking her emotions, or she'd heard it all before. My money was on the latter; this was a repeat. Perhaps her asking me had been a test of my integrity.

When I'd finished, I set my coffee cup on the table in front of me. I'd been using it as a prop. It had gone cold ages ago.

Diana's gaze followed the coffee cup, but she didn't move. Redmond hadn't said a word. I glanced at James. He watched his mother with guarded interest.

"You're a Ghost," Diana said, her voice a whisper. We'd finally got to the one small detail she hadn't known.

"I am," I said. I felt at a loss as to what to do with my hands. The air conditioner kicked in. I tucked a curl behind my ear.

Diana's gaze locked onto my earrings. I'd worn the grey-green studs James had given me. I rarely took them off. She inhaled and lifted her chin. If she admired them, she didn't say. One day soon, I'd tell her they were a gift from James.

"We can't stay," James said, standing. "Mason is waiting for us."

I stood, as did Diana and Redmond. James kissed his mother's cheek. "See you tonight," he said. I thought it sad that they didn't embrace. Perhaps James's aloofness came from his mother.

Diana once again offered up her china-doll smile, fully recovered, and extended me her hand. "I'm glad you dropped by, Emelynn. It was lovely to meet you."

"You as well," I said. She remained in place as Redmond walked us to the door. He patted James on the shoulder then offered me his hand.

James played the gentleman and opened the passenger door of the minivan for me. I hopped inside. He rounded the van, climbed in and twisted the key in the ignition.

"You failed to mention that meeting your mother was an *occasion*."

He backed out of the parking stall. "Don't let it go to your head. As long as the Tribunal controlled us, there was never going to be a significant other." That part wasn't news. He'd vowed to be the last male in the Moss line, cutting off the Tribunal's coercion of his family.

"But," he said, pulling into traffic, "circumstances have changed."

"Yes, they have," I agreed, happy to hear him sounding positive.

We continued north and somewhere along the way, Highway 29 turned into Highway 128. Outside of St. Helena, the countryside returned. Once again trees lined the road and the hills were quilted with flowering grapevines. I cracked the window and inhaled the fragrant air. The terrain grew steeper the farther north we travelled.

On a particularly twisted section of road, James took a left into a driveway I didn't see coming, and we climbed a sharp rise. We passed a Private Property, No Trespassing sign and kept going.

"Is this where the caucus is being held?" I asked.

"It's the back entrance. Where Mason's been staying."

The black asphalt was barely wide enough for two vehicles. I checked the GPS on my watch. We were headed southwest. After a final curve in the road, a striking manor house came into view. It was built of red and grey stone and lay at the edge of a clearing that abutted a gentle hill studded with ancient oaks.

James pulled up to the front door and killed the engine. "I'm going to leave you here and carry on to the winery to check on security. Mason will take you to the caucus."

"Will you come in?"

"Yeah. Mason and I need to go over a few things." James's gaze drifted past me. "Speak of the devil."

I turned in my seat and saw Mason approach. He opened my door.

"Welcome to Acadia Vineyards," he said. He pulled me into an embrace the moment I stepped from the van. He wore a T-shirt and jeans—black, of course.

"Acadia? I saw a sign for that miles back."

"Yes. That would have been the main entrance. It was closed to the public a few days ago for a private event. We'll give it back to them tomorrow. How was your trip?"

"I'm getting spoiled with the executive jet, but I love it. Could do without Sebastian's company, however."

Mason's smile reached the corners of his eyes. He released me and turned to James, who'd joined us. They shook hands, an improvement over the last time I'd seen them greet each other in my presence. "Grab your bags and come inside."

James turned back toward the minivan. I hesitated, stunned by Mason's words. "Are we staying here tonight?" I asked.

"Yes. Dad, too. Tonight is a celebration. I want my family here with me."

James returned with both our bags in his hands. I wrapped my arm around Mason's waist and gave him a squeeze. The fact Mason had included James was a huge step. "Thank you." They might never be best buds, but I'd take this newfound tolerance over their former animosity any day of the week.

Mason draped his arm around my shoulder, and we walked across the courtyard and into the two-storey foyer. The house was as impressive inside as it was outside though it wasn't as big or as polished as Cairabrae. Its rough-hewn charm put me in mind of knights and round tables.

"This is quite the castle. How did you find it?" The same red and grey stone lined the interior walls, and what wasn't stone was chestnut-coloured wood. To the right, a staircase wound up to a second-floor bridge that crossed over the foyer.

"It took a while, believe me, and we didn't pick the location for this place, though it is an attractive add-on. It was the Acadia winery we were after. You'll see what I mean tonight." He checked his watch. "Make that in a few hours."

We stepped to the left into a large drawing room, at the end of which stood a fireplace with a massive live-edge wood mantle. The high ceiling was also wood, made of recessed panels. If I had to name the style, I'd call it modern medieval.

We hadn't yet sat down before a familiar voice called my name. I turned to find Phillip standing at the room's threshold. "Welcome," he said, with a dip of his head.

"Phillip?" His presence outside of Cairabrae surprised me. I put my hands on my hips and grinned. "They're helpless without you, aren't they?" He might have blushed. I couldn't be sure because he ducked his head to examine his shoes. Phillip managed Cairabrae. It was a full-time job, and one he excelled at. I would have hugged him, but that would have made him uncomfortable. He'd always kept our interactions purely professional. It was his default setting with everyone, from what I'd seen.

"Is Consuela here as well?" I asked. Consuela was their cook at Cairabrae.

Mason answered. "No. She's not one of us. It's too dangerous." I nodded in understanding. Their former cook, Maria, who'd been more a family member than an employee, hadn't been one of us either. She'd been killed at Cairabrae.

"Shall I take your bags to your room?" Phillip asked.

"Perhaps I'll go with you," I said, and turned to Mason. "You two need to talk, anyway. Do you mind?"

"No. Go ahead," Mason said. "Come back down when you're settled."

Phillip took a bag in each hand and led the way out of the room and up the stone staircase. We crossed over the bridge and I slowed to take in the view. From the high windows on the foyer side, I could see the downward slope of the land and vineyards in the distance. On the other side, visible through a wall of windows in a formal sitting area, lay the upward slope of the grassy hill dotted with gnarly oaks.

"Spectacular, isn't it?" I said.

"Yes. It is," Phillip said. "Mason is staying there." He nodded to a closed door above the room we'd been in downstairs. I followed him in the opposite direction. "Stuart's in that suite," he continued, "and you're down here." It was the last door in the corridor.

"Let me get that," I said, offering to open the door. He stepped back with a nod and I walked in ahead of him. The same walls of red and grey stone and dark wood were present in here, along with the high wood-panelled ceilings. But where it felt warm in the vast room downstairs, in the confines of a smaller bedroom, it felt closed in. I rubbed my arms.

"I'll get a fire going," Phillip said, noticing my chill.

I glanced at the fireplace. Maybe it wasn't such a small room. "No need to rush. I'll only be in here a few minutes. But later tonight would be nice." I pictured James naked on the floor in front of the fireplace.

"Of course," Phillip said. He set our bags on a bench at the end of the bed and directed me to the bathroom. "I've stocked it with plenty of towels and the usual toiletries, but let me know if I missed anything."

"Thank you, Phillip. It really is great to see you. You're well?"

"Quite, thank you. Is there anything else?"

"No. I'll see you later?"

"Yes. I'll be here when you return tonight." He nodded then left. Always so proper.

A heavy brocade drape covered the window, and behind it, a sheer fabric muted the fading daylight. I walked over and tugged the drape open to brighten the room. It overlooked the hillside. I took my toiletry bag into the ensuite and set it beside one of the sinks. After freshening up, I headed back downstairs to rejoin James and Mason.

A bottle of wine and three glasses sat on the table between them. "Ah, you're back. Will you have a glass of wine?"

"Love to." I took a seat beside James. "What are we drinking?"

"A cab sav from J. Lohr in Paso Robles. One of my favourites. Sound good?"

I nodded and he poured. When we each had a glass in hand, he toasted. "To tonight."

I tipped my glass into his. "I'll toast to that. No more Sebastian barking orders at me."

Mason indulged me with a laugh. I settled back against the sofa. James remained perched on the edge, his elbows on his knees, holding his glass by the rim.

"Tell me about tonight," I said. "What's going to happen?"

Mason swallowed a mouthful of wine and sat back, relaxed, with his legs spread wide. "It starts with the caucus. The change of power happens first, followed by the meeting. My first agenda. Afterwards, we'll all head up to the winery to celebrate with the families and invited guests. When it's all over, we'll return here."

"How long's the meeting?"

"Traditionally, it's short, an hour at most. Tonight it'll run longer than that, but there's no getting around it."

"What do you mean?"

"I'd hoped this business with ICO would be done with, but there'll be questions. It'll take away from where I want their attention."

"On going public?"

"Yes. It's critical we set it up on our terms before we're exposed by someone's cellphone video on social media. Tonight's caucus is our first opportunity to really drive the issue home. I don't want anything to distract from that."

James pursed his lips and hung his head. Mason and I both noticed.

"You got something on your mind, James?" Mason asked.

"We are, as you say, in a fight against time with technology," James said. "But there's something you haven't considered."

Mason frowned. James tipped back a slug of wine. "When I was semi-conscious and strapped to a cot in Vector's lab, they'd send in two techs at a time to draw blood. You know what I heard them say?"

Mason didn't answer. I gripped my glass and prayed they weren't going to come to blows with whatever James came out with.

"They thought we were aliens. As in, not human."

Still frowning, Mason said, "A simple DNA test will disprove that."

"They had my DNA. All that did was make them wonder how we'd manipulated it to mimic human DNA."

It felt like a sucker punch. It had been weeks since James and I escaped Vector Labs. We'd talked about what they'd done to us many times and not once had he mentioned this alien comment. Mason sat forward.

James continued. "Human rights are for humans. Without that label, we have no rights. Not to life, liberty or any protection at all."

Mason nodded. "I'll give that some thought."

James took another gulp of wine. "I've got to go," he said, and set his unfinished glass on the table. "Thanks for the wine." He stood.

I leapt up as well. "I'll walk you out."

Mason remained seated. "We'll see you back here later?"

James paused then nodded. In the space of that pause James had crossed another major divide: willingly staying under the same roof as Mason.

"Back in a minute," I said to Mason. I followed James out of the room and across the foyer. He opened the front door, and the moment we were in the lee of the minivan I turned to him. "Thanks for agreeing to stay here tonight."

"Didn't want you to think Mason was the only one making an effort."

"I appreciate that, and not to sound ungrateful, but why am I only now hearing about the alien comment?"

James furrowed his brow. "I hadn't given it a lot of thought before coming down here."

"And you chose now to bring it up? Hours before the caucus? Are you trying to throw Mason off his game?"

He reached for me. "Not at all. Tonight will go ahead just as Mason planned, but he needs to consider that his proposal has some dangerous gaps. I'm afraid the suggestion we aren't human is only one of them."

I let him pull me into an embrace. "I like the dream he's selling, Emelynn. I'm just not sure I like the price we might end up paying."

The irritation I'd felt slipped away. "Tonight's just talk anyway," I said. "Right?"

"I hope not," he said, and kissed me. "At least not later, upstairs." He brushed a stray lock from my cheek. "I can't wait for this to be behind us."

"Me too." We kissed again and then I watched him K-turn the ugly minivan and drive out of sight.

Chapter Seven

Back in the drawing room, Mason stood gazing out the window toward the driveway. He turned when I came back into the room. "How is James?"

"You're asking me? You just spent a week with him." I dropped into the seat I'd vacated.

Mason returned to the sofa and sat. "He's skilled. Knows the security business better than I'd given him credit for, but there's an undercurrent to him, a rage that simmers just below the surface."

I jerked my head back. "That surprises you? After what the Tribunal put his family through?"

"I guess I'd hoped he'd moved past it. Especially considering how he feels about you."

"He's trying. It's not easy, besides which, he has his family to consider. All they know about me is that I'm a Ghost—that's an indelible black mark as far as they're concerned. I can't even fault them for it."

"You deserve better than that."

This is what it meant to have family. Support even if it was misplaced. "Thanks, but it's not about what I deserve. I love James. He's allowed to be angry about what he and his family have been subjected to. He'll work through it, and I think he's worth the wait."

Mason smiled. "I agree. I don't know many men who would step up and agree to help someone they so recently thought of as the enemy. I wouldn't be able to pull off this demo without him. He's going to be the magician behind the curtain tonight."

"I'm glad you asked for his help."

"I never thought I'd say this, but I hope you and James work out in the long run." Mason picked up the bottle of wine from the coffee table. "Can I top up your glass?"

"Sure." I gave Stuart credit for Mason's sentiment. He'd been building bridges. I'd have to thank him for that when I saw him. "When's your dad arriving?"

"He's on his way." He began to pour. "How's Laura?"

The question, casual as it was, hit me like a brick to my head—a painful reminder that my mother thought this man and his father had killed my dad.

"What's wrong?" he asked. I realized I'd once again failed to keep my emotions off my face.

"Nothing," I said quickly, cutting off his alarm. "I just ... forgot to call her."

"Call her now," he said, and set the bottle down. "You shouldn't make her worry. I'll wait."

"I'll text her," I said, and pulled out my new phone. I walked away from him and faked a text to her then tucked the phone back in my pocket.

"You said she's back in Toronto? Has she sold her condo yet?" He resumed pouring the wine and handed me my glass.

"Not yet. It just went on the market." I sat on the sofa opposite him.

"Then how about we toast to a quick sale?" He said, offering his glass. Mason's attentiveness to my mother's life remained a curiosity. She'd caused him no end of trouble, even before she'd learned his sister gifted me. I imagined his interest would die in the frost after he learned of her suspicions.

"To a quick sale," I said, raising my glass. I savoured a sip before I broached the *not-human* bomb James had dropped before he left.

"He made a valid point," Mason said. "But it won't derail tonight's agenda."

"I'm glad. Are you still announcing the end of the Redeemer threat?"

"Of course. It's the first thing on the agenda. I want to open on a positive note."

"It's also an ideal lead-in to a discussion on some form of democratic representation."

"Not tonight, Emelynn. I want laser focus on going public."

"But the end of the Redeemer threat is the perfect opportunity. Redeemers wouldn't have existed at all if they felt like they had a voice."

"I said no. If going public fails, there'll be time in the coming years to feel our way around the representation issue."

"In the coming years?" That sounded a lot like five more years of *not a chance in hell*. "Before you brush me off entirely, consider this: the Tribunal are only nine voices. No one knows their names. They use their wealth to buffer themselves from their communities. But there are thousands of Fliers. All of them are embedded in their communities, known to their neighbours. Think about it. Thousands of voices speaking in our defence versus nine."

Mason's expression looked pained. "I know you want to give everyone a voice. I applaud you. It's a commendable goal."

"It's more than commendable; it's the honourable thing to do, *and* it will prevent another uprising."

"Another uprising would take years to organize. In the meantime, I plan to convince the majority on the Tribunal to go public. When we do, the uprising issue evaporates. With no secret to police, the Tribunal's role evaporates, along with its power over our kind. Fliers can access the regular judicial system for justice instead. One stone kills all the birds."

"And if you fail to convince them?"

"Have some faith in your uncle. Talk to me again tonight, after the caucus. See if I change your mind."

Deflated, I leaned back and twisted my wine glass, staring into the red velvet liquid.

Mason shifted in his seat. He set his glass down and reached behind the sofa. "I have something for you."

"To shut me up?"

"As if that's possible," Mason said, sporting a smile. He slid a large box onto the table in front of me. "Open it."

"What is it?"

He raised an exasperated eyebrow.

I sat forward and reached for it. The box had no logo, no identifier of any kind. I lifted the lid. Inside, a gold seal secured a fold of tissue paper. I broke the seal and parted the tissue. He'd given me a jacket. I touched the soft leather. Black, of course.

"Try it on."

I stood and slid my arms into the silk-lined sleeves. It was tapered and fell to mid-thigh. I pulled the zipper up to my chin. It fit perfectly. "It's beautiful."

"It looks good on you. You'll fit right in tonight."

"Ah, so this is to make you look good."

"I believe what you meant to say was 'thank you.'"

I grinned. I couldn't help it. "Thank you. But don't think this is going to buy me off. I'm going to push you hard for representation whether you like it or not."

He raised his hands in surrender. "Consider me warned."

Mason looked toward the foyer. I felt Stuart's presence before he materialized. A Ghost in my presence felt like a tug on my psyche, as if someone were watching me. All Ghosts had an aura that other Ghosts could sense. Except for me. They couldn't sense me. I'd gotten that from Jolene; no one had been able to sense her, either.

Stuart materialized with a smile on his face. "Emelynn," he said, opening his arms. I went to him and snuggled into his grandfatherly embrace, blocking out all thoughts of my mother's indictment. God, I hoped she was wrong about them. Well-worn cowboy boots peeked out from the legs of Stuart's jeans.

"You had a good trip?" he asked.

"I did. You?"

"Yes. Phillip and I drove over last week. Beautiful countryside, isn't it?"

"Very."

"I see the jacket fits. Do you like it?"

"I do. It doesn't go with the capris, but yes, I like it."

I unzipped the jacket and laid it back in its box. Mason poured a glass of wine for his father and the three of us sat while Stuart relayed the latest security report.

"It was nice of you to invite James's family to the caucus," I said.

"It was time. Caucus has always been a time to showcase our unique strengths—kinetic gifts, memory manipulation—they're all part of what makes us strong enough to protect the others."

Phillip arrived with a charcuterie tray loaded with olives, cheese and deli meats. "Something to tide you over until tonight," he said, setting it in front of us.

He tucked the tissue around my new jacket and refitted the box's lid. "Shall I take this to your room?" he asked.

"Yes. Thank you."

By the time we'd finished the bottle of wine and made a sizable dent in the deli tray, it was time to dress for the caucus.

"Dad will escort you," Mason said. "I'll join you there."

I gave him a hug, wished him well and headed for the stairs. Up in my room, I dressed in Flier black; leggings, boots and a silk turtleneck. I combed my hair and pulled it into a high ponytail. After I applied a bit of eyeliner, mascara and lipstick, I felt ready. Nervous but ready.

Finally, I pulled out the silver filigree crystal-case necklace that held Mason's mom's crystal and fastened it around my neck. It sparkled in my reflection.

I donned the new jacket, slipped leather gloves in the pocket and headed down the corridor.

From the bridge, I saw Stuart standing in front of the bank of windows in the formal sitting area. He turned and looked up when he heard me. I continued down the stairs.

Stuart's white hair matched his shirt and bow tie. He wore a black tailcoat, and he'd traded his cowboy boots for a pair of patent-leather oxfords. He held his gloves in one hand. His gaze drifted to the necklace. "May I?" he asked, reaching for it.

He'd given Mason his wife's crystal to pass on to me before she'd been killed at Cairabrae. She'd suffered a debilitating stroke years earlier and hadn't used it since. He held the weight of the crystal case on the tip of his fingers and turned it, admiring the fine filigree work. He set it back in place and smiled. "Jeannette would be so proud to see you wearing this tonight."

I took his hand. "I met her only once, but she made an impression. I'm so sorry you lost her."

"That was a terrible night. We all lost something." He patted the back of my hand.

"I thought you'd be wearing black," I said.

"Not tonight, but I've got a black travel cloak."

"How do you feel about Mason's idea of going public?"

"You know how I feel. I support him wholeheartedly."

"I know you did before the massacre, before ICO and Vector Labs. Has any of that caused you to reassess?"

"I've considered all of it, dear. None of it would have happened had we gone public a year ago. The damage won't stop. Not until we're free of the chains of secrecy. Today's technology will expose us. I'd rather we do it on our terms. I'm not saying it's going to be easy. The Tribunal will fight us every step of the way. But it is the right direction. I'm sure of that."

"I wish I shared your confidence, Stuart."

"You will, Emelynn. We have far more to gain than we have to lose."

Stuart took my elbow and escorted me to a hall table where a satellite-image map had been laid out.

"What's this?"

"The caves at the Acadia winery. It's where we're holding the caucus." Stuart pointed out the residence where we were staying and the winery building where the reception would be held, roughly a mile away as the crow flies. The road James and I had driven in on was a twisted line that skirted the eastern edge of the large property. "The wine caves are here." He pointed to where someone had drawn a *T* in thick black marker. Two curved lines crossed the *T*, like smiles, instead of one straight one.

"You say it's a cave?"

"Yes. Man-made. Most wineries around here have them for storing and aging wine. Each arm of the cave is ventilated through an air shaft at the terminal ends. It's how we'll access the facility. The caucus takes place in the centre chamber." He indicated the vertical section of the *T* between the two curved crossbars.

"Access to the caves is through a portal at the base of the hill, behind the winery." He pointed to the bottom of the *T*. "We blocked it five days ago and put guards in place to monitor it. Only authorized personnel have been in or out of there since we arrived. The air shafts are hidden in the hillside and have been monitored since we've been on site. No one is getting in or out of there without our knowing about it. If anything unexpected happens, we'll escape through the air shafts."

"That's very reassuring."

"What happened at Cairabrae will never happen again."

"What about the reception?"

"We've removed the glass in the upper windows in the reception hall. If there's trouble and they can fly, they can escape."

"And the food?" The Redeemers had incapacitated us at Cairabrae by poisoning everything we ate and drank with ground amber, a Flier-specific toxin we were all susceptible to.

"It arrived this afternoon and it's already been tested. The wine is sealed. There's nothing to worry about. Mason's caucus will come off without a hitch."

"Please touch wood when you say that."

Stuart checked his watch. It was close to nine o'clock. "Time to go. You ready?"

"I suppose."

Phillip met us at the front door and handed Stuart a long black overcoat. Stuart slipped it on and pulled a dark watch cap over his hair. Phillip opened the door and we stepped outside.

"We'll fly down to the northeast air shaft and ghost in from there," Stuart said, pulling on his gloves.

I did the same. My gloves, like Stuart's, had been specially made with a pocket stitched into the palm—to hold a crystal. I made a show of removing the crystal from the necklace and tucking it inside my glove's pocket. I couldn't identify exactly why I'd kept the nature of my crystal secret, but something inside me—something I trusted—guided me.

"It's the first time we've flown together," I said. In normal families, first-time events would be the first time we'd skied or rode horses together. Not in our family.

"So it is." He lifted into the air and waited for me. The power of my crystal, the real one inside me, surged and sent tingles underneath my skin. I twisted free of gravity and drifted up to join him.

We rose above the treetops. The surrounding hills and distant vineyards painted a canvas I'd never tire of. Side by side, we flew a straight line. Five minutes later, we dropped down in long grass near a thick standpipe with a candy-cane bend, set in concrete.

I looked around. "I thought these air shafts were monitored."

"They are. We're surrounded by cameras and there's a greeter waiting below. I'll go first and see you inside."

He winked out of sight. When his aura was gone, I closed my eyes, squeezed my crystal and pushed my ghosted form through the screen at the opening of the pipe. It was fifty feet straight down. At the pipe's mouth, I passed through a series of air filters and into what looked like a utility closet with a control panel and a steel-grated door.

The air was thick with a sweet, musky scent reminiscent of port. Oak barrels in iron cradles stacked three high lined the walls down the length of the cave. Stuart stood on the other side of the grated door beside the greeter, but the welcome felt somewhat muted by the automatic weapon the man held at the ready.

"My granddaughter will be here momentarily," Stuart said to him. "Her aura is faint. Don't be alarmed if you don't sense her."

The greeter's expression held doubt, but he blinked when I re-formed beside Stuart. He recovered quickly. "Go ahead. The others are already here."

"Mason will be along any minute," Stuart said, then turned to me. "We must ghost again. When we reach the caucus chamber, don't re-form until you're called upon."

"How long?"

"Twenty minutes or so. Follow me."

Again, we ghosted. Polished stone paved the cave's floor. A layer of rough concrete covered its arched ceiling. Our destination curved out of sight. We drifted a hundred yards and still hadn't reached the centre chamber when I felt the first pulls on my psyche. Ghosts were close by. With each metre I moved forward, the pulling intensified, until I felt swamped by the sensation.

I stopped and whispered to Stuart, "Just a minute."

"What is it?" he asked.

"How many of us are here?"

"All of us."

"Every Ghost?"

"Every able-bodied one, yes. Can you feel them?"

"Yes. It's overwhelming."

"Take a couple of deep breaths. We've got another thirty yards until the centre chamber."

I followed him deeper into the cave. In the distance, light spilled into the corridor, split by iron bars that marked the end of the cave, or more correctly, I supposed, its beginning. I felt movement in the airflow.

I concentrated on Stuart's ghosted form and followed him through the iron bars. My heart pounded against my ribcage. Normally, I could sift through auras and differentiate Ghosts. I knew Mason's signature and Stuart's, even Sebastian's. But what I felt now was unlike anything I'd experienced in the past. The air in the centre chamber rippled in waves, surging and retreating. Bulges formed and smoothed out, like knees and elbows under a clear sheet.

The chamber before me spread out thirty feet across. Its ceiling, a complicated symphony of arches, stretched up and perched on top of pillars spaced generously around the edge of the room. Wall sconces dimly lit the perimeter. An iron chandelier hung from the centre of the chamber above an oversized rectangular table. One chair sat empty at each end. Four chairs lined each side. Seven of the eight side chairs were occupied by Tribunal members, and each one was dressed as I was, in black leather. I recognized them all from Cairabrae.

Lillian Spencer sat demurely with her hands out of sight. The demure element was intentionally disarming. Her steel-grey hair, cut to her chin, framed an elegant, fine-boned face.

Albert Vanderhoff occupied the seat to Lillian's right. He rested one arm across his stomach and the other stroked his chin. The scalp above his receding hairline glinted as if it had been polished. He gazed down his sharp, pointed nose to the empty chair at the head of the table.

Dillon Marshall was next. He wasn't more than five years older than I was. Dillon had replaced his cousin, Carrie, who'd been killed by the Redeemers. Dillon didn't seem to know what to do with his hands. He smoothed his hair then scratched his neck. His gaze darted around the table, never settling anywhere.

Beside him, Ivy Adams watched Dillon's fidgeting with disdain. She'd crossed her arms, and the fingers of one hand beat a tattoo against her ample girth. I expected any minute she'd bark at him to stop.

Across from Ivy, on the other side of the table, sat Rachael Warner. Like me, she'd worn her hair in a high ponytail. Her clasped hands rested on the table, and her head swivelled as she scanned the room with large, dark eyes framed in thick lashes.

Ron Evans was seated to Rachael's right. Thankfully, he'd fully recovered from a Redeemer's bullet to his back. The injury had amped up the guilt I'd felt over breaking his nose months prior. It was hard to believe he'd suffered either of those injuries looking at him now, with a hoodlum's skull-trim haircut and shoulders straining under his jacket.

Edward Kosikov filled the seat next to Ron. Though he still had the ruddy complexion of an outdoor enthusiast, he'd shrunk since I last saw him. He was a widower now, thanks to the Redeemers. He leaned over the table on his forearms. His hands were clenched, as was his jaw.

The eighth side chair, the one they'd offered to me, sat empty.

I felt Mason's presence as he entered the room and brushed across the ceiling. Those who were seated shifted in their chairs. He materialized at the end of the table, with Rachael on his right and Ivy on his left. He nodded a separate, silent greeting to everyone around the table before he sat down. He was a handsome man with the same pale-blue eyes as Jolene. Dark blond waves curled against the collar of his leather car coat.

Sebastian arrived last. I sensed him drifting into the chamber. He re-formed as far from the table as possible. The moment he did so, everyone around the table scraped their chairs back and stood. Sebastian didn't move until he had their undivided attention. He wasn't one to waste the opportunity to make a grand entrance. He strode forward, the heels of his boots echoing in the chamber. He wore an embossed leather duster. It should have looked ridiculous, but it didn't. It suited him. In his right hand, he held an elaborate sceptre reminiscent of royalty. In his left hand, he held a large book. It occurred to me that I might not have given the ceremonial aspect of this caucus enough thought. What came next? A crown?

When Sebastian reached the head of the table, he set the book down and I got a closer look at the sceptre. A white dove perched on a crystal cross embedded in the diamond-encrusted globe. The staff itself was made of gold filigree, similar to many of the Ghosts' crystal cases.

"Welcome," Sebastian said. He looked at the sceptre and cradled the globe in his gloved palm. When he lifted his head, he cast his gaze around the table. He called out in a clear voice, "Are you prepared to renew your allegiance to the Tribunal Novem and the laws we hold sacred?"

Everyone around the table answered as one with a shout. "Aye!"

The other Ghosts in the room stirred and the air heaved. Sebastian once again looked down at the sceptre in his hands.

He addressed the gathering in measured words. "Each of you at this table represents one of our nine founding families. Each of you has been granted one vote at this table. Are you prepared to discharge your duty?"

Again, a resounding "Aye!" rang out. The Tribunal members remained standing.

Sebastian's thumb stroked the sceptre. He carried on in his measured tone. "When our forefathers formed this governing body, they decreed the mantle of power be passed on every five years in accordance with the order set down at the inaugural caucus."

I'd never thought to do the math before, but the figures floated through my head now. Nine members and a five-year rotation; each family had a shot at the leadership every forty-five years; once in a lifetime for most. The odds of being of a sufficient age to handle the job when the opportunity arose must have been similar to the odds of winning the lottery.

Sebastian continued. "Tonight, the power to lead this body, to set our path forward and cast the deciding vote, passes from the Kirk clan to the Reynolds clan."

Sebastian called down the length of the table. "Mason McKenzie Reynolds, call your family."

Mason seemed to be aware of where his father and I were situated in the room, a feat I felt was beyond impressive considering how many auras were intertwined in the chamber. He looked right at us. "Show yourselves."

I swallowed. Stuart re-formed. I gaped at him but followed his lead and re-formed. Uncomfortable didn't begin to describe the sensation of a heated spotlight on us. Mason nodded at us then at two other figures who'd emerged from the ether. A man and a woman with dark cloaks draped over their shoulders. A couple perhaps? I didn't know them.

Sebastian addressed the four of us. "Have you chosen Mason McKenzie Reynolds to represent your clan?"

Stuart shouted "Aye," as did the other two. Sebastian looked at me and cocked his head.

"Aye, yes," I added. It came out like an awkward afterthought. Why hadn't Mason given me a heads-up about this ritual crap?

Sebastian turned back to Mason. "You have been chosen by your clan. Do you accept the mantle of leadership?"

"I do."

"Will you put the interests of the whole above your own?"

"I will."

Sebastian gave a small nod and inhaled. "So be it." He looked past the empty chair to his left and addressed Edward. "Edward Alexander Kosikov, call your family."

Edward's gaze fell into the void of the chamber. "Show yourselves," he said, and one by one, five Ghosts re-formed around us.

Sebastian skirted the empty chair to stand before Edward with the sceptre in his hand. "In the presence of your family, Edward Alexander Kosikov, do you swear allegiance to the Tribunal Novem and the laws we hold sacred?"

Edward went down on one knee. "I do." Sebastian held the sceptre out to him. He kissed it and then stood with his head bowed.

"You may now present yourself," Sebastian said.

Edward stepped back, turned and walked up to Mason. Again, Edward got down on one knee.

"Do you swear your fealty?" Mason asked.

Fealty? Seriously?

"I do." This time, Edward kissed the back of Mason's hand. When Mason nodded, Edward stood, walked the long way around the table and took up a post standing behind his chair.

Sebastian moved to stand before Ron and repeated the exercise. "Ronald Terrance Evans, call your family." Four Ghosts materialized, including Ron's brother, Gordon, whom I recognized. Ron swore his allegiance and then approached Mason to kiss his hand.

Sebastian made his way around the table, repeating the ritual with every member except Mason. With each member's pledge, more Ghosts materialized. By the time he stood before the last member, Lillian, there were close to fifty of us in the chamber. Many of them I had met at Cairabrae. We acknowledged each other with silent nods.

When Lillian had returned to her place behind her chair, Sebastian walked the length of the table and stood before Mason. Sebastian extended the sceptre. Mason slowly inhaled then reached out and accepted it. He straightened and called out so the chamber could hear. "Sebastian McDougal Kirk, are you prepared to renew your allegiance to the Tribunal Novem and the laws we hold sacred?"

"Aye," Sebastian said.

"You have been chosen to represent the Kirk family. As such, you have been granted one vote at this table. Are you prepared to discharge your duty?"

"Aye," Sebastian said.

"Sebastian McDougal Kirk, call your family." He did, and Tiffany re-formed, along with three others. Tiffany had tears in her eyes. In that moment, I felt a surge of empathy for her and Sebastian. It had been petty of me not to appreciate how difficult it would be for a man like Sebastian to hand over the reins of power.

Mason continued. "In the presence of your family, Sebastian McDougal Kirk, do you swear allegiance to the Tribunal Novem and the laws we hold sacred?"

Sebastian went down on one knee. "I do." Mason held the sceptre out to him and he kissed it.

"Do you swear your fealty?"

Sebastian took a breath. "I do," he said, and he kissed the back of Mason's hand. Mason nodded, Sebastian stood and Mason offered his hand. Sebastian shook it then turned and walked back to his seat.

The Ghosts who had re-formed in the chamber stood back from the table, giving it a ten-foot berth. I scanned the faces, picking out a few more I recognized. One of the faces stared back and stirred a memory. He looked familiar, but I couldn't place him, and I hadn't seen which Tribunal member he'd materialized in support of. I nudged Stuart and drew his attention to the man with the goatee who was now looking elsewhere. I mouthed, "Who's that?"

Stuart glanced in the man's direction then back at me. He stiffened. "Not here," he whispered. I turned back to the man with the goatee, but he'd vanished.

As I looked at the others around the room, I noticed splashes of colour peeking out from under black cloaks. The women wore jewel-coloured gowns that swept the floor, and the men wore white shirts and bow ties, like Stuart. In fact, the only ones dressed in black leather were the nine Tribunal members. And me. I chalked it up to my name being on the agenda in connection to the one seat at the table that remained vacant.

Mason walked between his chair and the table, rested the sceptre on the surface in front of him and took his seat. "You may sit."

Stuart touched my elbow. I turned to him. He tipped his head and ghosted. All around the room, the other Ghosts were doing the same. I squeezed my crystal and followed suit. The room swirled around me again as the Ghosts dissolved into molecules. Only the nine Tribunal members remained in corporeal form. They settled into their seats, and with the ritual behind them, the meeting began.

Chapter Eight

It is my great honour to open tonight's caucus with welcome news. The Redeemer threat is gone." Mason waited for the excitement around the table to die a natural death before he continued. "With the assistance of the Moss family, my father and I identified the last of their numbers and have since ensured they will never be a threat to you or your families again."

I shook my ghosted head. The Redeemers might never be a threat again, but if Mason didn't succeed in his attempts to go public, another group would take the Redeemers' place. And that group would be even more ruthless, having learned from the Redeemers. I couldn't help but think Mason was squandering a tremendous opportunity to introduce the idea of some form of democratic representation for all Fliers to quell another uprising.

Mason turned a sympathetic eye to Edward Kosikov. "They took your wife." He looked at Dillon. "They took your cousin, one of our own, and they tried to take another." Mason glanced at Ron Evans. "They robbed me of my mother, my father of his wife of forty years, and took many others. Though it is cold comfort to those of us who suffered at their hands, we can find solace in the fact that they paid for their treason. Our loved ones' deaths have been avenged. Your families can come out of hiding."

Excited chatter broke out once more, and even the Ghosts in the room contributed to the volume. At the far end of the table, Lillian stood. The voices receded. "An auspicious beginning to your leadership, Mason. Well done. You have our clan's gratitude."

The room filled with voices adding weight to Lillian's sentiment. Mason tipped his head, accepting the praise.

After Lillian sat down and the voices receded again, Mason continued. "The news is not as good with regard to International Covert Operations. As you are aware, ICO broke their contract with us and overstepped any possible interpretation of good faith when they abducted the two Fliers whose services we offered them. Sebastian Kirk called upon many of you to assist in his effort to eradicate them. Unfortunately, one of the signatories to ICO's contract, Canada's General Cain, escaped the cull."

Murmurs of alarm spiked. Mason raised his hands to quiet them. "Sebastian assures me he has a plan in place to find Cain and finish the job. And on a positive note, all data ICO collected about us has been removed from their computers, files and databases."

The murmurs started up again. Ron Evans didn't engage. Instead, he directed a question to Sebastian. "Overlooking the fact that we were not apprised of the missing general, what is this plan of yours?" All attention swivelled to Sebastian's end of the table.

Sebastian's smile suggested superiority. "We have wiped out Cain's support system. Without funds and tech support, he can only hide for so long. We've put in place a net to catch him when he surfaces."

"A net?"

Again Sebastian smiled at Ron as if indulging a precocious child. "We've put tracers on everyone he might contact when he gets tired of hiding. The moment he surfaces, we'll know his coordinates."

Sebastian then addressed the entire table. "The ICO agents who knew about us were eliminated swiftly. As you know, this operation spanned two countries and infiltrated the highest levels of their governments. It was no easy task. Cain's escape is well within the expected margin of error for such a complex operation and is but a temporary situation, I can assure you."

Ron kept up the pressure. "We know that when our representatives were held captive at Vector Labs, ICO learned that Ghosts could be detained in airtight spaces. Did your people find and destroy that specific intelligence?"

Sebastian raised his voice over the ensuing whispers. "Yes. ICO operates on a cell mentality—only the cell tasked with interacting with our two representatives knew about us. The data they collected was compartmentalized. We successfully located and destroyed it. However, as anyone in the intelligence community will tell you, when you're dealing with human beings, there are no guarantees; no absolutes."

Ivy spoke up. "Enough sidestepping, Sebastian. What are you saying? Spell it out." God bless her lack of social finesse.

Sebastian tried his best to hide a scowl. "Our grievous exposure at Cairabrae left us no choice—we had to engage with ICO or risk far greater damage. You were all aware that our contract with ICO could further expose us. We took that risk and lost: ICO betrayed us. With your help, my team cleaned up the mess. But there is no way to definitively plug all potential leaks. I'm speaking of the low-level file clerk who talks to her Friday beer buddies about the report she filed, or her beer buddy who tells his brother. My team did an outstanding job. Human skepticism will negate any unforeseeable leaks."

"How fortunate for us that our government is still afraid of being painted with a paranormal brush," Albert said, shoring up Sebastian's position.

Sebastian nodded. "Public opinion is a powerful influence working to our advantage."

In the silence that ensued, I had to congratulate Sebastian. He'd checked off all the contentious issues while simultaneously patting himself on the back and blaming the entire ordeal on our *grievous exposure*, as if he'd had nothing to do with it. We wouldn't have been exposed at all if Sebastian hadn't insisted on an ill-timed and frivolous cocktail party at Cairabrae. And for what? To satisfy the Tribunal elite's curiosity about the woman Jolene gifted? It always came back to me.

When would it end? The Tribunal had tracked down and killed every Redeemer without once considering, let alone addressing, the underlying irritant that had spawned them. Now they'd all but eliminated an entire elite government cell. Would going public have saved those lives? How would my covey in Vancouver feel about the deaths racked up on their behalf?

"Are there any further questions before we move forward?" Mason asked.

When the grumbling around the table subsided, Mason took control and finally began laying the groundwork for his raison d'être.

"We have another enemy at our gates," he started. "An intelligent force that constantly adapts and grows more powerful with every passing day. If you will indulge me for a moment, a demonstration will make my point far more effectively than words."

Mason stood and walked a slow circuit around the table. "Most of us use vertical laser sensors to monitor the perimeters of our properties. We set those sensors to identify trespassing heat signatures large enough to pose a threat. Larger than a raven, for example, or an eagle."

The unmistakable buzz of a drone grew louder as it approached from the portal end of the chamber. Heads around the table swivelled to search out the source. A white drone with four rotors circled the room before landing nimbly in the centre of the table. Its rotors continued to spin.

Mason spoke above the buzz. "But our laser sensors will not detect something the size of this drone. Further, this drone can be operated from five miles away, and it houses a powerful camera with telephoto and infrared capabilities. That camera can send high-definition live digital feedback to its operator, night or day."

Ivy tsked. "Drones may cause an interim disruption, but already governments are severely curtailing and limiting their use. The novelty will wear off, just like it did with those remote-controlled toys we were all so worried about a few years ago." She let out a derisive snort. "Before that, it was surveillance cameras that caused a stir. Turned out to be a non-issue. Even traffic cameras are focused on activity on the ground, not in the air."

"I might add," Albert said, "that drones communicate with their operators over a radio frequency. A simple RF jammer will take care of that." He pointed to the offending drone.

"You're right, Albert," Mason said. "But this drone is no toy and it's not operating on RF. The GPS coordinates of this room were programmed into it. An RF jammer wouldn't have stopped it."

"Even so," Sebastian said, "there's no mistaking the sound a drone makes. We can adapt our sensors to pick up a range of their sound signatures. As Ivy said, drones are an interim disruption."

The drone's rotors abruptly stopped. At the same time, two large projection screens began unfurling from the ceiling. When they were fully extended, everyone in the room could see one of them.

"It's hard to argue with Sebastian's point," Mason said. "Drones do emit a distinctive sound." Mason now stood behind his chair. He looked to the screens as they lit up with identical footage. I recognized the very table at which the Tribunal sat, filmed from a distance. As the distance grew shorter, I could tell that whatever had taken the video we were watching was airborne and had approached from the same direction the drone had. It had circled the entire room. But the footage wasn't live; it had been recorded when Mason had been seated. When the caucus had begun. Before the white drone occupied the centre of the table, as it did now. Confusion flitted across the faces of those seated.

Mason held out his hand, palm up, drawing everyone's attention. A bug the size of a grape floated in an erratic diagonal line from the iron chandelier above the table to rest in Mason's hand. It could have been mistaken for a moth.

"But what about this drone?" Mason said. "Did you hear it enter this chamber earlier to film our proceedings?" The drone took off again and fluttered around the table. I felt a pinch of pride knowing James was the one behind the scenes pulling the strings.

"This particular drone resembles a moth, but it could just as easily look like a mouse, a dragonfly or a cockroach," Mason said. "The technology is cutting edge and not widely available, but it will be."

"What is, however, widely available are these." Mason pulled out his phone. "There is more computer power in this cellphone than there was on the first spaceship to the moon. How many of you own one?" Heads bobbed around the table. "Indulge me, if you would." Mason stepped around his chair and laid his phone on the table. "Set your phones on the table before you." Phones appeared from pockets and were dutifully laid on the table.

"Sixty-five percent of Americans own a smartphone, and that number is increasing daily. Each one is equipped with a digital camera capable of taking high-resolution photos and video at the press of a button. Just as quickly, those photos and videos can be shared around the world on dozens of social media sites, blogs or news networks." Mason gazed around the table. "How long do you think it will be before someone films a Flier in action and posts it on social media?"

"Cellphone technology is not a new threat," Albert said. "Cellphone cameras have been around since the early 2000s. Smartphones since at least 2007. It's not been a problem."

"I agree," Mason said. "Up until now. Bear with me a moment longer. How many of you have photos on your phones of your kids' first flights? Perhaps your grandkids'? Or that time you took the perfect shot of a loved one mid-air? A selfie over a landmark? You think those photos are safe because they're locked behind a password, maybe fingerprint technology or face recognition software. But what if all of your protections aren't enough?"

Again our attention was drawn to the big screens. This time, photographs floated across them. Those at the table began recognizing the faces in the photos. Some reached for their phones and tried turning them off. A couple of people quickly removed their phones' batteries. But the damage had been done. The photos kept scrolling by. Most were benign: shopping lists, pet antics, laughing friends and shared meals. But some were the type Mason had warned of: Fliers mid-air.

The photos faded away. "The technology that so easily accesses your phone's photos can also access your phone's camera and mic." A number of phones on the table began playing back an overlapping chorus of Mason's words. "Up to now ... Bear with me ... Up to now ... Bear with me ..." The hanging screens lit up again, this time with video selfies of those who'd picked up their phones in a vain attempt to turn them off. Mason's words and the videos played on a loop.

Edward shoved his chair back and stood. Anger coloured his cheeks red. "This is a gross invasion of our privacy. Stop it at once."

The screens darkened immediately and the voice playbacks faded.

"I agree with you, Edward. It is a gross invasion of privacy, but it's one each of you willingly facilitated." Grunts of denial flared but Mason beat them down. He stepped away from his chair and began another slow circuit around the table. "When you arrived this evening, you were each asked by the guards to show your email invitation. To do that you had to open an attachment on your cellphones. That attachment unleashed the spyware that allowed us to control your phones. If this was a real attack, the perpetrator would now have all your contacts, all your photos, all the GPS data identifying the places you frequent—and you wouldn't even know it. If they infect your home computers, they will have the ability to turn on the computer's cameras anytime they choose to spy on you. They can turn on the computer's mic to listen to and record your conversations. Again, you would never know it."

Edward retook his seat, and Mason paused for effect. "Technology is the enemy at our gate. It is no longer a matter of *if* one of our kind is exposed. It's a matter of *when*, and that time is fast approaching."

"Hold on a second," Albert said. "As disconcerting as this demonstration has been, you had us at a disadvantage. We trusted the security you had set up. Otherwise, we wouldn't so easily have fallen for opening an email attachment. After all, every virus-protection program warns about opening attachments. In fact, the software we all use will immediately identify spyware and quarantine it."

"And yet your virus protection did none of that tonight," Mason said. He took a heavy breath, and I could feel his exasperation. It seemed no matter what Mason put forward, no matter how compelling his demonstration, some of them were hell-bent on ramming their heads back into the sand. Their stubborn refusal to acknowledge the danger technology presented was almost comical.

"Spare us the suspense, Mason," Sebastian said. "What is the purpose of this little demonstration of yours?"

Mason again paused. "I'll repeat what I stated earlier. It's only a matter of time before our existence is discovered. It already happened once, at Cairabrae, and we were not ready. That's how ICO got a foothold. The technology I've demonstrated today isn't going away; it's getting better." Mason returned to his seat at the head of the table. He settled his back against the chair, and let his hands dangle off the ends of the armrests. He gazed confidently around at the seated members. "What I'm proposing is that we plan for our inevitable exposure, and let it unfold at a time and in a manner of our choosing."

Alarmed voices rose like geysers. Sebastian scowled down the table at Mason. "Have you forgotten the pledge you took tonight? In front of all of us? You swore allegiance to the Tribunal Novem and the laws we hold sacred. Maintaining the secret of the gift is the one law we hold sacred above all others. If you are not prepared to uphold that law, then perhaps you are not fit to lead us."

"My allegiance to this body remains absolute," Mason replied. "But real leadership doesn't wear blinders or handcuffs. That law was put in place in a time when technology wasn't a threat. The purpose of that law was to protect us. Secrecy is no longer an effective means to that end. We need to think boldly and find a new way to protect ourselves."

"Are you proposing that we make a public declaration of our existence?" Lillian asked.

"I'm asking each one of you to consider the implications of going public. We ignore technology at our peril. Consider the damage another uncontrolled exposure presents. Think about what our lives might look like without the burden of this secret."

Albert spoke next. "I think you've lost your mind, Mason. Governments will never allow Ghosts to roam free. Our capabilities pose too big a threat to their security, their sovereignty."

Mason paused long enough that I grew concerned he hadn't anticipated this roadblock. He slowly drew his eyebrows together in an expression of profound bafflement. After a long delay, he spoke. "It seems I haven't made myself clear. I apologize. The ability to shed gravity and take flight is what I'm suggesting we make public. Exposing Ghosts is not on the table."

I gasped, but it was relief that sounded around the room. Shoulders relaxed and the low rumble of disapproval lightened to twitters. Apparently, Mason was more than prepared for this roadblock. I thought back to every conversation I'd ever had with Mason or Stuart about going public. Not once had either of them specified flight as the sole element slated for public exposure. Had I misunderstood their intent all along?

As I studied Mason, I felt a stab of his duplicity. Faced with a death sentence, even the innocent would be tempted to accept a lighter penalty. Is that what Mason had set up? Threaten to expose everyone and then offer a safety valve available only to Ghosts?

"Contrary to the Pollyanna version of an unveiling Mason suggests," Ivy said, "going public would be the end of this Tribunal. Every damn Flier who's ever had a grievance with us will seek remedy in the courts, and I don't need to remind anyone here that the non-Gifted don't share our version of justice, not even close. We'd be crucified."

"Only a handful of Fliers outside of our own ghosting circles know the names of those of us on this Tribunal," Mason countered. "The phone numbers that we provide to the coveys can't be traced back to us, so no one's going to be crucified."

What the hell was Mason doing? First he gives Ghosts an out and now the Tribunal?

"Perhaps," Albert said, "but regardless, Ivy's brought up an interesting point—or perhaps I should say an opportunity. Let me be clear, I do not support Mason's idea, but if he's right about this technology and our secret is exposed, we should be prepared to take advantage of it. Disgruntled Fliers may or may not be able to name us, but if they can and they seek remedy in the courts, they will self-identify. We can then make quick work of eliminating them."

My heart sank. I fought against a rising wave of panic.

"Albert is right," Sebastian said. "If Mason's prediction about technology is correct, the secret we've spent centuries protecting may be made public. But Ghosts won't be. The ghosting gene is shared by few and well hidden. Threat of our exposure is low. If the Tribunal doesn't have to waste its time and energy protecting the secrecy of the gift, we could concentrate our efforts on ferreting out Fliers who have a grievance with us or even know about us. Let the courts deal with Fliers' petty complaints."

"In fact," Albert said, "if the secret of the gift is made public, governments may do some of our work for us. They'll most certainly want to compile a database of names, which would be useful."

Ivy huffed. "That will happen as soon as one of the idiots demonstrates the power of a jolt. No government will let that weapon go unmonitored. They may even develop a method of controlling it."

"This idea of yours might have some merit after all," Sebastian said.

Albert nodded and pinched his chin.

My panic tipped into seething anger. Mason's plan wouldn't eliminate the Tribunal, it would make it stronger. And after they'd killed off all dissenters and had a list of names, they'd probably help the governments develop a method for controlling jolts, our only means of defence. With the Flier population hobbled, there would be no stopping the Tribunal, and now I had to wonder if they'd ever had Fliers' interests at heart.

Were they so blinded they didn't see that we were all Fliers? Was this how they'd want to be treated? I ached to shout out that their names would be on that government list, I'd make sure of it, but self-preservation silenced me. My faith in Mason now felt shockingly naive.

Mason shifted forward and rested his forearms on the table. "I am not calling a vote on this item tonight." He glanced around the table. For the most part, the faces that looked back were contemplative, accepting even. "This demonstration was intended to spark a conversation, which I'm confident it has done. But be forewarned. It will be on the agenda next time we meet, and at that time, I *will* call a vote. Meantime, I suggest you continue this conversation with your friends and families. My door is open to your thoughts and questions."

Mason checked his watch. "Thank you for your patience. I have kept you longer than I intended. There is just one outstanding item to address before we join our families at the reception."

The empty seat at the Tribunal's table was the one item left to cross off Mason's agenda. It taunted me from across the room. Take the seat and the Tribunal would own a piece of my freedom. Walk away from it and the Tribunal grew more powerful.

How would I feel if my friends' names ended up on a witch-hunter's list and subject to who knows what form of control? I thought about Avery and Victoria, Eden and Alex, and everyone else in my covey. They were mothers and fathers, daughters and sons, children and grandparents. They were hardworking, down-to-earth Fliers who saved for retirement and paid mortgages. And they had no one to look out for them around this table of arrogant elitists and no hope that it would ever change.

Mason spoke but I'd stopped listening. I drifted up and over the table and approached the empty chair. If I walked away, I was no better than the others at the table. My heart felt as if it were pounding to get free of my chest. My thoughts raced. Would James understand? Would my mother? I'd come here tonight to free myself from the Tribunal, but my conscience wouldn't let me. Change would never come from outside the Tribunal. The only chance to influence this fucking archaic body was to fight it from within. If that meant giving up a piece of my freedom for a while, surely it was a small price to pay, and nothing compared to what my covey—my friends—would pay if the Tribunal continued on the path Mason envisioned. I couldn't leave my friends to that fate.

I re-formed behind the seat. Mason stopped talking midsentence. Silence stole the air from the room. I circled the chair and sat down.

"My dear," Sebastian said, offering me a sympathetic smile. "I'm afraid it's too late. We were just—"

I looked him face-on. "I accept your offer. I'm claiming the seat."

"But—"

Mason cut Sebastian off. "The motion to withdraw the seat was not, in fact, complete, Sebastian, before Ms. Taylor accepted our offer."

Albert leapt to his feet. "This is preposterous! What does she know about Tribunal business? She was gifted, for god's sake. And how are we going to come to definitive decisions without a tie-breaking vote? We are the Tribunal Novem. Nine, not ten."

"I agree!" Sebastian said. "This offer was not well thought out. It was an overreaction. I move that we strike the offer and end this insanity."

The room exploded with angry voices. Mason stood, effectively silencing the room. He then turned on Sebastian. "You forget yourself. I lead this body, not you. You do not have the power to strike items off my agenda. The seat we offered merely needed to be accepted, and it has been."

Mason turned his attention to the others at the table. "Perhaps you have all forgotten what this *gifted* woman did for you. At great mortal risk, she engaged Carson Manse in a fight for all of our lives. She alone put an end to him. This *gifted* Flier recovered each and every one of your crystals—intact. Your offer to her was not an overreaction. It was the least you could do to express gratitude for your lives. Our gratitude. A minor adjustment to fix the tie-breaking vote issue is hardly an excuse to withdraw our offer."

Rachael Warner spoke for the first time that evening. "I agree. Our family, for one, has not forgotten Emelynn's contribution. We thank you, Emelynn, and welcome. I look forward to working with you."

Ron Evans spoke next. "Hear! Hear! My family is also grateful. Welcome to the Tribunal, Emelynn."

Sebastian remained stone-faced, as did Albert and Ivy. Edward and Lillian were hard to read. They were either horrified or on the fence. Dillon hedged his bets, spreading smiles all around the table.

"Emelynn ..." Mason started. "I'm embarrassed to say I don't know your middle name."

"Morgan."

Mason lifted the sceptre from the table. I pushed my chair back and stood.

Emelynn Morgan Taylor, you have been granted one vote at this table. Are you prepared to discharge your duty?"

"Aye," I said.

"Emelynn Morgan Taylor, call your family."

I was at a loss. I couldn't call Stuart—he'd already sworn allegiance to Mason. Calling Mason seemed grossly inappropriate given his role, and I'd never put James in that position.

"Bloody farce," Edward whispered under his breath. "She has no real family to call."

I straightened. "I call my Vancouver covey. I'd ask them to show themselves but they are not Ghosts and therefore not present."

Mason reached for the sceptre. "Fair enough. You will represent your absent covey. Present yourself."

I held on to my defiance and strode to stand before Mason.

"Emelynn Morgan Taylor, do you swear allegiance to the Tribunal Novem and the laws we hold sacred?"

I went down on one knee. "I do." Mason held the sceptre out to me. Though doing so repulsed me, I kissed it, just as the others had done.

"Do you swear your fealty to me?"

I couldn't believe I was participating in this archaic crap. "I do," I said, and kissed the back of his offered hand.

Mason turned his hand over to help me up. I took it with a glare he ignored. He dipped his head. "Welcome to the Tribunal, Emelynn."

Mason then addressed the table. "Within the month, I will present a proposal to address the tie-breaking vote issue. If you have suggestions you wish me to consider, send them along. Thank you for your time this evening. The reception awaits. This caucus is adjourned."

I felt the eyes of the room on me as those around the table vacated their seats and began to disperse. Mason turned to me and reached an arm around my shoulders. He tried to pull me close, but I crooked my elbow and pushed against his chest. I wouldn't embarrass him in this crowd, but I'd be damned if I'd let him think I was happy with him. He leaned in and spoke low into my ear. "Don't be angry. You've made me so proud. We'll talk tonight."

Mason released me and was soon swamped by people wanting to shake his hand. I turned away with escape on my mind but found Rachael and her husband, Marc, waiting. I accepted their well wishes, thanked her for her support and tried again to break away.

This time Stuart blocked my path. He'd read my body language better than Mason and kept his distance. "You made the right decision, Emelynn."

I balled my hands into fists. "I'm glad you think so. I doubt James will share your opinion." I walked away from him, but Ron and Gordon caught up to me. Gordon still wore his cloak.

"Where are you sneaking off to?" Ron asked. He wore a wide grin that ruined his tough-guy facade.

I stopped in my tracks. "This is all just a little overwhelming."

"To be expected your first time. You'll get used to it."

"Which part?" I asked. Gordon chuckled and Ron elbowed him in the ribs.

"Only the ritual, I'm afraid. The egos you'll never get used to."

He seemed so normal. They both did. I felt myself relax a bit. "I can't believe I broke your nose. I'm so sorry."

"Don't be," Gordon said. "He needed a dose of humility."

Ron edged his brother out of the way. "How about you let us escort you to the reception and buy you a drink?"

"I'm not going to the reception."

"Oh, but you must," Gordon said. "You'll be the talk of the room."

"Exactly," I said.

Ron stepped in front of me, blocking my view with his thick neck and broad shoulders. I looked up. "Don't run, Emelynn. You'll never beat them like that. Walk in there with your head held high. You earned your place at the table. That's a lot more than I can say for the rest of us."

His comment was most unexpected. I wavered. Maybe enduring thirty minutes of bullshit would put an end to some of the talk. Ron extended his elbow. I took it and we started for the portal.

Ghosts who'd been hanging back rushed past us. Those who'd re-formed nodded greetings. Some offered congratulations. I faked a smile, ducked my head and kept going.

We left the wine caves and headed for the glass-walled reception hall, which was lit up like a Chinese lantern. Gordon opened the door for us and we stepped inside. Classical music played. Gordon shrugged out of his cloak and handed it to a woman who already held an armful of them. He tugged the bottom of his white vest. Every man in the reception hall looked just like him. The women wore gowns in every colour imaginable. This was the formal affair Stuart had spoken of.

The only people in the room who weren't dressed in white tie were the nine—no, ten—Tribunal members. We looked like party-crashing thugs. And yet, without exception, it was the black-clad oddballs who held the guests' attention. Mason, in particular, looked swamped in an ocean of silk and chiffon. He didn't appear to mind.

Sebastian was likewise swarmed, though his admirers coddled whereas Mason's clung to him as if he were a rock star. Watching it nauseated me.

I looked back to the woman with the cloaks and realized what Mason had done. I hadn't had to wear black tonight. I could have worn a gown and covered it with a cloak like the others in that chamber. But Mason had set it up so I'd look the part when the time came. Indeed, we would talk tonight.

Furtive glances and whispers trailed us as Ron and I strolled the perimeter of the reception hall. Gordon snagged three champagne flutes. I searched the room for James but didn't see him. Ron stopped to acknowledge some people he knew. He introduced me by name, but they already knew it—a scenario repeated with regularity around the room. The whisper campaign spreading news from the caucus was well underway. Some of those who approached claimed to have met me at Cairabrae. They looked vaguely familiar, but I'd met a lot of people that night. I smiled my appreciation but didn't remember half the people who wanted to shake my hand.

But there was one man I knew. He stood alone and stared at me from a distance. I met his gaze and faltered.

"You know him?" Ron asked.

"I thought I did once." I changed direction and nearly bowled over a stout elderly man.

"Hey, Dad," Gordon said to the man. They embraced, and then his father patted Ron's shoulder and shook his hand. Ron introduced us.

The older man grasped my hand in both of his. His dark eyes twinkled from a boxer's face. "My wife would like to meet you."

At his urging, I followed him to a sitting area. His wife rose to greet us. "Finally, we meet," she said, after introductions were made. "I must say, ever since Ronny showed up with two black eyes, I've wanted to meet you."

Once again, I apologized, but that only made her laugh. "I hear you made quite a stir in there tonight."

That she hadn't seen it first-hand told me she wasn't a Ghost. We chatted for another thirty seconds before I caught sight of Redmond's figure cutting through the crowd. "Will you excuse me?" I said. "There's someone I need to see."

With their blessing, I moved off and caught up with Redmond. He turned when I called his name. "Redmond, have you seen James?"

From five feet away, his gaze zigzagged over my torso. "No."

An elegant young woman in an ivory off-the-shoulder gown approached Redmond, unaware he'd been speaking to me. "There you are." She kissed his cheek. Her chestnut-coloured hair was swept up in an elaborate twist. She looked much better than the last time I'd seen her. Redmond hooked an arm around her waist.

It was then that she noticed me. She looked from Redmond to me with apology. "I'm interrupting. Where are my manners? Please forgive me."

Redmond straightened and tightened his grip on her waist, holding her back. "Sandy," Redmond said, smiling stiffly. "This is Emelynn Taylor."

She froze, and in that moment I sensed that she knew my shame. Alexandra Moss was Sandy to her father, Sandra to her brother. And wife to my first lover. A fact that my lover had neglected to share with me at the time.

Her smile remained fixed, but she'd lost her words. "I, ah ..."

Her father came to her rescue. "It's okay, honey. You probably don't remember her."

Sandra had been drugged to the point of oblivion the night I met her. I remembered thinking that even in that condition, she was beautiful. That was before I knew she was Jackson Delaney's wife. Bad night all around.

After a few breaths, she recovered her voice. "You're right. I don't. I'm ... sorry. For what happened to you. I'm grateful. Thank you."

"Looks like we both survived," I said. She'd been held captive for months. Jackson had recruited my covey to rescue her, and I'd been shot during the ordeal. The wound hadn't hurt nearly as much as learning that Jackson had used me.

James's mother approached. Black-velvet appliqué adorned Diana's blood-red gown, lending her petite frame a larger presence. If she'd come tonight to look her family's tormentors in the eye, they'd not soon forget her.

"Diana," I said. Sandra shot a quizzical glance at her mother. It seemed Sandra hadn't known of my visit earlier in the day.

Sandra's gaze returned to study me as her mother engaged me in social banter. I found it hard to concentrate on Diana's words under Sandra's scrutiny.

I knew the moment Sandra saw my earrings. She fixated on them just as Redmond had done the first time I met him. Diana had displayed the same behaviour earlier today. Such an odd reaction.

"You're the woman James has been seeing," Sandra said, interrupting her mother.

"Sandra, darling," Diana said. Admonishment laced her words. She reached for her daughter. That's when I saw the ring she wore on her left hand. It sparkled with the same grey-green stone as my earrings.

"Do you mind my asking?" I said to Diana, nodding at her hand. "What is that stone?"

She pulled her hand back but then didn't quite know where to put it. She looked down at the stone in her wedding ring.

It was Redmond who answered. "It's a moss diamond."

Diamond? "Named for your family?"

"No," he said, with a puzzled expression. "Named for its colour. I'm surprised James didn't tell you."

"It's lovely," I said.

"Green is the rarest colour of diamond on the planet," Redmond said. "Our family's taken a special interest in the ones identified as moss, for obvious reasons. It appears that James located two more."

I raised a hand to an earlobe and finally understood the family's reaction. In their eyes, James's earrings marked me as one of them. When I'd imagined they were merely semi-precious crystals, two carats didn't seem extravagant, but now I felt self-conscious at the display. Conspicuous. So unlike James. Then again, he'd always been a man of few words. The earrings spoke for him.

Did his family already know James had compounded his sins? Not only did he care for a Ghost, but that Ghost had just joined the Tribunal. Standing before them in the black attire that identified me as a Tribunal member must have been a test of the Moss family's manners.

My clothes grew uncomfortably warm. I excused myself and went in search of James. When I couldn't find him inside, I slipped out the door and started for the portal into the caves. I hadn't made it ten paces when a figure stepped out from the gardens and into my path. I stopped and took a step back.

"Hello, Emelynn."

It annoyed me that I still thought he was handsome. He wore his hair too long and his confidence like a badge. His pale hazel eyes searched my face and took in my attire.

"So it's true. You are a Ghost."

I glared at him. "You still married, Jackson?"

He lifted his chin. "I wanted to say hello is all. Wish you well. I'm not here to apologize. Again."

"I'm not asking. I've forgiven you. I won't forget you hurt me, but I've moved on."

"Still seeing James?"

I shook my head and exhaled my annoyance in a huff. "Good night, Jackson." My mind lit up with memories as I skirted around him and continued to the wine caves. I felt desperate now. I needed to see James. Hold him. Beg for his understanding, for his forgiveness.

The portal doors to the caves had been closed and locked. I ghosted and pushed through them, rushing along the main corridor and into the centre chamber. It was empty. The drone had been removed from the table. I called James's name. It echoed off the high ceiling and around the room. Four grated doors marked the arms of the interior caves. I shouted James's name at the mouth of each one and got no reply.

Had he returned to the house? I ghosted past the iron bars to the cave Stuart and I had entered earlier. At the terminal end of the cave, the greeter's post was abandoned. I passed through the grated door and the air filters and pushed up the air shaft and out the candy-cane bend. Once free of the vent, I established my bearings and headed for the main house.

The sight of James's minivan in the driveway flooded me with relief. I rushed the door, passed through it then re-formed at the foot of the staircase. Hurried footsteps echoed down the hall above. James appeared on the bridge with his satchel in hand. When he saw me, his stride faltered, but only momentarily. He swept down the rest of the way and stopped in front of me.

"You're leaving?" I asked.

"I can't stay here. I'm going to find Cain."

"Now? No! Please. We need to talk."

"Oh? Now you want to talk?"

"I had no choice."

"I warned you about Mason and Stuart, about how manipulative they are, but you wouldn't listen. Thought you could handle it and now look at you."

"It's not forever. Just until I find a way to protect my covey."

"What about us, Emelynn?"

"Nothing's changed."

"Everything has changed. You said you weren't one of them—almost had me convinced. And now you are."

"I'm the same person I was this morning. It's a job, James. That's all."

"If you think it's just a job then you weren't listening. You swore an oath."

"It's a stupid ritual."

James's face was set in hard lines. He took a step forward.

I reached for his arm and grabbed his sleeve. "Don't go."

"I can live with the fact that you're a Ghost. You had no choice in the matter. But this? *This* was a choice. I don't know if I can live with it. I don't know if I can live with a fully sworn member of the Tribunal."

He pulled free of me and walked out the door. I heard the engine of the minivan start up and the screech of its tires as he peeled out of the driveway. And then I heard nothing.

Chapter Nine

I desperately wanted to run after him but my feet were rooted to the floor—a rat trapped on one of those horrid glue strips. It's hard to know if I stood there for one minute or ten. Eventually, I put one foot in front of the other and made my way into the drawing room.

If I hadn't felt so numb, I might have jumped at the sight of Stuart sitting in a chair tucked around the corner. He had a drink in his hand. He didn't get up and didn't say a word. I didn't acknowledge him. I walked to the bar and poured myself a Scotch. I tasted it then downed it and poured another.

"I'm sorry James reacted that way," Stuart said.

"Can't blame him, though, can you?"

"I'll talk to him."

"Don't. You and Mason have done enough damage."

"You made the right decision tonight, in spite of what James thinks. He'd have done the same in your shoes."

"Why aren't you still at the reception?"

"I saw James leave the party. Figured you might follow him."

I sat in a seat on the other side of the room, far away from Stuart. "I'm curious about something. The Tribunal go to great lengths to keep their identities hidden. Why be so public about it tonight?"

He swirled the dregs of his drink. "Showing themselves exposes their vulnerability. It also proves their trust in the ones selected to attend. Those who have been invited understand that they've been granted an honour. The Tribunal protects them, so they protect the Tribunal. If any of them were to be so foolish as to reveal an identity, they'd be dealt with harshly, not only by the Tribunal, but by all the others."

Another five minutes passed before Stuart spoke again. "Where does the name Morgan come from?"

"It was my dad's mother's maiden name."

"It's a Celtic name."

Again, silence stretched between us.

"Earlier tonight, Mason mentioned that some of us can manipulate memories," I said. "What did he mean by that?"

"He was referring to people like James and Redmond."

"There are others?"

"A few can plant memories. Others can erase them."

Handy. Maybe I'd get a referral. "Are those people forced to work for the Tribunal like the Mosses were?"

"No. The others are Ghosts; coercion isn't necessary."

Another five minutes passed. "Who is the man with the goatee? I've seen him before—not at Cairabrae but somewhere." I tried once more to remember where and came up empty.

"You've not seen him before."

"Why do you say that?"

"He keeps a low profile. He's an assassin for hire. Has no allegiance. Killed his own brother on a contract. He couldn't spell the word *honour* if you wrote it out for him."

"Does he have a name?"

"No."

The Tribunal probably kept Mr. No-Name Assassin busy. Exhaustion crept over me. I didn't have the fortitude to confront Mason tonight. I finished my drink and stood. "Good night," I said, and started for the stairs.

In my room, I closed the door behind me and stared at the bench where James's satchel should have been. I tossed my coat across it. The room was warm in the glow of a crackling fire. I tugged off my boots then fell into a chair in front of the fire and curled my feet up under me.

I pictured the hard set to James's face and replayed his words. He didn't know if he could live with the choice I'd made. I could still feel him twisting free of my grip and hear his heels on the stone walking out. My heart ached. It struck me then that *heartache* wasn't just a word.

I stared into the flames. How could James not understand the position I was in? He'd been privy to the conversation in that chamber tonight. Did he not recognize the power grab the Tribunal was setting up? The danger of a government registry? The glee in Sebastian's voice alone should have been a warning. How could James think I'd walk away from that threat without a fight? Perhaps he didn't know me as well as I thought he did.

Would my mother react the same way? Had I made a choice tonight that would drive away everyone I loved?

A knock at the door pulled me out of my thoughts. "Come in."

Phillip arrived with a tray. "Stuart told me you hadn't eaten. I thought you might like some dinner." He set the tray beside me. One covered plate sat upon it, not two. A missed meal wasn't the only news Stuart had passed along.

"That's kind of you," I said. "Thanks. And thanks for lighting the fire." Phillip scurried about poking the coals and set another log on the fire.

He accepted my thanks with a bow and soon left me alone again. I circled my knees with my arms, pulled them close and turned back to the flames.

Eventually, I crawled into bed. Pain flared around my heart as I thought about living my life without James. Who would I call when I'd beaten my best running time? When I needed to vent about Sebastian? Who would ever understand what I'd been through in the years after Jolene gifted me? The years I didn't understand why or how I lost gravity. Who would ever believe I'd been unaware that Jackson was married?

James had said he didn't know if he could live with my decision. I grasped at the hint of indecision in his words because losing James would be like losing a piece of myself. Tears came and went, and in time I fell asleep. It wasn't restful. I woke tired and lay in bed once again reliving my last conversation with James. Neither the sun streaming in through the crack in the drapes nor the hours that had passed eased the pain in my chest. I feared having to get used to it.

After showering, I stood at the foot of the bed and stared at my clothing options. Peach-coloured capris with a white T-shirt, or black on black. The capris looked too much like a fun day at the beach. I dressed in black—it suited my mood—and pulled on Mason's Tribunal jacket. I was one of them now. Might as well look like it. Hell, maybe I'd been one of them all along. I packed my bag and headed down the stairs.

The scent of toast sent me searching for the kitchen. I hadn't even looked at the meal Phillip had brought me last night, and now I felt famished. The kitchen was in the back of the house. Phillip wore a black apron and tended to two skillets on the stove. Mason and Stuart were seated and looked up at my arrival. Stuart set aside a newspaper and Mason set aside his tablet. Neither said a word. Phillip, wisely, pretended he hadn't seen me.

I walked to the coffee pot, poured a cup and took it to the table. Mason pushed the cream in my direction. I poured a dollop and stirred.

"I wish you'd stayed last night," Mason said. "I said some nice things about you in my speech."

"Yeah, I'm sorry I missed that," I said. My sarcastic tone didn't escape him.

"How long are you going to stay angry?"

I stopped stirring. "You manipulated me. Again. I want to know why and then I want to hear an apology. After that, I'm leaving."

Mason set his mug down and stared at it as if it had the answers. "Do you remember our conversation before your party at Cairabrae?"

"I remember you lied to me about Jolene. You bugged the first crystal-case necklace you gave me. You've never been honest with me about the Tribunal. But all of that pales in comparison with what you did last night."

Mason rubbed his forehead. "Man, you hold a grudge like no one I know. I did make sure we could locate you after I gave you Mom's crystal, but I never lied to you. I never misrepresented what happened with Jolene. We failed her, which pains us to this day, but I didn't lie about it. It simply never came up. We set things straight with you the moment we could."

"You mean the moment I caught you in your lie?"

Mason hung his head. Stuart dove into the fire. "As you witnessed last night, Ghosts are the only Fliers permitted in caucus. That's because Ghosts are the only ones who count in our world. We can't all sit at the table, but we can network and we can lobby. We influence what happens around that table. Jolene didn't have the fortitude to stand in opposition to the Ghosts she'd grown up with. She abstained. We tried to influence her, and you know how that turned out. But you ... you're different. You have grit and fire. You have no history with the other Ghosts. We knew you'd stand up for what you believed in. What was right. From the beginning, all we have ever done is endeavour to guide you."

"Manipulate me, don't you mean?" I said. They didn't bite.

Mason took up where Stuart had left off. "After Cairabrae, when we learned that the Tribunal would offer you a seat, Dad and I thought a miracle had dropped from the heavens. I was coming into power and you had an unfailing moral compass. Two votes instead of one."

Stuart took the baton. "Not since its inception more than two hundred years ago has the Tribunal ever made such an offer. You can't imagine how frustrated we were that you wouldn't even consider it."

"You can deny it all you like," Mason said, "but I know you didn't understand the significance of the seat the Tribunal offered you. Not until last night. How could you?"

"Are you quite done?" I said. They stared at me as though I'd grown a second head. "Where the hell was *your* moral compass, Mason, when you lied to my face and told me this plan of yours would neuter the Tribunal? For months now you've asked for my support and not once did you ever mention your plan didn't include exposing Ghosts." My voice had risen to a shout and it felt good, like a cleansing. "I will not stand idle while you protect Ghosts and the Tribunal at the expense of my friends and covey. Their names will not be written on some government register and I'll fry in hell before Ivy's idea to quell our jolts sees light."

At some point during my rant I'd risen. I felt the heat in my face like fire. My heart pounded and my hands were balled into tight fists. Stuart looked contrite, worried even, but Mason smirked. My temper blew, and a gasket lost its life. "What the fuck are you smiling about!"

No one challenged me on my language. "See?" Mason said. "Moral compass."

Now it was my turn to stare at him as though he'd grown a second head.

"This is politics, Emelynn," he said. "It's a negotiation. A constant back and forth. Last night I floated a trial balloon. Sebastian and his cronies knew it and took their shots."

"Shots? They annihilated your plan, and in the process I learned a very ugly truth. They don't care about Fliers. Their only interest is their own skin, their own families."

"Not all of them," Stuart said.

"Did you think it was going to be easy?" Mason said. "Maybe now you understand why we need you. Last night was just the beginning. I didn't expect to get everything I wanted in this first round."

"You got nothing and gave away everything. I thought you had some integrity. Where was your outrage when they suggested the idea of a Flier registry or controlling jolts?"

"Outrage isn't a very effective strategy. And we didn't get *nothing*. We now know who our strongest opponents are. And everyone who isn't opposed, or who's on the fence, will be home with their families right now discussing the idea of going public. Those conversations have never happened before. We lifted a taboo last night. When they've had time to absorb the tremendous freedom waiting on the other side of the secret, they'll come around. I'm sure of it."

"You took Ghosts out of the equation last night. They have no incentive to go public."

"I gave the dissenters what they needed to hear to keep the conversation going, move it into their homes. The ghosting gene may not become public knowledge, but Ghosts will want the same freedom as Fliers. Believe me, they'll accept nothing less."

"And what about the Tribunal? Everything I heard last night would make them stronger, not weaker. The proposed registry? The culling of Fliers opposed to them?"

"Sebastian and his cronies lost last night. Their threats were to save face, that's all. When the secret is out in the open, the Tribunal will have nothing to police that the courts can't handle. Their circle of influence will shrink to Ghosts and Ghosts alone. The important thing is that we now have our baseline. We negotiate from there. It may take longer than expected, but trust me, we will end up where I've envisioned."

"This is a game to you."

"It's one I'm good at."

"Manipulation. Yes. There's no denying that."

Mason tilted his head. "I also gave you what you needed to hear last night. We can't do this without you."

"You could have warned me."

"And I could have repeated how important it was for you to take that seat. But I might as well have bashed my head against a wall. You wouldn't have listened."

I dropped back into my chair. My head swam. I couldn't sort out if Mason had a point or if he was scary good at manipulating me. Phillip pretended we hadn't just had a screaming match that involved my saying fuck to his employers and set three plates down in front of us. The heavenly scent of breakfast sausage wafted up. Dollops of cheese and fried mushrooms oozed from an omelette peppered with black olives and green scallions. Salsa dribbled down the side of the eggs and pooled at the base of a heap of fried potatoes.

"If I find out you're lying to me, Mason, I will never speak to you again." Then I looked at Stuart. "Same goes for you. If anything he just said is bullshit, you tell me today. Because if I learn later that even a tiny detail of what I heard is a lie, I will disown you both." I picked up my fork.

Only the sound of cutlery against china accompanied our meal. I guess my threats had dampened any potential for benign conversation. Not that I minded. My head was still reeling. I felt as if I'd been sucked into a vortex, chewed up and spit out. If only I could talk to James. He was my sounding board and I'd never needed him more than right now. Where was he? I wondered. Would he ever forgive me? Or at least come to understand the position I'd been in, the choice I'd made? Regardless, I'd made a choice and there was no going back.

"What comes next?" I asked, breaking the silence. "I mean, with the Tribunal?"

They both stared at their plates. I felt my temper rise. "What are you keeping from me?"

Mason looked up. "You're aware that five members of the Tribunal actively carry out our decisions?"

"Yes, I remember." Five of the nine ... no, ten Tribunal members formed a subgroup that investigated grievances and enforced the Tribunal's rules.

"One of them, Rachael, has put in her five years. She can ask to be replaced any time now. Dad and I think Sebastian or one of his crew will put your name forward to replace her."

"Force me to get my hands dirty."

"I'm afraid so," Stuart said. "God willing, going public will put an end to all of it of course, but that may take a few years."

"It wouldn't be fair to accept special treatment," I said. "It would make me look weak. I'd be less effective, and it's not as if my hands are clean, anyway."

"We don't want that for you," Mason said.

"A little too late for that, don't you think? You two got any other surprises I need to know about?"

"No. That's it."

After we'd finished eating, Mason offered to drive me to the airport. Neither he nor Stuart had mentioned James's glaring absence, for which I was grateful.

Outside, Mason held open the passenger door of his Audi for me. I climbed in and fastened the seat belt. I nodded to Stuart as Mason made a wide turn at the base of the driveway.

Our conversation in that first thirty minutes felt stilted, as if Mason was afraid of saying something that would set me off. It was probably a prudent move on his part. In the second thirty minutes, I let go of the anger and loosened up.

"I'll have to tell my covey," I said. Mason didn't disagree. "They'll probably toss me out when they learn I'm one of you."

"They won't," Mason said, "but remember, the laws about Ghosts remain, at least for now. Your covey mustn't know we exist."

I gave some thought to how that conversation would play out. I'd also have to tell my mom. I'd promised her honesty and couldn't lose her trust.

"My mother will be horrified."

"Laura is a fighter, just like you," Mason said. "She'll understand."

"James didn't understand. He left me, and I'm not sure he's coming back." I hadn't intended to say that; the words had just leaked out, and tears welled in my eyes.

Maybe Mason didn't want to deal with the waterworks, or maybe he didn't care to discuss James with me, but whatever the case, he pulled me out of my despair with words that smacked me upside of my head.

"Sebastian's joining you on the flight back to Vancouver."

I swung my head in his direction and blinked, as if clearing my vision would somehow change his words. "Are you fucking kidding me?"

"Enough with the *fucking* already. Sebastian's still Tribunal. You think I'm going to suggest he fly commercial?"

"I would pay to see that."

"You might actually enjoy this flight. He'll be scrambling to ingratiate himself with you after his behaviour last night. I'd love to be a fly on the wall inside that plane."

"I'd rather he not speak to me."

"Open your mind to the game, Emelynn. See if you can score some points. You might not, but wouldn't it be fun to see him grovel?"

"I can't believe you treat this like a game, Mason."

"What's the alternative? Crawl into a hole? Shoot yourself? Your choice, I suppose. Personally, I wouldn't give him the satisfaction."

When we got to the airport, Mason parked at the departures door and jumped out of the car. He collected my bag from the trunk and approached. "Let me know how it goes with Laura. If she needs a punching bag or someone to shout at, call me." Mason's words stabbed my conscience.

This time, when he pulled me in for a hug, I let him. He handed me my bag and I turned away from him and sleepwalked through the doors. The past twenty-four hours had been so horrendous they'd pushed all thoughts of my father's plane crash and the Mansfield Group from my head. Now it was all I could think of.

The needle of my moral compass pointed to hypocrite. I'd just berated Mason and Stuart for lying to me and I was guilty of the very same offence. How would they react when they learned of the investigation? Would they disown me as I'd threatened to do to them? Memory manipulation was sounding better to me all the time.

Chapter Ten

The stilted conversation in Mason's Audi was nothing compared to the ice in the air when I entered the airport's executive lounge. Kimberley glowered at me. Sebastian didn't look up from his newspaper. Tiffany was absent. When the plane was ready, a co-pilot escorted us across the tarmac to the jet.

Kimberley started up the steps ahead of me and blocked the aisle while she engaged the pilot in an uncharacteristic show of good manners. I pretended her silly power play didn't annoy me. She eventually moved on and claimed the sofa in the rear of the plane. I ducked into a seat at the front. Sebastian passed me without a word and joined his wife. Suited me just fine.

After the usual pre-flight drill from the co-pilot, I plugged in my earbuds and pushed my seat back, hopeful sleep would claim an hour or two of the journey.

I did, in fact, nod off, but awakened at the soft crunch of leather. I opened my eyes to find Sebastian sitting across from me. I tugged out my earbuds. "Can I help you?"

He sat forward with his elbows on his knees. "You made a bold move last night. I didn't think you had it in you."

"You made that quite clear," I said.

"Perhaps I've misjudged you."

"Why do you hate me so much?"

"It's not personal. I quite enjoy your company. I don't, however, think you belong on the Tribunal."

"So you said."

He sucked in an impatient breath. "Gifted Fliers are a liability, not an asset. It's not your fault. You simply don't have the context. You weren't raised with the same experiences or expectations. Nonetheless, your handling of Carson Manse at Cairabrae was remarkable. I commend you for it, always have."

I snorted. "Commend? I don't think blaming me for what happened that night is what *commend* means. I never even wanted that party."

"The party wasn't the problem. The problem was that you revealed your gift. And to a law-enforcement officer no less. If you had let nature take its course, Jordan would have died when that helicopter went down. We could have avoided having to deal with ICO entirely."

"Is that what you tell yourself? Detective Jordan came back with reinforcements and paramedics who saved lives that night. Fliers' lives."

"Indeed. But we might have gained the upper hand without Jordan, in which case our secret would have survived intact."

"How many lives would that have cost?"

"It's not about the lives," Sebastian said. He rubbed his forehead. "I see that you and I have gotten off track again. We seem to do that a lot. What I was saying earlier was that I agree your bravery deserved to be recognized. I encouraged the Tribunal to offer you a substantial monetary reward. They chose instead to reward you with a seat. A seat that requires skills you don't have. They left me little choice but to mentor you. Sadly, your skills are still not at the level you'll need going forward."

I started to protest, but he stopped me. "Before you brush me off again, let me ask you ... Do you know what the expectations are of those who sit on the Tribunal?"

I didn't answer, but it didn't seem to matter.

"You will be expected to investigate crimes committed by and against Fliers. You'll be expected to take a position on the outcome of those investigations. And most importantly, you'll be expected to carry out the Tribunal's decisions. Even the distasteful ones you disagree with."

"Do you really think I don't know that? I won't tell you it doesn't trouble me because it does, but the seat is about more than that. It's about having a voice, contributing to a conversation."

"Like Mason's idea to go public? It's a foolish notion. History has already taught us that lesson."

Sebastian was nothing if not consistent. Mason had thought Sebastian would use the flight home to try to make up for his bad behaviour. I'm not sure Sebastian recognized his bad behaviour.

"You find that amusing?" Sebastian said, and I realized I'd been smiling.

"No. What I find amusing is you and me and this tug of war that goes on between us. How about we be honest with each other? I irritate you, you irritate me. This mentorship, as eye-opening as it's been, has also been tense and unpleasant. I'm done with it. I'm not working for you or under you. If you want to work by my side, show me some respect. I'll give it a shot, but I'm done being your lackey."

Sebastian sat back in his chair and crossed an ankle over a knee. With his elbows on the armrests, he pressed his fingertips together. "Where does this arrogance come from, Emelynn? This false confidence? Jolene was never this cocky. She knew her strengths, her weaknesses, her place. I wish she'd lived long enough to pass those traits on to you."

Her *place*? Sebastian was more than a dick—he was a relic. "Are you sure that's the hand you want to play?"

Sebastian swivelled his head away from me. He gazed out the window and I could practically hear the cogs grinding. All the while, he worked his fingers, pressing in and out. When he turned his head back to me, I saw something in his face I'd only ever seen once before and that was at Cairabrae: vulnerability. "All right," he said. "A fresh start. But this respect you speak of? It goes both ways."

"Like I said, I'm willing to try."

"As am I. Shall we toast to it?"

Sebastian excused himself and returned with two glasses of champagne. I glanced toward the back of the plane and saw a glass in Kimberley's hand, but she'd taken up a furious game of magazine-page-flipping and studiously avoided eye contact. Just as well.

What followed was one of the most unexpected and pleasant conversations I'd ever had with Sebastian. I weighed every word to check for deceit but found none. He talked about the renovation they'd done on their Point Grey home—even suggested I might like to come see how it turned out. He seemed to be trying to sell me on their architect, but I didn't mind. I admitted I'd been thinking about what he'd said on the flight down and would consider hiring one. It was a pleasant upgrade from our usual exchanges.

He asked how my mother's move was progressing and told me he'd looked her up and been impressed with the research she'd had published. I asked about Tiffany and learned she'd taken up with a man both he and Kimberley approved of.

And then he asked about James.

A smile froze on my face as a fresh lick of pain flared around my heart. "He's great."

Sebastian didn't seem to notice, or if he did, he let it pass. "I was pleased to see Redmond and his family accept our invitation. Another fresh start."

"Yes. Diana seems a force to be reckoned with."

"She'd have to be."

"What do you mean?"

"Ah, it's nothing. Petty of me to even mention it."

And yet he had. I quirked an eyebrow. Sebastian ran with it. "In his day, Redmond had quite a reputation. 'Anything in a skirt,' they said. Diana managed to rein him in, but his reputation lingers. Thankfully, James doesn't appear to have picked up his father's bad habits. I often wonder if James or Alexandra have any idea of their father's robust past?"

Robust? I had my doubts it was true—it hardly fit Redmond's style—but I guessed Sebastian had to get in one last swipe at the Mosses.

Sebastian smiled. He seemed to be enjoying himself. "We should have started fresh a long time ago."

I declined Sebastian's offer to have his limo drop me off. Kimberley hadn't thawed during the flight and I didn't want to subject myself to her arrogance in the confines of a car. Sebastian returned to Kimberley at the rear of the plane when the pilot announced our descent into Vancouver. The city below was lit up like a chandelier.

Once outside the airport, I jumped into a cab. The familiar landmarks separated me from the world of the Tribunal, from Mason and Stuart, from James and his *robust* father. Instead, my thoughts turned to Sam and my mother, to Avery and the covey. It felt as if I'd been gone a month, not two days. I checked the time. Eight thirty in the evening.

The cabbie pulled into the condo's circular drive. I paid him and jumped out. Colin opened the building's front door for me. It must have been a slow night on the front desk.

"Someone came by to see you yesterday," he said.

A spike of alarm registered. Cain? "Did you get a name?"

"I wasn't on the desk. Just heard she was cute. Blue hair."

So not Cain, but my tracker would have suggested I was in the condo. He could have sent someone to check. "Was she told I wasn't home?"

"Oh no. We don't share that information. We would have said there was no answer and to come back later."

"Thanks, Colin." I picked up my mail and headed for the elevator. Inside the condo, I dropped my bag and checked both phones. No word from James. I walked into the living room. Stars twinkled against the velvet night. On an impulse, I squeezed my crystal and ghosted. I rushed the balcony door and fought the offshore breeze to get to the roof, where I re-formed.

Cool evening air carried the scent of spring. I broke free of gravity and lifted up thirty feet, then fifty. Below, the streets morphed into a Lego village, the ships at anchor into Tonka toys. I turned west, flew out over the Pacific and channelled the speed Jolene had entrusted to me. I rejoiced in the endorphins and let my body take the lead. It was enthralling and dangerous; consuming and lethal. I hadn't worn my Ryders, and my hair blew straight back, loose. I knew with one wrong move at these speeds I'd cartwheel out of control, but the thought didn't frighten me tonight. I defied it and kept going.

Ever since I'd learned to control it, flight had been my escape, my nirvana. I felt invincible. No one could catch me up here. I used to think no one could hurt me up here.

But I did hurt. My heart felt shattered. Days ago, I couldn't imagine my life without James. Tonight that bleak possibility had taken hold and rooted itself in my gut. I thought back to my reluctance to accept his proposal. Perhaps I'd been right. There were too many obstacles in our path, and I'd just piled on another.

I slowed my reckless flight and turned for home. If and when James showed up I'd have to deal with the fallout from what I'd done, but I wouldn't grovel or beg for his forgiveness. I'd made the only choice I could live with. If he couldn't accept it, I would have to understand. And as much as it hurt, I would have to let him go.

Back inside the condo, I unpacked my bag. The bracelet with the tracker on it lay on the bathroom counter. I slipped it on. The reminder that Cain was still on the loose helped push thoughts of James out of my head.

I turned my mind to Avery and the covey. There was no question I had to tell them. Might as well rip off the bandage quickly and put it behind me.

It wasn't too late to call. I dug out the new phone and dialled Avery. "I'm home from the caucus," I said. "I have news to share. I need you to call the covey together as soon as possible."

"What's the news?"

"Mason made the announcement. You're free to tell the covey that the Redeemer threat is gone."

"They'll be relieved to hear it."

"I have other news for them as well that I'd rather not talk about over the phone."

"Does it have to do with ICO?"

"No. And you know nothing about ICO, remember?"

"Right. I don't even know the acronym," Avery said. "Will you enlighten me about this other item before the meeting?"

"I will. And Avery? Make sure Sebastian Kirk is included."

When I hung up, I texted Sam. *I need to see a friendly face. You still bunking at the station?*

I grabbed my keys, locked up and headed to the garage. A minute later, my phone dinged. *Yes. Bring food. Something deep-fried.*

The McBurgers and fries bag wafted tantalizing aromas as I arrived at the station. The officer on duty called Sam, and a few minutes later he came through the door with a white towel draped around his neck. His badge was clipped to the waistband of a pair of track pants.

"There's a gym in this place?" I asked.

Sam took the clipboard and signed me in. "How do you think I keep up this fine physique?"

The officer on duty rolled his eyes and Sam caught it. "Some of us don't even know which floor the gym's on." Sam handed the clipboard back with a grin and took the visitor pass. The officer was still chuckling when we pushed through the inside doors to the elevator.

Sam closed his office door behind us. I followed him to the sofa and set the takeaway bag on the coffee table. He dug into it as if he hadn't eaten in days.

"Did you run out of food?" I asked.

"You ever eaten microwaved dinners five days straight?"

"Point taken. Enjoy. But could I have one of the fries?"

He handed me the cheery red box of deliciousness and unwrapped a burger.

"Catch me up on the investigation," I said.

"You first," he said. "I'm eating."

Without revealing any confidential details, I explained what had transpired at the caucus. By the time my sin had been laid on the table, Sam was finished eating. He wiped his mouth with a napkin and leaned back.

"I don't understand what the problem is. You can't steer the bus if you don't have a hand on the wheel, and it sounds to me like those Tribunal characters are apt to drive the thing off the road."

Sam's take on events left me with a wide grin. If I stripped away the brutality of how the Tribunal dealt with offences, Sam was absolutely right. My spirits perked up.

"What does James think?"

And just as quickly, my spirits fled. "He's not very happy with me right now."

"Then you mustn't be telling me everything."

"I left out a few details. Nothing I can share." And nothing I could change. "How's the research going?"

Sam stood and walked to his desk to retrieve a spiral notepad. "I cleared the pilot. Mid-forties career pilot with instrument rating and a perfect record. Left a wife. She still lives in the home they shared. Fifty-thou life insurance. Mortgage was insured and paid off. The last passenger, other than your father, was a stockbroker. He left an offshore account and a few unhappy clients. I'm checking out the unhappies. Might scare up someone pissed off enough to act out."

It was the best lead so far and I latched onto it, knowing if it failed, the only passenger left to investigate was my father.

"Where are things with the Mansfield Group?" I asked.

Sam checked his watch. "Peter Caulfield and his crew are in the air as we speak. They've secured a vessel out of Prince Rupert and plan to be provisioned and underway to Haida Gwaii tomorrow."

Sam sat me in front of his computer and played the film clips Peter Caulfield had sent him of Mansfield's equipment in use. Drones carried Mansfield's specialized sensors over the water. When a target was identified, the team would send in an unmanned submarine to check it out.

"They've got six drones. Four of them will run a pre-programmed grid. Two are spares, and they have one submarine. They're going to work around the clock."

"They can operate in the dark?"

"So they tell me. Strong winds or rough seas could shut them down, but the weather looks good this coming week."

"A part of me hopes they don't find it."

"Don't let your mother hear you say that. Does she know you're back?"

"No. I didn't get home until close to midnight Toronto time. I'll call her in the morning. That reminds me, the front desk told me a blue-haired woman dropped by to see me yesterday. They didn't get a name."

"I take it you don't know anyone who fits the description?"

"No. Do you know if she showed up here?"

"You thinking Cain sent her?" he asked. I shrugged. "I can call up the station's front-desk video feed. If she showed here, Cain's a damn good bet. It'd be nice to know if he's making a move."

He called up the feed from three days prior to cover our bases, and we started fast-forwarding through it. It reminded me of the mind-numbing surveillance Sam and I had done at Vector Labs. Soon, I was yawning and Sam let me off the hook and sent me home.

I checked my phone before I crawled into bed. James hadn't called.

My dreams were salted with memories of James and visions of drones. I woke half a dozen times in the night and got out of bed with the sun. James hadn't reached out in the night. I pulled on my house-coat, made a pot of coffee and curled up on the sofa. I planned out my discussion with my mother. It gave me the illusion of control even though I feared the conversation might veer onto the rocks.

I refilled my coffee and sent her a message with the subject line *We ship same day free; Cialis, Viagra, Vicodin for $6.30*. She would know it was from me—not because of the randomly generated sender's name but because of the subject line, which would flag the message as junk and divert it to her junk email folder. The message meant I'd contact her on our encrypted phones at 6:30 a.m. my time, 9:30 a.m. her time.

Ten minutes later, I video-called. "Where are you?" I asked, not recognizing her surroundings.

"Alexandra Park. There's an open house today at the condo so I'm making myself scarce."

I warned her to get comfortable, and then I proceeded to tell her about the seat I'd been offered. It would have been so much more difficult had I not previously told her about the Tribunal. Because she was my mother, I could colour in the details about Sebastian, Mason and the other Ghosts, and about what had happened in the caucus that had forced my hand. None of that, however, made it easier for her to accept.

"I went there thinking I'd wash my hands of it, but given what happened, I couldn't. I took the seat, Mom."

"Jolene should rot in hell for putting you in this position."

"Jolene wouldn't have known it would come to this."

"She should have. Does this put you in danger?"

"My identity is protected, but honestly, I don't know."

"But you say you'll be able to cast a vote? One of ten?"

"Yes. It's not much, but I might be able to influence some of the others."

"Does this improve the odds that the Tribunal will hold Mason and Stuart accountable for your father's death?"

"Mom, please!"

"You promised me."

"I did. And I will honour my promise, but let's not talk about what-ifs. I can't think about that outcome right now." I changed the subject. "How's the handoff of your research coming along?"

"I'm stretching it out. Figure if I can't return to Vancouver until this Cain character is dealt with, I might as well keep busy. Any news on him?"

"None. We all thought we'd have heard by now but nothing yet. I'll call the moment I know."

"All right. Give my regards to James."

My words caught in my throat. "I—I will. I love you."

If it were nighttime, I'd have gone flying to clear my head. Since it was daylight, a run would have to do. I dressed and headed out.

Late in the morning, a text came in from Avery on the phone that had the trace. He'd set the covey meet for one o'clock at Clam Diggers pub. He'd played the phone game, giving Sebastian no reason to believe I had a second one.

I pulled the MGB into the pub's parking lot at 12:40 p.m. Avery's Porsche was already there. The covey met at the old converted two-storey farmstead that called itself Clam Diggers for a reason: when we needed discretion, we could reserve one of their two private rooms. One was the home's original dining room. I suspected the other had once been a library.

On my way to the front door of the old pub, I passed a motorcycle that reminded me of the one Alex Klause rode. I missed Alex and his girlfriend, Eden Effrome. They'd been there for me from the beginning, when I'd learned what I was. They'd helped teach me to fly, and Eden had become my closest friend in the Flier world.

They'd moved to Seattle at the urging of their families after Carson Manse put all of our lives on the line. I couldn't blame them, but I lost one of the few confidants I'd had when Eden moved. I made a mental note to call them as soon as I got home and tell them the good news about the Redeemers.

I jogged up the steps and through the dingy old foyer. The cliché décor included fishing net, which hung in dusty billows from the ceiling. Over the years, patrons had tossed beer coasters and baseball caps into the netting, crowding the dirty net floats and faded plastic starfish.

I walked toward the private room on the right—the one I imagined had been a library in a previous incarnation. We often met here when it was too chilly for the outdoor deck. The muddy-coloured carpeting might even have been original; it smelled of old nicotine and stale beer. An easel with a sign that read Private Function cordoned off the doorway to the room.

My presence today would surprise, maybe even alarm, some in the covey. I stopped short of the easel. The last time most of them had seen me was at Avery's, after Carson torched my cottage. They'd gathered to support me, but Carson's sniper had had other thoughts. His shots missed but made a mess of Avery's kitchen and terrified all of us. After that, I'd stayed away for fear I'd further endanger them. But now, with Carson's Redeemers gone, we could open a new door. *A fresh start*, as Sebastian would say.

I stepped inside. Avery and Victoria stopped talking when they saw me, and then the couple they'd been talking to turned around. For a moment, I lost my words. Eden and Alex stood there with silly grins on their faces. Eden and I rushed for each other and embraced. Alex put his arms around both of us and hung on.

"What are you doing here?" I asked through happy tears. "And what have you done with your hair?" The former redhead now sported a bright-blue pixie cut with long bangs that swept across her forehead.

"Do you like it?"

"It looks great. God, I've missed you."

"I dropped by your place but you weren't home."

"You should have called."

"We wanted to surprise you."

"You can tick that box!" We pulled apart and I rummaged through my pockets for a tissue. "Where are you staying?"

"With us," Victoria said. "We would have told you but didn't want to spoil their surprise."

"How long are you visiting?" I asked.

"We're leaving tomorrow, but Avery's news may change everything."

"Are you moving back?"

"If we can. Alex hates working for someone else, I can never get enough nights off, and I miss you and Vancouver and this covey that feels like family."

"How about we go to the Neon Turtle for dinner tonight and catch up," Alex said. "Like old times." He turned to Avery. "Are you and Victoria in? My treat."

"We'd love to," Avery answered. "May I have a word, Emelynn?"

Just as Avery and I stepped away, Sebastian entered the room. Victoria played hostess and introduced him to Eden and Alex. As far as our covey knew, Sebastian was just another Flier who'd moved into the neighbourhood. While Victoria bought us some time, I gave Avery a quick and dirty summary of my announcement.

He drew his eyebrows together. "What happened? Last we talked you couldn't wait to walk away from them."

"That didn't turn out to be an option." Sebastian was freeing himself from Victoria's circle. "I'll explain later."

"This is going to be a tough sell," Avery said.

I didn't have time to react before Sebastian strode over.

"Avery. What's this about?" Sebastian had resorted to his default setting of putting people on the defensive.

Avery's ingrained bedside manner kicked in. He smiled like a boss about to announce bonuses. "There's been an announcement concerning the Redeemers that you'll be glad to hear. And Emelynn has asked to share some news." He knew Sebastian was a Ghost and on the Tribunal, but he'd never let on to Sebastian that he knew. Avery had figured it out on his own, not through me, but if Sebastian heard, he'd likely accuse me of divulging restricted information.

"Is that so?" Sebastian said, sliding his gaze to me.

Kate Dennison and Deidra Lewis swept into the room engaged in animated conversation. The elementary school teachers were long-time friends. The moment they saw Eden and Alex, the volume of their conversation kicked up a notch. I jumped at the opportunity to join them.

Next to arrive was Gabe Aucoin. He carried a briefcase and wore a suit that suggested he'd come straight from a courtroom. He scanned the room and elected to visit with Avery and Sebastian rather than join our boisterous group.

Danny Thornton had no problem adding to the noise. He bounced into the room with his typical head of steam, offering hugs all around. He no longer competed in tae kwon do, but he could move faster in a fight than anyone I'd seen. He and Alex immediately paired off and starting talking cars. Danny sold them and Alex knew all about painting them.

When Avery called for our attention, I saw that Sydney Davenport had slipped into the room. Earlier in the year, Sydney's girlfriend had been murdered. Sam and I got tangled up in the investigation, and it caused a rift in my relationship with her that hadn't fully healed. She cautiously watched me from the side of the room.

Steve Elliott had also slipped in discreetly. The fact I hadn't seen him arrive didn't surprise me. He moved with stealth, blending his medium height, medium build and nondescript features into any background with ease. Steve closed the door to the room and stood as sentry.

We'd gathered in a semicircle around Avery. "Thank you for making the time to meet on such short notice," he started. "I know you all want to visit with Eden and Alex and get a bite to eat, so let's get the news out of the way. If you've noticed Emelynn amongst us, you may already know what I'm about to say. The Tribunal have at long last neutralized the Redeemers. You and your families can breathe a little easier." Relief floating on ripples of quiet excitement filled the room.

"And one more thing," Avery said, once again gathering everyone's attention. "Emelynn has some news she'd like to share."

I bit my lower lip, stuffed my hands in my pockets and walked to stand beside him. "Hi. It's good to be back. Now that news of the Redeemers is official, I need to fill in more of the history." I took my hands from my pockets but didn't know what to do with them, so stuffed them back in. "Weeks after Carson Manse's sniper took pot-shots at us in Avery's kitchen, he attacked again. It was during a gathering at the safe house Detective Jordan sent me to. Manse and his Redeemers murdered and injured many Fliers that night before he was stopped."

I shifted my feet. Swallowed. "I was the one who put an end to it. Put an end to him. It's not something I like to talk about. I don't even like to think about it, but he had to be stopped."

Empathetic whispers surged. I tamped them down. "I wouldn't be telling you this at all if I didn't have to. My role that night, in taking out Carson Manse, caused ... a change ... within the Tribunal Novem."

The room quietened in a hurry. "I know how you feel about the Tribunal. You're the ones who taught me what they were. How they operated in secrecy. How they meted out their version of justice with no opportunity to appeal." I studiously ignored the glare coming off Sebastian like a heat wave. "That's why even the mention of their name sets off a reaction.

"But what if we had a chance to influence them?" I said. "To have them hear our voices?"

"What you been smoking, Emelynn?" Danny said. "That's never going to happen."

"But it has," I said. "They offered me a seat on the Tribunal Novem. A thank-you for handling Carson Manse."

Confusion clouded their faces.

"What does a seat on the Tribunal mean?" Deidra asked.

"I've been given a vote. One of ten on everything the Tribunal puts to a vote."

"One out of ten is hardly influential," Deidra said. "What are they really after?"

"Their offer is sincere," I said. "They are grateful, even if some of them didn't support the decision to offer me a seat."

"You know who they are?" Gabe asked.

"I do. But their identities are protected."

"I say walk away," Kate said. "They're up to no good."

I spoke over the growing din. "I accepted the seat two days ago."

The room fell into silence again. "I told the Tribunal I'd represent my covey."

"Us? Great!" Deidra said. "So now if they don't like your vote they'll come after us."

"Emelynn, what have you done?" Sydney said.

"I took a chance! And no, Deidra, they won't come after you if they don't like my vote. The Tribunal protect their own. That includes all of you now."

"You believe them?" Kate said. "You should have taken a pass."

"It's not just a vote. I have the opportunity to talk to the other Tribunal members, to bring our voices to the table."

"They're never going to listen to the likes of us," Sydney said.

"I agree," Kate said. "If Emelynn wants to associate with the Tribunal, that's her choice, but I don't want my name or my family connected to them."

"I'm with Kate on this one," Deidra said, and Sydney was quick to add her name to that list.

"How do we know if we don't even try?" I said. "You think this opportunity is going to come again? If I throw it away then we're telling the Tribunal we're happy with the way things are. Is that the message you want to send?"

"I might add," Gabe said, "that the Tribunal already know who we are. Carson Manse is responsible for that, not Emelynn."

"Forgive me if I'm overstepping," Sebastian said. "I know I'm new here, but didn't the Tribunal just wipe out the biggest threat we've ever faced? And Emelynn must have some degree of trust in them or she wouldn't have taken the seat. Perhaps they've earned a show of faith?"

Sebastian was the last person I'd expected support from, and even though he'd taken liberties with the degree of trust I had in the Tribunal, I was grateful for his support.

"If I'd been offered the seat," Danny said, "I'd have taken it. Like Emelynn said, this opportunity isn't coming again. We throw it away and we're not in the game. We're not even in the stadium."

Alex stepped forward. "Every one of us has expressed concern about how the Tribunal operates. If this is our opportunity to change it, I say that's a good thing."

Glances and grumbles flitted around the room until Avery spoke out. "It may have been easier to accept Emelynn's decision if we'd been forewarned. Regardless, she now has a vote and she's offered to represent us. Unless and until we're proven wrong about this arrangement, I say we let it stand and support her decision. Does anyone disagree?"

Hushed conversations and foot shuffling ensued but no one raised a hand.

"We have our decision," Avery said. "Remember, we don't always agree, but we're stronger when we stick together. Please share Emelynn's news with discretion. Her head's above the parapet. Let's not make her new role any more difficult." He searched our faces for agreement before adding, "We're done here."

Avery walked to the door and opened it to call a waiter. I felt a moment of awkwardness standing there alone, wondering how much damage I'd done.

Eden and Alex were the first to approach. "You didn't tell me any of this," Eden said. "Why?"

The hurt in her eyes wounded me. "Killing Manse wasn't self-defence. That's not something I ever wanted to share. And that seat? I had no intention of taking it. I didn't change my mind until the day of the caucus."

As Danny approached, Eden snagged my sleeve. "You and I are going to talk about this."

I nodded. "Tonight, okay?"

Danny slapped me on the back. "You got cojones, girl. I like that. If you ever need backup, I'm here for you."

Danny and Alex stayed with me while Eden joined a conversation with Kate and Deidra. Gabe broke away from Sebastian to offer me his support and then left to talk with Sydney. When Steve joined us, he, Danny and Alex started into "old home week" memories. I extracted myself and sought out Sebastian.

"Thank you," I said.

He shrugged. "I promised you a fresh start. It looked like you could use the support."

"I appreciate it. I didn't anticipate such strong resistance."

"Apparently they don't think very highly of the Tribunal."

"This covey isn't unique in that opinion, but you already knew that."

"The fear, I expected. It's something we cultivate. When your numbers are small, fear is an ally. Their disrespect, however, is unfortunate."

"Perhaps we can change that," I said.

"You should have insisted they keep your name confidential. You've put a target on your head."

"I trust them. They may not agree with me, but they won't endanger me."

"I hope you're right."

Those who could stayed for a late lunch. Several tables had been pushed together. I took a seat with Eden on one side of me and Avery on the other. Talk of the Tribunal died in favour of lighter conversations between friends and the quick banter that always popped up when we got together. Lunch plates came and were cleared and our group thinned out as more people departed.

Eden leaned into my personal space. "We've been here an hour and you haven't mentioned James once. What gives?"

"James disagrees with my decision to take the seat. I'm not sure we're going to get past it."

"I'm sorry."

"Me too." The phone in my left pocket vibrated; the one Sebastian was monitoring. I glanced down at the screen. *Unknown Caller*. A moment later, Sebastian pulled out his phone. I fished a twenty out of my pocket and dropped it on the table.

"I've got to go," I said to Eden, as the phone continued to vibrate. "I'll see you tonight."

I waved goodbye in the general direction of the table and scooted out of the room with my phone to my ear. "Hello."

"Call your boyfriend off," the voice warned.

Chapter Eleven

"Who is this?"

"You know who this is. Call him off."

"Or what?"

"You don't want to know the answer to that question. Call him off. I won't tell you again."

The line went dead. I stood in the parking lot of Clam Diggers momentarily stunned. Whatever James had unearthed had pierced Cain's armour.

I got in my car and texted Sebastian. *You get that?*

Sebastian hurried out of the pub and got into a black Cadillac SUV. He pulled out of the parking lot without acknowledging my text.

James needed to know, but with this mountain between us, I hesitated to phone him. Instead, I sent him a text using the second phone. *Cain just called. You must be close. He told me to call you off.*

Next, I called Sam and relayed Cain's message.

"I doubt Cain's call will be traceable. Did you warn James?"

"I sent him a text."

"A text? Is this disagreement between you two serious?"

"I'm trying to give him some space."

"This isn't the time. I'll call him," Sam said. "I'll get back to you."

I put the car in gear and drove out of the parking lot. I hadn't driven a full block before my cellphone went off. This time it was a fire-engine ring tone—my condo's security alarm. With no chance of getting there before the police, I let it go through to 911 and stepped on the gas.

Moments later, my second phone rang. It was Sam. Trouble at my address had triggered a phone call to him. "It might be Cain," he said, as if that hadn't been my first, second and third guess. "Be prepared. He knows what you can do."

A police cruiser with its lights flashing had parked at the condo's front door. I parked behind it and raced inside. Colin paced a brisk line in front of the desk. The elevator's doors stood open.

I called to him as I raced by. "What's going on up there?"

Sirens sounded out front and an ambulance screeched to a halt. Colin had no time to answer me. He ran to open the doors. I sprinted to the stairwell and ghosted then blasted straight up to the top floor and re-formed. I pushed open the stairwell door and looked out past the elevator. My condo's door stood ajar. I approached it with caution and stepped inside. Immediately, my gaze was drawn down the hallway toward the living room. Lying on the floor, jutting out from the kitchen doorway, were the uniformed legs and sturdy boots of an officer. I raced forward and found a second officer performing CPR on the woman.

"I'm trained in CPR. Can I help?"

"Clear the way for the ambulance."

I rushed back down the hall and dragged the small hall table into my bedroom then propped the condo's door wide open. When I returned, I asked what had happened.

"Not a goddamned clue," the man said. His ears pricked up at the sound of the elevator's ding. He stopped his compressions and ripped the woman's shirt open. "Get the AED set up," he yelled, as the paramedics stomped down the hall. "She's not breathing. She needs defib right now!"

I backed into the dining room to get out of their way. I glanced toward the balcony door. It was open. Two more paramedics arrived with a gurney, and before they had the officer off the floor, half a dozen officers swarmed into the condo.

One of them approached me. "Who are you?"

"I live here. This is my place. I have ID in my pocket." After he nodded, I pulled it out and showed him.

"The condo's alarm gets relayed to my cellphone. I got here as fast as I could."

"Show me," he said. I pulled my phone from my pocket and showed him the call log. "Okay. Go with him," he said, motioning one of the officers over. He kept my phone. "Hold her until we find out what happened here."

WINGS OF PREY

The officer whose name tag read Nowak took me to a meeting room on the main floor. I'd never seen it before. He left me inside. I pulled out my other phone and texted Sam with an update.

An hour passed before the man in charge came down to see me. The first thing out of his mouth was an apology. "I'm Ortez. Jordan tells us you're one of his operatives."

He handed me back my phone. "Why is the GPS disabled on this?"

"The nature of my work requires that I take precautions. That's one of them. How is the officer?"

"She didn't make it."

His response jarred me. His words didn't line up with my she'll-be-fine conviction. "What happened?"

"The officers answered the alarm, found your door unlocked. Followed procedure. Cleared the place room by room. Officer Ingram radioed in the all clear but as they were leaving, they heard a noise in the kitchen. Ingram went to check it out. Next thing her partner sees is her falling flat on her back."

"The balcony door was open. Did the officers open it?"

"No. And her partner is sure it wasn't open when Ingram radioed in the all clear. We figure whoever attacked Ingram circled behind her partner and hid until they could escape off the balcony. Easy to do with that kitchen layout of yours and the tiered balconies. We're checking the units below yours now."

"I'm sorry about your officer."

Ortez stiffened, but he was only momentarily derailed. "There's a possibility Ingram and her partner interrupted a robbery, but given your work, it may have been more than that. You working any cases that might have prompted this? Any enemies we should know about?"

Enemies? Which one? "No." Cain maybe, but he'd have known that breaking in would be a suicide mission. Hardly seemed likely. A Ghost wouldn't need to use the door or the balcony. But a Flier would.

"I need you to come back upstairs and tell us if anything is missing. Unfortunately, you won't be able to stay there until the investigation is complete. It could take a few days."

Ortez accompanied me back to my condo. This time we donned booties and gloves before going in. The forensics team was already at work photographing the scene and dusting every surface for possible prints. I spared a moment to wonder if the fine black powder would wash off.

I sifted through every room with Ortez peering over my shoulder, but found nothing missing. Back in the kitchen, disposable packaging from the paramedics' efforts littered the floor. An open cupboard door revealed gaps where cereal boxes had been. Several brown-paper evidence bags lined the kitchen island, and a man in a jumpsuit was filling another bag with the contents of my fridge. It looked like a food drive.

"Why are you taking all that?"

"A hunch," Ortez said. "We're also bringing in a tech team to check for electronics. Someone was willing to kill an officer to get out of here. There has to be a compelling reason. We're going to find it."

Ortez supervised my packing of a small overnight bag. As a professional courtesy, and with my and Sam's reassurances that I'd be readily available, he let me leave. I left him my contact details and took the elevator down to the main floor. The front door had been propped open and Colin stood beside it looking out on the activity in the driveway. He jumped when I called his name.

He brushed away my apologies then we both stood and watched the activity. The back doors of a large police cube van hung open near our vantage point revealing neatly packed bins and metal lockers that put me in mind of an airplane's galley. Curious neighbours stood staring at the building. A swarm of officials in every conceivable uniform reminded me that emergency services come out in force when one of their own is killed. Some milled about while others searched the lawn and nearby shrubs.

Police and EMT vehicles occupied every parking space on the street and along the condo's driveway. My small MGB looked out of place in their company. I warned Colin that I'd be away for a few days then moved my car into the underground and walked back out. It would be easier to hide in the city for a few days without my car. I hiked down the street and caught a bus to downtown.

Shoppers crowded Pacific Centre mall. I slipped into the public washroom and ghosted. I wasn't taking any chances that someone was following. I drifted outside and around the corner to West Georgia Street and found my destination. I re-formed in a quiet alcove in the Hotel Vancouver. The grand old railway hotel was one of a dozen hotels within walking distance. Might as well be comfortable, I reasoned.

I checked in as Megan Fairchild using my newest fake ID. My former ID, Dana Christopher, had been compromised by ICO. The moment I latched the door to my hotel room I pulled out my phone and dialled Sam.

"Fairchild checked into the Hotel Vancouver. What's the latest on the break-in?" I dropped my bag on the bed.

"Nothing yet. Good call on Fairchild."

"It's a Flier, Sam." I parted the sheers and looked down to West Georgia Street while I explained my reasoning, but I couldn't answer the *who* question.

"Don't be so quick to dismiss Cain. He may have known you weren't home so you'd be no threat to him. Maybe he wanted to plant a listening device in your place to stay a step ahead. Someone with his training has the skills to rappel down the building. Would explain the open balcony door."

"True. Ortez is having my condo swept for bugs. If Cain planted one, he'll find it. Did you get hold of James?"

"Yeah. He's working up a profile on Cain's family," Sam said. "Figures he got too close to someone Cain cares about in Ottawa. James is flying out there. If Cain's panicking, he's gonna make mistakes. James will flush him out."

"And if it's not Cain?"

"Your first instinct pointed to a Flier," Sam said. "You thinking someone in your covey?"

"Not a chance. They were all there with me when the break-in was happening."

"Think outside the covey, then. Anyone else pissed with you right now?"

"In connection with me taking that seat, maybe, but I can't think of anyone in particular."

"All right. Hang tight. Let's keep in close contact."

After ending the call, I dialled Avery and told him about the break-in. "It's best I don't join you for dinner tonight. I'm going to lay low until we figure it out. Tell Eden I'll call her when the dust settles, would you?"

"I will, but I'll guarantee you Eden's not going to wait for the dust." Avery then asked me for the details I'd promised on why I took the seat. "For what it's worth, I think you made the right decision," he said, after I'd explained everything. It was worth the world to me.

I lay on the bed and flicked on the TV. My building was all over the news. The crawl read *Local police officer killed attending B&E at an upscale condo.* I listened to a reporter interview Colin and a few of my neighbours. Constable Ingram's official police photo flashed on the screen. She was a mother to two young children. I turned it off before I melted into tears.

Outside, the sky darkened. My thoughts turned to Cain's threatening phone call. In the melee surrounding the break-in, I'd put it out of my mind. I fetched the phone he'd called me on and saw I'd missed two calls from Sebastian. Shit!

I dropped into a chair by the window with my finger hovering over the call-back icon. The crushing dread I felt was a response born of our old relationship. I took a deep breath, envisioned the new respect between us and hit call back.

"Where are you!"

My hackles shot up. "I'm safe."

"Well ... good. That's good."

I breathed a sigh as his tone softened. "You saw the news?"

"I did," Sebastian said. "When you didn't answer my calls I expected you were dealing with the police."

"They've cordoned off my condo. I can't go back there for a few days."

"Come stay with us. You'll be safe here."

After picking up my jaw from the floor, I told him I'd already found accommodation. He didn't pry. We both knew the rules of the game. Tell no one.

"Going into hiding is prudent but probably not necessary," he said. "As you know, high-end neighbourhoods like yours are tempting targets for thieves." When he was my mentor, we'd spent time identifying high-value houses with security features he'd taught me how to breach. "The police likely interrupted a break-in."

"There's more to it," I said, and filled him in about the balcony door. I told him I believed a Flier was responsible.

He didn't agree. He reminded me not to complicate the situation. "If it looks like a duck," he said.

"Were you able to glean anything from Cain's call?" I asked.

"Not much. He's in Ontario, but we can't narrow it down any further."

"Ontario? I thought he was in BC."

"No. Ottawa is my guess. He's lived there for years, has family there. He'll be trying to re-establish a support network."

"Detective Jordan figures Cain panicked or he wouldn't have called."

"I wouldn't use the word *panic*. Men like Cain don't panic. He's military; a strategist. The call will have been calculated to throw us off. James has a bead on Cain's sister in Ottawa. He thinks Cain might try to relocate her. James is heading there now, but I imagine you already know that."

Perhaps if I'd had the cojones Danny credited me with, I'd have heard it from James rather than Sam. Truth was, I was a coward, afraid my next conversation with James might be my last.

After we hung up, I couldn't get Cain's being in Ontario out of my mind. Was the break-in at my condo Cain's attempt to make us think he was in BC? What if Cain wasn't in Ottawa but in Toronto doing his own digging to find my mother?

The extra layer of protection between Mom and me had never felt so important. I left her a Viagra message and waited an excruciating ten minutes to call her. No video this time. I didn't want her to know or even guess where I was.

She hadn't caught the local Vancouver news. The officer's death in our kitchen hit her hard. Before she jumped all over Jolene and her gift again, I reminded her it was most likely an interrupted B&E. I even used Sebastian's *walk like a duck* line. I should have known it wouldn't work. She immediately suspected Cain, and her second suspect was someone on the Tribunal. I couldn't fault her on her analytics.

"Just to be safe, Mom, why don't you stay with a friend for a few days?"

Thankfully, we agreed on that. I ordered room service and watched mind-numbing TV until I felt drowsy enough to sleep.

In the morning, I donned a baseball cap and left my room to find the hotel restaurant for breakfast and a change of scenery. I scrolled through the news on my phone while waiting for my meal. No new details on the break-in had been reported, but Constable Ingram's profile had been filled in. Christine Ingram left behind two boys, Christopher, aged six, and Kyle, aged four. Her husband appeared glassy-eyed, numb, and far too young to be a widower. I set my phone down and stared out of the window. His wife had died in my kitchen answering my alarm. Logically, I knew I wasn't to blame, but it was a struggle to not wear the guilt.

By the time Sam called, my table had been cleared. "I have good news, bad news and bad news. Which do you want first?"

"Glad I finished my omelette," I said. "Good first."

"The Mansfield Group started their grid search at seven this morning. They've hooked me into their system so I'm getting real-time information."

"That's impressive. What's the bad news?"

"Ortez found no evidence of someone rappelling off your balcony. Doesn't mean it didn't happen, just means they were good enough to not leave a trail."

"Cain might be in Ontario, but he could have sent someone else," I said.

"Yeah, you don't reach his level without skilled connections, and he had those long before his association with ICO. But a Ghost or a Flier wouldn't have left a trail either."

"What I wouldn't give for a little taste of normal right now. What's the rest of the bad news?"

"I cleared the stockbroker. The unhappies sued his estate but went away empty-handed when the broker was cleared of professional misconduct. The government confiscated his overseas account. I'm afraid that leaves only your father."

"Damn. I was so hoping there'd be someone else to blame if this turns out to be sabotage."

"Even if I find something in your dad's background, and there's no guarantee I will, it may have nothing to do with the Reynoldses."

"Thanks for that. It's what I'm praying for. Have you told my mom?"

"Not yet."

"I'd like to tell her. If you don't mind."

"Okay. I'll get started on your dad."

After we hung up, I returned to my room and arranged a call to Mom. Her curiosity blossomed at the news of Mansfield providing Sam with real-time reporting. "Skype him, Mom. He'll be able to share his computer screen with you."

Then I told her about Sam clearing the last passenger. "I'm sorry, sweetheart," she said. "I know this isn't what you imagined."

"No. You're right, but here we are." She asked for news about the break-in. I ran through my discussion with Sam, which didn't answer any of her questions, but I was glad to hear her confirm she was staying with a friend.

"Be extra vigilant, Mom. It won't be for long," I said, hoping that was true. "I love you," I said, and we disconnected.

I kicked off my shoes and lay on the bed. I'd nearly worked myself into feeling hemmed in when the phone rang. It was Eden.

"I wish you'd told me what was going on," she said. "You don't need to shoulder everything yourself, you know."

"My intention wasn't to shut you out. I know how you and Alex feel about the Tribunal. I didn't want to drag you into that, especially when you're so far away. Besides, it's not like I can talk about most of it." In fact, there was very little about the Tribunal that I could reveal.

"I'm glad you took the seat, even if the prospect of you being involved with them frightens us. I think it was terribly brave."

Her kindness was just what I needed. I desperately wished I could tell her about Cain and ICO, but those subjects were off limits. What wasn't off limits was Mansfield's search for my dad's plane wreckage. I told her the whole story, right from the beginning. It was an unburdening, confiding in a good friend who understood how I'd come to care for Mason and Stuart. She knew without my saying how much it hurt to think they might be responsible for my dad's death. And she'd known about Jolene as long as I had. She didn't take a side, just listened, which I appreciated more than she could know. It felt as if she'd never left for Seattle.

When I'd talked the subject out, she told me she and Alex had decided to move back to Vancouver.

"I've already talked to the HR people at the hospital," she said. "They're short of nurses. Alex is talking to the guy who's been running his paint shop. He wants to make him a partner and go into business together."

We must have talked for an hour. After we said our goodbyes, I jumped up and opened the drapes feeling grateful. I had my confidant back, and soon we'd be in the same city again. The day didn't feel so bleak any more. The phone rang and I reached for it.

"What's up, Sam?"

"Brace yourself. I have more news. The milk carton in your fridge was laced with enough opioids to kill you with your morning cup of joe."

My voice dried up. It was a hard feeling to place, knowing someone hated me enough to want me dead. *You should be used to it by now*, I thought bitterly. I wasn't.

Chapter Twelve

Sam hung up with a warning that Ortez would be in touch with me. When Ortez called, it was to ask me to come to the station. He said it was an interview, but I knew better. The opioids they'd found in conjunction with a death in their family meant I'd be questioned until an answer they could use fell out. My B&E had been knocked into homicide territory.

I stored my fake ID in the hotel safe and left the building the way I'd arrived, ghosting and travelling to Pacific Centre mall to re-form in the food court's washroom. I then walked to the street and hailed a cab to take me to the station.

Ortez led me to a windowless room where three solemn-faced detectives had gathered. They hunched over their notepads with pens at the ready. Sam wasn't present. He'd explained that when it came to investigating an officer's death, professional courtesy extended free rein to the team interviewing internal operatives. He would be subjected to the same questioning. Refusal would cause an irreparable tear in both of our reputations.

After introductions, I expressed my condolences.

"Thank you," Ortez said. "Ingram was a fine officer. We're going to find the person responsible. Whoever it was broke into your apartment and spiked your milk to kill you. That's where this investigation starts. With you."

He and his team waded in gently with the questions. I stuck to my official caseload, the most recent being investment fraud at the Chinese embassy, and before that, the drug trafficking case involving the Cooper brothers. They dug deeper and quizzed me about my inheritance and my recent trip to California. They asked about my relationships with the Kirks and Reynoldses, and with James and Avery.

Ortez leaned back in his chair. He upended his pen and tapped it on his notepad. "This isn't the first time someone has targeted you, is it, Emelynn?" His tone leaked frustration.

"No. Carson Manse was a madman, but he's no longer a threat."

"Looks like you've recovered from the injuries he inflicted." Ortez's statement felt like an indictment. Being whipped caused more than physical injuries.

"Are you questioning my mental stability?"

"I'm questioning everything." Ortez picked up his notepad. "Two of the four men responsible for your abduction were killed at the scene. One was never caught and Manse escaped custody. Is that right?"

I nodded and he continued. "The records show Manse and the associate of his who'd escaped were shot and killed by the Reynoldses' security team last year while trying to break into the family's estate in California."

"Manse and his associate were both armed at the time," I said. Theirs were the only two deaths officially associated with the massacre at Cairabrae. It was the deal agreed upon by the Tribunal and Cain's ICO team the night they struck their bargain.

Ortez closed his notepad. "I've read the records. Cut-and-dry self-defence. Doesn't it seem odd, though? The last two men connected to your ordeal, both dead? That's a tidy wrap-up, isn't it? Big bow on top. And shortly after that, you turn up working as an operative for Jordan."

The digging, I didn't mind. I'd expected as much. But his accusatory tone was an unpleasant surprise. "What are you suggesting?"

He reached across the table, grabbed a clear plastic evidence bag and dropped it in front of me. My bracelet had been stripped of the locket that had held ICO's tracker. I'd left the bracelet behind in the condo when I met with the covey.

"The only thing our sweep of your condo found was the RF transmitter hidden in a locket on that bracelet."

I feigned ignorance, told them I'd picked up the bracelet at a flea market in the States. "Perhaps the previous owner of that bracelet was the target," I said. I gave them a date for the purchase—a date when I'd been in California—but when I couldn't identify a specific flea market, they suggested I was lying. I should have known ICO's trackers wouldn't be off-the-rack varieties. They even brought Sam's integrity into question.

"What kind of an operative are you, anyway?" Ortez asked.

I didn't bite. Ortez rested his elbows on his chair's armrests and twisted his pen, studying me. "Constable Ingram's autopsy came in a few hours ago. Apparently, she suffered an aneurysm. A brain bleed."

Damn. It wasn't Cain. Could only be a Flier. "Why do you say *apparently?*"

"No one in this room believes Ingram died of natural causes. And you're not nearly as pissed off about this line of questioning as you should be."

I shoved my chair back and stood.

"Where do you think you're going?"

"Are you detaining me?"

"Not yet, but this investigation is not over. We'll be keeping an eye on you. There are way too many coincidences and unanswered questions where you're concerned, Emelynn."

"I'm sorry one of your officers died answering my security alarm. Her death is tragic no matter what the cause. In your rush to judgment, I hope you don't forget that someone tried to poison me. If I can help with that, let me know."

I turned and walked to the door. My hand was on the doorknob when Ortez spoke. "Your condo has been cleared. You can move back in."

His *I dare you* went unspoken. I walked out and avoided the temptation to go directly to Sam. He'd be next, no doubt, and with a lot more to lose than I had. I prayed he wouldn't give anything away.

I returned to my hotel room under a cloud. Fear and anger fought for space in my gut. Who wanted me dead? I ran through everyone I knew. I could think of a few Fliers who might be angry with me, some who didn't like me, but enough to kill me?

My thoughts drifted to the Mansfield Group and Dad's accident. Could someone have learned of the search for the wreckage? Someone who would be threatened by what we might find? I resisted thinking about the possibility that Mason and Stuart were behind it, but given my father's warning, I couldn't dismiss it. The thought made me sick to my stomach.

It occurred to me I needed to call Avery and fill him in. He needed to be prepared in case the police called him. The worry in his voice nibbled away at my conscience long after we'd hung up.

My cellphone didn't ring again until the next morning. It was Sam looking for my room number.

"It's 1508. Why?"

"Because I'm in the lobby and I'd rather not have to ask the front desk. See you in five."

When I opened the door, he was quick to get inside and close it.

"You're out of your bunker?"

"Yup. First chance I got after Cain got pushed out of the suspect pool." He'd obviously come to the same conclusion I had: only a Flier could have caused Constable Ingram's brain bleed.

"How'd your interview with Ortez go?" I asked.

"Much like yours, I expect." He tossed his jacket on the bed exposing the gun in his shoulder holster and the badge on his hip.

I ordered coffee and we compared notes. Afterwards, Sam sat back in his chair. "I'm impressed, Taylor. Six months ago you wouldn't have been able to contain yourself through an interview like that."

"Thanks, though I'm not sure getting better at taking abuse is a good thing."

"Don't be too hard on Ortez. He's a good cop. He's trying to do right by Ingram and her partner."

"Yeah, I get that. If I could hand over the guilty party, I'd do it. Sure would make my life easier. What are the odds that someone has learned what the Mansfield Group is up to?"

"Small, hopefully. We were clear up front about the need for confidentiality."

I thought about something Sebastian mentioned at the caucus: there were no guarantees when humans were involved. A seemingly harmless comment could expose us. "I wish I could say that eliminates anyone threatened by the search for Dad's wreckage. Has Mansfield had any hits?"

"None. And that reminds me. They want another payment. I'll send you their invoice."

Sam finished his coffee and set his cup on the table. "You told me that taking the seat on the Tribunal put a few noses out of joint. Anyone's nose in particular?"

"At least three, including Sebastian's, but I don't think it was them. If it was six months from now, maybe, but getting rid of me so soon after the caucus would be too obvious. Besides which, a Tribunal player wouldn't have botched it. I'd be dead now."

"That leaves us looking for a Flier, and odds are you know them."

"That's a comforting thought."

Sam laughed then stood and stretched. He walked to the window and pulled the curtain aside. "I spoke to Walter Gorman yesterday."

"Who's he?"

"The doctor who supervised your father when he was in residency. Gorman's in his late nineties now. He still remembers your dad, though. Had very nice things to say about him."

"That's good to hear. Thanks for telling me. What else are you learning about my dad?"

"Nothing that raises a flag. At least not yet. That may change when I move my focus to Jolene."

"Be careful. Searching for Jolene is what triggered Manse and the Reynoldses to find me. They won't like that you're digging into her past."

"Thanks for the warning."

My hand nervously strayed to the coffee-service tray and lined up the silver milk and sugar pots. "I think I should move back to the condo."

Sam whipped around.

"Hear me out," I said. "My hiding in here isn't getting us anywhere. But if I'm back home, whoever did this might be tempted to try again. I'll be ready for them next time."

Sam rested his hands on his hips and stared at the floor. "Ortez will be watching. Might scare whoever it is off."

"A Flier won't be using the front door."

Ortez hadn't even bothered with an unmarked. A cruiser was parked on the street outside the condo building when I arrived ninety minutes later. It was one o'clock. I stood in the hall outside the door to my condo. Sam stood beside me with a shopping bag in his hand. "You'd better have that lock changed," he said, as I inserted my key.

Inside, the place looked like it had a hangover from a frat party. I dropped my bag in the bedroom. Sam peered in from the hall. "I might as well get started," I said, looking at the mess.

"Me too," Sam said. "Where are your tools?"

I directed him to the shelf in the hall closet and set about straightening. Every drawer had been searched; every shoe, boot and garment had been checked. They'd been thorough but respectful. I lined up my shoes, straightened the hangers and tidied the drawers. A similar situation awaited me in every room, but the kitchen was by far the worst. I collected the medical waste from the floor and went to toss it, but the garbage bin was gone. I dumped the garbage in a shopping bag and added *waste bin* to the growing shopping list.

Next, I tackled the fingerprint dust. Mom had instructed me to vacuum up as much as I could first and use a mild soap-and-water solution to dissolve the rest. What did it say about our family that mother and daughter could share that particular cleaning tip?

My phone rang before I finished, but I didn't have to answer it. When I picked it up, the screen was lit with a live stream of the view from the rooftop door. Sam's face moved in to fill the screen and he waved. Moments later, he returned to the condo.

"How'd it look?" he asked.

"Good," I said, and showed him.

"If a Flier shows up on the roof, you'll know. The camera is motion activated and mounted in the door frame. Change the ringtone for it to something unique."

After Sam left, I found a barking-dog ringtone—sounded like a perfect fit. Then I finished cleaning and made myself a cup of tea. I curled up on the sofa and cradled the oversized mug. It occurred to me that having someone try to kill you wasn't unlike experiencing grief. The stages weren't linear, but I recognized them. Denial, anger, bargaining, shades of depression and, finally, acceptance. I planted my flag in the anger arena.

In light of our new pact, I phoned Sebastian with the latest news. He was suitably incensed that a Flier was responsible, but like me, had no idea who it might have been. He tossed out names like playing cards. Nothing stuck.

"I've got the perfect distraction for you," Sebastian said.

"I don't need a distraction. I need to figure out who's trying to kill me."

"Trust me. You'll appreciate this. I'll be there in an hour."

He hung up on me. I guess not everything about the man had changed.

I headed to the shower and scrubbed the charcoal-coloured dust from under my nails. With my hair still wet, I ran out to pick up some milk and coffee cream. The rest of the groceries would have to wait until after Sebastian's visit. A fresh pot of coffee was brewed when Colin called to tell me I had company.

Sebastian wasn't alone when I opened the door. His *perfect distraction* stood beside him.

"This is Ben Nicolson, the architect I've been telling you about."

I wasn't sure what I'd expected Sebastian's architect to look like, but a thirty-something rock star in Rag & Bone jeans wasn't it.

He clutched a laptop under one arm. I extended my hand. "Emelynn Taylor. Come in."

Sebastian walked his architect down the hall ahead of me as if he owned the place. They walked straight to the living room and stood in front of the view. I felt like the help coming up behind them offering coffee.

They didn't turn from the view until I set the tray on the coffee table. Ben raked a hand through perfectly dishevelled hair. He accepted the cup I held out to him and took a seat opposite the sofa. Sebastian took the other chair.

We had the you-have-a-lovely-place conversation followed by Sebastian praising Ben's work. Ben got points for looking embarrassed about it, and he wiggled out of the conversation with an offer to show me some of his recent projects online. He moved to sit beside me on the sofa and opened his laptop.

He took me through a half dozen impressive before-and-after layouts on his website, including the work he'd done on Sebastian's Point Grey home. He pointed out details I would have missed and talked about how important he felt it was to stay true to the original design. Sebastian refilled his coffee and turned his chair to the view.

Ben spoke with the fervour of someone who loved his work. "It's difficult to appreciate the results on such a small scale," he said, referring to his screen. "They're much more impressive in person. Perhaps I could arrange a time to show them to you?"

"Sure," I said, and briefly wondered if selecting an architect was like buying a car: kick the tires and take him out for a spin.

"Good," he said. "I hope you don't mind, but when Sebastian told me about the arson, and that you might rebuild, I did some research." He went back to his computer and opened a different file.

I pushed to the edge of my seat. "Where did you get that?" I said, looking at a black-and-white photograph of my cottage I'd never seen before.

"City archives. Your home was the first one built on the Cliffside bluff in 1918. Frank and Nelly Thomas were the original owners."

"This must have been taken when it was brand new," I said. "These trees are fully grown now, and there's a garage over here," I said, mesmerized by the photograph. "Would you please send me that?"

"What's your email address?" With a few clicks, he sent it on its way. "If you don't mind, I'd like to go out there and take a look at the property. Get a feel for it. Take some photos. See the neighbourhood."

"Please do."

You'd think I'd granted him a wish the way his smile lit up his face. "Thank you. I'll send you my preliminary thoughts. If they appeal to you, perhaps we can work together to build you a new home." He closed his laptop and stood.

I stood as well. "Thanks for making the time to come and see me today. I hope Sebastian didn't drag you away from another commitment."

"No worries. It's been my pleasure. I'll be in touch." He shook my hand.

Sebastian came to stand beside us. "I'll walk you out."

They turned down the hall and I caught myself wondering if Ben's jeans would suit James. James. I reached for my phone like an addict for a fix. It had been four days with no word from him. Was this really the end for us?

Thankfully, I didn't have long to wallow in that thought. Sebastian returned and handed me Ben's card. "He forgot to give you that."

"Thanks. He sounds enthusiastic."

"He's an impressive young man. Ambitious, but you have to be to stake a claim in his business."

I screwed up my face. "Renos?"

"Renos keep the money coming in, but it's projects like yours that build a reputation. Those projects don't come along every day."

"I hope you didn't promise him anything."

"An introduction is all. I trust it wasn't too painful." He raised an eyebrow.

I bit back a smile. Funny was new for Sebastian. I picked up the coffee tray and walked it to the kitchen. When I returned, Sebastian had wandered into the dining room and stood in front of Jolene's painting.

I joined him. "Mason told me you knew Jolene," I said. He'd told me Sebastian and Jolene had dated before Jolene met my father.

"Yes, a long time ago."

"Tell me about her."

"She was a mystery. Beautiful. Rebellious. Stuart hoped she'd choose someone like us to settle down with, but she seemed determined to find a match outside of our circles. Your father, for example. Tragic what happened to them. Jolene wasn't lucky in love. After your dad, she almost married twice. In Greece, she fell for a man who owned an olive plantation. Years later, in New York, she fell for a banker. They weren't Fliers. Would have been terrible matches."

"You're forgetting Carson Manse."

"Yes," he said, and spared me a glance. "He was the worst of her suitors by far."

"What happened to the man in Greece and the one in New York?"

He returned his gaze to the painting. "They didn't work out. It was hard on her, but it was for the best. Her life would have been so much easier with one of us. Someone who understood the life of a Ghost."

"Somehow, I don't think she'd agree."

"She deserved better."

"You loved her."

"I cared for her once. Jolene was fragile. I felt protective of her, especially after she lost her son. But I'd found Kimberley by then, and never looked back."

"I wish I'd known her."

Sebastian dragged his gaze from Jolene's painting and sighed. "Sadly, we can't change the past. I am, however, glad you and I have found a new accord."

"Me too."

"There are times I recognize Jolene's gift in you. Maybe that's why I put in the extra effort where you're concerned. And now that I've done my good deed for the day, I must go."

I walked him out. When I returned to the living room, I dusted off my laptop and looked up Ben Nicolson. He'd been careful about his public profile, filling it with photos of beautiful architecture and fine art rather than drunken party shots. There wasn't a bad photo of him anywhere. He must be one of those fortunate photogenic types, I thought.

Later that afternoon, a locksmith showed up. He was in and out faster than his bill suggested, but I was happy to have the lock changed. I wondered if I'd ever get the chance to give James a key.

With nothing left to keep me busy, I wrapped my head in a scarf, donned sunglasses and headed for the grocery store. The constable in the cruiser out front didn't recognize me as I passed by. It occurred to me they would know who Ben Nicolson was by now, though I doubted Sebastian had allowed himself to be tagged.

I'd made it back home and was folding the grocery bags when Mason called. I stared at the screen, torn between needing to answer it and wanting to keep him at bay. I answered.

"Why am I learning about an attempt on your life from Sebastian?" were the first words out of his mouth.

"Sorry. It's been crazy here since the break-in and the constable's death. The police are hovering."

"You are a Tribunal member. The consequences of this reach far beyond the police or their judicial system."

"Not right now. Not with the police on my doorstep. There's no need for your concern. Sam's involved and Sebastian's been around. I'm in good hands."

"They aren't your family. You should have called."

His words struck me dumb. Was he my family? It pained me that I couldn't be certain. It's why I hadn't called him.

"Emelynn? What is it?"

My voice hitched. "There's nothing you could have done."

A moment of silence followed. He then asked for a blow-by-blow of every detail of events before, during and after the break-in. He asked questions that might have convinced a less-jaded person that he hadn't been involved. It saddened me to know that was no longer me.

The conversation left me exhausted. I stared at my reflection in the bathroom mirror and wondered who I'd become. I still looked the same, but inside I felt hollow, numb, detached. For the first time since I'd put them on, I removed the earrings James had given me and returned them to the box they'd come in.

Chapter Thirteen

The fog in my head persisted despite the dawn of a brilliant morning. I took my coffee to the balcony and bundled up. Without a peep from James, I had to face the unpleasant facts. Never had his lack of communication spoken louder. How long would the pain of missing him last? Seeing his earrings, touching them, had always reminded me of him. Now their absence served the same purpose.

I desperately needed a new focus. One far removed from death threats and Fliers. I thought of yesterday's meeting with Ben Nicolson. Maybe Sebastian was right. Rebuilding the cottage might be the perfect distraction for me right now.

I found Ben's card and dialled his number. That afternoon, he took me on the promised tour of his favourite renovations, but we skipped Sebastian's. I didn't want any reminder of the Flier world today.

Some of the projects were rebuilds, others were additions. All of them inspired confidence. One was still under construction. Before we went in, he made me don a hard hat and a pair of steel-toed boots he'd brought along. I spared a moment to wonder where he'd borrowed a pair of steel-toed boots that almost fit.

He introduced me to the foreman and handed him a set of drawings. After our tour of the site, we retreated to a trailer, where the foreman had unfurled the new drawings. He whistled out the door of the trailer and a few minutes later, a woman wearing a tool belt joined us. Ben included me in the discussion about the work's progress and the possible sticking points.

When we finally returned to his truck and I got back into my own shoes, he suggested we go out to Cliffside Avenue in Summerset and take a look at my property together.

"Unless you have other plans," he said.

"Absolutely none. Let's go."

Ben left the truck on the road at the end of the cul-de-sac. "I want to approach it on foot, get a feel for it," he said, snagging his camera's strap as he stepped out of the truck.

We didn't say a word as we walked up the driveway. He stopped every few yards, turned left or right, snapped some photos then continued. When we got to the garage, he circled around it. He didn't look into the window or ask me to open it. He got to the top of the driveway turnaround and stared out toward the gap in the trees where the cottage once stood.

"You won't be able to build as close to the cliff's edge as before. New setbacks came into effect twelve years ago."

I stayed in place while he walked along the edge of the cliff from the south end to the north, looking through his camera's lens, recording every angle, every view. I loved that he treated the property with the reverence it deserved.

He appeared lost in thought when he returned to me. The wind had tossed his hair.

"Is there someplace nearby we can go for a coffee or a drink? I'd like to jot down some notes while they're still fresh in my mind."

"There's a Starbucks on the strip."

"The strip?"

"Sorry. That's local-speak for a popular section of Deacon Street. It's not too far."

We climbed back in his truck and made the short drive to Deacon.

He brought his camera and notepad into the coffee shop and set to scribbling away at a table while I continued to the counter and ordered two Americanos. I returned to the table and set his cup in front of him.

"Thanks." He took a sip and returned to making notes. A full ten minutes passed before he reached for his camera. "I don't mean to be rude. I'll just be a few more minutes." He then clicked through the shots he'd taken and made some final scratches on his notepad. "There, that should hold my ideas in place." He closed his notepad and set the camera down on top of it.

We talked for an hour, maybe more. He wanted to know what I

envisioned for the property, and then he teased out more details, like the number of bedrooms and bathrooms I wanted and the scale I imagined.

"Why do you call it a *cottage*?" he asked.

"My father told me the old couple who sold it to him referred to it that way. That must have been Frank and Nelly Thomas. I'm glad I know their names now."

"What else do you remember about the cottage?"

An unexpected wave of emotion hit me from out of nowhere. I looked away as tears welled.

"I'm sorry," Ben said. "That was careless of me."

"No. Not your fault." I blotted my eyes with a napkin. "I miss it is all. The last time I saw my father was in that house. I was twelve years old. All of my memories of him were tied to that place, and now it's gone."

"Did they ever catch the arsonist?"

"Yes. He's dead." The perfect distraction had run its course. "Will you take me home?"

Ben didn't notice the police cruiser that pulled in and parked on the street when he dropped me at my building. He offered another apology and a promise to get some preliminary ideas to me within the week. I thanked him for the day and headed inside.

A woman I knew as Mary was on the front desk. She wanted a firsthand account of the break-in but I had neither the energy nor inclination. "Ask Colin. He was here," I said, and continued on to the elevator.

Upstairs in the condo, I dug out my phone and dropped my bag on the kitchen counter. No one had called. I opened the fridge and looked at the roasted chicken. Later, I thought, and closed the door, settling for a glass of wine instead. I set a music playlist going, dropped into one of the chairs and swivelled to the view. As much as I enjoyed the warmer weather, it meant shorter nights and longer waits until darkness brought the promise of relief. Tonight, the sun wouldn't set until after 9:00 p.m.

At 7:00 p.m. Mary called from the front desk. "Detective Jordan is here to see you." I asked her to send him up and went down the hall to open the door.

I could tell by the stiff set of Sam's shoulders as he came off the elevator that whatever news he had for me wasn't good.

"Would you like to join me in a glass of wine?" I asked.

"How about a beer?"

I handed him a cold can and a glass and he poured his own. He took the seat beside me in the living room and we both stared out to the Pacific. He put the glass to his lips and drank down a third of it.

"What's on your mind, Sam?"

He looked at me in the window's reflection. "Your father wasn't the only man in Jolene's life who died unexpectedly."

I turned to him. "Who else?"

"A guy named Nick Pagonis, and another whose name was Arthur Curtis."

"Let me guess," I said. "One from Greece, the other from New York."

Sam swung his head to me. He narrowed his eyes. "How did you know that?"

"Sebastian told me. He said Jolene was unlucky in love."

Sam snorted. "Some would call her a black widow. What exactly did Sebastian say?"

I retold the conversation as best I remembered it. "Sebastian didn't say the men had died. He just said it didn't work out."

"That's one way of phrasing it. You need to prepare yourself, Emelynn. If not Jolene then someone she knew killed these men. And if you believe Sebastian, that Stuart wanted her to marry within the community, then Mason or Stuart could very well be responsible."

I stared back out of the window. His words wrapped around my heart and squeezed.

"I know that's not what you wanted to hear, Emelynn. But don't dismiss it."

"It wasn't Jolene. Not where my dad was concerned, anyway. It could have been Carson Manse," I said. "In which case, we'll never know. How did the other men die?"

"A drowning and a suicide," Sam said.

"Of course."

"The suicide was controversial. He jumped from the George Washington Bridge, which is monitored by CCTV cameras. I haven't seen the film myself, but the police reports describe the man as being loose-limbed and moving unnaturally."

"As if a Ghost were helping him along? That eliminates Manse."

Silence stretched between us.

"It could have been Sebastian," Sam said. "You told me he loved Jolene. Maybe he was jealous."

"Maybe, but it seems unlikely. He married Kimberley after Jolene took up with my dad, and they're still married. Besides, Sebastian's too proud to be jealous."

"I'm not ruling him out."

And the two I wanted to rule out, I couldn't. Sam's investigation was tightening a noose around Mason's and Stuart's necks, and I was the one choking. And if that weren't stifling enough, we were nowhere closer to finding the Flier who wanted me dead. "Any news from the Mansfield people?"

"Nothing yet."

Not that long ago, I'd hoped they wouldn't find Dad's wreck. Now I wondered if it even mattered. If it was sabotage, I'd suspect Mason and Stuart. If it wasn't sabotage, I'd still suspect them. Either way, I couldn't trust them around me or my mother.

We sat and watched the sun's descent. I poured another glass of wine and handed Sam another beer. I liked that we didn't need to fill the silence.

We both started when my phone rang. It wasn't the phone on the coffee table but the one still in my purse on the kitchen counter. The one Sebastian was monitoring.

He followed me to the kitchen. I dug out the phone and we both stared at the screen. *Unknown Caller.* "It's Cain," I said. I answered it and put it on speakerphone.

"I can only assume you didn't take me seriously when I told you to call off your boyfriend."

"But ... I did call him off."

"Then why is he standing in my sister's living room? You have forced my hand, Emelynn." Sam jumped and pulled out his phone. He must have had it on vibrate. "You have one hour to see that James gets on an international flight. I don't care which destination."

"Hello," Sam said, answering his phone. "Who is this?"

"That will be for you, Emelynn," Cain said.

My mother's voice came out of Sam's phone. "Emelynn! Emelynn!" Her panic stabbed me.

"I'm here, Mom! Where are you?"

The phone's reception was dampened by something covering the mic. Sam and I strained to hear. When Mom came back on the line, her voice was faint and broken by sobs. "I c-can't say. He told me to tell you ... he'll send me back to you ... one p-piece at a time ... if you d-don't do what he says."

Mom's voice cracked and the sound of her fear raged in my ears. "Don't you fucking hurt her!" I shouted into the phone. No one but Sam heard me. Cain and his accomplice had already hung up.

I covered my face with my hands and groaned in despair. Sam dialled a number and held the phone to his ear. "Cain's got eyes on you. Get out of there." He immediately called another number and repeated the message. James wasn't picking up.

Fucking hell. I followed Sam's lead and stabbed at my phone. I left James a voice mail and then I texted him. *Cain has Mom.* I prayed he had his phone on vibrate. I lost count of the number of texts I sent, one after the other, all with the same message.

Sam laid his hand over mine and stilled my fingers. "Breathe."

I looked up at him and drew in a ragged breath.

"Call Sebastian," Sam said. "See if he got a location."

Why hadn't I thought of that? I dialled Sebastian's number. It went unanswered. "Doesn't anyone answer their fucking phones!" I left a message and tossed the phone to the counter.

Sam stared into space, deep in thought. "What is it?" I asked.

"Cain had James in his crosshairs and instead of putting a bullet in him, he calls you."

I frowned. Sam had a point. Why wouldn't Cain get rid of the problem himself? There could be only one reason. "He wants James alive."

Sam nodded his agreement. "Cain's not finished with whatever he's doing."

I picked up the phone and checked the time. Seven minutes since Cain's call. "I'm going to Sebastian's," I said, and turned for the hall.

"You don't know where he is."

"Kimberley will know."

"If she's home."

I stopped in my tracks. Damn. I'd never felt so useless in my life. "I don't know what to do. I'm out of options."

"But James isn't. Have some faith."

I bunched my hands into fists and closed my eyes. We both paced. I had a phone in each hand and checked them at every turn on the floor. Ten minutes. The condo felt stifling. I opened the balcony door to let in some cool air. Fifteen minutes. My mother's life hung in the balance and I couldn't stand it.

"I gotta do something."

My phone rang. The traced one. Sam bolted to my side. It was James. "I'm on my way to the airport. Cain's following. He's brazen now. Out in the open."

"Please do what he says, James. Mom's life is on the line."

"I know. Gotta go."

He'd hung up. I stared at the screen until it went blurry with unshed tears. Sam came to stand in front of me and put his hands on my shoulders. He bent to look me in the eye. "He won't do anything to put your mom in danger."

The tears spilled over and Sam pulled me close. "If anything happens to her ..." I said, and then I melted into his embrace and gave in to the guilt. Sam didn't ply me with platitudes and I was grateful for that. Sometimes, knowing what not to say was more important than words.

He held me until I'd composed myself. "What now?" I said, pulling away and swiping at my tears.

"We wait."

We both checked the time. Twenty-two minutes. "Will Cain call back?" I found a tissue and blew my nose.

Sam shrugged. "Don't know. He wants to make sure you know he's in control."

I sat on the edge of the sofa with my elbows on my knees and held my head in my hands. Sam walked to the balcony door and went outside.

My phone vibrated. A text. Sam saw me reach for it and rushed inside. Sebastian had written *Stay off your phone so Cain can get through*. I showed it to Sam. "Guess that means he knows."

As I watched Sam read the message, something else occurred to me. "James called me on my traced phone. He was making sure Sebastian knew what was going on."

Sam grinned.

The next hour tested my fortitude like it had never been tested before. When I stood, I paced. When I sat, I fidgeted. I carried a tissue and wiped at tears that leaked without warning. I raised the phone's ringer to maximum volume. The sixty-minute mark came and went. I fought to keep dark thoughts from consuming me. *Have faith*, Sam had said. I repeated his words over and over in my head.

Almost two hours later, the phone rang. I jumped. "It's him," I said, and answered it.

"Your mother is in one piece. For now. Her fate is entirely in your hands. If I see any sign of James or another of your kind, she's dead. If anything happens to me or anyone in my family, she's dead."

"Please don't hurt her. She has nothing to do with this. Let her go. You can take me."

He laughed. "I like my odds with your mother better. Don't test me, Emelynn. I've been playing this game since before you were born. There isn't a trick I haven't seen or perfected."

"James has left. He's not coming back."

"You think I should take your word for it? You can't be trusted. Your people, if that's what you are, tried to kill me. You wiped out my entire team. Most were friends. You will pay for that."

"We already paid, or are you forgetting that ICO kidnapped me, kidnapped James. Used us like lab rats. You facilitated that."

"Fuente is responsible for that, not me."

"Who told Fuente about us?"

"No one on the team you wiped out."

"Bullshit. A CIA director went rogue and recruited someone in ICO. Your team is ICO."

"My team was going after those bastards."

I searched for the term I'd heard on the news. *Collateral damage*, they called it. Was that what he was insinuating?

"What? Got nothing to say to that?" Cain said.

"You knew for three months that someone had infiltrated ICO. You left James and me exposed for three months! That's how they got to us. And after we escaped, when you finally enlightened Sam, you wouldn't name names. That's on you."

"You and your people have the blood of innocents on your hands. When I'm ready, I will prove it."

"Ready? What does that mean?"

"You didn't wipe out everything. I have irrefutable proof of what you are. This time you won't be so quick to erase it."

He hung up. I stared at the phone. "Bastard!"

Almost immediately, the phone rang again. This time it was Sebastian. "You heard that?" I asked.

"Yes. I sent reinforcements to James after his initial call. Cain won't get away this time."

"You can't do that! He's got my mother."

"We'll find her."

"You'll get her killed."

"Your lack of faith is hardly fitting for your new role."

"Do not throw that crap at me, Sebastian. My mother isn't some sacrifice for the cause."

"I am well aware of that. We will not endanger her. Remember your training. Step back and look at the big picture. We are the hunters, never the prey."

"Please don't underestimate him. You did that once and he got away. You do it again and he'll kill her."

That night was the longest of my life. I woke in the early hours on the sofa with a blanket over me. I checked the phones. Nothing. I made a pot of coffee and walked down the hall to my room. Sam had tucked into my mother's bed. I used the washroom and splashed water on my face. For the thousandth time, I wondered if my mother was dead or alive. Where had James gone? What were Sebastian's men doing? The questions hammered relentlessly in my head.

When Sam woke, he banged around in the kitchen and then set a plate of fried eggs and toast in front of me.

"I can't eat."

"You're more clear-headed when you're fed, and you need to be sharp. Eat up."

Sam wolfed down his eggs while I picked at mine. "How long has it been?" I asked.

He checked his phone. "We're still within the first twenty-four." The first twenty-four. The most critical hours following a kidnapping. If Mom wasn't found in that time frame her chances of survival diminished exponentially with every hour that followed.

Sam's phone rang. It felt like an electric shock straight to my heart. He spoke briefly then disconnected. "That was the chief's PA. He wants to see me."

"What about?"

"He wouldn't say. I stalled him, but I can't put it off for long."

"Thanks for staying with me."

"We're partners, remember?"

We took turns with the pacing. Hours later, Sam went back to the fridge. This time he came out with roasted chicken sandwiches. "Hope you like mayo," he said, setting one in front of me.

"Do you vacuum, too?" I asked, and surprised myself with a smile.

A matching smile tugged at the corners of Sam's mouth. "You get cocky and I won't feed you."

We sat on the sofa and ate slowly, staring out the window. When dark thoughts swooped in I swatted them away. Not knowing was exhausting.

I pulled a blanket around my shoulders and dozed on and off in the early afternoon. How Sam managed to keep himself sane, I had no idea.

When the traced phone vibrated on the coffee table, I knocked over a glass of water getting to it. Sam was behind me in an instant and read the message over my shoulder. *Your mom is safe.* It was from James. I closed my eyes and sent a silent thank-you to the heavens.

Sam put his hand on my shoulder. "It's over."

Chapter Fourteen

We didn't have to speculate about what had happened for long. Sebastian phoned a few minutes later.

"We have your mother. She's been mildly sedated."

"Why? Is she all right? Where is she?"

"She's fine now, but she was frantic when they found her. The sedation was necessary to get her through airport security without raising suspicion. James is with her. They're in the air and on their way to you now."

"James? I thought he'd left the country."

"No. With Grace Shipley's help, he managed to plant a look-alike. I'm sure he'll explain it all when you see him. Their plane lands at ten this evening."

Grace? Was she why James had been so quiet? "I'll meet the plane. Thank you, Sebastian. Thanks for all you've done."

"You are most welcome, my dear. I look forward to seeing Laura again when she's safely home."

Safely home: two of the most comforting words in the entire English language. I wallowed in that comfort and inhaled relief by the lungful.

"I'm going to head out," Sam said.

I thanked him again and gave him a grateful hug before he left. I promised to let him know the full story as soon as I knew it.

After I tidied Mom's room, I jumped in the shower. She and James wouldn't arrive for hours yet. Would Grace be with them? I touched the facecloth to my empty earlobes. Jealousy stung like soap in my eyes.

The cruiser out front posed a minor problem. Mom and I had worked too hard to protect the connection between us. Cain had found out anyway, but I still wasn't going to expose her unnecessarily. When it was time, I ghosted out of the condo and re-formed blocks away. From there, I hailed a taxi to the airport.

I arrived twenty minutes early and went down to the departures level and bought a cup of herbal tea. It was something to occupy my hands while I waited. The moment their flight registered as landed, I took the escalator to the arrivals level. I kept my head down and stayed out of sight.

When they finally came through the doors, I dropped my cup in the trash and ran to them. James had his arm around Mom's shoulders. Her pale face lifted with a wan smile when she spotted me. James let her go and Mom and I embraced as if it had been years and not days since we'd last seen each other. I felt the heaving of her slender body and fought to keep my own tears at bay.

"Let's go home," I said, and loosened my hold.

I looked over at James. He shook his head. "I'm not going with you."

His words stung.

He spoke to my mom. "Laura, I need a private word with Emelynn." He took my mom's elbow and escorted her to a bench at the perimeter of the baggage carousel area. I followed. "We'll be right over there," he told her. "We'll just be a minute, and I'll have my eyes on you the whole time."

Mom nodded. James walked away and I followed him with my heart in my throat. He turned so he faced my mother and offered her a reassuring smile.

"You're limping," I said, having noticed him favouring his left side.

"Yeah. Didn't see the kick coming. It's nothing serious."

The dark circles under his eyes made me wonder if he'd slept. I held my breath.

He looked to the floor. So this is it, I thought. I wasn't ready. "What happened?" I asked, stalling for time. Time to prepare, to steel myself.

I'd interrupted his thoughts. He rearranged his features. "Grace knew just the guy to impersonate me. I sent him to Cain's sister's house on the pretense of an investigation. Sure enough, Cain showed himself. I would never have approached his sister if I'd known Cain knew about your mother." He glanced in Mom's direction again. "She's pretty shaken, but she's strong." He gathered his thoughts before continuing. "Sebastian's men subdued Cain until I was able to read him and learn the protocol he'd set up to check in with the kidnappers in Toronto. Cain knew where she was being held. That's how we found her."

"Thank you. I know how much you hate doing that."

He tipped his chin. "There's more." Once again, he looked away.

"What is it?"

"There's a child. A baby, I suppose. Not born yet."

The blood left my face in a rush. Though I knew the answer, I asked anyway. "Ours?"

"Yes. A surrogate is carrying our child."

I grabbed his sleeve. "Who? Where?" Half-formed thoughts skittered around in my mind unable to find purchase.

"I don't know, but I know the clinic they used. It's in California. I'm heading there now."

"What will you do when you find her?"

James's gaze flickered to one of my earlobes and then the other. He struggled from my grip and put his hands on his hips. "I don't know. I'll have to play it by ear. See how much she knows."

"This is the proof that Cain spoke of."

"Yeah. He was pretty proud of that. Your mother doesn't know. I gotta go."

My mouth gaped. He walked a brisk pace back to my mother and knelt down in front of her. I gathered my wits and rushed to catch up. "Emelynn is going to take you home. If you feel that panic coming on again, take the Ativan I gave you. Remind yourself that the men who took you and the men who were behind it are all dead. They can't hurt you again."

My mother flinched at the word *dead*. James patted her knees then stood and offered her a hand up. She took it and mumbled thanks as he hugged her. He then turned to me. "I'll call when I have news."

He walked away from us and jogged toward the departures level escalator. I watched his back until his tall frame disappeared. He hadn't even touched me.

I wiped my tears and turned to Mom. "Let's get you home."

I had her put a scarf around her hair and most of her face then took her hand. "Keep your head down," I told her. We walked out of the airport and got into a taxi.

It sped through the light late-night traffic. I had the driver drop me off a block away from the condo and assured Mom I'd be there waiting for her. When they were out of sight, I ducked into the shadows and ghosted then bolted for the condo.

The police cruiser parked in front of my building was an unwelcome reminder that whoever had tried to kill me was still out there. Regardless, Mom was safer with me than without me, and I didn't want her out of my sight. At least the police were close at hand if we needed help.

Back in the condo, I buttered some toast and made a pot of tea. Mom didn't want to talk about her ordeal. I didn't push. I'd been in her shoes. She'd talk when she could cope with it. She'd suffered no physical assault that I could see. She nibbled at the toast with little enthusiasm and soon excused herself and went to her room.

I phoned Avery and apologized for waking him. After I told him what had happened, he agreed to come by first thing in the morning and see Mom. I warned him about the police cruiser out front and asked him not to mention to Mom the attempt on my life. She didn't need any more stress. I didn't tell him about the surrogate; I couldn't get the words out of my mouth. We were as close as father and daughter. I knew he'd be devastated. I wouldn't ruin his night. I'd tell him tomorrow.

I checked on Mom as I walked to my room. She lay in her bed with a book. I closed the door of my bedroom before I called Sam. He wasn't asleep. I relayed the events as James had described them. Telling Sam about the surrogate was easier than telling Avery. He took it in stride and immediately went into solution mode. He made it sound simple: protect the surrogate, isolate her if necessary, and make sure the baby is delivered safely. He didn't get to the next part—the mom and dad and happily-ever-after-family part. Once again, he knew what not to say.

"I have some news of my own," Sam said. "The chief tells me the funding for my position has been reallocated. Not that he ever knew ICO funded it, but ICO must have figured out they had a dead cell and they're erasing their tracks. I've been laid off. I'm on paid leave until my twelve-week notice period runs out."

"Guess we knew this was coming. What will you do?"

"Don't know yet. Haven't been out of a job since I was fourteen. Right now a hammock and a cold cerveza somewhere warm sounds like a decent plan."

"Okay, but until you book that flight, you're on my payroll. That is, if you want to keep working on my father's case."

"Yeah, I'd like to see it through."

I checked on Mom again. She'd turned out her light and lay in the bed with her back to the door. Perhaps she'd taken the Ativan James had given her.

After I crawled into my own bed, the thoughts I'd been fighting since seeing James came rushing in. He hadn't kissed me or held me. We were going to be parents and strangers. The child growing in someone else's womb already had so many strikes against it. Our child.

Early in the morning, I got out of bed and pulled on a robe. I tiptoed down the hall and looked in on Mom. She lay curled on her side, still asleep. I made a pot of coffee and checked my phones. Carrying both of them was proving cumbersome. I no longer needed two, but I didn't feel comfortable asking James to remove the tracer from the first. I added *find a new IT maverick* to my to-do list.

When Mom came out of her room freshly scrubbed and fully dressed, I took it as a good sign. She didn't usually lounge around in her robe like I did unless she was sick. I made porridge for our breakfast with the intent to fill her with comfort food and surround her with familiarity. We'd just finished loading the dishwasher when Avery arrived. I excused myself to give them some privacy.

When I returned, she and Avery were sitting on the sofa. A prescription lay on the table in front of Mom, and Avery was scribbling the name of a psychologist. I'd overheard a little of their conversation but didn't let on. I sat in one of the swivel chairs opposite them.

"The psychologist is going to think I've lost my mind," Mom said. Avery raised his eyebrows and Mom caught on to what she'd said and laughed at herself.

"She's very competent. I think you'll be pleasantly surprised," Avery said.

"Thank you."

"Are you sure I can't get you a coffee?" I asked.

"Thanks, but no, I should go." Avery stood.

"Please, not yet. I have something I need to tell both of you."

Avery hitched his slacks and sat back down.

I gathered my courage and began. "When James was ... interviewing Cain, he learned that ICO implanted a surrogate with an embryo. Mine and James's."

"Oh, sweetheart." Anguish was plain on Mom's face.

Avery hung his head. "How far along is the pregnancy?"

"I don't know. James found out which clinic was used. It's in California. He was headed there last night. Said he'd call when he had more information."

"It can't be more than six weeks," Avery said. "The first trimester."

"How are you feeling about it?" Mom asked.

I picked a knob of lint from my sleeve. "I knew this outcome was a possibility, but I never really thought it would happen."

"The odds were stacked against it," Avery said.

"I know. It's not that I don't want kids—I do—but I didn't want them right now, and not like this. Looks like that choice has been taken away from me."

"There are options, Emelynn," Avery said.

I looked up. Would terminating the pregnancy be an option for James? Somehow, I doubted it. "If this baby is born, I want it. I won't have someone else raising a child of mine."

"How does James feel about it?" Mom asked.

"We didn't get much of a chance to talk about it last night, but I know he wants kids. He'll want this baby."

"That's a good start," Mom said. "A baby can be a blessing."

"Any child of mine will inherit the ghosting gene, Mom. I have no idea how to deal with that."

"So you'll learn. And I'll help you."

I smiled at her effort. A mother's love trumps all. I'd have to remember that.

"A word of caution, Em," Avery said. "There's a reason couples don't announce a pregnancy until after the first trimester. She could still lose it."

"You know, I hadn't realized it until just now, but I hope she doesn't, whoever she is."

After Avery left, Mom asked me if I wanted to talk about it. I didn't. I didn't want to think about a baby being born into a broken family. How would custody work between parents in two different countries? I wondered.

Mom had left her prescription on the coffee table. I glanced down at it and shook my head. "He prescribed Ativan? Do you know how many times I asked him for that and he said no?"

"It's only five pills," Mom said.

"It's a minor miracle is what it is."

Later in the morning, I told her that Sam had been laid off from the police department.

"I should call him," she said. "Thank him." She slipped back to her room. When she emerged, she told me the Mansfield Group still hadn't found the wreckage. They'd been searching for five days.

Sebastian called that afternoon. He wanted to come by to see Mom and offer his support. He wasn't her favourite person, but she agreed to his company. She said she owed him thanks as well. I suspected Sebastian's visit would also serve to interrupt the memory loop I knew was playing in her head. In time, she'd be able to unlink the fear from the memories and the fear would fade. The memories, however, I wasn't so sure about.

Sebastian continued his good-neighbour routine and checked in at the front desk. He showed up with flowers. Mom seemed pleased, or at least her smile was genuine.

The three of us went into the kitchen while she arranged them in a vase, but her small talk was full of holes. She finally gave up the ruse that everything was all right and asked Sebastian to tell her exactly what had happened.

We migrated to the living room and they stitched together their stories.

"I'd been staying with Linda," Mom said, turning to me. "You remember her?" Linda was one of Mom's oldest friends in Toronto. I nodded. "I should never have gone back to my apartment, but I needed some papers I'd left there. It only took a minute. I was in and out, but they must have been watching. I walked back to Linda's. It's a few blocks away. Didn't even notice the van parked along the sidewalk. A car alarm went off across the street somewhere and I heard shouting. In hindsight, I know that it was planned as a distraction. They pulled me off my feet and I didn't even have a chance to scream before the van was moving. Going back there was stupid of me."

"Laura, these men are ... were professionals. If they didn't get you there, they would have gotten you somewhere else."

"He's right, Mom. Don't beat yourself up."

"The plan to flush out Cain was already in motion when we learned he had you," Sebastian said. Sebastian's men must have given him an in-depth timeline of events, which he relayed to Mom. He didn't scrimp on details either, so I was glad I'd already told her about the surrogate.

Sebastian turned to me. "Such a shame things didn't work out between you and James."

My mother swung her head around. "Emelynn?"

I'm sure my face was frozen and probably the colour of ash.

"Oh dear," Sebastian said. "Seems I've misstepped."

"What happened?" Mom asked.

"What did James tell you?" I asked Sebastian.

"He didn't tell me anything. I read the signs. But perhaps I'm mistaken?"

"I don't care to talk about it."

That little bomb effectively ended our conversation. Mom thanked Sebastian for his part in freeing her and she walked him to the door. But she wasn't done with me.

She sat opposite me. "Is it true? About James?"

"He didn't agree with my decision to take the seat on the Tribunal. Hasn't spoken to me since. I'd hoped he'd come to see that it was the only decision I could make, but he hasn't. If it weren't for what happened to you, I probably still wouldn't have heard from him."

"I'm sorry. I know how much you care for him. If you need to talk, I'm here for you."

Mom and I didn't stir from the condo the rest of the day. With nightfall came the risk of a return visit from the Flier out to kill me. I didn't think Mom was ready for that news yet. I kept my phone close.

The night ground slowly past.

We had a visitor the next morning, but not the murderous kind. The front desk called to announce Ben Nicolson. I explained who he was to Mom before he knocked on the door.

He stood a step back from the door and massaged a roll of drawings. "I wouldn't normally drop by unannounced," he said, with his chin tucked in. "I couldn't find your number. Thought I'd leave this at the front desk, but they called up. If this isn't a convenient time ..."

"It's okay. Come in and meet my friend, Laura."

He raised his head and stepped inside. After I introduced them, Ben asked if we could use the dining room table. He unfurled the roll of drawings and we each took a corner to keep it flat.

"I used the city survey for the dimensions, so they might not be accurate. This is just to give you a rough idea. This is the setback line." He pointed out the property's features on the aerial view, though he didn't need to. I knew every inch of the landscape.

On the next drawing, he'd placed a building's footprint. It was parallel to the cliff, much like the original cottage had been. "This siting takes full advantage of the ocean view, but this second one," he said, peeling back a page, "is sited on a slight angle to the south, toward the park. You've got the space to do it and you'll get more sun. We'd have to rebuild the garage, but with the new setbacks, unless we move the house closer to your neighbour to the north, we'd have to do that anyway." Given my nighttime activities, distance from the neighbour sounded like a good plan.

He lifted that page without warning and the drawing underneath stole my breath away.

"This is an elevation drawing looking from the road." He continued to talk—something about the history of the property and the vision of the original owners—but I wasn't paying much mind. All of my attention was on the home he'd drawn. I recognized the Arts and Crafts style. It was the cottage, but bigger and with a second storey. A flagstone walkway led to wide steps and a big covered veranda that begged for a porch swing and sturdy wicker chairs.

"I love it," I said, then realized I'd interrupted him.

A smile stretched across his face. "This is your vision. I just put it together. The design software did most of it."

"It's perfect. What do you think?" I said, turning to Mom.

"Certainly has the feel of the original, doesn't it?"

"Let me show you the other elevations," Ben said. He turned back the drawing to show us the other sides of the structure. "You don't need to settle on this particular model. There are a number of suitable Craftsman designs. I can help you sort through them, but I don't want to push. You haven't even hired me yet."

"Well, let's fix that. Draw up a contract and I'll take a look."

He straightened. "I'll do that," he said, smoothing back his hair. "In the meantime, I can send you some floorplan layouts."

"I'd like that. Thank you."

"All right. I'll include some pricing to give you an idea of construction costs."

After he left, I couldn't wipe the smile from my face. "I'll have to thank Sebastian. This is exactly what you and I both need right now."

"Is he one of you?" Mom asked.

"Ben? No. He's refreshingly sweet and uncomplicated." The look on Mom's face made me smirk. "You look relieved."

WINGS OF PREY

"Can't blame me, can you?" she said, and we both started laughing. Our laughter grew more animated, and soon we had tears in our eyes. Happy tears. It felt wonderful, as if we'd opened a valve that was releasing the pressure of the past few days.

Later, each with a glass of wine in hand, Mom and I stood over the drawings. "The kitchen in this corner, I think," I said. "Master bedroom here."

She flipped back to the front-porch view. "I can see a nursery right here," she said, pointing to the second floor. Her words drew a surreal line in the sand. She noticed my stillness and looked up, offering me a smile as if it were an invitation. "You can turn it into a bedroom when the little one grows up." I stepped gingerly over the line, and we flipped between the big sheets and reimagined our future.

Chapter Fifteen

The next day marked the seventh day of Mansfield's search. They still hadn't found Dad's wreckage. Sam sent me another Mansfield invoice and checked in.

"How much longer?" I asked.

"They'll finish searching their initial grid today, but they've identified a secondary area outside the original grid. If they find nothing after that, we'll have to regroup. Make a decision."

By the time evening rolled around, Mom had a touch of cabin fever, so we went out for dinner. Our meals hadn't arrived before the barking-dog ringtone sang out. I quickly checked my phone's screen. James had come back. Hope surged through me like adrenalin.

"What is it?" Mom said.

"James is at the condo." I turned my phone to show her. "Sam installed a camera on the rooftop so I could see who's coming and going."

But my elation drained in an instant. "Damn it," I said, and pinched the bridge of my nose. "He doesn't know I had the locks changed." I dialled his number then pulled up the video feed again.

He hadn't yet opened the rooftop door. I watched him pull the phone from his pocket. He looked to see who was calling and immediately scanned his surroundings.

He put the phone to his ear and continued his scan. "Are you clairvoyant now?" He spotted the camera and stared into it. I knew every angle of his face, could feel the stubble on his jaw, the soft dip at the base of his throat.

"No. Just cautious."

"May I come in?"

"I had to change the locks. I'm out with Mom for dinner, but I can be there in ten minutes."

He looked away from the camera. "Don't interrupt your dinner. I'll see you tomorrow."

"Don't go." I cringed at the desperation in my voice.

"I have things to do. I'll see you tomorrow."

He hung up and moved out of the camera's range. I stared at the phone. Mom reached across the table and touched my hand.

"I should have told him about the locks earlier." It occurred to me that I hadn't told him any of it. Not about the break-in. Not about the poisoned milk. It had all happened so fast and at the same time as Cain's calls and Mom's abduction. What a mess.

The next morning was Mom's first appointment with *the shrink*, as she called her. She came out of her room wearing a lemon-yellow dress and beige pumps—an outfit that wouldn't have looked out of place at a church luncheon.

"What do you think?" she said.

"You look very nice, but I don't think the doctor cares what you wear."

"Maybe not, but first impressions are important."

"Would you like me to go with you?"

"No. I need to do this myself."

She took the MGB and I settled in front of my computer studying the floorplans Ben had emailed. He said he'd stop by this morning. I was beginning to understand what he'd said about how difficult it was to get a good feel for drawings on a small computer screen.

My phone rang. I jumped up to get it from the kitchen. It was Colin on the front desk. "Ben Nicolson is here. Shall I send him up?"

"Yes, please," I said. I tidied some dishes away and headed down the hall. Ben's face lit up the moment I opened the door.

He presented me with a contract. It was a preliminary arrangement covering sixty hours of his time.

"If we work well together and you like my work, we can extend the contract through construction."

"I already like your work," I said. "Do you have a pen?"

He pulled one from his pocket. I signed the contract on the coffee table, dated it and returned his pen. "I think we should celebrate."

"What do you have in mind?"

I stood. "How about some crappy champagne? It's been in my fridge for months."

"How can I turn that down? You make it sound so appealing." He followed me into the kitchen and opened the bottle. I dusted off two champagne flutes and he poured.

"To rebuilding the cottage," I said, and tipped my glass into his.

We took our drinks out to the balcony. The breeze felt warm, like a kiss from the summer still to come. "Do you think it'll be ready by Christmas?" I asked.

He laughed. "Not a chance. Maybe this time next year."

I heard my phone ring and excused myself. It was Colin again. "James is on his way up."

For a brief second my spirits soared and I allowed myself to think James might share in our celebration. I let the thought go. Wishful thinking was worse than foolish. It hurt.

I opened the door and invited James in. Though I craved his touch, he maintained a polite distance. He stared at the champagne flute in my hand. "What's the occasion?"

"I'm rebuilding the cottage. Just hired an architect. Come in and I'll introduce you."

He stepped inside tentatively. "I didn't know you were considering rebuilding."

I paused. Had I not told him that either? "Mom suggested it after Molly's baby shower. I didn't give it more thought until Sebastian mentioned an architect he knew who might help me sort out my options."

"Sebastian?" James said.

"On the flight to the caucus."

James followed me down the hall. Ben turned as we approached and I introduced them. James shook his hand and held it longer than necessary and I knew why: he'd be picking through Ben's memories.

James declined a glass of champagne and asked Ben how he'd met Sebastian. An integrity check.

"His realtor recommended me. I did a walk-through with Sebastian and his wife at the Point Grey property before he bought it."

Ben upended his flute. "I must go, and not because of the terrible champagne." I smiled at his good-natured dig while he shook James's hand. "Good to meet you, James."

"I'll walk you out," I said, and we left James on the balcony.

When I returned, James had closed the balcony door and stood inside, stone-faced. "What are you doing?"

"I beg your pardon?"

"I didn't realize Sebastian had started a dating service."

"Ben's an architect, James. Nothing more."

"He's Sebastian's minion."

"Is that what you saw when you shook his hand?"

James stared at me with his hands on his hips. "I found the surrogate. She's a womb for hire. Was implanted ten days ago. Has no idea whose baby she's carrying. She's paid in instalments plus expenses every trimester and gets a nice bonus for a safe delivery. Her house is now bugged as is her phone. I'll keep close tabs on her."

"And when the baby comes. What then?"

"Have you changed your mind about having kids?"

"I never said I didn't want them, James. What the hell is happening to us?"

"You're asking me? I've been gone ten minutes and you let Sebastian set you up on a date?"

"I'm not dating Ben. Can you say the same about Grace?"

"Grace is a colleague. But maybe I should date her. At least she's no one's puppet." He might as well have slapped me across the face. His nostrils flared. He held up his hands. "You're not wearing my earrings. You changed the locks. You didn't need a sledgehammer, Emelynn. I got the message."

"I'm not sending a message and I'm no one's fucking puppet. Ben is not a date. He's an architect. If you looked at his drawings you'd see that. The locks were changed because I had a break-in, and I took the earrings out because you left me, or maybe you just cut off communication. How the hell would I know the difference! And how long do you think I should sit around and wait for you to pick up a phone?"

"Ten minutes would have been nice."

"The caucus was ten *days* ago. Have you changed your mind about the decision I made?"

"No."

"Then I guess none of this matters, does it?"

He stormed past me. I watched him leave and didn't have a word to say to stop him. He thought I'd chosen the Tribunal seat over him, when it was never an either-or decision.

I felt gutted. I dropped to the sofa and couldn't even muster tears.

It was finally sinking in. It was over. I realized then that I'd felt gutted since the day of the caucus, when he'd left me. I loved him, but I had to concede that maybe that cheesy line about love not always being enough had some merit.

When Mom returned, I hadn't moved from the sofa. I donned a smile mask just like hers and asked how her session had gone. She sounded subdued, distracted. She excused herself and went to her room. I dragged out the vacuum and started on the floors.

The condo sparkled by the time I propped my phone against the lamp and fell into bed, but the pain of losing James refused to subside. He'd left a wound too raw to touch, one that required more than time to heal. I retrieved my computer and composed an email to him. It was a goodbye, an apology and an explanation he wouldn't accept but one I had to express. He and I might be done, but I couldn't let it go without telling him that I hadn't chosen the Tribunal over him. That I understood his perspective, how much he and his family loathed the Tribunal I was now a member of. I signed it with love and pressed send. Tomorrow, I'd courier the earrings back to him. He'd want them one day for whoever replaced me.

Morning started earlier than expected with a phone call from Sam.

"Mansfield's found something. They're prepping the sub now."

I jumped out of bed and woke Mom. We sat in our robes at the kitchen island with my phone between us, waiting for Sam's next update. We burned through a pot of coffee and enough banal conversation to bore us both stiff.

I decided to tell Mom about James; get it over with. "James came by yesterday," I said. "If I wasn't sure before, I am now. We're done."

"I'm so sorry, sweetheart."

"It's going to make this baby business a lot more complicated."

"You'll work it out."

"Never thought I'd be a mom in my twenties, let alone a single mom."

"You've got me. I'll be here to help."

"Thanks. You don't happen to know where the switch is that I can flip to stop thinking about him, do you?"

The phone rang. I put Sam on speaker and Mom and I leaned in. "They found it. The call letters appear to match. They're photographing the fuselage for analysis."

"What do you mean by the call letters appear to match?"

"The tail section was separated from the main fuselage. The call letters were severed."

"Do they have a preliminary finding?" Mom asked.

"They're not speculating, or at least not sharing it with me. They're back in the air with the drones looking for the tail section. It could be a while."

"Where was it found?" Mom asked.

"In their secondary search grid. Northeast of their original estimate. I'll email you the coordinates."

"Why was the plane outside of the original grid?"

"Mansfield suggested it could have been a blip in the weather, or drift."

"Did they ... were there ... any bodies?" I asked.

"No. It could be a while before they find the rest of the wreckage. I'll be in touch."

Mom and I took turns showering so we could babysit the phone. I popped bagels in the toaster. "Do you think Sam meant hours or days when he said it could be a while?"

My other phone rang from down in my bedroom. I raced to get it. It was Sebastian.

"Did I interrupt something? You sound out of breath," he said.

"No. I ran for the phone is all." The two-phone shuffle was getting old. "What's up?"

"I spoke with Ben earlier," he said. "You made a good choice."

Though I didn't want to, I heard his words through James's *puppet* filter. "He did a good job on some rough sketches. Our contract is only for some preliminary work."

"That's wise," Sebastian said. "You should probably go through a tender process for the construction. Might get a better price."

I processed Sebastian's words. If Ben were Sebastian's minion, as James had suggested, Sebastian would be pushing him onto me, not suggesting I consider others.

Sebastian continued. "Ben tells me he met James. Does that mean you two have worked things out?"

"James came by to tell me about the surrogate."

"Yes. The final loose end. I'm sure finding her is a relief to both of you."

"Relief? I suppose, but it's a long way from over."

He didn't argue. After we hung up, I decided I'd give Sebastian my new number the next time I talked to him and put an end to the two-phone shuffle.

At dinnertime, Sam called back. We had him on speakerphone. "They found the tail section. I'm sorry to say it, but you were right, Laura. Mansfield's expert says there is no doubt. The plane was blown apart from the inside. The detonation severed the tail section. That's where the luggage was stowed. The explosives were likely in with the baggage."

Mom and I sat in numb silence.

"You two okay?"

"Yeah," I said. "I just ... I can't believe it."

"I can," Mom said.

"Sam, how long until Mansfield can get us a written report?" I asked.

"I'll check into it. You all right, Emelynn?"

"No. Has your research turned up anything else?"

"Nothing that changes my opinion. It was either Jolene or someone who had an interest in the men Jolene was involved with."

"Why are you two still saying *someone*?" Mom said. "We know full well who's responsible. Mason and Stuart Reynolds."

"Get the written report to us as soon as you can," I said. "I want to see the evidence for myself."

After we hung up, Mom stared me down. "You made me a promise."

"I know. I—I need to see that report."

I retreated to my room to escape her scrutiny. The solitude didn't help. What I needed was someone to talk to. Someone who understood the stakes. But I didn't want to talk over the phone. The moment it was full dark, I donned my flying gear.

Mom looked me up and down when she saw me. "Going somewhere?"

"To see Sebastian. Try to get some perspective."

"I know this is the worst possible outcome, Emelynn. And I'm truly sorry."

"Don't be. This result is not what I wanted, but knowing the truth is better than fooling myself. I'll do what needs to be done. Just give me some time, would you?"

I started to leave and stopped myself.

"What is it?" Mom asked.

WINGS OF PREY 165

"There's something else you need to know," I said. "The break-in here wasn't just a B&E. Someone poisoned the milk in the fridge."

Alarm registered on Mom's face. "Is that why there's a police car parked outside day and night?"

I shouldn't have been surprised that she'd noticed. "Yes. But I think whoever did it is one of us."

"A ghost?" Mom said, shifting to the edge of her seat.

"No, a Flier. If they show up on the rooftop, the camera up there will send a signal to my phone," I said, holding up the phone. "I'll call you right away. And if I do, leave the condo immediately."

She nodded and stood, straightening her shoulders. I admired her bravery in light of what she'd been through. I hugged her then headed down the hall and ghosted. Up on the roof, I got my bearings and flew to Sebastian's Point Grey neighbourhood. I landed in deep shadows adjacent to one of his neighbour's eight-foot hedges and texted him my new phone number knowing he wouldn't answer an unknown caller.

He called right away. "Why the new number? What's going on?"

"Something's come up. I need to talk to you."

"We're having a dinner party. Can it wait?"

"No. My father's plane wreckage has been found. It wasn't an accident."

The silence on the other end of the phone told me he understood the implication. "I'm sorry to hear that. I hadn't realized the investigation had been reopened."

"It wasn't. It was a private search."

"You?"

"I had my reasons. I need to talk to you. May I come over?"

"Yes. Give me ten minutes."

I hung up and walked the half block to Sebastian's home. The modern glass-and-concrete structure was the polar opposite of the charming wood-and-stone Craftsman model that Ben had suggested for me. It occurred to me that the differences were reflected in our personalities as well.

At the appointed time, I rounded Sebastian's driveway and walked down the path to his door. He was waiting for me and opened it before I raised my hand to knock. He put his finger to his lips and ushered me down a marble hallway and into the library, where we'd met on another occasion. He snicked the door closed and walked to the far end of the room. I followed.

"Kimberley and our guests are in the dining room. I've excused myself, but I mustn't take too long. Tell me what's happened."

I told him everything: my father's dire warning, Sam's discovery of Jolene's dead lovers, the hiring of Mansfield and finally, their determination that Dad's plane had been blown up. He didn't interrupt but checked the time more than once. When I'd finished, Sebastian walked away with his hands on his hips and stood at a distance staring at the floor. After a moment's contemplation, he dropped his hands to his sides and returned.

"Do you have proof of the sabotage?"

"Mansfield is preparing a report. I haven't seen it yet."

"And you think one of the Reynoldses is responsible?"

"Or Jolene. But I don't think she would have hurt Dad. She loved him."

"I agree. Jolene didn't have it in her to hurt anyone. Stuart and Mason, however? Both are highly trained. Powerful. They were both oddly protective of Jolene. Treated her like she was made of glass. I don't like to think ill of them, but they are the most likely suspects." He crossed his arms and drummed his fingers on his biceps. "Off the top of my head, I couldn't tell you which one of them was on the Tribunal at the time of your father's accident, or which family was leading it, but I can find out. If the Tribunal was involved, there would have been a vote. The Reynoldses may have misled the Tribunal, presented evidence that it was a case of someone learning about us or being careless with our secret. Either would have earned an assassination."

My heart sank. Had Mason and Stuart known about my father's research into the second lens in Fliers' eyes all along? Had they used that to order his death? I fought off tears.

"Do you plan to take your evidence to the Tribunal?"

"Yes. I made a promise to my mother. My father didn't deserve this."

"Do you understand the repercussions of doing so? Does Laura? The penalty for an unsanctioned hit on a Tribunal member's family is a life for a life."

Tears welled. I blinked them away.

Sebastian took my hands in his. "Hold your mother off. It's dangerous for her to get involved any further. I will help you bring this to the Tribunal, but it's going to take a few days to put the pieces together. Can you manage your mother?"

"I think so."

"Good."

The door clicked open. Kimberley called Sebastian's name and poked her head inside. Her eyes opened wide. She slipped inside and shut the door.

"I hadn't realized Emelynn had joined us," she said, staring at our hands. Icicles clung to her words.

Sebastian squeezed my hands before he let go. "We'll sort this out," he said, and turned to his wife. "Couldn't be helped."

Kimberley pinched her lips. "Our company is asking for you."

"Emelynn was just leaving," Sebastian said. "I'll be but a minute. Please let them know I'll be right there."

Kimberley turned on her heel and stomped out.

"I don't know what I've done to offend her," I said. "I didn't mean to cause trouble."

"Kimberley is temperamental. She'll be fine. Let me walk you out."

He opened the library door and I stepped out ahead of him. We heard a toilet flush nearby and a man emerged from a door further down the hall. He spotted us. Sebastian stiffened. The man tilted his head and made the decision to come our way rather than return to the party.

"We wondered what was keeping you," the man said, staring at me from under a furrowed brow.

Sebastian sucked in a breath. "Wade Hofmann, this is Emelynn Taylor."

Wade. I'd heard that name before, but I couldn't remember where. I offered my hand.

Wade squinted as he shook it. "Taylor?" he repeated, as if my name were a curiosity.

"Have we met?" I asked. "You look familiar to me." Something about his face stirred an unsettling memory I couldn't quite grasp.

"We haven't met. But I've seen you." He flashed a flirty smile despite being older than my father would have been. "I saw you at the caucus." I'd met a lot of people at the caucus.

"Emelynn was on her way out," Sebastian said.

"Then I won't keep you. Nice to meet you, Emelynn," Wade said, and his gaze flicked to Sebastian before he turned back the other way. So, Wade was one of us. I wondered if he'd checked in with Avery, which was customary.

On the flagstone outside the front door, Sebastian assured me that he would call the moment he was ready to move forward.

I walked back to the road and turned into the shadows then disappeared into the tree canopy. I flew straight out to the Pacific and took a long, circuitous route home. As the wind tugged at my hair, I tried to reconcile the different versions of Mason and Stuart: supportive uncle, nurturing grandfather, calculating murderers. They were puzzle pieces that would never fit together. I felt their love. I felt the love they had for my father. How could I have felt that if it wasn't real?

I remembered the night I'd met Mason. Even then, it had felt as if he were guiding me. Sure, I'd known he could be deceptive: planting a bug in the crystal case he'd given me, keeping secrets about his family's rocky relationship with Jolene and, most recently, setting me up to wear black at the caucus. But was it malicious? And Stuart supported him at every turn. What did that say about Stuart?

What did it say about me that I could be so completely taken in? And yet I still couldn't harden my heart to either one of them. How long would I live in denial? How long until it sunk in?

Sebastian was right about one thing though. Mason and Stuart were Tribunal, the strongest of our kind, skilled and powerful. They'd be dangerous when they learned about Sam's research and Mansfield's discovery. I hated to think what would happen when I dropped that bomb at the feet of the Tribunal.

Mom had waited up for me. "What did Sebastian have to say?"

"Not a lot. Murder doesn't shock him quite as much as it does the rest of the population. But he did offer to find out who the Tribunal players were at the time of Dad's accident." I caught myself. *Dad's accident.* "Dad's murder," I said, correcting myself.

"That won't change the outcome."

"No, it won't, but I want to know the names of every single person who was involved. If I'm going to avenge Dad's murder, it won't be in half measures."

"It pains me to hear you talk like that. You sound like one of them."

"I am one of them."

Chapter Sixteen

Mom was on her phone when I emerged from my bedroom the next morning. A pot of porridge sat on the stove. Our bowls and the brown sugar were laid out on the counter beside it. I poured a cup of coffee and couldn't help but overhear Mom's conversation in the living room. She was talking to Sam about Mansfield's findings. I topped up her mug and carried the coffee pot back to the kitchen.

As usual, she'd dressed and looked fresh, ready to start the day. I looked as if I hadn't slept and were preparing to crawl back into bed. "Did you learn anything new?" I asked, after she'd hung up.

"The Mansfield Group is demobing."

"Demobing? Is that some secret code?"

She smirked. "Demobilizing. Packing up and heading home. Sam says to tell you Mansfield will send a final invoice that has to be paid before they'll release the report."

We drank our coffee while I watched the news crawl with the TV on mute. Mom scanned the news on her phone.

"Can breakfast wait until I've showered?"

"Sure," Mom said.

"I won't be long." I placed my mug in the kitchen sink and headed back to my room.

I was dressed and combing through wet tangles when my phone rang. It was Colin. "Mason Reynolds is here. Shall I send him up?"

I froze, and my voice caught in my throat. Had Mason found out?

"Emelynn?"

"Of course. Yes. Send him up." I raced out of my bedroom and down the hall.

Mom heard me coming. "Shall I dish—"

"Come with me. Hurry." I tugged her up from the sofa.

"What is it? What's going on?" She had a death grip on her phone but let me lead her at a trot down the hall.

"Mason is on his way up. He may already know about Mansfield. You can't be here." I pulled her into my room and stopped short, darting my gaze around. "Bathroom or closet?"

She stared back at me, stunned.

"Closet," I said, and pushed her toward it. "Hide behind the clothes and stay quiet. Turn the ringer off your phone." I closed the door on her hoping she'd break out of her shock and do as I'd said. I rushed back to her room and closed that door, too. Then I heard Mason's knock.

My heart raced. I could feel the flush in my face. I deliberately slowed my steps and drew deep breaths. I halted in front of the door, schooled my face and took one last breath, then opened it.

"I wasn't expecting you," I said. Mason stood on the threshold with a bakery box in his hands. "Why didn't you tell me you were coming?"

"That's an interesting question, Emelynn. Why didn't you tell me Cain had abducted your mother? I had to hear it from James."

"Why would James—"

Mason cut me off. "Are you going to invite me in?"

I shut up, opened the door wide and established my strongest block. "By all means."

He looked to my mother's closed door as he walked down the hall. "Is she resting?" he asked, and set the bakery box on the coffee table.

"She's not home."

"Will she be back soon?" Disappointment laced his words.

"No. Not for a while."

He bent to the box, picked it up and stepped toward the kitchen.

"What are you doing here?" I asked.

He jerked his head back. "I've come to see your mother and check on you." The furrow on his forehead deepened. "Are you all right?"

"Yes. Of course. Why do you ask?"

"You're acting odd. Which brings me back to my earlier question. What's going on with you? Why didn't you tell me about Cain?"

"I ... it all happened so fast. We're still catching our breath. It slipped my mind."

WINGS OF PREY

Mason frowned. "Slipped your mind? Like the break-in? That's what you want me to believe?"

"It's not as if you could have done anything. James and Sebastian were handling it." He turned for the kitchen again. I rushed behind him and jerked to a stop.

His gaze fell on the bowls Mom had left out. He swivelled his head in my direction and then walked to the stove and lifted the lid off the porridge. He touched his palm to the side of the pot. "Where's your mother?"

"I told you. She's not here."

"You're lying. Shall I go find her and ask her why?"

"No!" I took a breath and closed my eyes. Stupid answer.

"Start talking, Emelynn. What the hell is going on?"

"It's nothing. We—had an argument."

"So why did you say she wasn't home?" He tipped his head, waiting for my answer.

"We weren't expecting company. She's not—dressed." Another stupid answer. I took another breath and gathered my wits. "Listen, this isn't a good time. Why don't you come back later?"

"I'm not going anywhere until you tell me what's got you so rattled."

"I can't."

Again, he tipped his head. "Can't or won't?"

"Does it matter?"

"Is someone threatening you? Your mother?"

"No. Please, just go."

"Damn it, Emelynn!" He stepped forward and I jumped back. He stopped and frowned. He took another step forward and I dashed behind the kitchen island. He straightened. "I am not leaving. You can either tell me why you're reacting like this," he said, waving his finger between us, "or I'll go ask your mother."

I rubbed my face with my hands. He'd boxed me in. "Stay here. I'll be back in a minute, but not if you follow me." I turned to leave then glanced back. He hadn't moved. He raised his hands in submission. I took a chance and darted down the hall. I grabbed Mom's coat and the keys for the MGB then raced to my bedroom closet. She'd crouched in the corner behind a curtain of clothes. I swept them aside and held out her coat, motioning for her to put it on.

"Mason knows you're here. He knows something's up. I've got to get you out of here. Put these on," I said, shoving a pair of my shoes at her. They'd be too big but they'd have to do. She slipped them on. I handed her the wallet with Megan Fairchild's ID. "I'm going to hold your hand. When I ghost, you'll ghost too, and then I'm taking us down to the parkade." She swallowed. "You'll be fine." I took her hand. "You with me?" She nodded.

I squeezed my crystal and ghosted. Mom began to fade and she yelped. I shushed her and pushed us through the closed bedroom door then out the front door into the hallway.

"Ready?" I whispered. She didn't answer. I blasted us through the elevator doors and down the shaft to the basement and a corner I knew was blind to the security cameras. I dropped her hand and re-formed. When she materialized, she'd lost the colour in her face. Her breaths came fast and shallow.

"Breathe," I said, grabbing hold of her shoulders. She nodded wordlessly. "Get in the car and drive. There's a couple hundred dollars cash in the wallet. I'll phone you when Mason is gone."

"Be careful."

"I will. He can't touch me when I ghost. I'll be fine. Now go."

I waited until she'd started the engine then ghosted and returned to the condo. I found Mason in the kitchen right where I'd left him.

"Did you get your mother away safely?"

The kitchen walls closed in. I walked out of there and into the living room. Mason followed. He rounded the sofa, sat on the edge of it and leaned forward.

I checked my block and didn't take my eyes off him.

"Dad's plane wreckage has been found. It wasn't an accident. Someone blew up his plane."

Anger clouded Mason's features. "Who?"

The words dried up in my throat. Mason leapt to his feet and I recoiled.

He leaned forward. "Tell me," he said, raising his voice. I opened my mouth but nothing came out.

I balled my fists.

He straightened and a look of confusion came over him. "You think it was me?" I remained silent, ready to ghost. "You think I killed Brian? Are you mad?"

"Dad warned Mom. He told her your family was powerful. That if something was to happen to him she was to take me and run."

"Brian was a big brother to me." Mason took a step forward.

I took a step back. "Don't do this," I said.

A pained expression clouded his features. "I loved your father. Mom and Dad loved your father. We were devastated when he and Jolene lost their son."

"Your family never wanted Jolene to marry outside of our kind."

Mason frowned. "Where are you getting this crap from?"

"Your father wanted her to marry a Flier."

"Because it was safer for her, but he never interfered with her choices. Ever."

"What happened to the man from Greece she was going to marry?"

"Nick? He drowned. Losing him plunged Jolene back into depression. We thought we were going to lose her as well."

"And years later, Jolene's fiancé from New York?"

"What fiancé?"

Ah, perhaps she'd learned her lesson by then and wasn't sharing the happy news. Hadn't helped, though. "His name was Arthur Curtis. He committed suicide."

Mason took a step back and sat again. He dropped his head in his hands.

"And then my dad's plane blew up. That's three for three. A clean sweep of every non-Gifted man Jolene ever loved."

Mason didn't speak and I didn't move.

"I didn't kill your dad or the others, and neither did my father."

"You've lied to me before."

Mason whipped his head up.

"If you presented a case against my father to the Tribunal, I'll find out about it."

"We didn't. We didn't attend the Tribunal the year your father died. I remember because it was the year my mother had her stroke. The same year Jolene disappeared. Hard to forget a year like that. We gave our seat's proxy to Ruby Church. She was Rachael Warner's aunt. You can check."

"I will. But that doesn't mean you or Stuart didn't have my father killed."

"Who filled your head with this vile garbage?"

"I want you to leave."

His shoulders slumped. He looked up, resigned. "You are being misled. I suggest you look carefully at the motives of whoever is feeding you your information. I would predict if you accused them of what you're accusing me, you wouldn't still be standing."

He ghosted and within moments his aura was gone. My knees gave out and I dropped into the chair behind me. The receding adrenalin left me shaking.

I prayed Mason didn't find out Sam was behind the investigation. And now that Mason knew, I'd have to act quickly. But first, I needed to be sure Mom was safe. I found my phone and called her.

"Emelynn?"

"It's me," I said. "He's gone. I'm okay."

"Oh, thank god. I've been so worried."

"Where are you?"

"UBC. Koerner Library."

"Stay there. I'm on my way."

I threw together an overnight bag for her and ghosted out of the condo. I re-formed inside the library and found her at her old cubicle, on the lowest level of the building. She sat in her chair with her coat on, clutching the wallet I'd given her. She jumped up when she saw me and we embraced. When her shoulders finally relaxed, I pulled away. None of the other desks in the study room were occupied. I closed the door.

"Here," I said, and set her bag on the counter. "Should be enough for a few days. Buy whatever else you need."

"What happened?"

"I told Mason about the sabotage. He didn't give me a choice. He denies he had anything to do with Dad's acci—murder."

"Of course he does," Mom said.

"He'll be searching for the evidence to destroy it."

"You can't let him do that."

"I won't. But I can't be fighting Mason and worried about you at the same time. I need to know you're safe."

"What can I do?" she asked.

"Don't go back to the condo and don't come back here. Take a taxi downtown. Get the cabbie to drop you near the Sinclair Centre and find a hotel. There are lots around there. Any one but the Hotel Vancouver." I took my wallet from her hand and pulled out the Megan Fairchild ID and credit card. "Check in using this ID and credit card. Text me when you're settled but don't text the name of the hotel. I'll be able to find you."

"How long?"

"Give me three days. If you don't hear from me, call Sam. If you have to leave a message, don't use your name. Use the name on this ID, Megan Fairchild. If you have to go out, change coats. Pick up a hat or scarf, wear sunglasses."

"What are you going to do?"

"I'm going to get my hands on Mansfield's report. Make sure Sam is out of the line of fire."

"Be safe, sweetheart."

"I intend to. Don't take your usual exit out of here. Find another one and leave right away. I love you, Mom."

I took the keys to the MGB and walked out the main entrance. On the way to the car, my phone buzzed. A message had come in. It was from Mason—a contact number for each of the nine Tribunal Novem members. He hadn't prefaced it with a note.

The moment I got in the car, I called Sam. "You at home?" I asked. He said he was. "I need Mansfield's report."

"They haven't sent their invoice."

"I don't care about an invoice. Call them. Get a price and I'll send them their money. I'll explain when I get to your place. I'm on my way now."

When Sam opened his door, his gaze skirted around me before he invited me in. It wasn't until he'd closed the door that I noticed he had his gun in his hand. He shoved it back in its holster. I followed him to the living room. Sam's townhome had been one of the show suites decorated à la Martha Stewart. He kept it neat, but the décor didn't fit his no-nonsense personality.

"I can't reach anyone from Mansfield," he said. "They're probably on a flight by now."

"Damn it!"

"What is it?"

"Mason knows Dad's plane crash wasn't an accident." I laid out what had happened. "It won't take him long to find out Mansfield was conducting the search," I said. "We have to get Mansfield's report before he destroys it."

"I have no other way to contact them. They closed down the live feed from the ship yesterday. We're going to have to hang tight until they get in touch."

"Have you tried through their website?"

"The website contact is Peter Caulfield, and I've already left him a message. Mansfield is a small operation."

"I don't think you're safe here, Sam. Mason might retaliate if he learns you had a role in this."

Sam heaved a sigh. "I hear that hammock calling my name."

"You should go. Today."

"No. Not until we get that report. I'm safe as long as you're within touching distance." He looked at me with a wry smile.

Though I didn't say it, it felt good to have someone like Sam in my corner. We retreated to his den and he checked on the flights out of Prince Rupert, where Mansfield had chartered its ship.

"They're flying commercial. It's a two-hour flight to Vancouver, and they have a connection there." He checked the time. "If they're in the air now, they'll be landing at three o'clock. Let's hope they check their messages between flights."

I pulled out my phone. "I have to tell Sebastian. He's going to be pissed I've tipped off Mason." Sam nodded and I dialled. "That's strange. No answer." I left Sebastian a message a heartbeat before another thought formed. "Oh no! What if Mason thinks Sebastian is behind this? He probably went straight there. I should have called Sebastian right away."

"Or he's on the toilet. Give him a minute."

"No. He would have picked up no matter what. I need to get to him."

"To do what?" Sam said.

"What if Sebastian or Kimberley are lying on the floor? This is my doing. I need to check on them."

Sam slowly nodded. "All right. But you're not going anywhere without me."

"Then let's go."

We took Sam's vehicle, and for once it wasn't one owned by the Vancouver Police Department. He drove a gun-metal-grey Ford pickup. We parked half a block from Sebastian's home. "Give me an hour. I probably won't be that long, but I don't want you coming in there. You can't defend yourself against these people."

"I haven't forgotten," Sam said. "But if you don't come out of there in an hour, I'll be calling every news outlet in the city for the story of the century."

I cracked my window. "I'll see you soon," I said, and blinked out of sight. I squeezed out the window and drifted across the street and down the block. As I sifted through one of the neighbour's hedges, a black BMW sports car raced far too fast into Sebastian's driveway. It squealed to a stop at the front door. The man who emerged was Wade Hofmann. He looked like someone who'd just had his car keyed. As he approached the front door, he did a surreptitious 360-degree sweep of his surroundings then ghosted.

I started, momentarily taken aback by the brashness of it. I followed him inside. He had re-formed and was strutting toward the back of the house calling Kimberley's name. She came down a staircase he'd already passed. I never thought I'd be relieved to see Kimberley looking so well.

"Wade. What are you doing here?"

He turned to face her. "Looking after my interests. How big is this mess your husband's cleaning up?"

"He wouldn't say, but it's got him scrambling." And too busy to answer his phone. Kimberley crossed her arms. "How did you find out?"

"He put me on notice. Told me it's Tribunal. Sanctioned. Wouldn't elaborate. What do you know?"

"I think it's Mason Reynolds. When Emelynn Taylor was here the other night I overheard some of their conversation."

"Mason Reynolds? Ah, that is music to my ears." Wade rubbed his hands together as if a perfectly grilled steak had been laid in front of him.

It hit me then: Wade Hofmann had shaved off his goatee. He was the assassin from the caucus ... and Sebastian was lining him up to kill Mason! I wished I hadn't figured that out.

"No wonder Sebastian wasn't anxious to tell me who the target was. One less ace up his sleeve." Wade crowded Kimberley but she didn't back away. "Doesn't solve your little problem though, does it? I'm surprised you haven't taken matters into your own hands."

"You think I haven't tried?"

Haven't tried? What was she talking about?

"Well, well. Tell you what." He brushed a blonde curl off her cheek. "You round up those photographs Sebastian's holding over my head and I'll make that little problem of yours go away."

Kimberley kept her arms tightly crossed. "Even if I could, Sebastian's got copies. I'd never find them all."

"That's a pity. If you change your mind, you know my price." His flirty smile nauseated me. He stepped back. "No need to let Sebastian know I dropped by." He winked at her and then walked straight to the front door and let himself out.

Kimberley stayed in place, closed her eyes and took a deep breath. It sounded to me as though she was working against Sebastian. And what little problem did she need to solve? Wade had made it sound like an assassin could take care of it. Was the problem a person? Me, perhaps? I knew it irritated her that her husband had chosen to mentor me, but it was hardly a big enough offence to warrant killing me. Still, could she be the one behind the B&E at my condo? The poisoned milk?

Kimberley retreated up the stairs. What were the photos Sebastian had on Wade? Wade had been a dinner guest the night Sebastian introduced me. I'd thought they were friends, but now I wasn't so sure. And Wade's car—the black BMW—I'd seen that car here before, too, earlier in the spring on one of my runs. Maybe entertaining assassins came with the job of Tribunal leader.

Nothing about Kimberley's conversation with Wade sat well with me. I wondered if the answers lay in the photographs Sebastian was using to manipulate Wade. If Sebastian was keeping the photographs in the house, they'd likely be in a safe. Fortunately, Sebastian's mentoring had included how to locate safes.

I checked the library first and then the formal dining room. No results. I swept around the great room at the rear of the house and the open-concept kitchen adjacent, and then I skirted the rest of the main floor. The furnishings were modern and perfectly in tune with the clean lines of their home. I'd have complimented Kimberley on a job well done if I weren't currently wondering if she wanted me dead.

Continuing the search upstairs in the master suite was the logical next step, but the idea of entering Sebastian and Kimberley's private quarters made my skin crawl. However, short of abandoning the search and any hope of finding possible answers, I had no choice. At the top of the stairs, I found their bedroom door open. New-age music drifted out from another doorway down the hall. I followed the music and found Kimberley in a room that had been adapted into a yoga studio. She sat cross-legged in a meditation pose.

I left her and returned to the master bedroom. The sparsely furnished main room held no safe. Nor did I find the rack of whips I half expected. But the expansive dressing room coughed up the prize, a built-in model, camouflaged behind a rack of hanging clothes.

If Sebastian had taught her the tricks he'd taught me, I'd never fool her into opening it, but I had to give it a try. I pushed the garments aside to expose the safe, opened the dressing-room door and then passed back out of their bedroom and into the hall. I re-formed and slammed the bedroom door closed then ghosted again.

Kimberley burst out of her yoga studio and stopped short, gazing toward the closed door. She called out Sebastian's name and moved tentatively toward the bedroom. With her hand on the handle, she stopped to listen then slowly turned it. She peeked inside. "Sebastian, are you home?" When she got no answer, she pushed the door open and scanned the room, stopping at the open dressing-room door. "Wade, is that you?" She approached it with caution. Kimberley wasn't a Ghost; she wouldn't be able to sense one. Finally, she stepped inside. She saw the safe and immediately checked to see if it was open.

With a furrowed brow, she started moving the clothes hangers back into place. I thought I'd run out of luck, but then something changed her mind and she shoved the hangers aside again. She punched in the code, opened the safe and immediately pulled out a manila envelope. She flipped through the contents and sighed with relief. With a shake of her head, she returned the envelope to the safe, reset it and pulled the hangers back in place in front of it.

I waited until she disappeared into her yoga studio again before I returned to the dressing room and re-formed. I punched in her code, opened the safe and retrieved the envelope. Inside were several five-by-seven surveillance photos of a man I didn't recognize. I took out my phone and snapped photos of them all. In some he had a beard; in others, he was clean-shaven. His hairstyle varied as well. One of the photos—a studio portrait—showed him as a young man.

When I finished, I returned the envelope to the safe, reset it and arranged the hangers the way Kimberley had left them. I then ghosted and got the hell out of there.

When I got back to Sam's truck, he had his notepad out and a pair of binoculars on the dash.

"I'm back," I said, warning him before I re-formed.

"Who was the visitor?"

"Wade Hofmann. Stuart told me he's an assassin. Is that his licence plate?" I asked, nodding to the number he'd jotted on his notepad.

"Yeah. Wouldn't hurt to know a little more about him. What'd you learn?"

"Kimberley is alive and well. She told Wade that Sebastian was out. She didn't elaborate, but I got an earful from Wade and Kimberley's conversation."

After I told him what I'd heard, Sam said, "I wonder if Kimberley can account for her whereabouts during the time of your break-in? Do you have a photo of her?"

"No. I had one, but it's in my room at Cairabrae." A room I'd never set foot in again.

"Shouldn't be too difficult to get another one. Wouldn't hurt to put a bug in Ortez's ear. Maybe she'll show up on camera somewhere she shouldn't have been."

"We need Sebastian," I said. "Please don't piss him off."

Sam furrowed his brow in concentration. "If she's working against Sebastian, I'm doing him a favour. But don't worry, Sebastian will never know who brought Kimberley to Ortez's attention. Remember that charity event you attended last year? The one in the Cooper brothers' case?"

"At Cecil Green House?"

"That's the one. Ortez is, no doubt, looking into your acquaintances. As I recall, Sebastian and Kimberley attended that event. There'll be official photos and plenty of candid shots."

"Good thinking! You're unusually clever for a civilian."

"Yeah. Should have been a detective," he said with a wry smile. "Show me those photos you took." I pulled them up on my phone and passed it to him. "You know him?"

"No, and there was no name on the envelope or the back of the photos."

"Send them to me. I'll call in a favour—now there's a line I never thought I'd use." He shook his head. "If he's known to police, facial recognition will ID him."

Chapter Seventeen

Despite my objections, we drove back to Sam's place. He needed his computer and bristled at the notion of going into hiding. I followed him to the den. He fired up his computer, got on his phone and sweet-talked someone on the other end into helping us ID the man in the photos. He sent off the portrait shot; it was the sharpest of all of them.

Though I was tempted, I didn't call Sebastian again. I'd already left him a message. I told myself I didn't want to distract him, that he'd call when he could, but guilt about handing Kimberley to Ortez was part of my reluctance.

We moved to the living room and Sam plopped into a worn recliner that appeared to be the only piece of furniture he'd brought to the decorating party.

"Mason sent me contact details for the Tribunal members. I should call one of them. See if he was lying to me about the year my dad died."

"You do that. You hungry?"

"Starved." I thought of Mom's pot of porridge gone cold on the stove at home. Sam extracted himself from the recliner and walked back to his kitchen. I watched him pop open the fridge door and lean on it, staring inside.

I scrolled through the names on Mason's list and stopped at Ron Evans. I felt as if Ron and I had connected at the caucus. I texted him my name and number and asked him to call me as soon as he could.

Minutes later, he called. "Emelynn. Good to hear from you. How are you?"

After we exchanged pleasantries, I got to the point of my call. "Do you recall a time when a Tribunal seat was vacated and a proxy given to another member?"

"Surely you're not ditching us already, are you?"

"No. That's not why I'm asking."

"All right. Yeah, it happens. Carrie and Rachael gave their proxies to one another from time to time. Ivy has given a standing proxy to Sebastian. Why are you asking?"

"Do you recall a time when the Reynoldses vacated their seat?"

"No, but I can ask my father. He served for twenty years before I stepped in. Somehow I can't imagine the Reynoldses giving anyone their vote. It's about as likely as Sebastian Kirk giving up his."

"Would you check with your father? It's important. And one other thing: is a record kept of what the Tribunal votes on?"

"Sure. There's a ledger. Sebastian would have passed it to Mason at the caucus." I remembered Sebastian had arrived at the caucus carrying an oversized book along with the sceptre. Great! I thought. By now, Mason will have erased any evidence from it.

I thanked him again and we hung up. I looked over to the kitchen. "The Tribunal's ledger of recorded votes is in Mason's hands. I'm trying very hard not to jump to conclusions over here." What was Mason thinking? That I wouldn't check?

"Assumptions will lead you astray," Sam said. "Follow the evidence." He stood in front of his stove with a spatula in his hand. "Get the pickles out of the fridge, would you?"

He'd made grilled cheese sandwiches. I set out plates and added dill pickles to both and a blob of ketchup to mine. "Want a beer?" Sam said, opening the fridge and snagging a bottle.

"No, thanks." I'd never developed a taste for beer. We took our plates to the table. A text came in from my mother. I glanced at my phone. "Mom's safe. For now, anyway."

I was at the sink playing Molly Maid when Sam's phone rang. His body language told the story. He massaged his forehead and then ran his hand over his brush cut. "What the hell happened?" He listened for a moment. "You have it backed up, right?" He listened again. "Good. Let me know when you have it."

He stuffed his phone in his pocket. "That was Peter Caulfield. Someone rifled through the Mansfield Group's baggage. It arrived in Vancouver missing a critical component: the hard drive with the data from their search for your dad's wreckage. Peter spent the last hour with YVR authorities, who guaranteed him the baggage had been secured and under surveillance on the tarmac. They reviewed the surveillance film. No one touched their baggage."

"No one they could see. I guess we know now where Mason's been hanging out. Damn! Did I hear you say Mansfield's data is backed up somewhere?"

"Yeah, they uploaded it before they left the ship. They're catching a connecting flight and will recover it when they get back to their office."

"So we're back to waiting?"

"Afraid so."

An hour later, Ron Evans called me back. "I stand corrected. Dad recalls that Stuart bowed out for a while after his wife suffered a stroke, ten or fifteen years ago. He doesn't remember who got Stuart's proxy."

A part of me felt disappointed. Mason's treachery would have been easier to accept on top of another lie. "Okay. Thanks for your help."

"If you don't mind me asking, why is this important?"

"I'm trying to get to the bottom of something is all I can say right now."

Before we hung up, Ron promised to help in any way he could.

"Looks like Mason was telling the truth about his family's absence from the Tribunal the year Dad's plane crashed. Not that it changes anything. Just because they didn't know about a sanctioned hit on my father, or vote to support one, doesn't mean they didn't do it."

Sam found a baseball game on television. The boys of summer had been at it for two hours before his phone rang again. The end of the conversation I was privy to did not sound positive. By the time Sam hung up, I knew Mansfield hadn't been able to retrieve the data.

"What happened?" I asked.

"They were able to download the files from their backup site, but they'd been overwritten with garbage. Whoever did it hadn't been able to erase the files, so they corrupted them. Peter is doing all he can to recover the data, but he's doubtful. He wants to know if we care to involve the police."

"There's no point. If Mason is determined to cover his tracks, the police won't be able to stop him."

"For what it's worth, the wreckage is still there. Peter has the coordinates and a photo of the partial call letters on the main fuselage in his notes."

Our heads snapped up at a knock on his door. "Are you expecting someone?" I asked.

He stood. "No, but they're knocking. That's got to be a good sign." Regardless, he pulled out his gun and motioned for me to follow him.

Sam stood to the right of the door with his gun down by his thigh. I stood to the left, slipped my hand over his in case we needed to ghost, and kept out of sight as he wedged opened the door.

Sam didn't say a word. It was Sebastian's voice I heard. "Did you think we didn't know where you lived? You were thoroughly vetted before you ever started working with Emelynn."

I pulled the door open and showed myself.

"I thought I might find you here," Sebastian said.

"Why don't you come in," Sam said. He wasn't smiling.

Sebastian stepped inside and addressed Sam. "I think it's time we stopped the pretense that you don't know who or what I am."

"Let's not," Sam said. "It's better for my health if I don't know." He turned and led the way down the hall to the living room.

"You got my message?" I asked Sebastian as we trailed behind Sam.

"Yes. Where is your mother?"

"She's safe," I said. "Where were you?"

"Indisposed."

Sam once again sat down in the recliner.

Sebastian took a seat on the sofa. I sat opposite him. "The groundwork is in place to bring your case forward to the Tribunal. Naturally, with an allegation as serious as an unsanctioned hit on a Tribunal member's family, I'll need to review your evidence in advance. If it's satisfactory, I'll trigger the meeting as soon as you're ready."

I dropped my head in my hands.

"What is it?" Sebastian said. "Have you changed your mind?"

"No. Dad's plane was blown up, I just can't prove it. The hard drive containing the data was stolen from Mansfield's baggage and their backup files are useless."

Sebastian leaned forward. "Surely they've got some way to recreate their findings?"

"Short of returning to the site of the wreck, no," I said.

Sebastian's face hardened. "You can't expect me to condemn another Tribunal member without solid proof, Emelynn. It would be suicide. How soon can this group get back out to the site?"

"I don't know," I said. "I'm not even sure they'd be willing to go back now that they know someone doesn't want the wreckage found."

"I'm sure Mason will be happy to hear that," Sebastian said, tipping his head with an air of superiority. He stood. "You should never have told him. It was a mistake. One you'll have to live with."

"There's got to be another way to prove he killed my father." I wanted to scream in frustration.

Sam rose from his chair. "We've got nothing more than a loose collection of facts and three deaths surrounding Jolene, none of which have been ruled homicides. Circumstantial at best."

Sebastian looked down at me. "That's not nearly enough. I'm sorry, Emelynn. Find another way to prove it, and I'll do all I can to help."

With frightening clarity, another thought occurred to me. "Mason's going to hunt me down."

Sebastian swept away my fear with a swipe of his hand. "You're no threat to Mason without evidence of his guilt. It's a harsh introduction to life on the Tribunal, Emelynn. You and Mason may be enemies now, but enemies abound in our circles. Ask for his forgiveness and keep him close. If there's a silver lining to this fiasco, at least now we know we can't trust him."

Sebastian headed for the hall and Sam walked him out. How would I ever explain this to Mom?

When Sam returned, he went straight to the fridge for another beer. "Is he gone?"

I did a quick check. "Yeah. He's not here."

"He is one cold, calculating son of a bitch."

"I'll never ask for Mason's forgiveness. Not knowing what I know. This can't be over. I have to talk Peter Caulfield into going back out there."

"Do you think that's wise? You'd be putting his team in someone's crosshairs."

Sam's phone dinged. He took it out and looked at it. "It's Dino from the station. He's found a match for the photo." I'd met Dino before. Sam scrolled and paused. "Well now, isn't this interesting."

Sam passed me his phone. The photo Dino had sent had an Interpol stamp across the top and the name Otis Hofmann printed across the bottom. There was no doubt the image was the same man from Sebastian's stash of photos.

"Hofmann? This is Wade's brother. Stuart told me Wade killed a brother. I wonder if he has more than one?" I handed Sam his phone.

He starting dialling and walked back to his den. I heard him address Dino.

I found the studio portrait of Otis Hofmann on my phone, sent it to Ron Evans and then dialled his number.

"Hello, Emelynn."

"I need your help again. I've sent you a photo of a man. Do you know who he is?"

"Just a minute," he said. "Got it. Where'd you get this?"

"I can't say. Do you know him?"

"Sure. Everyone knows him, or knew him. His name was Otis Hofmann. He's one of only a handful of Ghosts the Tribunal has ever ordered assassinated. My father told me about him. His own brother took him out."

"When?"

"Geez. You're testing my memory today. Ten years ago, maybe more."

"What did Otis Hofmann do to earn that sentence?"

"He'd been testing the Tribunal's resolve for years, stealing major works of art. We're talking the Louvre, the Met, the British Museum. High profile. The thefts were risky. Outrageous. Authorities actually have his face on film. The final straw came when the police uncovered a ring of Fliers helping Otis fence the stolen art."

"Do you know if the Tribunal ordered Otis's gift ... reassigned?" I couldn't think of another way to say it. James had told me the Tribunal had a history of stripping the accused of their gift before they were executed.

"Interesting you should ask that question. Strangely, no. They didn't. It was the one condition his brother insisted upon when he took the contract. Still, taking money to kill your own brother? The man has no conscience."

"Yeah. Thank you, Ron. I appreciate the information."

"If you don't mind me saying, you don't want to be messing with these people, Emelynn. Wade Hofmann is trouble."

"So it seems. Thanks again."

Sam returned shortly after I disconnected. "Dino tells me Otis Hofmann was found barbecued in his car seventeen years ago."

"That's not possible," I said. I pulled out my phone and flipped through the photos I'd taken. "Here. He's getting into an SUV. Sure doesn't look seventeen years old to me."

Sam took the phone from me. "You're right. That's a Lincoln MKX. Not more than three years old."

"Wade didn't kill his brother after all," I said. "Sebastian knows it, and from these photos, he's known it for a while."

"That's what Sebastian's holding over Wade. But why hasn't he turned Wade in to the Tribunal?"

"Maybe he wants an assassin in his pocket. He did say enemies are plentiful in our circles."

"Or they're playing a game of chicken," Sam said. "Maybe Wade's got something on Sebastian."

"Do you have Wade's address?"

"His vehicle is registered to a numbered company, but Dino dug down and got me an address. How about we take a drive?"

"Why not? One break-in a day is hardly enough to keep my skills up." I stood. "Let's go."

Wade lived in a posh condo on West Hastings Street. Parking proved impossible. Sam pulled into a loading zone.

"Do you know how to sweet-talk your way out of a ticket?" I teased. His dead-pan stare drew a laugh out of me. I ducked down in case anyone was watching then blinked out of sight.

I made my way into Wade's building through the glass front doors and headed to the elevator shaft. Once inside, I rose to the sixteenth floor and poked out into the carpeted hall. Elegant wall sconces threw dim light across the floor. Six-inch moulding framed each door. Wade's unit was 1607. I pushed through his door and found myself in an entry hall that opened into a spacious living room.

Wade's voice drifted from a room to my left. I made a quick circuit of the living room and pantry and found no mail, nothing to hide a safe behind and very little food. With Wade still occupied elsewhere, I re-formed in the kitchen and quietly opened cupboard doors. Most were empty. It was as if he didn't live here. The bedroom and bathroom to the right of the living room were likewise void of anything more telling than a receipt. Which left the room Wade occupied—another bedroom, no doubt.

Even though I knew he couldn't sense me, being in ghosted form around him still unnerved me. He lay on the bed with his cellphone to his ear. Fortunately, he was dressed. Unfortunately, he was caressing his crotch. He flirted with whoever was on the other end of the phone, laughing softly and coercing the person to join him. It gave me the creeps. A little like watching Hannibal Lecter talking to Clarice Starling.

"I'll make it worth your while," he said. "Promise."

I checked the wall behind the bed, where a large painting hung. Nothing there. Nothing on top of the dresser.

"Blow him off," Wade said. "He's got nothing on me."

The ensuite was surprisingly clean.

"Tomorrow then," he said. "I'll meet you at the Bayshore. Let's say eight o'clock. Drinks then dinner then me."

I checked the walk-in closet and came up empty-handed. Expecting pay dirt twice in one day was perhaps overly optimistic. Time to go, I thought, and pushed back into Wade's bedroom.

He leapt up off his bed. "Bimbo better be worth my time," he mumbled, stuffing his phone in his pocket.

If only I could have warned the poor woman. Instead, I got out of there as quickly as I could.

"It's just me," I said, as I re-formed in Sam's passenger seat.

Sam reached down and started the engine. "What'd you find?"

"Not a thing. I don't think he lives there. There's nothing personal lying around and it's too clean."

"Not a bad set-up. Guess the killing business still pays well," Sam said.

"Checking his place was worth a shot, but we're no further ahead. We've still got nothing."

"It's late. How about we call it a night and tackle it fresh in the morning?"

Sunshine wouldn't fix this, I thought, but it was late. "Your place or mine?" I said. Sam swung his head in my direction. Surprise and confusion warred for top billing on his face. "I need to be within touching distance of you, remember?"

His brow smoothed and he nodded. "You could try to not look so relieved," I said.

He laughed, did a shoulder check then pulled out.

We stopped for Thai takeout and ended up back at Sam's. "I have better beer," he told me. After our late dinner, I stretched out on his sofa with the pillow and blanket he'd given me. He took the recliner, swearing it wouldn't be the first time he'd slept in it.

Chapter Eighteen

The night was relatively restful, considering the bed and the number of Ghosts we'd pissed off. As the sun rose, I left Sam snoring softly and went to the bathroom. He'd put out a facecloth and toothbrush for me. Like a Best Western, I thought with a smile that faded as frustration with my predicament settled in again.

When I returned to the living room, Sam was leaning on the open refrigerator door. He'd changed his shirt.

"You're up," I said.

"You know you mumble in your sleep?"

I raised a doubtful eyebrow.

He shut the refrigerator door. "There's a restaurant around the corner that serves breakfast."

We headed outside. Tall yellow irises bloomed in a garden bed along the way. Soon summer would be here. I longed for warmer nights to fly to my heart's content.

Inside the restaurant, Sam nodded a greeting to the waiter and walked to the back of the room. He seated himself beside the fire exit, his back to the wall. He'd obviously been here a time or ten. The waiter brought over two coffees. "How are you today, Detective?" Sam didn't correct him. He ordered eggs. I ordered French toast. I stirred cream in my coffee and savoured my first sip.

"I've been thinking," Sam said. "Even if we had the report from Mansfield, what have we really got? Three of Jolene's lovers died. We might make a case that two of the deaths are suspicious, but none of them can be definitively tied back to the Reynoldses. It's only your mother's testimony about your father's warning that makes the connection, and that conversation occurred twenty-odd years ago."

"What are you saying?"

"I know you promised your mother you'd take this to the Tribunal if the crash turned out to be sabotage, but even if the Mansfield Group were able to recover their data, we don't have enough evidence to determine anyone's guilt."

"Then we need to find another connection. Something that ties my father's death to the Reynoldses."

"No. We need to find something that ties your father's death to his murderer. Keep your mind open or you'll overlook the clues that don't confirm what you believe."

I took a deep breath. "Confirmation bias. Mom talks about that in relation to her research. Okay. I'll keep my mind open. Where do we start?"

"With Wade Hofmann. He's in the right profession, has the right connections and something doesn't add up about his relationship with Sebastian and Kimberly. I'd like to stir that up. See what happens." Sam frowned. "What the hell are you finding so funny?"

"Do you remember when we first met? You were investigating a string of missing persons. You employed the same tactics back then. Stirring up shit. Only that time, I was on the pointy end of your stir stick."

Sam smiled. "Yeah, now that you mention it. Feels like a lifetime ago."

"Do you ever wish you'd never learned about us?"

He didn't answer right away, just stared down at the napkin in his hands. "What I experienced the night you ghosted me out of that helicopter, what I witnessed, changed me. It made me realize I'd worn blinkers my whole life. I don't want to wear those blinkers ever again. I'm glad I know."

"Me too. I can't imagine going through this without you. We make a good team. You might even be rubbing off on me—I know something we can use to stir up shit with Wade." I picked up my coffee cup and Sam made an impatient rolling motion with his hand that made me laugh.

"When I was in Wade's place last night, he was talking to some woman on the phone. Told her he'd meet her tonight at eight o'clock at the Bayshore Hotel. Maybe I should intercept him."

We walked back to Sam's place after breakfast and worked out a plan. I'd need to go home to collect a suitable outfit—something to get and hold Wade's attention while I planted the seeds that might bring Sam and me closer to the truth about my father's murder.

Sam drove me to my condo and parked a half block away from the cruiser. "That used to be me," he said. "He thinks he sees what's going on, but he hasn't a clue."

"Give me fifteen minutes," I said, and ghosted. I drifted down the street and into the condo building then up the staircase. Elevator shafts were faster, more direct, but staircases were less intimidating, and cleaner. Once in the condo, I re-formed and turned off the alarm. I did a quick walk-through. Everything seemed in order. The pot of cold porridge still sat on the stove. The two cereal bowls and dish of brown sugar remained where my mother had set them.

It felt impossible that it was just yesterday morning I'd accused Mason to his face of killing my father. I remembered Sam's warning. Had I already applied confirmation bias? For the first time since Mansfield had made their finding, I let myself consider that maybe it wasn't Mason. The hope that swelled hurt like hell. I cut it off before it crippled me. As long as the possibility that Mason could be guilty existed, I had to be strong. My father deserved nothing less.

I put the bowls and sugar away and fed the congealed mat of oatmeal to the garburator then washed up the pot. In my bedroom, I sorted through my options and picked out a simple black dress with a deep-V front and a pair of stilettos that were torture to wear but would keep Wade's attention. I grabbed my makeup bag, reset the alarm and ghosted back to Sam's truck.

"Get everything you need?"

"Right here," I said, looking to my bag. He put the truck in gear and we headed to his place with the dull prospect of an entire day of waiting ahead of us. Mom was on my mind again as we approached Burrard Street.

"Do you feel like going downtown and finding Mom? It's not yet been three days, but I'm sure she'd appreciate knowing I'm all right."

"Good idea," Sam said, and he pulled into the turn lane.

I took out my phone and searched for a list of downtown hotels. Starting from the top, I dialled each one and asked to speak to a guest by the name of Megan Fairchild. On the fourth call, I got a hit.

"She's at the Pan Pacific," I said, and waited for my call to be connected. When she picked up, I brushed off the barrage of questions, asked for her room number and told her we were on our way.

"How's she sound?" Sam asked.

"Anxious."

"On the off-chance one of your Ghost buddies is following us, let's not give her location away."

He chose a parkade near Waterfront Station, blocks away from the hotel. "I'll play decoy. There's a cigar shop around the corner. I'll be there if you're looking for me. Otherwise, I'll be back here in half an hour. Give my regards to your mom."

"Thanks, Sam." I ghosted and made my way out to the street. I drifted above the pedestrians and pushed onto Canada Place with its iconic five sails and the adjacent Pan Pacific Hotel. Once inside, I found a public restroom and re-formed.

I took the elevator to the ninth floor and knocked on my mother's door. "It's me, Mom," I said, as soon as I saw the shadow of her feet under the door. She opened it and I quickly moved inside. We embraced, and I couldn't tell whose sigh was deeper.

She broke away. "Come," she said, taking my hand. "What's happened? Tell me everything." We sat in the two chairs by the window. The sheers beneath the curtains were closed, muting the mountain view.

Her expression darkened as I unpacked the details around the Mansfield Group's missing hard drive.

She stood and crossed her arms then turned her gaze out the window. "We should have involved the police from the start. Called in the media."

I looked away from her. I'd originally steered her off that path fearing the Tribunal's repercussions if Mansfield's investigation threatened to expose our kind. "Maybe you're right. And now, with the ledger in Mason's hands, we might never know if the Tribunal was behind it."

"Looks like it doesn't matter who sanctioned your father's murder."

"They only got Mansfield's data," I said. "The evidence is still there and we have the coordinates."

"Whoever got that data also has the coordinates. How long until they make sure the wreckage is never found again?"

"I wish I'd never told Mason about finding Dad's plane wreck. I'm afraid all I've done is made a powerful enemy."

"He's always been your enemy. You just didn't know it."

I knew she believed that, but it didn't ring true to me. Maybe I'd done the ostrich thing after all. "Sam thinks that even with Mansfield's report, we don't have a strong enough case."

Mom turned back to face me. "What do you mean?"

"Dad's warning is the only thing that ties his death back to the Reynoldses. We need more." I told her about my visit to Sebastian's and the conversation I'd overheard between Kimberley and the new player, Wade Hofmann. "Wade's an assassin. He might be the link we're looking for."

Mom finally sat back down. "Sam and I have a plan. We're going to shake Wade up and see what drops out. It might take a few more days. Can you hang tight here?"

"I'll do whatever it takes to see this through. Your father deserves justice, as do the other men on that plane."

I checked the time. "I've got to go. Sam's waiting."

"Be careful, sweetheart."

The waiting continued at Sam's. He found a game on television. I lay on the sofa and tried to read, but it was no use. I couldn't concentrate.

Sam's phone rang. "It's Ortez," he said, and answered it. After listening a while, Sam said, "Good call. I appreciate the update." They exchanged pleasantries and then Sam hung up.

"Kimberley Kirk's Lexus showed up on a traffic camera in your neighbourhood. She was headed westbound on Sixteenth Street at Wesbrook Mall ninety minutes before your break-in."

I sat up. "Kimberley?"

"She claims she was shopping. Has a time-stamped receipt from a grocery store in the neighbourhood to prove it. Ortez got the impression she wasn't being entirely honest. He's going to keep lifting rocks."

"What the hell have I ever done to that woman? Why would she want me dead?"

"Maybe Kimberley's the one who's jealous, not Sebastian."

"Of me? I'm no threat to her."

"You've got her husband's attention. Maybe that's enough. Is she a Ghost?"

"No." I tried to remember when this hostility with Kimberley had begun. It was after Cairabrae. After Sebastian started mentoring me. "She told Wade she'd tried to take care of her *little problem* herself. She must have been referring to the break-in at my condo. If it was her, she's signed her own death warrant."

"Or someone else signed it for her," Sam said. "Have you ever had the impression Sebastian wanted to be rid of her?"

"No, and Sebastian was with me and the covey at the time of the break-in. He might not even know what she's done."

"Might have done. Let's hope Ortez comes up with something more. Meantime, we can chip away at Wade."

Sam ordered Chinese food for dinner. Afterwards, I got dressed and put my hair up. I came out of Sam's guest room with the stilettos in my hand; no need to start the torture any earlier than necessary.

"That'll get his attention," Sam said, looking me up and down. "Not sure he'll believe you were stood up, looking like that, though."

"Thank you. But my date wouldn't have seen all this gorgeousness."

"True," Sam said. "I checked on Wade's reservation at the Bayshore. Looks like Romeo booked dinner and a room. I'd wager he'll be hanging out at the bar. I'd better head out."

I checked the time. Almost 7:00 p.m. Sam left in his truck. His plan was to park underground at the Pacific Centre mall and lose any possible tail in the shopping crowd. Ten minutes later, I called a cab to pick me up at the restaurant around the corner from where we'd eaten breakfast. I ghosted to the restaurant as a precaution.

A text came in from Sam as my cab pulled up to the Bayshore. He was in place in the lounge, and so was our target. Sam's instincts were bang on. A doorman directed me to the lounge. With each step toward the bar, the heels of my stilettos connected with the hard marble. We wanted Wade to come to me of his own volition, so I didn't scan the room on my way for fear I'd make eye contact.

I set my purse on the polished granite bar and settled onto a black-lacquered bar stool. The bartender approached. "What can I get you?"

I ordered a Scotch and pulled my phone from my purse. My drink arrived, but not Wade. I checked the time: 7:35 p.m. Perhaps he hadn't seen me arrive, or didn't recognize me. If he didn't approach soon, I'd have to *bump* into him, which wouldn't be as convincing.

But I needn't have worried. I felt his presence behind me before he spoke. "Drinking alone?"

I turned in my seat and let my expression speak for me.

"Wade Hofmann," he said. "We met at Sebastian Kirk's." He held a martini in his hand and cut a handsome figure in a well-tailored suit. Very James Bond.

"Yes, of course. Sorry—I didn't recognize you. Are you staying here at the hotel?"

"Meeting someone. How about you? You waiting for a date?"

"Not anymore. He didn't show. I'm consoling myself with a drink then I'm going home."

"Stood you up? What a fool," he said. "I've got a few minutes. May I join you?"

"Sure. Much better than drinking alone."

Wade set his martini on the bar. "You created quite a stir at the caucus," he said. "The first gifted Tribunal member."

"I didn't know that. Guess I have Albert Vanderhoff to thank for making sure everyone knew I was gifted and not born."

"Albert's an elitist. He can't help himself."

"I guess you've known the lot of them your whole life."

"Indeed."

"Did you ever know the woman who gifted me? Jolene Reynolds?"

A smile of remembrance crossed his lips. "Yes, I did."

"What was she like?"

"I didn't know her well enough to say. She was a looker though." Wade sipped his drink.

"I wish I'd known her. I remember her only vaguely. Did you know she and my father had a son? They were going to get married. Unfortunately, their son died and their relationship fell apart."

A puzzled look crossed his face but he quickly recovered. "That's tragic, but like I said, I didn't know her well."

"*Tragic* sums up Jolene's life. First she loses her son and then three of the most important men in her life are killed, one after the other, including my father." I looked down to the bar and twisted my glass.

"I'm sorry. My condolences."

"It was a long time ago." I tasted my Scotch.

"If you don't mind me asking, how did these men die?"

I looked up from my glass and waited until I'd caught his eye. I wanted to gauge his reaction. "They were murdered." He appeared taken aback. I couldn't tell if it was genuine.

"Are you certain?" Wade took another sip of his drink.

"Yes, and I'm going to prove it."

"And how might you do that?" Wade asked.

"I don't know yet." I lifted my glass. "I'm hoping Sebastian can help."

"Sebastian?"

"We've grown close these past few months. He offered. Says he knows some people."

"Yes, he certainly does." Wade took a healthy sip of his martini and then toyed with the olive spike.

"What do the authorities believe happened to the three men?"

I cocked my head. "Do you think that matters?"

"Perhaps not." Wade gazed over his shoulder toward the clock behind the bar. "I don't mean to be insensitive, but three deaths surrounding one woman? I would suggest you look no further than Jolene."

"Jolene wouldn't have hurt my father."

Wade offered an apologetic shrug and then stripped the last olive from its spike and popped it into his mouth. He slid off his bar stool. "My date will be waiting. Don't want her to think I've stood her up." He reached a hand to my shoulder. I felt the warmth of it through the fabric and it chilled me. "I'm sorry about your father. I hope you find the answers you're looking for."

"Thank you," I said.

"Enjoy the rest of your evening, Emelynn."

"You too." I watched him pull out his phone as he left the bar. I had a feeling his date would be eating alone.

I glanced around the bar. Sam was nowhere to be found. I texted him *Where RU?* and headed to the ladies' room.

He texted back. *Wade's at the valet desk. Follow him. I'm going to get the truck.*

I ghosted inside a washroom stall. It felt good to get my weight off the stilettos. The valet desk was inside the glass entry doors. Wade stood outside, one hand in a pocket like a GQ model. If this was Wade frazzled, he'd chosen the right profession. When the valet arrived with his black BMW, Wade palmed him a bill and slid in behind the wheel. I took off straight up and kept him in sight.

The moment Wade got caught at a red light, I raced ahead and found a rooftop on which to re-form. I texted Sam. *He's eastbound on West Georgia at Bute Street.*

The light turned green. Sam texted back. *I'm ahead of him on Thurlow.*

I ghosted again and dropped down to keep on top of Wade's car. He got into the southbound turn lane at Thurlow. I searched for Sam's truck. After Wade made the turn, I saw the truck pull out from the curb and signal the turn.

I dove for it and blew inside. "I'm here," I said, and settled into the back seat. I re-formed under cover of the darkened back windows. "You got him?"

"Yup. He's ahead half a block. If I had to guess, I'd say he's headed straight for Point Grey. Did you find your bag?"

I'd already pulled out the clothes and ditched the high heels. I wiggled out of the stockings and pulled on my yoga pants and boots. The dress proved awkward to shimmy out of in the back seat of the truck, but I managed. I pulled on a black tunic and tucked my dress clothes away in the bag.

"Where are we?" I asked.

"On Nelson. He's going to turn south on Burrard and head for the bridge."

Sam was right again. Wade was on his way to Sebastian's. The moment Wade signalled his turn onto Fourth Avenue, Sam pulled back and increased the distance between us.

"Tell me about your conversation with Wade," Sam said.

I repeated the back and forth. "Sebastian's going to be pissed," I said. "I hope I haven't pushed too hard. I need him."

Wade pulled into Sebastian's driveway. Sam rolled past and parked a few blocks down. "Good luck," he said.

I pulled out my phone and set the recorder going. "Insurance," I said, tucking it back in my pocket. I ghosted then breezed out of Sam's truck and rushed back to Sebastian's. Once inside, I followed raised voices to the great room at the back of the house.

Sebastian's voice rang out. "You and I have a deal. That includes you not coming by without an invitation, so this better be good."

I drifted up to the ceiling as I entered the vaulted room that lay open to the kitchen. Sebastian remained seated in an Eames lounge chair, his feet stretched out before him on a matching ottoman. Wade stood just inside the room, his feet shoulder width apart and his hands fisted at his sides. Over in the kitchen, Kimberley cowered beside the open dishwasher door with her back to the counter.

"Did you think I wouldn't find out who Emelynn Taylor was?" Wade said with a snarl in his voice.

Sebastian responded with nonchalance. "It's not a secret."

"No, and yet you never mentioned she was Brian Taylor's daughter."

A cold shiver ran through me. "I had an interesting conversation with her tonight." Sebastian perked up. "She's somehow learned Jolene's lovers were killed, including her father." A dangerous silence hung in the air.

Sebastian splayed his fingers on the armrest. "She has no proof."

"She seems to think you might help her find that proof. Why would she think that?"

"She asked me to help her. I said I would." He chuckled and looked down to his fingers, which were caressing the leather armrests. "She believes Mason Reynolds is responsible."

Sebastian's mirth felt like a sucker punch. I'd thought Sebastian believed me. Apparently, he didn't.

Wade straightened. "Does she, now? Kimberley was right, then. The contract's on Mason Reynolds?"

Sebastian's fingers stilled. He kept his gaze in place, but I looked over at Kimberley. She seemed to shrink even smaller.

"Without proof of a crime, it can't be sanctioned," Sebastian said.

"You told me this was a sanctioned hit."

Sebastian shrugged as if it didn't matter. "I didn't say it was Mason Reynolds. In fact, I didn't give you a name. Regardless, the pay should more than compensate." What was Sebastian doing? Testing Wade?

"In case you hadn't noticed, I don't need the money. I'm also rather fond of breathing. I'm not touching an unsanctioned hit on any Tribunal member."

Sebastian glared up at Wade. "You losing your edge, Wade? Not good enough to take out one of us?"

"You think I'm gonna fall for that shit? Why don't you keep it in the family? I understand your wife has no qualms about unsanctioned hits on Tribunal. Maybe you should ask her."

I swallowed. The last of my doubt about Kimberley's guilt fled: she was the one who'd tried to poison me. Sebastian slammed his feet to the floor and stood. "Do not forget who you're talking to."

Wade staggered back a step and then ghosted. Sebastian must have jolted him. He wouldn't get another one in with Wade in ghosted form.

Wade's voice came out of the ether. "You want to make an enemy out of me? You're not the only one holding cards." I'd bet my life one of those cards was Wade's knowledge of what Kimberley had done. What else did he have on them?

"The jolt was for your insolence. I have no desire to make another enemy, but you will show me respect."

WINGS OF PREY

Wade re-formed. "Noted. Now, what are you going to do about Emelynn Taylor?"

"She's neutralized for now. I'll keep an eye on her."

Neutralized? The dick was back. So much for the new respect between us.

"And Reynolds?" Wade asked.

"He could be a problem, especially now that he knows about Jolene's lovers. If you change your mind about the hit, let me know."

Wade crossed his arms. "No disrespect, but you're a real bastard, you know that?" He disappeared, but he hadn't left.

Sebastian sat back down and casually picked up a book. Kimberley didn't move. Moments later, Wade's ghost was gone and I heard the squeal of tires outside.

Then Sebastian turned a steely glare to Kimberley. "When were you speaking to Wade?"

Kimberley tucked a lock of hair behind her ear. "He came by after you contacted him about the contract. I had no idea he didn't know it was Mason. He tricked me."

Lying bitch.

"Is that so?" Sebastian said. Kimberley busied herself with the dishwasher. Sebastian ghosted and reappeared inches away from her. "You were never a good liar. Why are you and Wade keeping secrets?"

"I'm sorry. I didn't want you to know I'd screwed up again."

Again? Was the first screw-up breaking into my condo? Poisoning my milk?

Sebastian reached his hand to her chin and lifted her face to his. "He's a dangerous man. If you let him get between us, I can't protect you."

"It won't happen again. I promise." She reached her arms around his waist and he pulled her close.

I turned from them and left the house, reeling. Back in Sam's truck, I played the recording.

"You're not wrong about Kimberley," Sam said. "I don't know her motive, but my gut tells me she's good for the break-in. Send me that recording."

"I can't understand why I'm such a big threat to her. And how is this connected to my father's death?"

Sam didn't speculate. "If Mason is Sebastian's target, there has to be a reason."

"Apparently it's not because he's convinced Mason had my father killed," I said. "Maybe it's Mason's politics he doesn't like, or maybe Sebastian is just testing Wade's loyalty to the Tribunal."

"No. Sebastian made a point of telling Wade that Mason knew about the deaths of Jolene's lovers. It sounded to me like Sebastian was using that to bait Wade."

"You think Wade killed them? Killed my father?"

"Fits his job description."

"Wade also knows that I'm aware of the murders."

"Yeah, and Sebastian never did name his target."

Chapter Nineteen

We sat in silence, each in our own thoughts.

"We're missing something," Sam said finally. "Wade's motive is easy enough to figure out—killing is just a payday for him—but Sebastian and Kimberley? They're a riddle." Sam turned to me. "When you were in their safe, what else did you see?"

"I didn't go through their things. I went right to the envelope Kimberley identified."

"Can you get back in there? You might have missed something. Something that would explain their behaviour, point to a motive."

I exhaled in a puff. "If they're not in their bedroom, I can."

"Take pictures of everything. Even if it doesn't look important."

"All right." I ghosted and drifted back into Sebastian's house. He and Kimberley were seated in the great room. I prayed they stayed put and headed upstairs.

Their bedroom door hung open. I breezed inside and straight to their dressing room. Unlike last time, the door was ajar. I re-formed inside and gently closed the door. It would help dampen any sound I made. I prayed it was enough because if Sebastian became suspicious, I'd never see or even hear him coming. I pulled the clothing aside, entered the code and opened the safe.

Someone had been inside it since my last visit. A black box the size of a large deck of cards sat on top of the manila envelope of photos. I picked it up and examined it. It was a hard drive, and I bet I knew whose. My hands started to shake. Questions I had no answers for swirled in my head.

I tucked the drive in my pocket and searched through the safe. I snapped photos of Kimberley's jewels and the deed to the house. With each flash of the camera, I feared someone would see the light leak out around the door frame. Still, I pushed on. They had Mansfield's drive. What else were they hiding?

Their family anthology was inside, but it was too lengthy to photograph in its entirety. I took shots of the family tree and what looked to be their holdings. I snapped the front page of their passports and some business documents. There were also records of provenance for some artwork and a couple of old coins. I photographed them as well.

When I was done, I put everything back the way I'd found it and closed the safe door. After rearranging the clothing in front of the safe, I ghosted and pushed out of the dressing room. Their bedroom was blessedly still unoccupied. I re-formed and opened the dressing-room door, leaving it ajar, as it had been when I arrived.

I checked that the drive was still in my pocket then ghosted again and drifted down the stairs and back out the front door. Relief didn't hit until I was back in Sam's truck. I re-formed. Sam gave a start. I pulled the drive out of my pocket and showed him.

"Is that Mansfield's?"

"I can't tell."

Sam took a photo of it and another photo of its serial number and sent them off to Peter Caulfield. Despite the late hour, Peter took less than ten minutes to confirm it was his. After Sam promised to have it couriered to him, he hung up.

"If Sebastian looks in his safe, he'll know this is gone," Sam said. "He might suspect you took it."

"There's not a lot I can do about that tonight. Tomorrow I'll buy another one to replace it and hope he can't tell the difference."

"No. Let's do it tonight." He reached down and started the truck. "There's a Staples at the university. They should have something similar enough to fool him."

"What's one more break-in?" I said, as Sam pulled out. "Kimberley has access to the safe, but she's not a Ghost; she couldn't have taken Mansfield's drive without being seen. That leaves Sebastian, unless he put Wade up to it. Why would Sebastian do that?"

"The man's a manipulator and obviously well versed in the art of blackmail. That hard drive has already neutralized you, and if Mason is guilty of an unsanctioned hit, it's a compelling weapon to hold over his head."

"If he has the means to control Mason, why would he want him dead?"

"I don't know, and we don't know if Mason is Sebastian's target, but we're getting closer. Didn't you mention that Wade said something about Sebastian losing an ace if Mason was eliminated?"

"Yeah, it was back there at Sebastian's, when Wade confronted Kimberley. Wade said 'one less ace up his sleeve,' meaning Sebastian's sleeve."

"That suggests keeping Mason alive might somehow benefit Sebastian. Maybe Kimberley did indeed get it wrong and Mason isn't the unsanctioned Tribunal hit Sebastian was talking about."

"Are you thinking Sebastian was talking about me? You can't be serious?"

"You were a threat to his wife before she tried to kill you. And if you prove Mason killed your father, Sebastian loses some sort of an ace. So yeah, I'm serious."

"Sebastian went out on a limb for me. He mentored me."

"I know, but so did Mason. What's that tell you?"

"I need better friends?"

Sam laughed. The levity was a welcome reprieve, but it felt like laughter at a funeral.

Behind the computer counter at Staples, I found a hard drive with the same brand name and design as the one I'd taken from Sebastian's safe. Kudos to me. I could now add *common thief* to my resume.

Sam drove us back to Sebastian's. Hitting Sebastian's home three times in one night was a test of my nerves. I ghosted out of Sam's truck and returned to the house. Sebastian and Kimberley were no longer in the great room. Unease gripped my shoulders as I drifted up the stairs. I found them upstairs in their bedroom and cursed silently. Sebastian lay in the bed propped up on pillows. The sound of running water came from the ensuite. It would be impossible to replace the drive tonight. I spun away from the sight of Sebastian's naked chest and returned to Sam's truck with the news.

"Shit!" he said. He pulled out and started back toward his place.

"You have to leave," I said. "Go find that hammock. If Sebastian discovers the drive is missing, you're in danger."

"So are you," Sam said.

"But unlike you, I can get away from him."

"Hiding's not my style."

"Screw the heroics. Don't be a moron."

Sam didn't respond—unless pursed lips and a clenched jaw counted.

As we once again approached Burrard Street I thought of my mother. "I have an idea."

His foul humour came through in just one word. "What?"

"Ditch your truck, pack a bag. Megan Fairchild will book a room for you near Mom. You can protect Mom, and you and I can keep looking for answers."

He glanced at me. "Much better," he said, and stepped on the gas.

Back at Sam's place, I called Mom and asked her to arrange a second room, preferably close to hers. Sam came down the stairs with a worn backpack.

"You ready?" I asked.

He hiked one strap of his pack over his shoulder. "More than I was the first time you did this."

I offered him my hand. He rubbed his palm against his thigh before he placed his hand in mine. His gaze was on our clasped hands when I ghosted. He didn't falter even as his body disappeared.

"This is fucking unbelievable."

I warned him to stay quiet. We slid through his front door and I dragged him a few blocks away to a back lane. In the shadow of a dumpster, I dropped his hand and re-formed. After he re-formed, he patted his body down, as if he'd find it missing parts.

"Come on. Let's get a cab," I said. He stumbled behind me.

When we got to Mom's room at the Pan Pacific, she'd already picked up the key to a room across the hall. I showed her the hard drive I'd recovered from Sebastian's safe.

"I knew that man wasn't to be trusted," she said.

"I'll courier this to Peter Caulfield in the morning," Sam said. "It's late. I'm going to get some shut-eye." Mom gave him the key and saw him out the door. I plopped onto the bed Mom hadn't been using.

After Sam left, Mom cozied up beside me. I told her what Ortez had learned about Kimberley being in my neighbourhood around the time of the break-in. "I don't know what her motives are, but Sam agrees that she's likely responsible."

Mom shook her head. "Sebastian, his wife, Mason, Stuart—they're immoral, evil people." She took my hand in hers. "You have to get away from them before they find a way to kill you."

She'd left out Wade. I stared at her simple wedding band and debated telling her that Sam and I suspected it was Wade who'd killed Dad. I decided not to. It was speculation at this point. Besides which, Wade didn't operate on his own. Someone had hired him to do it. The Tribunal and the Reynoldses were on the list. Awash in cold dread, I etched two more names on the list: Sebastian and Kimberley. "Do you want company tonight? I don't feel like going home."

She was happy to have me stay. After the lights were out, I lay in bed thinking. If I walked away from my seat on the Tribunal, I could, as Mom had said, *get away from them*. But what kind of a life would that be? Hiding and living in fear? What about Mom and Sam? They'd be condemned to the same fate. I didn't have a death wish, but living like that didn't sound like much of a life for any of us.

Walking away wasn't the answer. What I needed to do was find out who'd ordered Dad's assassination. I had Mansfield's data, so I had the proof my father was murdered, and I had Sam's research that identified Jolene as the pivot point. But I had nothing to connect Dad's murder directly to the Reynoldses or the Kirks. Or had the Tribunal ordered it?

I knew Wade had the answers, but he wasn't about to incriminate himself. I had no leverage with Mason, but I did have it with Sebastian: Kimberley's attempt on my life was a death sentence for her if the Tribunal learned of it. The danger in using that leverage lay in how involved Sebastian really was.

I thought back to my father's warning. He'd named the Reynoldses, not the Kirks. Though Mason denied it, preventing Jolene from marrying someone non-Gifted was a compelling motive to murder her suitors. Jealousy on Sebastian's part didn't seem as compelling a motive, not after what I'd witnessed tonight; he wanted to protect Kimberly. He cared about her. And Kimberley may have wanted me dead, but if she were jealous of Jolene, she'd promote a marriage, not kill off her prospects.

I compared their motives. I weighed my choices. I had to place a bet.

By the time the sun rose, my resolve had hardened. I'd make a deal with Sebastian. Even if Ortez was able to prove Kimberley's guilt, I'd let it go. Sebastian could deal with Ortez's evidence any way he wanted and I'd not take it to the Tribunal. That would also nullify anything Wade had on Kimberley. In exchange, I wanted what he knew about my father's murder—there was no doubt in my mind that he knew something. If Wade had done it, he would pay, and so would the person who'd ordered it.

Mom called for room service and Sam joined us for breakfast. While we ate, I told them my thoughts. "I know this plan isn't perfect, but the Reynoldses had more to gain by Dad's death than the Kirks, and the only one I have leverage with is Sebastian."

"It's a crapshoot is what it is," Sam said. "And you're assuming you can trust Sebastian. That's a mistake. You'll always be a threat to him."

"Not if no one can prove Kimberley tried to kill me," I said. "I'll make sure of it. I'll destroy Ortez's evidence myself if I have to." I stood and walked to the window. "We have to do something." I parted the sheers with my fingers and looked down to the street. "We can't stay holed up in here for the rest of our lives, and we can't undo what we've done. I don't see another way out."

"Maybe we need to take a step back," Mom said. "Replace the hard drive to hold off Sebastian, and give this plan of yours more thought."

I turned to face them. "I've been thinking about that hard drive, too. I'm the one who's been wronged, not Sebastian. So what if he finds out I took it back? He stole that drive from us. I can turn it around. Make him defend himself."

"Bad idea," Sam said. "If Sebastian's the one who ordered the hit and you confront him like that, he'll kill you."

"No, he won't. Not as long as I hold the proof."

"Jesus, Emelynn," Sam said. "You're holding a torch to a powder keg."

"I know, and it scares the crap out of me. But he already has the physical advantage; if I let him manipulate me, he's won the head game, too. I can't let that happen. I'm not completely powerless, and when he learns I've got the hard drive, he'll realize something else: that I know he can't be trusted and I'm not afraid of him."

I sat back down. Mom was perched on the edge of her seat. I reached a reassuring hand to her knee. "Giving this more time only delays the inevitable. I have to do this and I'm the only one who can."

Though Mom and Sam didn't like my decision, they understood it.

After breakfast, I left them and took a cab to Sam's place, where I'd left the MGB. Getting inside and firing up the ignition felt like reclaiming a tiny bit of my life. I stopped for groceries and drove past the police cruiser and into the underground.

Colin sat behind the front desk. I approached to ask how he was doing. The shock of a high-profile crime so close to home still had a grip on the building. I added my concern, collected my mail and took the elevator to the top floor.

The normalcy of it felt like staking another claim to my life. I slid my key into the new lock and the moment I opened the door, the joy I'd felt washed away. I closed the door behind me and stared at the chaos before me. The alarm beeped a reminder. I shoved the garments that belonged in the hall closet out of the way and punched in the disarm code. I sensed for a Ghost signature and found none. I slipped from room to room, but whoever had rifled through my place was gone.

What a mess. Not a cupboard or drawer had been spared. The scope of the disarray made me appreciate the respect and restraint the police had shown. I wondered if Sam's place had been hit as well. Had Sebastian already opened his safe? I remembered Sam's advice about confirmation bias, and though I pegged Sebastian for this *rearrangement* of my condo, I knew I needed to keep my mind open.

I closed the refrigerator door, set the groceries and the dummy hard drive on the kitchen counter and headed to the bedroom to start straightening the disorder. I put my clothes back on their hangers and paired up the shoes. I sorted and refolded clothes, muscled the mattress back onto its box spring and remade the bed.

The bathroom required more than tidying. I headed to the kitchen for the cleaning supplies. The moment I opened the broom closet, the sense of Mason's ghost hit me. I swung around as he took form in the dining room. Our eyes met before I ghosted. He could kill me as quick as a thought, but not if I was in my ghosted form.

He jutted his head into the kitchen and looked around, his expression perplexed. "What the hell happened in here?"

"What do you think?"

"It didn't look like this last night."

"What were you doing here last night?"

"Looking for you. You weren't home." With each step he took, glass crunched under his feet. "Did they find what they were looking for?"

"I couldn't tell you."

"Well, at least they didn't get this," he said, and laid out his mother's crystal case with care. The crystal gleamed inside it. "You forgot to take it with you."

I had no words. He'd witnessed my biggest secret. The one I'd vowed never to reveal.

"If you're not going to use it, you should keep it in a safe," he said. He walked out of the kitchen and into the living room. He hadn't so much as glanced at the hard drive lying on the counter in front of him.

I drifted into the room behind him. He stood in front of the windows, staring out at the Pacific.

"How long have you known?" I asked.

"I didn't know for sure until now, but I suspected it from the night I found you outside Carson Manse's trailer. It's why I had you swallow the amber before the paramedics evacuated you. Didn't want you exposing our secret on the treatment table."

"You never said anything."

"I did. I asked you about it twice—before I taught you how to ghost and again after the Redeemers' attacked at Cairabrae. You hedged, both times."

"I remember." I felt like I should apologize, but I'd never wanted him to know. I'd never wanted anyone to know. In a world where I was outpowered, every advantage counted.

"Jolene was the same. I found out when we were children and promised her I'd never reveal her secret. I never did. Not even to our parents."

"I don't know what to say." Had I been wrong about Mason?

"I'd like to apologize," Mason said. "Trust is a delicate thing and I've been careless with yours. It pains me to see you frightened of me and pushing me away. It's Jolene all over again."

"Why did you come here?"

Mason turned away from the window. "Someone tried to kill you. And now this?" He looked pointedly at the mess. "I'm worried about you, Emelynn. You've pulled away from me and Dad. From James. Who's left?"

"Don't pretend you don't know why you and I are estranged, and James is none of your business."

"Let me ask you this. Your father knew about the gift, about Ghosts. Did he tell your mother about us?"

"Of course not. He'd never endanger her like that."

"So if he knew about the Tribunal, he wouldn't have disclosed that either. In fact, he couldn't identify anyone but Dad and me for fear he'd put his family in danger. I don't fault Brian for the warning. He didn't have a lot of leeway. Laura did the smart thing hiding you away after he died."

His analysis threw me off-kilter. What else could Dad have said to warn Mom? If he'd named others on the Tribunal, would she have tried to find them? Put herself in danger? Could Mason be right?

He picked up a pillow and set it on the sofa. "What were they looking for?"

I drifted into the kitchen and re-formed. It was a terrible risk, but I had to know. I picked up the dummy hard drive, established my block for what good it would do me and walked out to the living room to face Mason. A wisp of a smile formed on his lips.

"This," I said, holding the hard drive out to him. He didn't move.

"What's on it?"

"Proof that my father was murdered."

"Who was looking for it?"

"I'm not sure, but I have my suspicions."

"Do you care to share?"

"No. But I will tell you that Wade Hofmann is staying in town."

Mason's face hardened. "Where?"

Sam wasn't the only one who could stir a pot. I set the hard drive down on the coffee table, pulled out my phone and sent Mason Wade's address. "What are you are going to do?"

"You'd better put that somewhere safe," Mason said, motioning toward the hard drive. "You're going to need it."

I frowned, and Mason seemed to read my mind. "I told you before. I'm not the one you're looking for. I didn't kill your father, and I would never hurt you." He ghosted and his aura disappeared.

I dropped to the sofa. Had I been wrong about Mason? Had my accusation been a cruel mistake?

Chapter Twenty

With the phone still in my hand, I dialled Sam. When he answered, I told him someone had been in the condo and had tipped the place upside down. Then I told him about Mason and his take on my father's warning.

"What do you make of it?" Sam asked.

"I don't know. He's fooled me before. But I have to admit, he's got me questioning myself, and he made no attempt to get the hard drive. Told me to put it somewhere safe."

"The real drive is on its way to Peter Caulfield. He should have it tonight. How did you leave things with Mason?"

"I pulled one of your moves and gave him Wade's address."

"More like you pulled a pin on a grenade."

"The fallout will answer some questions—I'm just not sure which ones."

After we disconnected, I looked down at the drive on the table. We'd have our answers soon.

I returned to the kitchen and froze at the sight of the crystal case on the counter. Had I even thanked Mason for returning it? I felt ashamed that I'd been so reckless with it. I tucked it in my pocket, picked up the cleaning bucket and the vacuum and got back to work.

It was late afternoon before I coiled the vacuum hose and put the bucket of cleaning supplies away. I'd made another list of items to replace. The teapot was the one that bothered me the most. It had been an old Brown Betty, like the one Avery had, and was the only one I'd ever had that didn't drip.

I dropped a tea bag in the bottom of a mug and flipped the switch on the kettle. When the tea had steeped, I took the mug out to the balcony. Along the way, I snagged the hard drive and stuffed it in my pocket. Leaving it out in plain sight felt like courting trouble, and I'd had enough of that already.

My thoughts turned to Mason. My accusation had hurt him. It had felt good at the time. Justified. A small payback for Dad. But that tiny smile on Mason's face earlier today, when I'd shown myself, played on my conscience. He'd been relieved to see me trust him. The hope that I'd been wrong about him swelled again.

I pulled my phone out and replayed the recording I'd made of Wade and Sebastian's conversation. I reversed again to the part where Sebastian goaded Wade about the unsanctioned hit. The part where Wade suggested Sebastian ask Kimberley to do it because she had no problem with unsanctioned hits. This time, I focused on what wasn't said: neither Sebastian nor Kimberley had denied that she'd attempted an unsanctioned hit ... mine.

I prayed it was enough to leverage Sebastian.

My stomach grumbled. I'd have to think about dinner soon. Mom was probably ordering room service. I unfolded myself from the deck chair and headed inside, but nothing in the fridge appealed to me. I ate a bowl of cereal.

As night fell, I ached to go flying and take the edge off the waiting. But before I got around to it, my phone rang.

"Sebastian Kirk is in the lobby," Colin announced.

Finally. The waiting was over.

"Send him up." He'd checked in downstairs, so he was either playing a game with me, or he didn't yet know I had the hard drive. I put my teacup and cereal bowl in the dishwasher, checked my block and walked down the hall to open the door.

"Hello, my dear," Sebastian said. He leaned in and pecked me on the cheek without a hint that anything was amiss. He walked in and headed to the living room. I shut the door and followed. He'd dressed in black, and I wondered if he'd flown over.

"I tried the detective's place first. I'm surprised to find you here. Do you think it's wise?"

"What do you mean?" I asked.

"Are you forgetting someone tried to kill you?"

"That's hardly the kind of thing you forget. I've decided to take my life back. Whoever it was is an amateur. If they come back, I'm ready for them."

He nodded as he removed his leather gloves one finger at a time and bunched them in one hand. "I have some news that should ease your mind. The final loose end from the ICO debacle has been taken care of."

"What final loose end?"

"James didn't tell you? He was so pleased." I offered him a blank stare. "No? Well, I hope I'm not speaking out of turn and spoiling the news. The surrogate in California who was carrying your child has lost it. She's no longer pregnant."

"No! What happened?"

"I don't have the details." He furrowed his brow. "Are you upset? I thought you'd be pleased."

"How could you think losing a child would please me?"

"You have to admit, the circumstances were hardly ideal. It wasn't even your doing."

"The baby was still mine. Ours." I dropped to the sofa. I'd thought James wanted the child. That he'd been pleased about losing it hurt more than the loss that had just changed my life's course. Again.

Sebastian took a seat opposite me. "I'm sorry, my dear, but this is for the best."

For the best? He'd used those words before, when he'd mentioned Jolene's relationships hadn't worked out. Before I knew the men had died. His comment had been callous. And, if I thought the worst of him, self-serving.

He straightened his gloves out against his thigh and refolded them. "Has the Mansfield Group made any progress restoring their data?"

"No, but I have." I pulled the hard drive out of my pocket and laid it on the coffee table in front of me.

He looked at it and hollowed his cheeks. "I thought as much. Kimberley told me about the safe. You've learned well."

"Why did you take it?"

He offered a glib smile. "You'll have to forgive me. I've been greedy. I saw an opportunity and I took it. Thought I could use it to wring something out of the Reynoldses before you sealed their fates and closed that door."

"What would you have wrung out of them?"

He stroked his gloves. "I hadn't decided. A vote, perhaps. I don't suppose you'd let me have it back?"

"How about you and I make a deal?" I reached for my phone, found the recording of him and Wade, laid it on the table and pushed play.

"You think I'm gonna fall for that shit? Why don't you keep it in the family? I understand your wife has no qualms about unsanctioned hits on Tribunal. Maybe you should ask her."

I pushed stop.

Sebastian glared at me. His nostrils flared. "How dare you!" Spittle flew from his mouth.

I'd thought I could ghost fast enough. I was wrong. He tipped his head and before I vanished, searing pain licked up my spine and exploded. His next few words landed garbled in my brain. I picked out *insolent* and *gross invasion* as I recovered.

"Did you think I wouldn't use everything at my disposal?" I said. "Isn't that what you taught me?"

"Show yourself."

"The amateur who tried to kill me was Kimberley. Unless you'd like to deny it?"

Sebastian slapped his gloves against his thighs and then shot to his feet. "Who else has that recording?"

I re-formed. "If you ever jolt me again, you're going to find out." I sat down to hide the shake in my legs. "I'm willing to overlook your wife's attempt on my life—for a price."

"You set Wade up to confront me."

"I believe that was another early lesson of yours. The most expedient way to get rid of your enemies is to pit them against one another? Did I get that right?"

"I'm not your enemy."

"You're acting like it."

"What is it you want in exchange for your silence?"

"I think you know who killed my father. I want to know who, and I want to know why Kimberley wanted me dead."

Sebastian turned from me and walked to the balcony door. He stroked his gloves. "And if I tell you this, you will forgive Kimberley's indiscretions?"

"I will."

"Then it's a deal." He turned around. "Wade Hofmann killed your father."

"On whose orders?"

A smug smile bloomed on Sebastian's face. "That wasn't one of your conditions, but I could be convinced to negotiate."

Bastard!

His expression didn't change as he continued. "I believe you wanted to know what motivated Kimberley. She was jealous of Jolene, even after Jolene disappeared. When you turned up and I agreed to mentor you, Kimberley thought I was replacing Jolene with you. Ridiculous, I know, but there you have it."

He may have outplayed me, but there was more than one way to get to the truth. "If that's true, your wife would have been pleased to see Jolene happily married to someone else. That knocks her out of the running for ordering my father's murder. Who does that leave?"

He held out his hand. "You give me the hard drive and all copies of that recording, and I'll tell you."

I looked down at the hard drive and the phone sitting on the coffee table. He didn't know the hard drive was empty, or how many copies of the recording existed. I could give him what he wanted without losing either. The temptation gave me pause, and in that pause, my instincts kicked into high gear.

"You are very good at what you do, Sebastian. I can see why the Tribunal values you so much."

He inclined his head, accepting my praise.

"My father's warning to my mother identified the Reynoldses, but Dad wasn't one of us. He might not have known all the players."

"Your father knew what we were."

"Mason mentioned that. He also told me you were very supportive of Jolene after she lost her son. You visited her regularly. Helped her through that terrible trauma. You were married to Kimberley at the time."

"Kimberley isn't a Ghost. She could never understand the bond Jolene and I shared, even after it was over."

"It must have been difficult for Kimberley to see you and Jolene together, knowing about this bond you shared."

"Yes," Sebastian said, nodding. He sat back down in the seat opposite and crossed his ankle over his knee.

"Given this bond you had, you must have been pleased when Jolene and my father split."

"Not at all. I felt Jolene's pain. Hated to see her unhappy. But it wasn't meant to be."

"Because he wasn't a Ghost?"

"Don't take offence, my dear, but he wasn't even a Flier. She was out of his league and then some."

"And Nick and Arthur? Was she out of their leagues too?"

Sebastian uncrossed his leg and leaned forward. "I don't like your insinuation."

I leaned away from him and crossed my arms. "Detective Jordan said something a while back that stuck with me. It was when we first learned that General Cain had hung us out to dry. Sam said *It's always the little shit that trips you up.* Did you know that when I mentioned Nick and Arthur to Mason, he knew all about Nick but he'd never heard the name Arthur?"

"He was playing you."

"Or you are." He raised an eyebrow. "And you're the one with an assassin on call."

A storm engulfed Sebastian's face. He blasted a jolt at the hard drive and it blew apart. The coffee table shattered, and the pyramid of decorative stone balls beneath it rolled out in every direction. I ghosted and flew up to the ceiling before he could change his focus.

He spun around trying to sense me, and then he sensed someone else. Mason. He re-formed behind the sofa and his gaze went from Sebastian to the shards of glass and black plastic between them.

"Where is Emelynn?" Mason said.

"I imagine she's right here." Sebastian checked his wristwatch.

"Was that the hard drive?"

"Yes. You can thank me for saving your hide. She'll never be able to prove her father was murdered."

Mason chuckled. "You've been busy, Sebastian. Picking at frayed edges with your charm and innuendo, driving a wedge between Emelynn and her family."

"If you were her family, you wouldn't have had her father murdered."

"Is that what you've been telling her?"

"Actually, that's what she told me."

"Is that so? That's not the story I just heard."

Before I could process what was happening, Sebastian's body blew backwards, his limbs akimbo, and he slammed into one of the concrete columns between the big windows. Mason had jolted him, and Sebastian hadn't been expecting it.

Mason kicked one of the stone balls out of his way and stepped toward him, but Sebastian ghosted before Mason could jolt him again. Mason spat out his words. "Wade Hofmann sends his regards. He told me all about the marker you have on him, and the deaths you ordered: Nick Pagonis, Arthur Curtis and Brian Taylor."

Sebastian re-formed behind Mason and threw a jolt into his back. Mason stumbled forward, caught himself and spun around. It hadn't been a lift-of-the-jaw jolt, like the one Sebastian had treated me to—it had been a killing jolt. If I'd been on the receiving end, I'd be dead. Mason's block was much stronger than mine. I backed into a corner of the ceiling.

"You think the Tribunal will believe the word of an assassin?" Sebastian said. "One who's betrayed them?"

The two men squared off against one another. Titans, fully armed, fully shielded, playing a deadly game.

"Why'd you do it, Sebastian? Because she rejected you? You couldn't have my sister for yourself so you killed any man she wanted?"

"That's absurd. Do you hear yourself?"

"You turned my sister's life into a nightmare. I hold you responsible for her death as well."

Mason and Sebastian walked a slow circle in lockstep. They were in a battle one of them wouldn't walk away from.

"You have no proof."

Mason flinched. Sebastian's shoulder twitched. They were testing each other's blocks.

"I'm confused about one thing though," Mason said. "Nick, I understand. He and Jolene were to be married. I never knew Arthur, but Emelynn told me they were engaged, so I get that one, too. But why Brian? He and Jolene were long done. He'd married another woman. Had a child."

"Why do you think Jolene was in Vancouver?" Sebastian said. "She was sniffing around Brian again. She wanted him back. Jolene threw her life away! I could have strengthened her bloodline, but she was determined to dilute it with someone unworthy."

"So you had him killed?"

"I saved her from herself."

I gasped.

Mason stopped circling. "Thank you. Now I have my proof."

I drifted down from the corner and re-formed behind Mason, using his body as a shield. Words rose like bile in my throat. "You bastard!"

"Emelynn," Mason said. His voice was a warning.

I glared at Sebastian, who'd locked his gaze with Mason's, his face set in grim determination. The air between them rippled with unspent power.

"You're wrong about Jolene," I said. "She wasn't after my father. She hadn't even spoken to him."

Mason shouted my name and in that instant, Sebastian pushed forward. Mason cartwheeled backwards and pancaked me against the wall with a thud. Something crashed to the floor.

Sebastian pressed his advantage and nailed Mason again. The jolt hit Mason and leaked around to me. I screamed and ghosted.

Sebastian smiled, and it must have been enough of a distraction to give Mason an edge. Mason retaliated, knocking Sebastian over the sofa and into the debris from the ruined coffee table. Sebastian rolled and jumped to his feet. He gripped a stone ball in his hand and launched it at Mason. It connected with his collarbone with a sickening thud. Sebastian followed it up with a second ball that hit Mason in the shoulder. Mason staggered backwards, into the dining room.

Though his face was ashen, Mason stood his ground. He kept the table between them, circling it as he blinked to regain his focus. Sebastian was gloating now and it sickened me. I re-formed behind Sebastian and hit him with the most powerful jolt I had in me. It barely registered with him. I ghosted as he turned in my direction. Mason reached for the dining room light fixture and sent it hurling at Sebastian's head. It caught him in the temple. He followed up with a powerful jolt that drove Sebastian back into the living room. He landed on the floor at the end of the sofa.

Mason gave away his injured left arm by holding it still as he circled behind Sebastian, wincing with each step. He kept one of the swivel chairs between them as a buffer and stopped with his back to the balcony. Sebastian grasped the arm of the sofa but didn't have the strength to drag himself up. Blood dripped from his temple to the floor. He shook his head. "Don't do it," he said. His gaze dropped to the floor. He looked broken.

Though hurting, Mason stood tall, impassive. I wanted to go to him, to beg his forgiveness and tell him how sorry I was, but shame and guilt overpowered me. Mason took his eyes off Sebastian and searched the room.

"I'm here," I said, from the corner by the hall. Mason couldn't sense me, but his gaze followed my voice. I drifted down to the floor and approached. I didn't realize our mistake until it was too late.

Mason's body sailed backwards into the balcony door, shattering it. He landed in a sheet of broken glass on the balcony outside. I raced to his side. His eyes bulged and he struggled to breathe, but it was the sound of barking dogs that stopped me cold.

I turned to see Sebastian get up and stand over my phone, which had landed face-up on the floor when the table shattered.

"About bloody time," he said, and then he vanished.

I floated back inside and looked down at my phone. James was on the rooftop. His hand was on the doorknob when he stopped and turned around. Sebastian stood just a few yards behind him.

I scooped up the phone and blew out the shattered balcony door and up to the rooftop.

I heard Sebastian's voice before I reached them. "Perfect timing, James."

"What happened here?" James said, his attention on the blood trail evident from Sebastian's temple to his jaw. "Is Emelynn all right?"

"She's fine. She'll be here in just a moment, I'm sure."

I raced my ghosted form to James's side and whispered in his ear. He jumped at the sound of my voice. "Sebastian killed my father. He's going to kill you. Get out of here."

James's face hardened, and he dropped his right hand to his side. I'd never known him to be without the gun he kept in a belt holster at the small of his back.

"I wouldn't do that if I were you," Sebastian said. James stiffened. His nostrils flared.

"Emelynn, show yourself," Sebastian called out. "I know you're here." He scanned the rooftop through squinted eyes. "He can't outfly me or get to his gun fast enough to save himself. You're all alone now, Emelynn. No one's coming to your rescue. Mason won't survive my jolt. You've alienated Stuart. James is outmatched." James rolled his shoulder back.

"What do you want, Sebastian?" I asked.

"One last bargain. You for James. Show yourself and I'll let him go."

"Bargain? With you?" Laughter bubbled out of me. "I can see how that bargain's going to turn out. I show myself, you kill me and then you kill James. Or, I don't show myself and you kill James. I'm not seeing the upside."

"James is no threat to me. I'm quite prepared to let him go. That's my offer. Take it or leave it, but make up your mind. Your neighbours will be investigating the disturbance before long and I won't wait." Sebastian made a show of checking his watch. "It's decision time, Emelynn. Do we have a deal?"

Anger vibrated off of James. "Not that deal," I said. "How about this one? Your life for James's. Or did you forget that I still have a bargaining chip."

"You have nothing, Emelynn. Any evidence you thought you had has been destroyed." He fluttered his fingers for emphasis. "The Tribunal will not back you."

"And the recording I played for you?"

"What? Wade's accusation against my wife? You're more misguided than I thought if you think the Tribunal will take his word against mine."

"Actually, I'm counting on them taking your word. All of them. Especially when I share with the Tribunal the part of the recording where you goad Wade into an unsanctioned hit on a Tribunal member."

Sebastian scowled.

"You didn't think I recorded only the bit about Kimberley, did you? Do you want to rethink my offer? You for James?" I drifted away from James as I spoke, and James's gaze followed my voice.

"Where is this recording?"

"On the phone in my pocket."

"Who else has a copy of it?"

"The detective. I can convince him to erase it."

"How do I know you're telling the truth?"

"You don't, but you can check when you get the phone."

"And if I let James go, what's to stop you from staying in ghosted form and double-crossing me?"

"That one's tricky. How about we both set down our crystals and step away from them?"

"Don't do it, Emelynn," James said. "He can't be trusted. You know that."

"I accept your deal," Sebastian said. "You may go, James."

"Emelynn? What are you doing!" James shouted.

"James, please. Go. Quickly."

"He's going to kill you."

"He's going to try." I re-formed. Sebastian had too much pride to renege on his word in front of James. "Please, James. I love you, and I'm sorry for everything, but you have to go."

James fisted his hands. "Damn it, Emelynn!" His mouth was a thin, hard line when he spun away from me and nearly took the rooftop door off its hinges. It slammed shut behind him.

Now I had to stall for time because I had no doubt that all I'd bargained for was a head-start for James. Sebastian would go after him.

"Thank you," I said.

"No need. James is of no consequence to me. Now hand me your phone."

"Crystals first." I put my hand in my pocket and unclasped the case. The crystal came loose in my fingers. I removed it from my pocket and showed it to Sebastian. He freed his from his leather glove and held it like I held mine.

"Set it down and step away from it," I said. We locked gazes as we each bent to the rooftop and released our crystals. It felt like an old western movie as we each slowly, and in sync, stepped away.

"Your phone."

I pulled it out but made no move to hand it over. "What is it about me that brings out the worst in you?"

"You're an irritant. A fraud."

"And you're a consummate politician. An irritant like me should be a piece of fluff on your lapel."

"You are unworthy of Jolene's gift. What she did, gifting you, was unconscionable. It goes against the natural order. Her gift belonged with one of us. Instead, she threw it away. Gave it to the non-Gifted, to the prey. It's an insult. You were never the hunter, Emelynn. That was an inside joke. You were always the prey."

"No wonder you hate me. How it must have galled you to think your fate would be delivered to the Tribunal on the wings of prey, Sebastian."

"Thankfully, that travesty has been averted. The phone," he said, holding out his hand.

He'd take his shot at me the moment I released the phone. But if he did it too early, the phone might not survive his jolt. "You've got a serious case of god complex. There's treatment for that."

I pulled out my phone and offered it to him.

WINGS OF PREY 221

"What's the code to unlock it?"

My gaze flicked a few degrees to the right and behind Sebastian's head. James had come up behind him with his gun drawn. I hadn't intended to give him away, but he'd surprised me. Sebastian saw the movement of my eye.

Though I'd started to ghost, I hadn't made it far enough when Sebastian's jolt hit me. The pain was instant and crippling.

I remember seeing the astonishment on Sebastian's face a split second before his head kicked sideways.

I remember seeing the flash from James's gun as his shot entered Sebastian's temple.

I remember the agony of dying.

Chapter Twenty-One

Darkness held me in suspended animation interrupted only by erratic shots of light that hit my brain like spikes, driving me deep into the depths of hell.

Consciousness returned in waves, ebbing and flowing with a distant tide. Mumbling voices disturbed my sleep. The words were a jumble from an alphabet I didn't know.

Hands brushed my arms and my face. Fingers worked their way into my scalp. More words pushed their way into my head. They were comforting words, but I didn't know why.

A faint peeping grew louder with each tide until it became an incessant beeping. With great effort, I opened my eyes to a bright blur of light and shadow. The light hurt. I closed my eyes against the pain and surrendered to the night.

The pain in my head brought me out of the blackness. I cracked my eyelids and the stabbing light leaked in. Raised voices spoke in tongues and quieted. I focused on the beeping, waiting for darkness to claim me again, but this time it remained out of reach.

I felt fingers on my forehead. My eyelids were pried open in turn. I blinked against the intrusion.

A blurry face pushed in. "Can you tell me your name?" A sense of déjà vu washed over me.

"Emelynn," I said. My voice sounded unrecognizable, gravelly, as if it belonged to someone else. Someone who smoked a couple of packs a day.

This was not hell. It was a hospital. I'd survived. Emotions welled up and tears threatened.

"Welcome back, Emelynn. I'm Dr. Buchanan."

I would learn later that Dr. Buchanan was the neurosurgeon who'd drilled holes in my head to relieve the pressure from the blood collecting between my brain and my skull. He'd also performed surgery to mend the leaking aneurysms in my brain.

I'd beat the odds by surviving, but I didn't get off without paying a price. The resulting stroke had rendered my left side weak. Dr. Buchanan felt hopeful it would improve with time as my brain rewired itself. "You're young and healthy," he repeated more than once. He'd used those same words to precede his astonishment at the astronomical odds of my suffering such a catastrophic medical emergency, one he labelled *multiple life-threatening subarachnoid hemorrhages*.

For five days after the surgery, painkillers warped my reality. I existed in a world of sleep and haze. Mom had been in my room the day I recovered consciousness, and it seemed she never left my side. Other than Avery, she was the only person besides hospital staff allowed in my room. She was family. My only family. I couldn't form the words to ask about Mason. The unrelenting pain in my head was my punishment, my regret and my shame.

Avery was often with Mom when I opened my eyes. They'd stop talking when they realized I was awake then coo and fuss over me until I drifted off again. After a week, I was stepped down from the high doses of painkillers. The surgeon told me I had to learn to live with the headache, that it could last six months or longer. If it lasted the rest of my life, I would bear it as the sentence I deserved.

When the narcotics were out of my system, I was moved out of the critical care unit into a private room. Ortez was waiting for me. I told him I remembered nothing. He volunteered what I already knew—that James Moss had killed Sebastian Kirk. They fingered Sebastian for the break-in at my condo and for the death of their constable. It was close enough. They found Kimberley hanging from a rafter in their Point Grey garage. Suicide, he'd said. I didn't correct him.

Shortly after Ortez left, Sam arrived.

Mom patted my hand. "I'm going to stretch my legs, get a coffee."

Sam took her seat beside the bed. "How are you?" I asked.

"Isn't that my line?" Sam said with a chuckle. Laughing made my head hurt, but I managed a smile. "Your condo looks good. Your mom's been busy setting it right. She had the balcony door replaced."

"I thought Mom had moved in here at the hospital."

"Avery convinced her to go home after the surgery. He knew you'd be out of it for a few days. I went over to check up on her and she dragged me out shopping for your new coffee table. You'd better like it 'cause I'm not doing that again."

"You heard about Kimberley?"

"Yeah. Ortez told me."

"Why aren't you in a hammock somewhere warm with a cold beer?"

"That's next. I wanted to see you first. How are you?"

"I'll be fine."

"That's not what I asked."

"The headache's not going anywhere. My left arm is weak and my left leg isn't taking direction very well."

"They had you up and walking?"

"I wouldn't call it walking. Shuffling is more like it, and that's only with support. I'm not even allowed out of bed without assistance."

Sam looked down at his hands. "Your surgeon asked me not to bring up what happened. Thinks it could be too traumatic. Might set you back."

The image of Mason lying on his back flashed in my mind. I turned my head away from Sam and a sob escaped. My vision blurred and warm tears wet my cheeks.

Sam laid his hand on mine. "I'm sorry, Emelynn. When you're ready, we can talk about it."

"Stuart must hate me," I said, between sobs. "It's my fault. I should have listened to Mason."

"You're being too hard on yourself. You set out to right a wrong. You followed the only clue you had. No one faults you for trusting your father's word, your mother's conviction. You got to the truth in the end. I didn't get there any sooner than you did."

"A man I loved is dead because I got it wrong. I'll never be able to fix that. I can't even apologize."

Sam frowned and touched his fingers to his lips. "The doctor was right. Your memory is playing tricks on you. I'm sorry. I shouldn't have brought it up."

"My memory is just fine," I said, sniffling now. "I know what I've done."

Sam handed me a tissue. "No, I don't think you do. You never loved Sebastian, not even close. You owe him nothing. And as for Stuart, he would like nothing more than to get in here and see you."

Now it was my turn to look confused. "Why are you talking about Sebastian? I loathed the man."

Confusion crossed Sam's face. "Who were you talking about? Mason?" Hearing his name sent more tears rolling.

"Mason is fine, Emelynn. Broken collarbone, mild concussion, but he's fine."

My voice hitched. "He's alive?"

"Last I saw him," Sam said.

I closed my eyes and wept. Mom chose that moment to return.

She rushed to my side, opposite Sam. "What have you done?"

Sam must have been mortified. "She thought Mason was dead. I told her he wasn't."

Mom bent down to me. "Dry your eyes, Emelynn. No crying. You know what the doctor said. It'll make your headache worse."

She was right. The pain in my head had shot into the red zone. I took the tissues she offered and practiced the deep breathing I'd been taught.

"I'm sorry, Sam," I said. "Last time I saw Mason he'd been blown through the balcony door. He couldn't breathe. Sebastian said he wouldn't survive."

"He'd recovered when James got there. Didn't know where you'd gone."

"He probably doesn't want to see me again, but I have to apologize to him."

"He would love to see you," Mom said. "I couldn't keep him out of the ICU."

"I never saw him there."

"He wasn't sure how you'd feel about him, given everything that happened. He didn't want to upset you. Let me call him."

When Mason arrived, my mother hugged him, Sam shook his hand and then Mom and Sam left us alone.

"I didn't know they made black slings," I said. He stood inside the door and advanced with tentative steps. He approached on my good side and I extended my hand. He took it then leaned down and kissed my cheek.

"Can you ever forgive me?" I asked.

"Already have," he said.

"I don't deserve it," I said, and the waterworks started again.

Mason brushed the tears away. "Your mom tells me you shouldn't do that," he said. He sat in the bedside chair. "I understand why you thought it was me. I don't blame you or your mom. How could she know? And Sebastian was fanning the flames every chance he got. I should have seen it sooner."

"I need to apologize to your father as well."

"My father doesn't know he was included in your suspicions."

"You didn't tell him?"

"No. And I never will. Just like I'll never tell anyone about your crystal. Promise."

I bit my lip and took deep breaths to keep the tears away.

"I don't suppose you've heard from James?" I asked.

"Is it true that you're seeing someone else now? An architect?"

"No," I said, disheartened. "I hired Ben to help me design a new cottage. James got the wrong impression."

"James told me you accused him of stepping out with Grace Shipley."

"Yeah, I did. Are you and James buddies now?"

"We had to stick around for questioning by the police. Went out for a few beers. For what it's worth, I don't think you and I were the only ones Sebastian was driving a wedge between. He worked pretty hard on you and James as well."

"Divide and conquer?"

"You were his target. He wanted you isolated. I think you should reach out to James. See if there's something worth salvaging."

"He can't accept that I took that seat on the Tribunal."

"Talk to him."

"What's going to happen to Sebastian's seat?"

"The Kirk family and their heirs have been permanently removed from the Tribunal Novem."

"That was fast. How did Tiffany take the news?"

"She was relieved. The Tribunal offered to execute her. She has your mother to thank for sparing her."

"My mother?"

"You know how this works. The wronged parties are offered restitution. You weren't able to respond, so they called on your mother. I told them I'd stand with whatever decision she made." My mother had made the right call. She'd followed her own moral compass—the same one she'd instilled in me.

The hospital put me up for a few more days then sent me home in a

WINGS OF PREY 227

wheelchair. Mom had outfitted the condo with mobility aids and rehab equipment. I had a walker, forearm crutches and a cane; exercise balls and adjustable exercise steps; and grab bars and poles for every conceivable scenario.

A steady stream of visitors came by. Eden and Alex showed me photos of the condo they'd bought near the hospital. They were staying with Avery and Victoria until they could move in. Molly and Cheney brought flowers. She was overdue to deliver her baby and couldn't wait to pop, as she put it. Stuart made a trip up and I shed more tears, though he didn't know why.

Ben Nicolson dropped by with a bottle of Veuve Clicquot. He offered to tear up our agreement in light of his prior relationship with Sebastian. I refused the gesture. Mom and I liked his work and we didn't believe he had an ulterior connection to Sebastian.

The others in the covey came by, usually in pairs. My mother was probably orchestrating the flow so I wouldn't tire. I didn't mind. It felt nice to have someone looking out for me.

At nine sharp, three times a week, a physiotherapist came by and worked with me until I cried uncle. Progress was frustratingly slow and the headache persisted, but Avery and the physiotherapist were both convinced I'd eventually regain full mobility.

When Mason returned to Vancouver, I asked him to take my mom out for a nice dinner. She resisted, but I told her one evening alone would do us both good, and she'd earned a night off.

After they left, I poured a glass of wine and settled on the sofa. I opened the small box that held the earrings James had given me. I'd never gotten around to returning them.

I'd given considerable thought to what Mason had said about Sebastian driving a wedge between James and me. Sebastian hadn't helped matters, but if I was honest with myself, I had to admit he'd only hammered at issues that already existed between us.

It had been a month since my surgery and James hadn't reached out to me. Then again, I hadn't reached out to him, either. I had thought I'd get over him and move on, but the ache of his absence persisted. Not a day passed where I didn't miss something about him. I loved him, and it wasn't going away.

I'd imagined my life without him, and that life felt empty. I pulled out my phone, held my breath and dialled his number.

Epilogue
(One Year Later)

"Mom, please. Stop fussing."

"I'm not fussing. You can't go in there splattered in mud. Stay still."

"I should have worn slacks."

"Don't be absurd. It's a wedding."

"I'm sure I wouldn't be the first."

Mom continued to dab at the hem of the dress with a damp paper towel.

"Are you sure you can't walk? We can take our time, go slow. Avery would be so pleased to see you walking."

"Avery sees me walking plenty."

Mom dropped the paper towel in the garbage bin. She sighed and dropped her shoulders. I hated seeing her disappointed. "I'm not getting much sleep, Mom. I'm exhausted. My left side's not strong enough today. I'd end up walking in circles or falling on my ass, and everyone will be watching. I'd rather not."

"Will you at least stand for the photos?"

"Absolutely. Now can we go?"

The interior of the church demanded reverence. My gaze was drawn from the warmth of the polished wood floors up to the prisms of light shining in through the magnificent stained-glass windows and up again to the high wooden arches.

The ushers stepped aside as Mom and I approached. Normally when I had to use the chair I wheeled myself around, but today Mom had insisted on pushing me. We headed up the centre aisle. Flowers decorated the curved rows of chairs on either side.

The minister stood at the front of the church with Avery at his side. Avery looked as handsome and nervous as I'd ever seen him. He smiled as we made our way to the front and then offered me a hand out of the chair. I took a seat in the front row, reserved for immediate family, on the groom's side of the church. Mom pushed my chair out of the way and joined me.

Soft choral music played. Everyone from the covey was here. The members and their families filled the chairs on the groom's side to balance the guests on the bride's side. I turned in my seat and exchanged hushed hellos with those closest. Mason appeared at the back of the church and looked around until he spotted us. He looked handsome as well today, his blond hair a stark contrast to his charcoal suit.

He nodded hello to Avery and sat on the far side of my mother. "Parking was impossible."

A few minutes later, James arrived. That tiny thrill of relief I experienced each time I saw him still hadn't gone away. He wore to perfection the steel-grey suit I'd chosen for him today, and he took my hand as soon as he was seated.

"You doing okay?" he asked.

After I assured him I was, he turned to say hello to Eden and Alex, who were seated behind us. I took in the strong angle of his jaw and the crinkle at his eye created by his smile and thanked god he'd answered his phone that day I reached out. We'd both been miserable, wallowing in the ruin of our relationship. I hadn't been able to travel, so he'd come to me, and day by day, we repaired the damage.

The organ music came to an end and the congregation shifted in their seats. When the music started up again, the maid of honour appeared on Gabe Aucoin's arm. Behind them, another bridesmaid and groomsman lined up. Avery and the minister turned to watch, and the unmistakable chords of Wagner's "Bridal Chorus" began.

The entire congregation stood as Victoria made her way up the aisle on the arm of her father. She'd chosen a form-fitting dress that flared below her hips, and pointed satin shoes poked out beneath the hem with each step. She radiated happiness. I thought she was absolutely gorgeous, and her father beamed as though the world were watching. A diaphanous veil trailed behind her. Victoria's mother stood across the aisle from me, tears in her eyes and a handkerchief bunched in her hand.

It was a beautiful ceremony. I cried, though I tried to hide it. James slipped me a tissue and rolled his eyes. After the wedding, we drove the short distance to the Shangri-La Hotel, where the reception was being held. We stayed through dinner and the first dance. I was about to suggest to James that we leave when I saw Mason take Mom's hand and pull her to the dance floor. She protested, but I could tell she was having a good time. They, too, had mended fences. I'd never seen her laugh as much as when she was in Mason's company.

"Let's go," James said, sensing I'd had enough. We thanked our hosts, wished Avery and Victoria a safe honeymoon and headed home. I fell asleep on the way and woke to the sound of the garage door rumbling open. I left the wheelchair in our new Volvo and went inside on James's arm.

The house still had that new-wood scent. I inhaled a breath of it deep into my lungs. Ben had delivered exactly what he'd promised in the plans—a modern version of my old cottage—and I loved every inch of it. We'd moved in a month ago, and Mom had taken over the condo so as to be close to the university, though she had a suite here with us as well.

We made our way up the stairs to the bedroom.

"I'll be back in a minute," James said, and left me to undress. When he didn't come back, I knew where I'd find him.

I slipped on a housecoat and walked down the hall to the nursery.

"I relieved the nanny," James said. "She's gone to her room." He lounged in the overstuffed armchair with Briana cradled in his arms. Sebastian's words had been a cruel lie. Our little miracle had been delivered safely almost four months ago. She had copper highlights in her hair, like her mother, and eyes that promised to be the same changeable blue-green as her father's. It was impossible for me to believe there'd been a time I'd not been ready for this tiny girl we'd named after my father.

"This came for you," James said, pointing to a box on the table beside him. "Alison brought it up before she went to her room. No return address."

I picked up the box and peeled off the outer wrapper. Inside were business cards. I unfolded the note on top. *When you're ready – Sam.* I handed James the note, slipped one of the cards out and smiled. It read *Jordan Taylor Investigations.*

Thank You

Thank you for reading *Wings of Prey*. If you enjoyed it, please tell a friend or consider posting a short review where you purchased it. Reviews help other readers discover the books and are much appreciated.

—JP McLean

Excerpt from The Gift Companion

Lover Betrayed is Jackson Delaney's story. His role in *Secret Sky* was controversial, pivotal and demanded to be told. Love him or hate him, you won't forget him. *Lover Betrayed* is *Secret Sky* Redux.

Lover Betrayed

When his wife leaves him for his half-brother, Jackson Delaney flies into high gear to find them. He dives headlong into dangerous intrigue involving the feared Tribunal and unscrupulous thugs from his past, in a quest for justice at any cost. When that quest leads him to a mysterious young Flier with no knowledge of her arcane gift, Jackson's vengeance gets the better of him and may cost him something worse than his life.

Read on for an excerpt ...

The oppressive heat was unavoidable, omnipotent, like the man in the casket. We followed dutifully behind, our steps out of time with the rhythmic clops of the black hearse horses. White lilies hugged the casket, quivering to the drum roll of a jazz band's lively rendition of "When the Saints Go Marching In," an absurd funeral favourite. Tourists in waist pouches and flip-flops, unsure of the show, whispered behind finger curtains and stole glances under furrowed brows and baseball caps. I understood their uncertainty. The father I'd loved and loathed died without warning, too soon to recognize his mistakes, let alone fix them.

"This is a goddamn freak show," I said. "I'd never have agreed to it if it wasn't spelled out in his will."

"But it was," Sandra said. "You and your father may have had your differences, but you're a good son, Jackson."

"Was. I *was* a good son."

"You always will be," Sandra said. My wife's fingers felt cool in my hand, despite the heat. She looked up at me, her blue eyes hidden behind sunglasses and a loop of black netting that covered her face. I eased the pressure off her hand with an apology, ignoring the bead of sweat that crawled down my spine.

It took thirty minutes for my father's slow funeral procession, wafting the cloying scent of flowers, to wind through the streets of New Orleans. We'd walked an unpleasant mile behind the coffin before passing under the iron arch of the cemetery. Like a shrimp trawler with its net out, our parade snagged tourists and curiosity-seekers in its wake.

The music took on a sombre tenor only when we mounted the slight rise, which housed the Delaney tomb. The last time I'd seen the tomb open was fifteen years ago when we'd laid my mother to rest. Following long tradition, her coffin had been discarded and her remains dumped into the bone heap below to make way for the new arrival. One day, my coffin would displace my father's in a similar ritual. Would I also succumb to a stroke before I'd finished living my life?

I was a teenager when my mother died. There were times now when I had to see her picture to remember her face, but I had no trouble remembering her love. She'd bathed me in it, cooking my favourite crawfish boil, which my father hated, and baking pecan pies he wouldn't touch. She liked that I'd inherited her hazel eyes. Dad had said she coddled me, or at least that's the excuse he used to justify his tough-love approach to parenting. I doubted I'd ever need a photograph of my father to remember him.

The priest raised his voice over the crowd while photojournalists captured video of the mourners. Tomorrow, they would justify the intrusion in the name of news. Equally unwelcome tourists snapped cellphone photos they'd later show their friends at home in some macabre recollection of their good fortune in stumbling upon a genuine City of the Dead funeral.

I looked out over the perspiring faces. Tourists aside, my father would have been pleased to see the calibre of mourners who'd braved the August heat to pay their last respects. Top-echelon politicians and business people mopped their brows and donned sombre expressions, hopeful that the priest was nearing the end of the ritual. Half of the men gathered were better candidates for a casket. My father wasn't yet sixty. It shouldn't have been his time.

After the casket was laid in place, I bid him a final farewell and then nodded to the cemetery workmen, who kept their wheelbarrows at a respectful distance. As soon as they moved in to seal the tomb, the mourners began to scatter.

Jimmy Marchant was the first to approach. Sweat was beading on his red face and dribbling down ample jowls that melted into a thick neck. His jacket was soaked through, but he hadn't loosened his tie. He'd be a proper southern gentleman for my father one last time if it killed him.

He pecked Sandra on the cheek before offering me his hand. "Sorry for your loss, buddy. Your father's left a big hole on half the boards in Louisiana." Jimmy was born and raised in New Orleans. He spoke with a Yat accent, pronouncing "boards" with a barely perceptible *r* and "Louisiana" as "Loo-ziana."

"Thanks, Jimmy." In his younger years, Jimmy could have passed for John Goodman's brother. My father respected Jimmy Marchant for his legal counsel and even more for his discretion. Jimmy understood my father's definition of doing business. It entertained him, and earned his firm a lot of money, especially when my father bent the law. I was in Jimmy's debt for making sure no one knew how often that had happened. "I hope you'll join us at the Omni tonight. Let Dad buy you one last drink."

"Wouldn't miss it. Matthew Delaney knew how to throw a party and I intend to honour my promise: your father's wake will be one to remember." He leaned close. "And well lubricated," he added with a conspiratorial wink.

I forced a smile and shook Jimmy's hand. One final spectacle to endure.

Dad had made a good and loyal friend in Jimmy. I'd known Jimmy all my life and had my own reasons for liking the man. It was through him that I'd met my wife, Alexandra, or Sandra, as she preferred to be called. Like Jimmy, her father was a lawyer, and Redmond Moss was well connected. After Katrina, Redmond used those connections to generate funds to help rebuild. Sandra Moss distributed her father's funding out of Jimmy's donated office space. When Jimmy recruited my father's development expertise, I was the lucky son of a bitch who got to work with her.

I took Sandra's elbow and turned toward the first in a long line of idling limos.

"Kyle, Anthony, you'll ride with us, of course," Sandra said, addressing my old Stanford classmates who'd flown in for the funeral. Kyle Murphy lived in Dallas so knew enough to wear a light coloured suit. Anthony Dimarco was New York through and through. His navy Brooks Brothers was a choice I suspected he now regretted.

The driver opened Sandra's door, and we followed her into the blessed air conditioning.

"Jackman—how the hell do you live in this heat?" Anthony said, using my college nickname as he mopped the sweat from his brow with a limp pocket square. He tugged his tie loose.

"Northerners," Kyle quipped.

The driver pulled out, leading the train of limos to the hotel.

"I'm serious," Anthony said, supplementing his pocket square with several tissues he'd yanked from the limo's complimentary supply.

"You get used to it," I said, sparing a glance at Sandra. She'd smoothed her hair into some complicated knot the heat didn't seem to touch.

"Will you be staying long?" Sandra asked.

"Only if you dump that lousy husband of yours," Kyle said with a lecherous smile. Anthony swatted him. "What? We all know she's out of his league."

"Oh, and you think she's in yours?" Anthony said, raising his eyebrows.

Sandra looked down at her folded hands, fighting a smile. They'd met her on our wedding day. The last-minute introduction had been unavoidable, but Kyle and Anthony had taken the piss out of me about it. They insisted she would have chosen either of them over me if they'd been introduced earlier. The truth was, if Sandra and I hadn't wed quickly, and quietly, her family would have tried to stop us. It wasn't just that she came from old money and I came from new—it was that her father didn't approve of the way my father had amassed his fortune. Redmond Moss was not a religious man, but he was a judgmental bastard who held firmly to the belief that the sins of the father should be visited upon the son. Thankfully, Sandra had a mind of her own.

The driver pulled up in front of the Omni hotel, where a black-capped doorman hurried to open Sandra's door. The limo's cool air dissipated in a suffocating wave of heat. We hurried inside.

"We're going to freshen up," Sandra said, removing her sunglasses. "We'll see you in an hour or so?"

"For sure," Kyle said. Anthony already had his jacket off and his tie in hand.

Sandra took my arm and we headed to the elevators. Back in our suite, she kicked off her shoes. "That went well, don't you think?" she said.

I removed my jacket and flopped on the sofa. "A few more hours and it'll be over."

"Don't wish it away too fast." She stood in front of a mirror untangling the netted hat from her hair. "After all, the Delaney board will be there and so will most of the city's politicians, not to mention the governor."

"And your father?"

"He'll be there. Mom as well. Etiquette dictates, as you know." Etiquette and old money went hand in hand. Sandra should know; she'd been raised on both.

"Have you told them about my plans for Delaney & Son?"

She dropped her hat on the coffee table and sat beside me. "No. I want them to hear it from you."

After the initial shock of Dad's death had worn off, Sandra and I talked through the night about what came next. I didn't keep secrets from Sandra—her discretion was impeccable, so she knew about Dad's *strategic donations*, as he'd referred to them, and his propensity to *eavesdrop* when he thought it would win him an advantage. I was ashamed of that. I told her I wanted to be a better man, to behave respectably and with honour. To do things right.

"Cleaning up Delaney's reputation will take a long time. Years probably."

She turned in her seat. "The fact that you want to is what matters. And soon you'll be the one making the decisions, not your father. Dad will see the difference. He'll come around."

I took her hand and brushed my thumb against her wedding band.

"I hope it's not a mistake. My father may have been short on scruples, but he knew how to make money."

"And so do you, but you know how to do it without compromising your integrity."

I lifted my head in a flash of annoyance. "My father had plenty of integrity."

She stiffened. "Of course. That was careless of me to say."

I dropped her hand and stood. "I'm going to shower."

"I'm sorry."

"I know. It's been a tough week." I squeezed her shoulder in passing. "We'll get through it."

After changing into fresh clothes, we took the elevator back down to the ballroom.

The scent of flowers nearly knocked me over. I doubted there was a lily in Louisiana outside of this room. Was this the measure of a man? Personally, I'd never understood the flowers. A man had died. He'd lived and breathed business, not flowers. Flowers were something his guilt trotted out on Valentine's Day. Why not a genuine tribute to the man when he was still alive? A fine bottle of bourbon? Midfield seats at a Saints game? A favour he didn't have to pay for?

My arrival dimmed the raucous laughter. Jimmy, finally free of his jacket, raised his glass in a silent toast from across the room, and held it aloft. One by one, everyone in the ballroom did the same. Say what you want about my old man, he made an impression. A rocks glass landed in my hand. I stared at the amber liquid and fought the lump at the back of my throat.

Slowly, I raised my glass. "To Matthew Delaney," I said. "A formidable businessman, a generous benefactor, and my father. May he rest in peace." A collective shout rang out and then bubbled away.

Conversations resumed, backs were turned and bursts of laughter rose above the ambient noise. Sandra stroked the back of my arm. "That was lovely."

Lovely? Anger crawled up my chest, prickling my neck. I scanned the crowd. Every gluttonous supplier, every slippery politician, every Barbie Doll wife, and every major charity bold enough to send a representative had benefited from my father's acumen and generosity. They still were, sloshing back the best the bar had to offer. What had Dad gotten? Flowers he would hate and a toast from a son who couldn't even say he loved him. He'd taught me everything he knew, and it wasn't enough.

My love for him was rough around the edges. In time, it may have softened, but we had no more time.

I quaffed my drink and another magically appeared. Condolences flowed, abundant as the liquor, and one after another, Dad's impressive circle of influencers, friends and rivals approached me to pay their respects. Marcel Cadieu, a Louisiana senator and early convert to my father's way of doing business, was one of the first to slither up.

"My wife, Claudette," he said, making an unnecessary introduction. "Please accept our sympathies, Jackson. Louisiana has lost a great man." Marcel hid his animosity behind a politician's smile. He'd never figured out how my father had learned of his affair with a sandy-haired gentleman half his age. Marcel had been so careful; he and his lover had never acknowledged one another in public, not so much as a wayward glance. They'd checked into separate but adjoining rooms on the forty-second floor of the Sheraton in New Orleans. Yet my father knew the sandy-haired gentleman had spilled his flute of Cristal out on the balcony that fateful night. Dad had a photograph to prove it. And if he knew that detail, then he knew everything.

Marcel immediately became a staunch supporter of Delaney & Son. But while he championed Dad's development projects, he quietly initiated and then backed the strongest anti-drone legislation in the country. If only he knew that a drone had not been necessary.

Carl Prudhomme, also a convert, waddled up with a hearty handshake. He was head of Industrial Rod and Steel in Lafayette. My father had ensured his loyalty and a favourable pricing structure after Carl heard a recording my father played for him. Apparently Carl and two other major steel suppliers had taken a midnight trail ride into the wilds of Carl's eight-hundred-acre ranch outside of Vidalia in Concordia Parish to discuss their new pricing scheme. My father had been eager to point out that collusion in any form would likely be frowned upon in Louisiana's legislative circles. Carl had had little choice but to tip his hat, but soon afterwards, he fired his ranch hands and hired new security. Not that any of that would be an obstacle to one of our kind.

With Sandra on one side and Jimmy on the other, we received the mourners. They dropped their smiles to shake my hand, and offer condolences. Sandra's father, Redmond, and her mother, Diana made their obligatory appearance and soon after disappeared. But not all the guests wore fake smiles. My father was a generous man who loved a good party and treated his friends well.

The line of grievers marched on and my father's acquaintances crawled by, kissing my wife and patting me on the shoulder. I grew tired of repeating what felt like my mantra: "Yes, I am proud of my father's legacy." And to those few who needed to hear it, I added, "Yes, I look forward to taking Delaney & Son in a fresh, new direction."

After the handshakes and back pats subsided, Jimmy headed to the bar and Sandra excused herself. I searched the room for Kyle and Anthony. They had been welcomed into Jimmy's clutch of insiders at the bar, many of whom were Dad's closest friends. I joined them and we put a dent or two in some of the finer bottles on offer and listened to my father's friends tell ribald stories of Dad's exploits.

My father had chosen to lead a public life, and some of the tales were ones he'd leaked himself. He'd manipulated the media as handily as the men he'd kept markers on, cashing them in when it suited his game. And it didn't suit his game to have the public know his other persona: the man who grieved when my mother died; the man who stayed by my side until I conquered my deadly fear of heights; the man who helped me bury Razz, short for Razzmatazz, the crazy black lab he'd bought me for my fifth birthday. Sadly, his tender moments had been as rare and fleeting as a *loup-garou* sighting in the bayou.

This game he played ensured that, to his face at least, people referred to him as a maverick, a shrewd negotiator, a visionary. But in the backrooms and bars, they called him manipulative, contemptible and crooked. That was my legacy. I was the *& Son* of Delaney & Son, and now I had to clean up the mess.

Standing in the midst of the huddle of men at the end of the bar, I watched Sandra work her way through the mourners. She clasped a hand here, stroked a shoulder there, smiled a blessing with a nod of her head. She charmed every man in the room and befriended every woman, and she was mine, my oasis in the quagmire of grief and guilt my father's death had stirred.

A little after midnight, Sandra approached the table where Jimmy had been reminiscing about Dad and the early days, when it was still just Delaney Developments. He'd been developing strip malls back then and married to his first wife. I loved those stories best. Dad hadn't yet felt the sting of betrayal or learned to like the feel of dirt on his hands.

The wake was just warming up and wouldn't end until dawn. Sandra offered the men a shy smile and then leaned down to my ear. "I think we've done our part, Jackson. Let's go."

Her sweet vanilla scent pulled me out of my chair. It always put me in mind of my mother's bread pudding, something else I could never resist. My father once told me Sandra was too good for me. His callous comment had angered me at the time, but not because he was right. He considered her a feather in the Delaney cap, but he never once acknowledged it was me, the & Son, who'd won her.

I excused myself and followed her to our suite, freeing the mourners to drain the bar and speculate about what would happen to the dirt Dad had on most of them.

Acknowledgements

Writing The Gift Legacy series has been an exciting and rewarding journey. What began as one book quickly morphed into a trilogy, which grew into a series. Along the way, I've met many generous, insightful and supportive people. *Wings of Prey* and the other Gift Legacy books benefited considerably from their thoughtful input.

I am indebted to beta readers Jean, Eleanor, Kathy, John, Gee and Sue. To Elinor, who was instrumental and supportive throughout the rebranding of The Gift Legacy series. To Nina Munteanu, who has edited and improved every Gift Legacy book. Nina is also a writing coach and author (https://ninamunteanu.me). To Rachel Small of Rachel Small Editing, who polishes prose like no one else (www.rachelsmallediting.com). To the Denman Writers' Group, whose members critiqued scenes early in the process. To the owners and staff at Abraxas Books on Denman Island, who have supported me from the beginning.

To each of you, thank you. You inspire me, humour me, and drop my jaw with your kindness, your generosity and your enthusiasm.

Thanks to the design team at JD&J Designs for *Wings of Prey's* enticing book cover design.

Last, but never least, heartfelt thanks to my husband and family for your unwavering support. None of these books would have made it into print without you.

All errors in the research and writing of this novel are entirely my own.

Glossary of Terms

Covey: A group of Fliers who are geographically connected. Older coveys were and still are connected by family rather than location. All Fliers belong to a home covey and are expected to check in with coveys in areas they are visiting. Coveys are a source of information and are trained to protect their Fliers.

Crystal: All Ghosts need a crystal to achieve ghosted form. The two exceptions to this are Emelynn Taylor and the woman who gifted her, Jolene Reynolds.

Flash: Fliers can use the second lens in their eye to produce a flicker of light within the eye that other Fliers recognize.

Flier: A human either born or gifted with a mutated gene that allows him or her to shed gravity and take flight. The gene can also manifest with additional facets, such as memory reading and telekinesis. The mutation produces a second lens in the eye.

Founding families: The nine founding coveys are comprised of the oldest and strongest families within the Flier community. Centuries ago, these family coveys founded the Tribunal Novem to police the Flier ranks.

Ghost: A Flier with the ability to dissipate into molecules too small for the human eye to see. Ghosts are rare. The process of turning into this form is called ghosting. All members of the Tribunal Novem are Ghosts.

The Gift: The mutated gene that allows a Flier to shed gravity. The mutation produces a second lens in the eye. The gene can also manifest with additional facets, such as memory reading and telekinesis.

Gifting: The process of transferring the gift, in whole or in part, from one Flier to someone else. The receiver can be any human. The process strips the donor of the element gifted. When the entire gift is given, the process weakens the gift-giver and is fatal half the time. Giftings are strictly controlled by the Tribunal Novem. A Flier who has been gifted is considered a second-class Flier.

Jolt: Fliers can use the second lens in their eye to produce a wave of energy along a spectrum from sparks, which are like static shocks, to jolts, which are painful and can even be fatal. The degree of energy produced depends upon the Flier's particular gift and varies from weak to strong. A fatal jolt causes a brain bleed (hemorrhage or aneurysm), which is medically classified as a stroke.

The Redeemers: A group of Fliers who feel they have been wronged, or are not represented, by the Tribunal Novem. Their goal is to replace the Tribunal Novem. They are led by Carson Manse.

Rush: Fliers can use the second lens in their eye to produce a stimulative energy that falls within the low-end of the spectrum of energy they are able to produce. It's sexual in nature and used to heighten sexual arousal. Referred to as the/his/her rush.

Spark: Fliers can use the second lens in their eye to produce a wave of energy along a spectrum from sparks, which are like static shocks, to jolts, which are painful and can even be fatal. The degree of energy produced depends upon the Flier's particular gift and varies from weak to strong.

The Tribunal Novem: Judge, jury and executioner in the Flier world. They are comprised of one representative from each of the nine founding coveys. They are always Ghosts. Their identities are not known within the Flier community. The Tribunal's leadership rotates every five years. At any given time, five Tribunal members provide day-to-day investigation and enforcement.

Discussion Questions

Spoiler alert: These questions contain spoilers that will ruin the story for those who haven't yet read the book.

1. At the end of the previous book, when Emelynn is compelled to tell her mother about the gift, she discloses only the "positive" aspects of it. In this book, Emelynn is caught in her lie of omission. Was it a mistake for Emelynn not to have told her mother everything immediately? How would you have handled telling Laura about the gift?

2. Emelynn's mother suggests that using the media to publicize their search will prevent the Tribunal from sabotaging it. Is the same strategy that whistleblowers use? Is it a sound strategy generally? Is it a sound strategy in Emelynn's case? Why or why not.

3. During the caucus, drones and other technology that actually exists are demonstrated. Do you think this technology is dangerous? Why? How might authorities curb their misuse?

4. James leaves Emelynn after the decision she made at the caucus. Was James justified?

5. Mason forgives Emelynn her accusations and actions, despite how serious they were. Is this out of character for Mason? Do you think Emelynn got off lightly?

6. Do you think Emelynn is worthy of being credited with having a moral compass? Why or why not?

7. Detective Coulter turns his back on the laws he'd previously sworn to uphold and joins ranks with Emelynn's kind. Is this behaviour in keeping with his character?

8. The author sets the series in the cities of Vancouver and Bodega Bay, the Napa Valley and the fictional town of Summerset. Which of these locations would you most like to visit?

9. If you were casting the role of Emelynn's mother, Laura Aberfoyle, which actress would you choose?

10. Are you satisfied with the way the series ended? Is there an alternate ending you'd like to see? Would you like to see the series continue?

11. If you could ask the author one question, what would it be? Would your organization or group like to arrange an author appearance in person or online? If so, please contact the author at jpmclean @jpmcleanauthor.com.

A printable version of these discussion questions is available at www.jpmcleanauthor.com/extras.

About the Author

JP (Jo-Anne) McLean is best known for her contemporary fantasy series, The Gift Legacy. Reviewers call the series *addictive, smart and fun.*

The first book of her Gift Legacy Series, *Secret Sky* (originally titled *Awakening*), received Honourable Mention at the 2016 Whistler Independent Book Awards. In 2016, JP's body of work was included in the centennial anthology of the Comox Valley Writers Society, *Writers & Books: Comox Valley 1865–2015*. Her writing has appeared in WordWorks Magazine, Wellness and Writing blog, Mystery Mondays blog, and many others.

JP holds a degree in commerce from the University of British Columbia, is a certified scuba diver, an avid gardener and a voracious reader. She lives with her husband on Denman Island, which is nestled between the coast of British Columbia and Vancouver Island.

She enjoys hearing from readers. Contact her via her website at www.jpmcleanauthor.com or through her social media sites. Reviews are always welcome and greatly appreciated.

- Sign up for her newsletter ~ www.jpmcleanauthor.com
- Find her on Goodreads ~ www.goodreads.com/jpmclean
- Like her on Facebook ~ www.facebook.com/JPMcLeanBooks
- Follow her on Twitter ~ @jpmcleanauthor